This book is dedicated to the people who use their gifts to make the universe better one choice at a time.

THE PEOPLE'S CHAMPION

A Protector Project novel

Jenna Lincoln

ALSO BY JENNA LINCOLN

Book One in
The Protector Project series

The Protector Project

www.BOROUGHSPUBLISHINGGROUP.com

PUBLISHER'S NOTE: This is a work of fiction. Names, charac
places and incidents either are the product of the auth
imagination or are used fictitiously. Any resemblance to ac
events, locales, business establishments or persons, living or dead
coincidental. Boroughs Publishing Group does not have any cont
over and does not assume responsibility for author or third-pa
websites, blogs or critiques or their content.

THE PEOPLE'S CHAMPION
Copyright © 2017 Jennifer Gottschalk

ISBN 978-1-54682079-6

ACKNOWLEDGMENTS

A belated but very important acknowledgement goes to Bev Robin, mistress of words. Thank you, Bev, for your early notes, full of kindness and insight, on *The Protector Project*.

Thank you to my beta readers for the feedback, questions, and ideas. While *The People's Champion* might have been slightly less raw when you got it than the earliest versions of my first book, you took on those 150K words with positive enthusiasm. Handing a manuscript to beta readers might be a little like taking a baby for that first haircut—you just hate to touch those infant locks, but you hope something even more wonderful will be revealed with a little trim.

Thank you to the Boroughs Publishing team with extra love for all my fellow authors. Thanks to Chris Keeslar for the fantastic cover and thoughts about the title. Extra special thanks to Michelle Klayman for taking over the editorial reins for this book and making it shine.

Thank you to my friends and to my friends of friends, native speakers of the languages in the book, who helped with the bits and pieces of language translations: Jackie Alden, Jen Lin, Nora Kayali Paynter, Nahla Mossallati and Samra Shummy. While I did my best to capture and reproduce their work with fidelity, any mistakes in translation are entirely mine.

Huge hugs and showers of gratitude to teachers Judi Holst and Michelle Oslick and to librarians Amy Tempel, Kristen Donegan, Carolyn Leahy for bringing my books into your schools. Thank you to Denise Johnson, Cathy Walker-Gilman, and Pamela Nocerino for the opportunity to do author visits in your classrooms. As a young-adult writer, receiving authentic feedback from my target audience is more valuable than an extra knife in a close fight.

None of this would have been possible without my incredible work family. Thank you for your unflagging interest in and support of my writing. Huge hugs to Barb, Denise, Ian, and Summer. Long distance hugs and special thanks to Valerie.

Like Mara, I have excellent luck in aunts. I want to thank my Aunt Lynn and her wonderful friends for the cheering and support as my first book came into the world. I also want to thank my Aunt Merry for sharing my books with family, and friends, as well as the teachers and students at Charles Silvestri Junior High.

Finally, with thanks forever, to my mom, dad, sister, and brother for your ironclad support. My imagination would not soar half so high without the solid grounding you provide. Most of all, thank you to my husband and daughters who have to live with me while I'm distracted, muttering, leaving odd notes around the house, and forgetting important items at the grocery store.

Thank you to the creators at the American Natural History Museum and volunteers at the Denver Museum of Science and Nature for the traveling exhibit: "The Power of Poisons." Wow, I learned a lot from that exhibit and picked up several excellent reference books. And no, that has nothing to do with what distracted me at the grocery store. At all.

THE PEOPLE'S CHAMPION

Chapter 1

In the pale light of early morning, Mara hurried into a fitted shirt and shorts then took off. Cushioned shoes made no noise on the molded plasticene floor of the dorm as a sensor in her wrist unit triggered the proximity lock. Once in the much brighter hallway she said, "Access History two oh one, Citizens and Government lesson fifteen." The tiny mikes attached to each of her ears began to play Dr. Elsebet Iskindar's voice.

"During class today we will discuss the original charter document of the Commonwealth colonies…"

Listening to lectures as she exercised helped Mara excel in her studies. She was so hungry to learn, in such a hurry to acquire knowledge. Dr. Iskindar's presence as a lead instructor had been one of many surprises at their new school. When the professor had departed Satri, Dalin and Mara were left wondering about Iskindar's role with the Queen's government, and Jameson had been even more suspicious. Yet, months later on the first day of class, she'd acknowledged Mara with a warm smile and said, "Miss De La Luz, how lovely to see you again."

Nothing was lovely at this school. But the classes were usually the best part of each day.

Everything had been in place for Mara and Dalin to return to Satri once they'd finished helping with the transitions for the Protectors. Mara intended to start her advanced studies at one of the universities. Dalin's plan was to resign from the militia and join her at school to follow his interests in science and energy innovation.

But just as she had before, the Great Tree of Satri changed everything for Mara. Radically.

The gontra *sapling on the edge of the battlefield had grown strong enough to open a connection to the Mother Tree on its own.*

She could see it, smell the gontra sap just as clearly as if she were there now. Then one day the Tree appeared as Mara was watering and checking the soil around the sapling. Black empty eyes, curling brown-gray hair, swirling marks running over dark brown skin, the Tree spoke. "Daughter. I need your help," she said, reaching out one slender hand to brush Mara's temple.

As it did nearly every day, the guilt and regret coursed through Mara. Flushed with the success of bringing down the Protector Project, she'd planned a new life for herself. She'd looked forward to being embraced by a family she'd grown to love. And, out of everything she'd dared to dream, spending time with Dalin had been at the top of her list.

That was where the guilt and regret came from. The Tree had compelled her, but the death tolls had compelled both of them. Dalin had been working with Jameson, culling key facts from reports assembled across the remaining war projects. On the same night she'd told him about the Tree's demand, he'd showed her the latest data. The worst part was the copy of orders, directly from the Queen's Council, stating the other war projects must increase casualties due to the loss of numbers from War Project Seven on Asattha.

Hand trembling, she'd reached for the page. Her fingers tapped the numbers, much as she'd counted and recounted the marks on the floor in her old room. "We did this, Dalin," she'd whispered, throat closing with horror. "Our actions caused these deaths as sure as if we'd struck the blows."

"Queen Vanora gave the orders—"

"Because of us," she cut him off, honor demanding she take responsibility.

The numbers, the casualties, peoples' lives tallied up in neat columns—it was too much. If she would fight for the Protectors, shouldn't she also fight for the children of Tian, Dorado, and Hépíng Xīng?

Mara pushed up the pace of her jog, following the slight curve to the left as she ran the exterior wing of the Queen's Military Skills and Strategy School, the Queen's Mess, as the students called it. After listening to Iskindar's lecture again, Mara chose other chapters from the textbook to review.

Her reading skill was developing quickly, but to understand text as complex as those chosen by Dr. Iskindar, Mara preferred listening. By the time the lecture and the chapter review concluded, Mara had finished her run and most of her weight-training regimen in the exercise hall.

The hall was a social hub in the early afternoon, and sometimes Mara picked up a double workout. But most mornings she just needed to run and study in peace. The huge atrium was a mix of new and old. The Queen liked new, but the King had liked old, as had the Kings before him. The dominant philosophy of the past hundred years was along the lines of "train how you'll fight." So no fancy muscle stimulators or high-tech workouts. And the validity of the thinking played out in the field. Nothing was going to keep a soldier fit like sit-ups, push-ups, and running.

The new tech stuff was really just updated biometric versions of machines from the mid-twenty-first century; at least that's what Dalin said. When he emerged from the upper locker room, Mara watched as he selected the simulated chest press and lay down on the bench without a wave or any acknowledgment.

They didn't have to be in uniform dress for exercise, and though Dalin could wear any uniform better than most soldiers with his lightly muscled build and lean height, he looked equally good in his short-sleeved black t-shirt and light gray pants this morning.

She tucked those thoughts away even as she looked at his face for a fraction of a second too long. The Queen's Mess was much stricter about male/female friendships than the Protector compound back home, while generally ignoring female/female and male/male relationships. One of the many stupid, pointless rules, given love could take root anywhere.

"Friendships with the possibility of romantic or sexual involvement cause tension and distraction in the ranks," was the caption on a large sign with a picture of two ambiguously gendered people leaning close to each other. Mara licked her lips as her partner continued his workout. Tension and distraction were familiar companions, especially when Dalin was around.

After the "at your age" lecture, teachers separated the new students by gender and delivered lectures on contraception and sexually transmitted diseases. None of the soldiers were under sixteen at the Queen's Mess, and most appeared to be closer to twenty. But it was all part of orientation and the long list of ways to get dismissed permanently from school.

They'd still been in the Northwest Protector compound when they'd decided to join up, to get themselves recruited into the Queen's elite training program. Their plan had made sense sitting alone together, on Dalin's bed, poring over reports and other intel. The best sabotage was from the inside and the school was adjacent to the palace. It seemed like a bonus that the best place for causing real damage to the Commonwealth was also a school. Mara could study and Dalin could teach.

Returning to her workout, Mara started with abdominal crunches on the mat, a good physical punishment to go with her guilt and frustration. Though it wasn't part of the plan, Annelise and Gunder had come along as well. They'd adapted to the Mess better than many of the first-year students, much better than Mara in a lot of ways.

With an inner groan, she flipped over and started push-ups.

Every time she thought about that morning months ago with the Tree, her head hurt, as if tendrils of compulsion were burrowing through her brain all over again. But it was worse to think about the death tolls and their complete lack of progress toward slowing the casualty rates, let alone stopping the war experiments for good.

Mara reached out to Dalin's mind through rapport, their mind-to-mind communication. *"Hey, need a spot?"*

Dalin's reps continued in smooth up-and-down motions. Finally, he stopped the machine and sat up. *"Why don't I spot you?"* he sent. His gray eyes crinkled with a small smile. Their ability to speak through mental rapport was the only way to have a private conversation because surveillance was everywhere.

After her push-ups, Mara didn't need the chest press but ten more reps couldn't hurt. She wiggled under the weight bar, her head right at the edge of the bench. *"These machines were made for smaller people, I think."*

Dalin tapped the start key. *"You're bulking up, but not that much,"* he said with a broader, appreciative smile.

Mara grunted as the second rep came down. Her arms shook under the heavy weight.

"Stop thinking about how we got here," Dalin sent.

Easier said than done. "Can you decrease the resistance?" she asked aloud. Too much silence between them with accompanying nods or smiles might give away their ability to speak privately, a luxury Mara refused to lose.

He tapped a few keys. "Sure, sorry, I was—*admiring the view*." He sent her a quick image of herself, hair falling out of her braid, tan cheeks pink from exertion, dark blue eyes focused on the weight.

"*Mara,*" Dalin said. "*Your points are low.*"

Mara sighed. "*I know. I don't like the way they score fights. And I can't stop worrying about the other people dying across the Commonwealth because the Protectors are free.*"

Dalin rested his hands on the bar as Mara lifted it. Pale stubble climbed his chin and cheeks, lighting the hollows of his face. "*Look, I'm still verifying the most recent updates from Jameson. We're going to get traction here, I promise. In the meantime, we don't know what happened to the last group that didn't earn the points needed to stay at the Mess. Washing out might not be the easy dismissal you think it is.*"

Out loud he added, "Just stay out of the bottom third, okay?"

Dalin keyed in the end sequence and walked to the bicep curl machine. Mara coded into the tricep machine just next to it. Speaking through rapport was Mara's only opportunity to be honest.

"*But if I can get dismissed safely, will you stay?*"

Dalin paused with the weight bar under his chin. "*The senior student, junior faculty position I have here is… It's odd. No one else has my rank as far as I can tell. I don't have access to the Queen's council files. Yet. I can get to the numbers, but not to the reasons behind the kill count requirements. I need more time, maybe until the end of the year. Which is why you need to get your points up. I don't want to be here without you. I don't want you to be anywhere without me.*"

Mara smiled as warmth suffused her chest. Aloud, she said, "I miss being outside. I miss my horse." She finished the last rep, arms and shoulders tired and sore. "*I can't locate the Laskan Tree from inside this school. We can't even touch a true energy source. We need to get out of here. Try a different location, a different arm of the bureaucracy.*"

Dalin glanced over, his silver-gray eyes warm. *"You're my partner. Where you go, I go. Your safety is my duty and my responsibility."*

Mara raised an eyebrow. *"My safety?"*

Dalin's mouth curved into his trademark grin. "I miss some things even more than fresh air and horses." He sent an image of the two of them kissing in Elana and Jameson's kitchen.

Mara's lips tingled. "Like your dad's cooking?" she said for the benefit of anyone listening in.

"Exactly."

Chapter 2

Annelise turned for Mara to adjust her fight suit. Mara checked the seals and tightened the shoulder gussets. Every centimeter had to be snug or the readings could be off. The tight fit allowed the sensors to not only measure the impact and precision of each hit, but also heart rate, respiratory rate, and hormones secreted through the skin. The newest suits, worn by upper-level students, measured, tracked, and recorded neuro impulses as nerves microfired in anticipation of an incoming blow landing or one being landed on an opponent. That data dumped into the combat simulation programs.

Annelise's usual riot of curls was slicked into a tight bun. All around them other girls were working in pairs or small groups getting into fight suits in the locker room. "Don't drop your hands," Mara said with one last tap on her friend's suit. "You relax too much sometimes and leave your face unprotected. Some of the girls fight dirty." Hushed, tense voices bounced and echoed off the syncrete floor and tile walls.

Annelise spun around, the fingers of one hand curved like claws; she pretended to rake them across Mara's cheek. "I know," Annelise said with a laugh. "I been learning a few tricks. They expect it."

Mara caught her friend's wrist. "What are you talking about?"

Annelise put her hands on her hips, amusement fading from her blue eyes. "How many points do you need to get out of the well tonight?"

Mara swallowed and sat down on the hard narrow bench that ran the length of their locker row. "Almost two hundred."

"Sixty points a win and you only get three fights. You have to do something decisive, like you didn't do last week or you're gone." She began checking the seals on Mara's suit. "You need to do something drastic," Annelise pressed, lowering her voice as several more students came down their row. "Do it in the first fight and create some healthy fear." She slapped Mara on the shoulder and sat down to slip on the rubberized fighting booties.

"I don't want to hurt anyone," Mara said.

"Well, they want to hurt you," Annelise said. "C'mon, sister. You're a fighter. A warrior. Remember?"

Mara closed her eyes and reached for the Tree or another source of living energy within the planet. For the space of a breath she felt a flickering something, an almost presence. Then a locker slammed and broke her concentration. If the Great Tree of Satri had a sister Tree on Laska, only the Light knew where.

Annelise tugged her hand. "Two minutes to get to the Box."

Mara grabbed her spare gear and weapons and followed her friend. The teachers and researchers rarely allowed weapons in the Friday Fights. But on the only weapons-optional occasion this quarter, the five Protectors on the benches had all been prepared. And because they always carried weapons as part of the rule of preparation, they'd all won.

Both girls' names changed from red to green on the competition board as they entered the crowded bench area. The lightly padded benches were uncomfortably narrow, each section scarcely wide enough for one fighter and her gear underneath. Several healers in yellow uniforms picked their way among the female fighters to check on injuries, strained muscles, and the like.

Mara claimed a bench spot with her pack and began a final gear check. The only thing missing was her water bottle. It wasn't under the bench or loose in her bag either.

"Need something?" a healer inquired.

"Water bottle's gone," Mara said, certain the healer didn't care.

"We have spare water today," the healer said, handing over a tall, full container. "Hydration won't be a variable, so you can have as much as you want."

Mara thanked her and took a long drink.

"Anything else? Injuries you're concerned about?"

Mara shrugged. "I'm only concerned about losing."

The healer looked Mara up and down. "You'll be fine." She stepped over a weapons bag and continued down the row.

"Wait," Mara called. "Are you from Kels?" The small female's yellow braids swung as she disappeared around the corner.

"Sit," Annelise tugged her hand. "They're about to announce the first names."

The Friday Fights were promoted as a fun exhibition for the senior level students, visiting scientists, anyone the Queen wanted to see her latest prospects. Inside the rings, the atmosphere was more serious than fun. The pressure to show off new moves and score a lot of points was high.

Unlike other exhibition matches, the fights in the Box were for an audience. Occupying a huge part of the fight complex, the Box held ten fighting rings divided by movable walls. The spectators sat in high seats and could observe at least three fights from a given vantage point.

The fighters could only see their opponents, the two judges and the four walls. Every other Friday for the past six weeks, Mara had gone into the Box when her name was called and merely held her ground for three rounds without actively fighting. Occasionally she lost a round to a more motivated or crafty fighter, but more often than not, Mara's lack of points stemmed from her lack of interest in earning any. She was here to end the war experiments and find the Laskan Tree, not fight.

Tonight she had to earn the win points plus more somehow. Mara perched on the bench bouncing her knees and sipping water. Her padded gloves hung from a strap on her waist. As the buzzer signaled the first pairs to start, her heart rate picked up and she swallowed hard. Some kind of awareness tickled Mara's mind as she tried to focus on her mental preparation. What? What was…? Her mental shields felt fine but her heart now raced as though a threat was near.

"Sit still," Annelise whispered. "Remember, they're getting all of this through your suit."

Mara planted her feet on the floor and straightened her back. She took measured breaths in the pattern Zam, her former combat instructor, had taught, visualizing energy flowing into her arms and legs. The announcer's words didn't register as she fought to bring her mind and body into alignment.

"That's you, sis. Just called your name." Annelise stood and helped Mara with her gloves.

Tripping over the doorway, Mara stumbled into the ring, blinking at the bright lights shining down into the square space. Her opponent, a medium-size female with dark skin and a white braid, waited behind the red line on the far side.

One way to win was to force the other fighter across the red boundary. Just touching the line was a point deduction. The faster the win, the more points earned. Mara chomped on her mouth guard and charged across the line as the buzzer sounded. Her opponent jumped into a front handspring, telegraphing her intent to lock her legs around Mara's neck. Something slowed the girl's momentum and Mara caught her ankles, dumping her on her head.

As the girl pushed off the floor, Mara kicked toward her face. The girl's hands flew up and Mara changed the direction of the kick, catching her opponent squarely in the ribs hard enough to send her flying backward. One hand touched the red line.

"Finish it," Annelise yelled.

Two strides took Mara to the prone fighter's side. With one arm tight against the windpipe and vein, she choked her into unconsciousness.

The buzzer blared and healers rushed out to take the fallen girl from the Box. Mara squinted at her score, but the numbers floated and blurred. She scrubbed a hand across her eyes and walked back to her place on the bench. Annelise swung a hand to clap Mara's shoulder but her hand stopped, stuck in midair.

"Are you shielding?" she whispered.

"Try to punch me in the face," Mara said, her voice coming out fuzzy and strange.

Annelise cocked her arm back and popped a jab toward Mara's nose. Four centimeters away, her fist caught, dragged, and stopped. "Holy Mother of the Light," Annelise breathed. "None of us have been able to…"

The healer with the braids ambled up. "Good fight," she said. "How's the hydration?"

"Uh," Mara fumbled for her bottle. "I'm good."

"Great," the woman responded and moved on.

"Does she look like she's from Kels?" Mara asked.

Annelise frowned at the woman's back. "Never seen her before. But what did you do? I want my shield back too. I'd be almost unbeatable in my division."

Mara swigged down some water. "Don't know. I mean, I always reach for it, that's habit. I guess I just found some energy source.

You try." If it was the Laskan Tree, finally, she could get dismissed from the Mess and start that part of her mission.

Annelise screwed up her face in concentration. The next fight ended with the buzzer and Annelise's name was called. "Hit me," she said.

Mara flicked her on the ear.

"Ow! Okay, plan B, win the hard way." Inside the Box, Annelise handled her opponent with a flurry of inside moves and finished with a spin kick to his head.

"Wow," Mara said when Annelise plopped back on the bench. "Why aren't you in the advanced class?"

Annelise was still breathing hard. "I keep askin'. They keep saying 'soon.'" She stood and craned her neck toward the tiny holoimages of the other fighting squares. "Has Gunder gone yet?"

"I haven't heard," Mara said. At the next buzzer, the point display flashed. She'd earned sixty points for the win plus five for the girl's hand on the line and fifteen for the knockout. Mara leaned forward to look down their row. Once everyone fought in Round One, the next round would change up the order.

The three minutes in the fight could feel like forever. Sitting through twelve of those three-minute fights passed much more quickly. There was never silence in the stands or on the floors. Staggered start times meant no shortage of action.

Annelise was called again. She took a shot to the nose and blood flowed immediately. A judge stepped in but Annelise waved him off. She spat a red wad on the floor and motioned for her opponent, a larger girl with heavy fists, to resume. The girl lumbered forward and Annelise feinted back twice, luring her opponent out to the center. Then she darted around and jammed a sidekick into the back of the girl's knees. When the girl staggered, Annelise jumped onto her back and rode her to the ground, slamming the girl's sweaty face into the mat an extra time. Annelise marched out of the ring, the gentle girl from the settlements she had once been long gone.

"You could've broken her back," Mara said.

Annelise swiped at her nose. "They'd fix her. The injuries are just temporary pain."

Maybe Annelise was right? And Dalin? The board showed her low point count. She had to win the next two matches with an extra something. Otherwise she would wash out to an unknown future.

The only way to get control of her immediate future was to win tonight.

Mara was rubbing her temples when her name was called for the last fight of the second round against a girl from her math class. The girl had a heart-shaped face, but her friendly smile had vanished.

They bowed and then closed in on each other almost immediately at the center of the floor. The girl from math class tried to catch Mara in a hold, long arms blocking and trapping. Mara stomped on her instep and kicked her in the pelvis. As she flailed, the heart-shaped face contorted and she landed a heavy slap across Mara's jaw. Mara's head snapped to the side, her left ear ringing, vision blurring. As she stumbled clear, she reached for the shield and energy surged around her.

Turning, she found the girl from math class replaced by a Gaishan in a black uniform and battle mask. Mara yelled and took two running steps into a high, flying sidekick aiming for the dead center of the mask. The Gaishan tumbled backward, crashing into the wall and landing in a heap. What sick joke was this? To throw a masked Gaishan in the ring with a Protector? Some "ancient enemy" variable? Mara stretched her fingers toward the mask and it disappeared. Only a broken girl, pretty face slack and bruised, was in the Box with her. Mara's outstretched hand shook.

"Back off," the judge ordered. "Nice kick. The healers will take it from here."

Mara covered her mouth and stumbled toward the door. Her stomach heaved and she tasted bile. When a light hand touched her shoulder, Mara flinched away.

"That's going to bruise," said the same blonde healer. "Here." She reached up and pressed a moist cloth scented with lavender and *bejul* to Mara's jaw. "Hold this on it for a while."

"Why are you helping me?" Mara asked, but the words were garbled through her mouth guard.

The woman smiled. "Drink the rest of the water. It'll make a difference." And she pushed back through the crowd of fighters toward the stairs.

Mara rested one knee on the bench while she swished water around in her mouth and then chugged the rest. Her cheek throbbed and her head spun. Sweat trickled under her arms even though the fight suit was supposed to keep everything tight and dry. What did healers and scientists know about real fighting?

She tried to breathe, tried to find calm, but all she could think about was Queen Vanora, the mother of all Darkness forcing them to fight; turning kind, sweet Annelise into a killer.

They had to remove Vanora and her council from power and find the Laskan Tree. A two-part mission that had seemed so clear.

From the only enclosed seats in the arena, the Queen could watch any of the fights. Her bodyguards, called the *vishakanya*, were a tight group of preteen girls who always wore long sleeves, long pants, and gloves. They usually attended on Fridays, but always sat just outside the high curtains. No one was supposed to know if the Queen was actually present, but Mara could always feel when Vanora's poisonous energy tainted the room.

Mara's name rang out for the second fight of the third round. She growled and stomped into the ring. Gunder emerged from the opposite door carrying a sword.

His eyes widened. "They called weapons," he yelled at one of the judges.

"Bow," the judge ordered.

Automatically, Mara and Gunder bowed to the judges and to each other. Mara stepped across the line, shield up. If only Gunder could use rapport. She nodded and gestured him forward, trying to let him know it was okay.

Gunder slid his sword behind the red line and stepped forward with his hands in tight fists at his cheekbones.

Mara swung a slow uppercut at Gunder's jaw. He stepped aside and threw a cross punch at her face. Mara slipped out of the way, but Gunder's fist caught the edge of her shield.

"C'mon," someone yelled. "This isn't pattycake." The display showed fifteen seconds gone. Mara began an intermediate four-punch, three-kick combination all the Protectors knew. Gunder caught the rhythm and blocked everything. He started the next sequence, extending his kicks and adding jumps. The audience approved.

None of his blows really got through Mara's shield, but she faked reactions as she would in a simulation, big enough to make it look like Gunder had the advantage. But she had to win. The round was already half over.

Mara slid under the tall boy's arm and wrenched his elbow high. "Will you let me win this one? I can make it look like I choked you out." Spit sprayed with the words as she tried to talk around the mouth guard.

"Go for it," Gunder said, bending and throwing Mara forward onto her hands and knees.

She blinked sweat out of her eyes and a man appeared next to Gunder. She sprang to her feet, hands up. Sometimes the teachers added an extra fighter in the ring to make the last round livelier. But this guy didn't look like a first year anything. His combat suit molded to his broad, heavily muscled shoulders. Bright blue trim circled his neck and wrists and he gripped a short sword with practiced ease.

Before Gunder and Mara could react, the man stabbed Gunder in the side and shoved him across the red line. He kicked Gunder's sword to Mara. "No more playing," the man snarled. "You're here to prove you're good enough to fight for the Commonwealth and defend our Queen's life." On that last word, he charged and swung his sword over his head.

Mara blocked the strike and shoved her heavy opponent out of the way. Where were all the healers? Why was Gunder still on the ground and bleeding without help?

The man faked a side strike and kicked Mara squarely in the stomach. Even cushioned by her shield, the blow doubled her over. She pitched forward and smacked her head on the floor. She scrambled to her feet, the walls spinning. But her opponent wasn't there to finish her; he stood over Gunder both hands wrapped around the hilt of his sword.

"This waste of flesh must die for his incompetence." He raised his voice to carry into the stands. "Everyone who fights for the glory of our Queen!"

The crowd noise surged with both jeering and approval.

Mara threw herself between Gunder and the vicious fighter, taking most of the killing blow on her left shoulder. The pain lit up her nerve endings and hijacked her perception until there was no sound, no feeling beyond the agony. The fool had turned his back to wave at the approving crowd.

She rolled onto her good shoulder and then up to her knees. Gunder's eyes were closed, his face too pale, but he was breathing.

She cast a shield over her unconscious friend. And with that casting, more power surged through Mara's body. She rose slowly and deliberately. When the fighter turned, she kicked him hard enough to break ribs. His face contorted and blood bubbled from one corner of his mouth.

Was he speaking?

His sword came up to the guard position. With unnatural speed, Mara disarmed him with a chop inside his elbow and a brutal wrench on his wrist.

"Not playing now," she said. Mara dove for Gunder's sword and sliced across the back of the man's legs, cutting both suit and muscle. He dropped heavily to his knees.

"Yield," Mara ordered.

The man bowed his head.

"*Mara.*" The smallest sound like the tap of a pebble tossed at a glass window. "*Mara, you're a Protector...the Light.*" She inhaled as the roaring crowd broke through her concentration. She changed her grip on the sword and slammed the butt into the man's temple. Spectators screamed, stomping and clapping.

Mara turned slowly, her left arm hanging useless and her unwound braid flopping over one shoulder. She panted, heart racing, hoping to see Dalin's face in the stands, needing a beacon to guide her back to herself. Instead, Queen's guards boiled through both doors, blocking her exit.

"No," someone yelled. "She won."

"Boo," more voices joined in jeering at the guards.

"*Mara, run!*"

Chapter 3

The Friday night fights started the usual way and Dalin, sitting with some of the fight instructors, didn't notice anything atypical until Mara's first round. But when she threw her full weight and strength into a kick, smashing her opponent on the bridge of her nose, he surged to his feet.

"What was that?" one of the instructors exclaimed. "Never once seen that side of her in class."

The referee had to shoo Mara away after the win. Exiting the Box, her steps were unsteady. He couldn't go to her as he wished. He couldn't go to her, and it never got easier to wait and watch. Instead he reached toward her and felt…a shield? Her energy signature had always been bright and clear, like a high country stream. Now it was tinged with something sharp and bitter.

By the time Mara's third round began, Dalin had moved well away from the other spectators to a corner of the stands, just inside the stairwell to the fighter's bench area.

Fortunately, they sent Gunder in the Box with her. It was a relief when Mara looked like herself, fighting in traditional Protector patterns with him. But the Queen's Champion entered the Box mid-fight, sword drawn, and stabbed Gunder without ceremony. Instantly, Dalin stopped wondering about the odd taint in Mara's energy and instead hoped that it would help her survive.

Usually light on her feet despite her size, Mara's steps were heavy and deliberate. Her clear intent was to protect Gunder, but that righteous ass of a champion was speechifying about the Queen's glory and worthiness. He was going to use her, make an example of her. Dalin's mind raced through his options as he counted and checked his weapons, gaze never leaving the fight. This would not happen, this could not happen. She wouldn't die in the ring at this useless school.

Mara rose from her crouch over their fallen friend, dark energy flaring. She fought like a goddess of war. And though he was an accomplished fighter, the Queen's Champion fell like a sacrifice before her strength and skill. As she raised her sword for a killing strike, Dalin raised his own hands as though he could stop her. *"Mara, you're a Protector. You protect the Light."*

A scream from the vicinity of the Queen's viewing box snapped Dalin out of near-rapport with Mara. The *vishakanya* looked incredibly pleased by the spectacle except for the leader who began issuing orders to the nearby adult guards.

"Mara, run," he sent, filling the command with urgency.

She ran, leaping for the wall and scrambling over it, favoring her injured shoulder. Half-tripping down the stairs, Dalin landed just in time to see her disappear with one of the healers. He reversed course, joining a group of jeering fourth-year students. The air crackled with anger at the Queen's order to send guards after Mara. He started to push through the next group when a tall blonde grabbed his arm and pulled him tight to her side.

"The Furies got this, Romeo."

Dalin tugged to get his arm free but she locked her grip.

"Don't fight me now. We're all going to do what's expected. Furies take care of the best female fighters in the Mess. Teachers stay out of the way or get dead."

The shock of being threatened galvanized Dalin. He broke her grip and kicked at her knee simultaneously. But the blonde stepped around him and laughed.

"Nice move. You've been pulling punches too long."

Dalin lashed out again, his hand a flat blade. She blocked him, grabbed his hand, and said, "Don't ruin a good thing. Stick with your role. Find out the plans and how to get her back in class without punishment. We're covering her retreat. Go on."

It was a role. He didn't care about the norms of behavior at the Mess for teachers or anyone else. Mara was hurt and he needed to get to her. He pushed away from the blonde and tripped the nearest guard. Another tall female stuck out her fist as the next guard rushed forward, catching him on the chin.

"Ouch, you ran into my fist. Guess I have to defend myself," she said. She grabbed another guard and swung him into Dalin. He pulled the baton from the guard's belt and cracked it across his shins, putting the weight of his anger into the blow.

"Fight!" the tall female called. "Help, the guards are attacking students." She laughed as a cluster of students joined in and then another.

The Mess earned its name again today, Dalin thought with disgust. He'd been working his way into the system slowly, playing by the rules. Stupid. He lashed out, not caring who he hit as he fought his way toward Mara.

* * *

"Look at your points," someone yelled as Mara rushed past. She spared a glance at the nearest holodisplay. Her name in massive letters. Five hundred points for beating that extra fighter.

A blurred figure in yellow waved from a doorway. Mara ran despite the haze dampening her thoughts, recognizing the dark-skinned woman with the Iloel tattoo around her ear and down her neck, a woman who had been kind to her in her first few weeks at the Mess. "Come, daughter, come, *tifla*," the woman whispered.

She gestured down a narrow dark hall. Mara darted inside and when the Iloellian healer closed the door, its seams disappeared into the rock foundation of the fight complex. The sounds of fighting and cheering muted instantly.

Mara's heart would not slow. Her damaged shoulder burned and three fingers on that hand had gone numb. The healer stopped Mara in a dimly lit alcove and brushed gentle fingers across the gash at the top of her left arm. Healing energy flowed into the injury. Light exploded behind Mara's eyes and she dropped to one knee.

"Listen to Sangita now. You must hide in the city," the woman said, her hushed musical voice still loud in the narrow passage. "The Queen will want to study you or punish you. It is the way of the royal family, passed down to her by her grandfather."

"Why?" Mara looked up into Sangita's concerned face.

She released Mara's shoulder with a gasp and made a warding sign. "Lady. Forgive me. I am not worthy."

Still on one knee, Mara shook her head. "What? I, you, you are helping me—"

"Your eyes," the woman said, voice tinged with reverence. "The Tree Mother walks with you."

"Are they…?" What had happened during the fight?

"Black as the night sky. I am blessed to behold you thus."

The all-black eyes of the Tree. It had happened before, but she'd been in deep rapport with the mother Tree on Asattha. Mara struggled to her feet. She couldn't go to her dorm with those eyes. Where would she be safe? Where was Dalin?

A door far down the narrow hall banged open with a shout.

"Go." The healer shoved Mara toward a different door, this one tucked behind a support beam. "Hide yourself."

Mara ran, flexing the fingers of her left hand. Her shoulder hurt less. The hidden door caught and then opened on the second push. She popped out into a crowd of students with fifth-year markings on their uniforms. "Hey, good on you, beating the Queen's Champion," one said and slapped Mara on the back.

"'Bout time someone took down that smug bastard. Always preaching about glory."

They swept Mara along with them. She kept her eyes down, suddenly aware she still wore the fight suit.

"Didn't they leave off chasing you yet? Unbelievable." A strong hand clamped around Mara's right arm. "C'mon, let's get you an exit." The voice was low, female, and full of the comforting tones of command. An exit sounded like the right decision.

The stranger pulled Mara through a busy open hall and out into a paved courtyard. The heat of the day had disappeared into a cool desert night. A fountain trickled in one corner. Mara pressed a hand to her forehead and tried to lean against the wall, but her feet slipped in the rubber shoes.

"Oh those useless booties *de basura*," the female said. "Take them off."

"What?" Mara's head was spinning again. She blinked, trying to focus on the older student's face. "Do I know you?"

"Soldier, shoes off. Now."

Mara dropped to her bottom and tugged off the booties, something she'd needed to do anyway. The tile radiated soft warmth under her sweaty feet. She took a deep breath, wrestling against the weakness flowing through her body and mind.

The tall blonde student sat and unlaced her shin-high combat boots. "Take these. You need to head into Crown City. Get a couple of clicks between you and the Queen's Guard." A tiny diamond stud sparkled on the outside of one of her nostrils.

"Aren't we the Queen's Guard?" Mara couldn't get her brain to function. Sensory impressions of the air temperature, the scent of boot polish, and the musical tinkling of the fountain were a backdrop to her confusion. She needed to ask this stranger for help and then depend on her to give it, something the months at the Mess had taught her to avoid.

The blonde soldier laughed and ran a hand across her shorter-than-regulation hair. She handed the boots to Mara. "No, chica, we do the hard work. The guards just look pretty."

It was hard to hear sounds of pursuit through the general crowd noise inside the fight complex as students and visitors were dismissed to quarters. She couldn't seem to shake the brain fog. Was that shouting for her?

"Great fighting, by the way," the soldier said. "All the girls in my squad were cheering for you."

Mara's teeth started to chatter. She clenched her jaw and finished lacing up the boots. "Thank you." She didn't want to look up, afraid her eyes were still black.

"I'm Fentress—"

"Thank you, Fentress." Mara risked a quick chin tilt and smiled.

"Go cool off in the city. Find a place to hole up for a day or so until the Queen forgets you broke her toy and gets a new one." Fentress stood and offered a hand.

"Isn't that AWOL?" Even as she asked, Mara began inching toward the gate in the far wall. She wanted to run. But she didn't want to jeopardize the reason she and Dalin were here in the first place by breaking the rules.

"Winners can request leave. I'll file it for you. *Vete*. Get outta here, Mara."

Agreeing with the logic, but worried and still hazy, Mara took off at a jog out through the ornate metal gate. She cut down an alley and ran past a series of stone arches before emerging at the top of a hill overlooking the sparkling lights of Crown City. Rising directly above the military school was a much steeper slope with the blazingly bright palace at the peak.

She curled and uncurled her toes in the borrowed and slightly large boots. Lose herself in the city wearing a sensor-laden fight suit? No weapon, but at least she could shield. Maybe that would prevent the sensors being tracked? She needed real clothes.

Just down the hill, the closest neighborhoods were small estates and mini-palaces, some complete with patrolling guards. Mara picked fruit from an overhanging branch, the tart sweetness washing away the bitter taste of whatever had been in that water bottle.

As the houses decreased in size, so did the width of the roads. Citizens moved behind windows, but the streets were relatively empty until she hit the outskirts of the market district. Mara paused at a public fountain to splash her face and neck with water and redo her braid. She sidled over to the darkened window of a dress shop, hoping to check her reflection. If her eyes were normal, she would go back and hope for the best. What stared back were wells of shadow.

Looking into the Tree's eyes was terrifying. Mara shivered, skin hot and freezing at the same time. The image wavered and the Tree herself stared back from the window's surface.

Mara reached out then stumbled back, barely catching her balance. What was happening? How was this possible?

Keep walking. Cool off.

It might have been her own mind, or it might have been Dalin. Her brain was so fogged, she couldn't be sure of anything.

She continued downhill seeking narrower streets, darker shadows. But as she wandered, her steps grew uneven, balance failing. Sometimes she'd stagger into a wall or a storefront, sometimes a person. Her vision would blur, than flare white with bright spots. Her head pounded with the uneven rhythm of her steps.

"Hey, *sharmuta*, need a little help?" The rough voice and ugly word belonged to a squat, ugly man wearing a belt full of weapons.

"I—" Mara's tongue stuck to the roof of her mouth. "Yes, need help," she slurred.

"Someone's running a little wild. When they let you soldiers out of school, you get wild." The ugly man's companion thrust his pelvis on the word "wild" and erupted with cackling laughter.

"No," was all Mara could manage.

"Yeah, *aahera*, that's how it feels. We can help you. But it'll cost something."

She braced a hand on the stone wall. The ugly man moved in close enough for her to smell his fetid breath and greasy hair. Mara choked and gagged.

"We're going to take that fancy tech suit from yous and help ourselves." His friend giggled and closed in on Mara's side.

Her stomach heaved and she vomited bile onto the ugly man's trousers.

"Hey," the man shouted. He slapped at Mara and caught her shield. With jerky movements she managed to grab his arm and punch him in the face. The ugly man rocked backward, slipped in the vomit, and fell.

His companion snatched at Mara, but she captured his wrist, twisted it, and slammed him head first into the wall.

Ugly man rose to one knee, fumbling for his weapons. Mara kicked him hard enough to lift him partway off the street. She leaned over the prone attacker and slid one of his knives from a sheath.

Her eyes burned and her instincts clamored to kill both men. Taking advantage of a sick soldier, a Protector? What was darker than that? She brandished the knife, growling low in her throat.

"Easy, *eazayzaa*. You don't want to do that."

Mara swung around and was immediately dizzy. She couldn't separate the owner of the voice from the dark walls. Words formed in her mind, but all that came out was raspy gibberish.

The calm voice from the shadows said, "Here now, filly, have some water." A hand extended a canteen.

Mara accepted it and sniffed before taking a long pull to rinse her mouth and spit it out. Satisfied it didn't taste of anything but water, she drank the rest down, dribbles coursing over her chin as she gulped.

Swiping the back of her hand across her mouth, she said, "The Commonwealth would be better off without these criminals." She waved the long knife toward the prone men.

"And you've brought justice to them." The dark man emerged, pulling the shadows with him. The moonlight brightened the planes of his face, revealing a sculpted beard and a sharp nose. He reached out slowly, as though to pat Mara's shoulder, and took the knife with dexterous speed. "My place is along this way, but we got a rule about no weapons. You can sleep it off in the back room."

When the man tugged Mara's hand, she stumbled into his shoulder. His linen shirt smelled like *terche* peel and cloves with maybe a hint of horses.

* * *

By the time Dalin fought through the students and guards, Mara had disappeared along with the tall, blonde soldier. When he shouted through their mental connection, demanding, pleading with her to respond, he got nothing but the tiniest spark. Mara was alive, but unreachable.

Out of options for an immediate solution, Dalin decided to attack the cause of Mara's disappearance. What had happened to her physically? What had triggered her shielding and her radical behavior change?

He stopped outside the door to his room and checked for signs of entry. The single thread across the latch was intact. The corrosion on the door hinges hadn't sprinkled to the floor either. Even if an intruder were stealthy enough to detect his thread and replace it, only the rarest and most subtle of thieves would think to sweep a few specks of paint and rust from the floor.

Inside he searched again, checking for any new monitoring devices. A dubious upgrade from his room at Northwest Protector House, the quarters had a kitchen/dining/living room and a separate bedroom and washroom. The flat industrial gray paint and micro-thin carpet hid most of the dust, but his half-empty bookshelf collected and displayed plenty. From a military housing perspective, he couldn't decide if the privacy or his own cooling unit was the greater luxury. Though his corner room, far from the training floors and classrooms, had been given to him as an afterthought, its out-of-the-way location was ideal. Even better, it was nestled against two of the Queen's Mess's thick foundation walls so only the hall side was vulnerable to casual or amateur eavesdropping.

The founding King had been a successful biohealth entrepreneur. But his paranoia, fostered in a tech-heavy time, had grown to something more. Tech use in the Commonwealth was easily a full century or more behind tech progress outside the Commonwealth.

More importantly for Dalin's purpose today, tech security was at least a century behind as well.

He'd have to go to the data storage center, and for that he'd need a reason. The justification he'd held back upon arrival at the Mess was the need to complete his several-years-delayed comparative analysis of the war projects. His research had been authorized through a joint council. Today was the day to bring that out and begin anew.

Retrieving fiber paper copies of the necessary documents, Dalin tucked them into his largest pocket before adding a few weapons to strategic places on his body, some visible, others not about his person.

Through rapport, he'd been able to determine Mara's whereabouts, but he couldn't get a lock on her completely. She had been heading into Crown City, wearing one of the infernal fight suits, and was likely without a weapon, unless that Fury had given her one.

Mara was sick or drugged or both. Tonight had revived the torture and the nightmare of the years and years watching her fight the false Gaishan while Dalin was forced to observe, prohibited from aiding her.

Finally being able to fight by her side and give her the truth had brought some peace. For an all-too-brief time, he'd had the relief, comfort, and satisfaction of knowing she was where she belonged: with him. Seeing her learn and thrive, he'd tasted hope for both their futures.

But when she had been in pain and was reeling from the Mother Tree's compulsion, he knew he'd do anything to keep his partner safe. His commitment to the eventual revolution was a guttering match compared to the roaring bonfire of need to protect Mara at home on Asattha, and now here at the most dangerous military school in the Commonwealth.

He rebuilt the shields around his mind as he focused on his path through the massive school complex, a visual and physical timeline of the Mess's history. The original red brick used for the main portion of the school had never been re-created. Newer passages were a mix of local stone and syncrete, ribbed with riveted steel supports at regular intervals. In some places, new halls had been built as arteries of older halls.

The data storage center broke out from one of the longest hallways between the school and the palace. Not too far from the open labs, teachers and techs could be found at the terminals during work hours. After the excitement of tonight's fight, and the evening meal, he was guaranteed a place to work even if he wouldn't be alone.

The access codes in his wrist unit allowed him entry into the data center. A group of students crowded one corner of the big space, whispering and typing into at least three terminals. Several large windows on the south wall reflected evening sky and a few points of light far below in Crown City. From the many available workstations, Dalin selected an area far from the students, but not at the opposite end of the room. Though he'd never seen the place full, over fifty users could be working at the augmented desks at a given time.

The stations stretched in long rows, small walls between each sending a message about individual work having a higher value than collaboration.

The scrape of his chair across the dark wood floor caused two of the data center monitoring techs to glance his way. Dalin smiled and nodded. Cameras were conspicuously mounted in every corner of the room and along the high ceiling. Much more subtle devices were embedded in each desk.

Starting about age ten, his father had begun challenging Dalin to access lab data from the files at his father's workplace. Nothing secret, of course. Not at first. But over time, Dalin's understanding of the storage and transmission architecture grew. He learned to improvise and, more importantly, he learned to cover his incursions. By then, the local schools held no challenge and Dalin's father had taken over instruction. Finally, at thirteen, Dalin was cleared to attend university classes.

Here at the Mess, the algorithmic structures underlying the programming were far less flexible than the nearly organic structures that ran across the southern half of his home planet, Asattha. The rigidity made everything easier to circumvent—unlike the physical hallways of the Mess, the data pathways were straight and predictable.

Dalin logged into the desk to his left and initiated a search program about the war projects. At the desk in front of him, he set up a mirroring search to run in the background then opened up one of his subroutines to begin his real quest.

The next time he looked up, the data center was silent except for the humming of the air coolers and tapping of his fingers on the keys. He stood and stretched, surprised to be entirely alone until he checked the time. Three hours had passed since his arrival. Dalin stood, turning his head left and right to test the kinks in his neck. His searches had yielded nothing new, no chemical wrinkles in the current protocols. Covering a yawn, he meandered over to the corner where the techs had been hours before. With a series of keystrokes, he logged in as an administrator and opened the recent history on the machine.

At first the pages read like nutrition and hydration logs. But as he dug deeper, rerunning the most recent searches and reference links, a cold tightness wrapped around his chest. And by the time he'd sent himself the full measure of data, the icy fury in his mind threatened to burst through his shields. The potential for damage caused by the experimental drug and the utter lack of regard for the lives impacted by the experiments, for Mara's life, filled his soul with the darkest anger he'd ever known. The drug went straight to the spinal fluid. Even a blood transfusion wouldn't, couldn't change what had been done to Mara.

Unclenching his fists, Dalin gave the voice commands that opened the camera feeds and adjusted the time loops until the records showed him sitting in one place the entire time. He reset the history of every workstation in the lab, logged out as an admin, and then logged out as an instructor.

It was fortunate these tasks were automatic because if he let himself think any harder, he would smash the desks instead.

Chapter 4

Mara opened her eyes in a room lit only by candles. She tried to sit up, but the sudden, sharp pain in her head and shoulder kept her down. Nausea rose. She leaned over the cot and threw up in the bucket placed next to her head. Shaking, Mara clasped the soft, clean-smelling blanket and tried to breathe slowly.

"Relax, sweetheart. Your body signed up for detox while your brain was still off duty. It's gonna be like this for a while." The person speaking entered her field of vision and lifted her good shoulder. "Drink this. It's lemon water with a little mint. Should help."

Unsure why he was helping, but feeling some level of comfort that he didn't mean her harm, she swallowed a few sips, sweating with the effort of holding her head up.

"Must've been a fun night," the man said, a touch of wistfulness in his tone. He sat the glass of water on the concrete floor within reach of the cot, but away from the bucket.

"No." Mara cleared her throat. "Not like that." She squeezed her eyes closed, trying to concentrate. "I was fighting and the guards and I won, beat an extra fighter. My partner said to run."

"That's how you got the cut on your shoulder? Up at the school?"

"Protect my friend," Mara tried to sit up as apprehension about Gunder jolted through her. "He was stabbed."

"You were alone in Lower Town. I tracked you for a while before I intervened. If you had any friends with you, they're long gone."

"No one. Ran with me," The spinning walls picked up speed. "Partner told me— I saw the Tree and my eyes—" She lost herself, gasping in the dark.

* * *

A deep boom shuddered through the floor and walls. Mara woke less nauseated, maybe even a little hungry. Sitting up with caution on the low cot, she looked around the large, simple room. Sunlight filtered through shades on several high windows and lit a full-size bed, a desk and chair, and four large metal footlockers. Small, colorfully patterned rugs covered much of the bare syncrete floor.

Another boom rattled the windows. Mara winced and the motion jolted her shoulder. The noise could be the spaceport, but that was almost ten kilometers from the Mess. She pushed up a little more and the sheet fell away, leaving her in a long, linen tunic, something that might have been a dress on a shorter person, and linen shorts. One of the orientation lectures had warned all the new students about the dangers of Lower Town in Crown City. But aside from the half-healed shoulder and her sick stomach, which was no fault of anyone here, Mara was unharmed.

The person she assumed was her rescuer lay sprawled face down on the bed, one arm tucked under his torso. Fine scars crisscrossed much of his muscled back, right down to the waistband of his trousers. In sleep, his dark face looked almost as young as the fourth- and fifth-year students. She tiptoed across the cool floor to the door in the far wall. The handle turned silently but the hinges squealed when she tugged.

"Going somewhere, *habibti*?"

Mara dropped her hand away from the door. "Do you have a shower?"

"I do." The man turned to face her, leaning on one elbow. "But you'd need to manage it on your own. Nearly threw out my back wrestling you out of that suit." Fresh from sleep, his Origin English was tinged with an accent.

She stiffened. "My fight suit—"

"It's all right, sweetheart. The blasted thing's in an iron box." He nodded toward the footlockers. "Didn't know if you wanted or needed to be found just yet."

Mara didn't know either. Better not to think about it. "Shower? I can manage."

The man slid out of bed, short dark hair bristling and messy. Linen pants hung low on his hips. "Shower's going to cost you. Breakfast won't be free either."

Mara lifted her chin as the man padded closer. He hadn't hurt her when she was incapacitated, so she held her ground. They were exactly eye-to-eye. "I don't have any currency or anything for trade."

"Well now, don't be too sure about that." His mouth lifted in a half smile, his expression less than honorable. "Lower Town accepts many payment options. What I want is your story."

Mara let out the breath she was holding and relaxed the fingers of her empty sword hand. "I accept your price."

The man stuck out his hand. "I'm Rafiq."

"Mara," she said, shaking on the agreement.

The door opened to a hallway of corrugated metal walls and more high windows. Many crates and boxes were stacked at irregular intervals. Rafiq pointed out the two closest doorways. "That's the shower, and that's the regular guest room. Bureau and closet should have suitable clothes. Well..." He considered the tunic dress that ended high above Mara's knees. "If nothing in there fits, you can borrow something of mine." He grinned and a dimple flashed in one cheek. "Chow's that way. Find me when you're finished."

Mara nodded and headed to the shower. She checked her eyes in the cloudy mirror. Back to their normal blue, Light be praised. But as she lathered with the citrus-scented shampoo, she wondered how to pay Rafiq's price without knowing the full story herself.

The dresser in the guest room yielded two drawers full of clean, nearly new undergarments, both men's and women's. She also found a shirt with almost long enough sleeves and finally settled on a pair of pants that fit in every way except length.

As she laced up the borrowed boots, worry about her circumstances churned her fragile stomach. "*Dalin?*" She mentally threw his name, imagining the school, picturing him there. After thirty seconds, Mara called Dalin's name again, consciously putting more energy into the shout.

"*Mara?*" Relief came through with Dalin's voice in her head. "*Are you hurtfinesicksafe?*" The words blurred together across the transmission of thought.

Mara braided her wet hair. *"Safe,"* she sent. *"I'm safe for now. Are you all right?"*

"I am now."

She smiled. *"All clear? Can I return?"*

"Soon. No class today or tomorrow." Wherever he was it was cold, his mental voice chilly as well.

"I have assignments to complete. I need to keep my points up—"

Strained laughter from Dalin. *"You have more points than anyone in the Mess."*

"What?" Mara sent confusion along with the question.

"Hey, you're sick," Dalin said, his mental voice steely with concern. *"How? Where?"*

"I'm in a safe place. Something they gave me was toxic. That's what you probably sense, my body trying to expel whatever it was."

Even at the beginning of their use of mental rapport, Mara had been able to get information from Dalin's body and senses. With practice, they had learned to open the channel in both directions.

"Be careful." His warmth and worry wrapped around her like an embrace.

"Little late for that." Mara grimaced.

"Mara, rest, stay safe," he said as he released the connection.

Before she went in search of the promised chow, Mara did a quick search for weapons. No energy weapons or spare swords were visible on the walls or shelves, not even a knife or dagger. Unwilling to risk a more invasive search, she picked her way down the crowded hall then opened the far door into an alcove separated by a high half wall from a much larger room. The ceiling was higher, also made of corrugated metal and lit by large circular lamps in wire cages. Fans turned in slow circles to move air heavy with the smells of frying meat and eggs. The door clicked behind her, seams and hinges disappearing into the wall. *Curious.* Mara rolled back her shoulders, the hurt side still aching, but not as bad as last night, and walked into the main room.

People, dressed mainly in the orange jumpsuits of spaceport workers, occupied five of the small tables. Rafiq sat alone, rocking back on two legs of his chair and sipping from a mug. He waved Mara over.

"Tea? Or food first?"

"Tea and food?" Mara replied. The cooking smells weren't making her sick, which was an excellent sign.

Rafiq stood to speak with a large man wearing a stained white apron. He gestured toward the chair across the scarred wooden table. Mara's host now wore a black linen shirt, unbuttoned to his sternum, and loose black linen trousers. His shoes only had one strap across the toes and made a flap sound when he walked.

The man in the apron slid a mug of strong-smelling spiced tea and a basket of bread in front of her.

"Thank you," she said.

"Thanks, Geraldo," Rafiq added.

Geraldo grunted and wiped his brownish-pink, sweating face on one sleeve. He shuffled back toward the counter on the near wall.

Mara nibbled a piece of the fresh flatbread and took a tiny sip of tea, uncomfortably aware of Rafiq watching her. Something about the man was predatory, but also vaguely military. He held himself ready, just like she did.

"You're from the school. Queen's Mess."

Mara took a much larger bite and nodded.

"But not Laska, originally."

"No," she said with her mouth full.

He waited a beat. "You were in the Friday fights?"

She eyed him over the rim of the mug. "Yes."

"And they drugged you for experimental purposes." The flat statement caught Mara by surprise. Was this common practice? Common knowledge?

Her cheeks heated with frustration. It was impossible to keep the rule of preparation here. "I don't know what happened to me."

"Well…" Rafiq tipped back his chair and dangled one shoe from his toes. "If you'd made a habit of indulging in substances and charging around Lower Town in a fight suit, we might've met before this." His posture was overly casual, but his gaze was intense.

The soft bread stuck in Mara's throat. "Never been off-site," she mumbled, gripping the heavy mug a little harder.

Rafiq narrowed his eyes. He dragged one thumbnail down the side of his beard and under his chin. "How old are you? Sixteen?"

"Seventeen, almost eighteen. Why? How old are you?"

"As my *maman* would say, 'Old enough to know better.'" He grinned, showing all of his white teeth.

It was hard to resist smiling back.

Geraldo slid plates in front of each of them and dumped forks, spoons, and napkins in the center of the table.

"Any chance you'd bring some lemon water?" Rafiq dropped the chair onto all four of its legs and smiled up at the massive man.

"Get it yourself, Rafe. We got paying customers in here." Geraldo's meaty hands spread to include all the tables.

"Sí, *cocinero*." Rafiq ambled to the counter and filled two tall glasses with water, adding sliced lemon to each.

Mara dove into the curried potatoes and scrambled eggs, her mood lifting with each steamy bite. After a while she didn't bother to notice Rafiq watching her. Finally she pushed back her empty plate and took a long drink of water. Four tables had occupants now all eating and talking quietly. Her eyes felt heavy and she yawned behind her hand.

"How's the stomach?"

"I apologize for my…illness earlier. If there are things that need cleaning—"

"Do you do dishes?" Geraldo interrupted, appearing to take the plate.

"Be glad to," Mara said. "That was the best meal I've had since I left home." She stood and stacked her plate on top of Rafiq's.

"Home is where again?" Rafiq asked, steering her toward a swinging door to the left of the bar.

"I'm from Asattha."

Both Rafiq and Geraldo froze.

"Asattha, you say." Rafiq assessed the dining room. The sixteen guests were all still eating or talking to each other and their dining companions. Geraldo moved his bulk between the main room and the kitchen door, effectively shielding the two smaller people.

"You owe me a story and that is one I'd love to hear." Rafiq nudged Mara into a kitchen with deep metal sinks along one wall and freestanding open shelves in the middle.

"Not much to tell." Mara plugged the drain and started filling the right-hand sink, just as she would on kitchen duty at the Protector compound. To her left was a modern dishwashing unit nicer than any other piece of equipment in the place, nicer and newer even than the one in the de Forest's kitchen. She reached for the first platter in the stack, ran it under the water and then fit it into the lower rack of the washer. Her hand froze over the next platter. "Your water keeps running? Up at the school everything is on a timer. How? In Lower Town I thought, I heard..." She raised her eyebrows and shook her head.

"Not much to tell. Really." Rafiq loaded glasses into the top rack of the dishwashing machine with exaggerated precision. "Pay the right people, get what you need. Geraldo's cooking is good. Add clean plates and forks plus drinking water? That equals customers."

Like most kitchens, the room was full of weapons. Somehow the awareness of the danger and the opportunities for violence gave Mara clarity about staying alert while deciding whether she could trust these two men. They trusted her to not pull a cleaver from the rack and slash at them. They hadn't attacked her either. Her soldier's instincts said she wasn't in danger, but it was always good to know where the knives were.

While they loaded a morning's worth of dishes, Mara began the story of the Protectors, of growing up inside the compound. The warm water and the steady rhythm of the work soothed her. Slowly she relaxed into the telling, smiling about Elias and the stable children, sighing over missing her horse. She handed the last glass to Rafiq.

Her face clouded as she scanned the unfamiliar shelves of food stores. "My partner and I had some ideas about what we could accomplish here. But we've made no progress. I was hoping to wash out of Queen's Mess, try something different at the end of this cycle but—"

"But you heard the students who wash out don't always survive."

Rafiq pulled the plug from the sink and Mara stared into the swirling water as soap bubbles and food bits circled the drain. She gripped the metal edge with slippery hands as everything blurred.

"Hey, let's get you back to the guest quarters. Let that food and water work some magic."

"Magic," Mara repeated, her shield flaring and wrapping around her.

With a soft finger snap near her ear, he said, "You don't need that here, sister. Just relax."

The energy hummed through her, but she felt so tired. She didn't want to fight anymore.

"Mara."

Looking down the drain reminded her so much of looking down into the root network of the Great Tree.

A loud crash of metal pans was followed by a man's voice barking out commands. "At ease, soldier. Release shield. Now!"

Mara dropped her shield, stepped her feet shoulder width apart, and put both hands at the small of her back.

"Back to quarters, soldier. March."

Part of her was ready to run again, but the rest of her consciousness responded to an officer's command. Rafiq took her arm as she marched all the way back to the cot. When he let go, she toppled like a felled sapling.

Chapter 5

When Mara woke again, the light was less bright and she was alone. Next to the cot, someone had removed the bucket and replaced it with a crate, water and several pieces of bread sitting on top.

This time Mara felt less like she was waking within a dream and more like she was part of reality. She drained the water glass and wiped her mouth on her sleeve. Everyone she'd met in Satri, the capital of her home planet, had food, running water, homes, small or large. But she'd assumed Laska, and especially Crown City, would have decadent luxuries. So far, the Queen's Mess and Lower Town were only slightly better off than the settlements.

Which didn't exist anymore.

That was done now.

The Protectors were free, the war experiment ended.

But the numbers coming in from the remaining war experiments were so high. She'd once thought fifty-three soldiers an unacceptable loss. According to Jameson's network, deaths had increased tenfold on Tian and Dorado. Though those experiments weren't full of children, most of the combatants were younger than twenty-five, but not teenagers.

Her fault.

She stood and folded the blanket, placing it next to the small pillow. She wasn't dizzy and breakfast had stayed in her belly. Time to head back to school, return the fight suit and the borrowed boots.

The bed across the room was made military-style, blankets pulled tight as any Protector's. The desk under the windows was clean, not a single stylus cluttering the surface. Why had this man pulled her out of the alley? He'd made it clear that in Lower Town rewards were taken, not given.

The drawers full of clothes in the guest room made it seem as though taking in strays was a habit. Intrigued, Mara nibbled a piece of flatbread and crouched down to inspect a small bookshelf tucked against the far end of the desk. She plucked out a battered volume, its spine lined with white creases, and inspected the cover.

A man brandishing a weapon smiled as he held a woman in a short dress against his side. The woman faced the man, her shiny red lips parted in…interest? Maybe she was talking. The words on the cover were made with curved, dotted symbols. Mara replaced the book and pulled out another.

Many of the covers were similar. Sometimes the man held a sword, sometimes he had no shirt. The woman had a weapon on one cover, a dagger, but she was at a greater disadvantage because she wore only undergarments. The title, written in Origin English, read "Dark Deception."

"Oh that one's a favorite," Rafiq said. "Book's in great condition too."

Mara glanced up at her host, surprised she hadn't heard his flapping shoes. "Does she have to fight to get her clothes back?"

His wide smile was dazzling. "Yes, I believe she does."

"I hope she gets a better weapon," she said and re-shelved *Dark Deception*. She pushed up from the floor and wiped her palms on her pants.

Rafiq sat in the desk chair and gestured for Mara to take the chair on the side opposite the bookshelf. "A certain type of collector is always searching for that sort of book. I've found I like them for myself now and again."

"You are fortunate to have so many books. This eating house must do well." For the first time since she'd put on the fight suit, Mara felt like herself again. But even though Rafiq had helped her, her instincts were on high alert.

Rafiq nodded, his smile fading as he leaned back in the creaky desk chair. "Listen, I went up to the Queen's Mess while you were resting. People aren't talking about the fights much. The staff is working on a big event, a funeral, actually."

Panic raced through her and she started to stand. "Who? A boy, a student?"

"Easy." Rafiq laid his warm palm on her arm. It was exactly the tone of voice and weight of touch to use with a skittish horse. "The funeral is for the Queen's Champion. This one lasted a lot longer than his predecessors. But I guess he lost a fight and then killed himself out of shame. Official story is he died in battle, but the kitchen staff tells it like it is."

"Queen's Champion?" Mara pressed her hand to her stomach. Light, what if it had been a funeral for Gunder? So much could have happened while she was incapacitated.

"Big guy. Follows the Queen around like a shadow. Special blue on his uniform?"

"We never see the Queen."

"Word is, this huge guy, a proven fighter, was defeated by a student from the Mess, a female student." Rafiq raised his eyebrows, dark eyes shrewd.

Images from her fights clicked through Mara's mind.

"Could that female have been you?"

Mara sat back. "I fought an extra fighter in my last round. Sometimes the teachers do that to increase the challenge." She tried to make the images fall into order and failed. "I think I was already ill by that fight. All I really remember is that the other fighter was going to kill my friend. He said something like soldiers should die for being weak. So I shielded both of us..." Mara narrowed her eyes. "Wait. How did you know about shields?"

Rafiq stroked his beard. "You mean earlier? When I ordered you to lower your shield?"

Alertness shifting to mild alarm, Mara nodded. None of the students, no one at the Mess, talked about the war experiments.

"I have an associate from your part of the Commonwealth, from Satri. Haven't seen him in a while, but he sent a message about some kids he knew enrolling at the Mess. Asked me to keep an eye out. Though my eating house does well, I have other business interests and one of those is importing rare goods for discerning collectors. Some of my clients collect...information as well as *objets d'art*. A few are extremely interested in the variables of the war experiments. When a report comes my way, I read it to determine the value of the information and set a price."

"You learned about energy shields from a stolen report about Protectors?"

"Very thorough with their reports, the Queen's Military Science Corps."

In response to Mara's puzzled expression he added, "I believe you called them the Browns."

Though surprised, she left questioning his depth of knowledge for a later date. The shouts of street vendors and the clatter of small vehicles drifted in through the window. The door was closed but the smell of baking bread permeated the air, all reminders she was not where she was supposed to be.

"My associate has clearly kept most of his valuable information to himself. A female Protector from Asattha is a rare creature indeed. I'm looking forward to the rest of your story over dinner." Rafiq's smile took on a predatory cast. "I assume you are staying until the school reopens?"

"You collect stories." She thought of the well-stocked guest room. "Do your collectors collect people?"

His expression flattened and darkened like someone had shuttered every window at once on an otherwise lovely house. "I don't take that kind of work." He tipped the chair forward, front legs crashing loudly on the hard floor.

"Clothes, meals, and a bed don't come for free. Tonight you will pay the rest of my price." Rafiq stalked out of the sleeping room and let the door slam behind him.

Well then. She hadn't meant to, but she'd offended him.

Dalin had warned her to stay away from school and now Rafiq confirmed it. It wouldn't have been her first choice, but the back room of an eating house in Lower Town was a great place to lie low. Except for her unpredictable host, she almost liked it here. If Rafiq's associate from Satri was her Uncle Jameson or someone in his network, it would confirm her instinct that she was relatively safe. For the moment.

Pacing bookcase to door, bed to door, Mara assessed her condition. Head clear, sore joints and muscles manageable, stomach full, body and hair clean, clothes clean. Her shoulder still needed attention, but her fingers weren't numb anymore. Bored and used to being, well, useful, she didn't want to stay in the back room. And absent restraints or a locked door, Rafiq couldn't make her.

Information and the movement her body needed to heal were right down the hall. Ready to defend her decision, she made her way to the main room of the eating house.

She found Geraldo shuffling his bulky frame through tables, many more occupied than empty. Catching up with him on his way into the kitchen, she asked, "Where's Rafiq?"

"Stormed out somewhere. Something about a part for the cooler. Typical. Dinner rush is just getting started." The cook swung his thick arm in a semicircle to encompass the tables full of people.

"I can help," Mara offered.

Geraldo's dark eyebrows arched toward his hairline. "You look more like a fighter than a waitress, *prima*."

"I can pour water and bring full plates out. Take empty ones back to the kitchen." She needed to move. And she didn't like Rafiq's insistence that she owed him.

The giant cook shrugged. "Yeah, that's better than nothing. Start with that group over there. Work your way around the room."

Mara listened to the customers' food orders as she filled glasses with water and tea. In the kitchen, she dropped dirty plates in the soaker and repeated customers' words to Geraldo. He glided along the long double grill with the grace of a fight master, flipping and chopping meat and vegetables.

Time became a loop, one long winding walk between the sixteen tables and the kitchen.

When a customer ordered something stronger than water or tea, Geraldo would put down his spatula and mix liquids and ice behind the bar counter.

Mara handed over two plates of *masala dosa* and one *huevos rancheros*. Forks, spoons, water, and all the diners were set. She dropped into a chair right next to the kitchen door, legs and back as tired as after a long training session or a forced march.

The kitchen door opened a fraction. "How's it?" rumbled Geraldo.

"Everyone's eating. No new customers." Mara yawned and rolled her shoulders.

"Let's get you fed." He wedged the door open farther. "Anything you want. You earned it."

She thought about the plates of delicious food she'd carried over the past hour. She would gladly eat any of it now that her stomach was functional. "I'll take whatever you have extra of. Don't go to any trouble."

"Tonight's special for the guest." Geraldo nodded. "Get yourself some tea and it'll be right out."

Mara pulled a clean brown mug from the rack and filled it with steaming mint tea. A group of men in flight suits waved at her on their way out.

"Hey, Rafiq," one said. "Like your new staff. Sure beats looking at you and that cook all the time."

Rafiq, on his way in, paused when he saw Mara clearing the dirty plates. He exchanged a few words in another language and slapped a few palms. "Don't know if we're keeping her yet or if she's just passing through."

Lumbering out of the kitchen like a bear from a cave, Geraldo said, "Rafiq?" Seeing his business partner, he lowered his chin. "Nice timing, *jefe*, we're back down to two tables."

Rafiq adjusted the long bag slung over his shoulder. "So you put our guest to work?" He emphasized the word *guest* as he closed in on Geraldo.

"You left. She offered."

"Right. I did." Rafiq took Mara's mug and walked to the nearest table. He plunked it down in front of a chair and pointed at her. "Sit."

Mara glanced at Geraldo. He shrugged and banged through the kitchen door.

The owner of the eating house filled a mug for himself and dropped into the opposite chair. He sighed. "Please. Sit."

The overhead light cast smudgy shadows under his eyes and cheeks. Stubble grew in the shaven and sculpted areas of his beard.

She continued to stand, crossing her arms over her chest. "I put myself to work to pay down my debt, the debt you say I owe." She reached for the steaming mug and took a sip, undecided about sitting down.

The last two groups called farewells as they headed to the door. Geraldo popped his head out and waved.

"Geraldo, man, you make the best green chile outside of Dorado," one of the younger men said.

"Family recipe." The cook bowed and returned to his domain.

In the sudden absence of diners' voices, the wheezing of the air chiller and the squeaks as the ceiling fans turned suddenly grew loud. She hooked a foot around the nearest chair and pulled it closer before she sat down outside her host's reach.

"I was a little forceful earlier," Rafiq said. "Human cargo is a sensitive subject." He looked up through his long lashes.

She guessed this was an apology, but it underscored how little she knew about the man in black linen. Clearly he had reasons other than kindness for helping her.

Sipping the tea but keeping her eyes steady on the man across the table, Mara said, "I have to go back tomorrow during the funeral. And I don't want to owe you."

His full lips curved and his eyes lost some of their seriousness. "Of course. Helping you has paid some of my debt to the Light. The choice to gift me with another part of a story is yours."

Geraldo pushed the swinging door with his hip and brought them two overflowing plates. "Two specials."

"Thank you," Mara said. "Are you going to eat?"

"Maybe. Already been eating all day, it's why I love my job." He smirked at Rafiq.

Her host retrieved forks, knives, and napkins for both of them. "That trader was right. Geraldo does make the best green chile anywhere off Dorado." Rafiq dug into his food with enthusiasm but managed to keep his beard and shirt immaculate.

Mara tried a bite of the spiced potatoes and mashed beans covered in thick yellowish sauce. The texture was soft with different amounts of chewy, the high notes of spice and low notes of sweet meshed in delicious harmony. No wonder the special had been so popular tonight.

"Good yeah?" Rafiq dabbed at his chin. "He threw in some of the *dosa* potatoes. The meat is *pollotro*. A genetically modified relative of the chicken."

"I have a friend who would love this." Dalin would analyze it but he would be happy while he was trying the new cuisine. She began to eat faster as she realized how hungry she was. Unlike her years as a Protector, she ate three times a day at the Mess. Her body now expected a regular food intake.

"This wasn't the first time I found a soldier from the Mess stumbling around in an alley. But you're the youngest and the prettiest," he said.

As the spice built on her palate, a light sweat beaded her forehead. Mara wiped her mouth and gulped some water. "Still don't know how I got here. You dragged me from the alley?" That didn't seem right. But she knew how sick she'd been.

Her host shrugged and sipped some tea. "On the road to recovery now."

"I wasn't myself and…those men would have hurt me, if you hadn't come along." Twin spots of shame burned on her cheeks. "I wasn't prepared. I didn't defend…" She trailed off in a mumble, pushing potatoes into a pile with her fork.

"Sweetheart, those bastards up at the Mess drugged you out of your head." He rocked his chair onto its back legs. "Never seen anything like it. Your eyes were all black and you were burning up sick."

"What about my eyes?" Mara snatched both hands to her lap to hide her agitation.

"Well, they're blue now. Blue as Daniel's Lake back where I grew up. But in the alley, I could've sworn they were black through and through, like holes in your skull. That happen to any other fighters lately?"

"I don't know." She wiped sweating palms on her pants.

Rafiq considered this, tapping one booted foot against a chair leg. "You're the first Protector I've met. But I guess now that the experiment's done, more of you will make it off planet."

"We didn't know it was an experiment. I grew up thinking it was a real war." Now that Rafiq had changed the subject, she settled enough to resume scooping beans and green chile into her mouth.

"Yeah, once Iloel fell apart I hoped Asattha would be next. Sure, kids are reckless and stupid enough to fight half decent. But that's no excuse for putting them on the battlefield with weapons."

Mara stiffened. "I never put my fighters at risk and my senior Protector did not risk me."

"You sound sure." Rafiq rocked and drummed his fingertips on the table's edge. "That's a gift, certainty."

She wasn't certain, had never been certain. That was why she'd left the Protector compound with Dalin looking for answers. And that was partly why they'd come to Crown City and the Mess. Once she helped the Tree and they had more answers about how to stop the increase in deaths, they were going to find a way to make things better. For good.

"First time I held a weapon I was twelve. My mom's service piece. I was chasing my little sister with it when Mom caught me. She beat me within a centimeter of my life and I deserved it."

Interest sparked, Mara asked, "Did you grow up here? Is your mother still a soldier?"

"Nah." His mouth twisted in a rueful grin. "I grew up a long way from here. Mom's not a peace officer anymore. But my sister is."

Geraldo emerged with a tray. He placed a small bowl in front of Mara and slid a platter full of the special in front of himself. After dragging over a chair and settling his immense frame, he reached into a pocket of his apron and pulled out a wad of currency. "Here you go," he said, shoving the wad over to Mara. "Your share of tonight's tips. Dessert is fried donut and coconut milk."

The crumpled currency displayed pictures of Queen Vanora. In Satri, she'd begun to learn about currency and when it was used instead of trade.

Rafiq reached for the pile and smoothed out the colorful plastic fiber rectangles with his long brown fingers. He counted the bills and laid them in a neat pile, making sure each was face up and going the same direction.

"You may not need cash now, up at the school," he said, responding to Mara's frown. "But it could be useful in the future."

"Girls like to buy extra stuff," Geraldo chimed in. "Dresses, perfume, fancy ribbons for your hair, jewelry." Seeing the skeptical expressions on their faces, Geraldo hmphed. "What? They do."

"Couple more shifts like tonight, you'd have enough for a good field knife or a down payment on some better boots." Rafiq folded the pile neatly and passed it to her with a nod toward her feet. "Those don't fit you very well."

Mara swallowed past the lump in her throat. "You helped me when I...I couldn't..."

"That deal's with him, not me," Geraldo said. "Customers liked you, tipped big. Would've been a hard night without an extra set of hands. You earned some squeeze, simple as that."

Chapter 6

The command for an all Mess faculty and staff meeting hit Dalin's wrist unit two hours before dawn. He was nearly awake anyway. Worry about Mara had kept him up half the night. Instead of trying for more rest, he resumed poring over the research data. The first shift in the Mess Mess opened an hour later, so after a quick meal he hurried to shower and shave.

The missive hadn't specified dress code, but his family believed in erring on the side of formality. Dalin put on a fresh uniform, tucked the corresponding hat under his arm, and headed for the Box.

Anger pushed his long legs into an even faster pace than usual. Fortunately, his slower-moving colleagues cued him to modify his speed. Middle of the pack was always the rule at the Mess. Extremes on either side of average attracted unwelcome attention.

Arriving with the second wave of staff, Dalin found a seat in the risers with a good view of the speaking area and the door. Though the smell of stale sweat still hung in the air, the fight boxes were gone, leaving a large, open expanse of floor. In the yellow glare of the overhead lights, most of the adult faces around him looked tired.

They'd had only one other all-staff meeting since they'd arrived at the school. The main content had been a beginning-of-the-year set of reminders and warnings, including no fraternization with students, and the allowable reasons for awarding or subtracting points.

Dalin opened the message about the meeting again and touched the top edge of the virtual note. A scrolling list of recipients appeared, but not the name of the sender. A different name caught his eye.

Bryant Kucala hadn't been quite as young as Dalin at the university of Hépíng Xīng, but certainly younger than most of the other students. What began as fierce competition developed over time into grudging respect and friendship. Bryant was a pompous, self-aggrandizing teacher's pet, but his presence had made Dalin feel less alone, in the rare moments when he allowed himself to recognize his own isolation.

Was Kucala faculty? How had they not run into each other before now? This could be exactly the break they needed. The Kook was not only a data freak, but also a control freak. If anyone might know how to get the files from the Queen's Council... Dalin shifted on the hard seat and sat up, not openly scanning the crowd but attending to more of the faces of those entering.

At precisely five minutes prior to the start of the meeting, a slim, black male walked through the door and looked up, straight at Dalin who raised a hand in greeting. At the university, Bryant's sport had been swimming. Then, as now, he kept his head shaved. As the man approached, he did not smile, but his eyes lit with interest.

"Tree," he said.

"Kook," Dalin replied.

And with that, he settled into the chair next to Dalin, attention firmly on the podium below.

Sixty seconds later, the dean of the Queen's Military Skills and Strategy School marched to the center of the floor and made a sharp turn to face the assembly. Sir Valji Varatanum came from lesser royalty on Laska and had been a courtier in King Chandragupta's court. Rumors said he'd witnessed Vanora murdering her grandfather, but that wasn't documented anywhere.

This morning, the man looked all of his years and more, his brown forehead deeply creased, his white eyebrows sagging over his dark, sunken eyes. Though every aspect of his white suit and red sash fit perfectly, lay perfectly, the clothes gave the impression of a fresh coverlet pulled over a rumpled bed. Lord Varatanum cleared his throat. "Change is an important value in our Commonwealth. Change based on science or on necessity."

Not everyone in the audience hid their surprise as well as Dalin. Mutters drifted down through the rows.

"Recent events have served to remind all of us, and most particularly our divine Majesty, that our Commonwealth can be divided by, not only distance, but beliefs. Therefore, her highness and the royal council have proposed a change in the procedure to select a new champion." Varatanum paused and wiped his forehead with a white handkerchief.

"For the first time, the tournament to win the place of Queen's Champion will be open to all comers. Any citizen may enter. Therefore the registration period has been doubled and construction will begin this morning on housing for competitors traveling to Crown City from other planets in the Commonwealth."

"Registration opens today. The requirements for tournament participation were developed by one of the Queen's advisory groups, led by Dr. Iskindar. Copies are being delivered now. The requirements will be posted on every student desk as well. Dr. Iskindar?"

Elsebet Iskindar stood and strode to the center of the room, the layers of her dark gray robe shifting as she walked. She and Varatanum nodded to each other and he moved to the far side, near the door.

While Dalin agreed with nearly all of Dr. Iskindar's academic work, he occasionally worried about her need to survive politically in Vanora's court. She had such a massive role in the school, how had she managed to visit Satri so recently?

"You were called here this morning because it is both our hope and our fear that many of the students from this school will register to compete. The requirements of participation are lengthy, and as the faculty, you must be able to provide clarity and answer questions."

Perhaps owing to the seriousness of the occasion, Dr. Iskindar's braids did not click as she paced back and forth in front of her colleagues. She wore no beads and no jewelry except the silver hoops in each ear.

The muttering and whispers began immediately and continued without shushing from any source for over a minute. With a slight nod toward Kucala, Dalin said, "What do you—"

"Later," Kucala interrupted, shifting his face and shoulders away.

"It is a single elimination tournament, once the tournament portion begins. But until then, training schedules will likely disrupt class schedules," Dr. Iskindar said.

A large groan rose collectively from the faculty and louder grumbling as well. A few hands shot up.

After a slow, deep breath, Dr. Iskindar brought her palms together, fingertips pointing up. She nodded. "I understand and share your concern. This academy is a place of learning. How will we guarantee the necessary information has been acquired by students preoccupied with this tournament?"

Dalin assumed his unarmed and armed combat classes would be more well-attended than ever, but the history, literature, mathematics, and science classes probably would suffer during the tournament cycle. Mara would be glad to have more individual attention from her teachers.

"While I commend your commitment to the students, I ask that you think first of your Queen," the professor continued. All the hands dropped and the side conversations went silent.

Dr. Iskindar scanned the group, slowly moving her head from left to right. "Our ruler is the knot at the center of this Commonwealth binding us together. She has lost her champion." Bowing her head, she was silent for a count of five. "And while the *vishakanya* create a living safety net for the Queen's person, her champion is a symbol of strength and readiness to fight on behalf of not only the Queen, but all citizens of our system."

* * *

Toward the end of his second class, Dalin received a summons to the research labs. He led the students through a shortened cooldown and stretch before asking them to store the edged weapons and depart in an orderly way. "Five points to everyone tomorrow," he promised. The topic of the new tournament rules had kept conversation going most of class. Not a single student appeared to be grieving or concerned about the funeral scheduled for the following morning.

A quick trip through the faculty locker room and Dalin was once again crisp and prepared, though his heart picked up speed as a brief worry about the possible discovery of his late-night foray into the data storage center crossed his mind.

The lab number on the summons was on the far side of a restricted hallway. Dalin had to show the virtual communication to the sentry before being allowed to proceed. These labs weren't just for the Mess; this was where the War Project variables were monitored and adjusted.

Seven sets of doors, five bright and two dark, lined the hall. The project on Iloel had been over for decades. He hoped the other dark door represented Asattha. And though the public credit for the end of the war project on their home planet had gone to a rebel group calling themselves the King's Men, he and Mara had struck critical blows. Which meant, even though he wanted to disagree with Mara's logic and her sense of responsibility, they had a share in the sharp rise in deaths across the other war experiments.

If the darkened labs represented Asattha and Iloel, the lit doors represented the heart of cruelty at the center of the Commonwealth. Human lives, generations of human lives, did not need to be sacrificed for security, should never have been sacrificed in the name of security.

With no wood, brick, or plaster in sight, this part of the Mess appeared quite new. When Dalin paused at the door marked D-1 and knocked on the frame, he couldn't help but stare in astonishment. The equipment inside rivaled anything he'd seen or even heard rumors about. Bryant Kucala lifted his head and motioned Dalin inside.

"Tree. Thanks for dropping by."

About half a meter inside the door, Dalin walked through a static field, a milder version of the dome once placed over the Northwest Protector compound. Not only did he feel the slight pins-and-needles sensation on his skin, he felt it against his mental shields also.

In response to the question in his expression, Kucala said, "It's a clean room. Nothing comes in or out without my permission."

Dalin nodded. "The energy field—"

"Smaller, tighter version of a dome field."

The old, anticipate-and-answer-questions-ahead-of-time habit was something Dalin had disliked about Kucala. He tried again, reminding himself to be patient. "Why—"

"Are you here? Because you left some fingerprints when you snooped in the local data last night. I wanted to ask you what you were looking for before I reported you."

His former schoolmate sat on a rolling lab stool in front of a large lit table screen. He tapped icons both floating on the screen and above it until the same tables and reports Dalin had downloaded the previous night appeared in the air between them.

The only thing Kucala cared about, besides being the smartest person in the room, was his sister. "How's Wren?" Dalin asked.

With an odd tick, he snatched his hands away from the evidence and held them flat against the edge of the table. "Wren is well," he said quietly. "She's gone. Away."

Wren was by far the happier of the twins. Just as bright as her brother, she inherited all of the interpersonal skills and, even more unfortunately for Kucala, all the ability to enjoy the simple pleasures of life. When they'd been at school together, Wren had been Dalin's first friend. The first person to take pity on the youngest, tallest student in their classes, the first to introduce him to their group, a mix of scientists, swimmers, and a few musicians.

Dalin searched Kucala's face carefully. "Gone away," Dalin repeated. "That's how they got you here and that's the bargain you struck. Your imprisonment for her freedom."

Standing abruptly, Kucala knocked his metal stool to the tile with a loud crash. He turned his back on Dalin and hurried to a small cooling unit in the corner. "Would you not do the same for your sister?" he asked. "Give your freedom to guarantee hers?"

He pulled two bottles of water from the unit. "Thirsty?" He held one out to Dalin.

After a pointed glance at the data hovering over the table, Dalin asked, "Where is Wren?"

Kucala wiped his sleeve across his forehead and gulped down more than half the bottle. "I didn't realize how long I've been thirsty." He cocked his head to the side and raised his eyebrows.

Dalin stared back. Years ago Kucala might have won a staring match. But not today.

Kucala looked away first. With slow precision, he opened the second bottle of water and drank it down. Finally he said, "My sister is sequestered with a group you crossed paths with recently. I'm working for them as well as my current employer. That is the bargain." The words poured out in a low, mumbling rush.

"The King's Men?"

"The very same." Kucala removed the two empty bottles and straightened every physical file on his table.

"Still working on your old round-the-clock schedule then?"

"Except when my routine is disrupted by a snooper."

Right. They were back on solid ground. "The female in this data," Dalin gestured toward the numbers. "She is my partner. Protectors are assigned—"

"In pairs. I know."

"Do you know who chose her or what the intended course of this particular experiment is?"

Kucala righted his stool. With a large arm swipe, he sent the number screens back to the table and opened additional virtual windows in the middle of the room. "They picked a pool of likely candidates to make the final rounds of the tournament. Additional candidates will be chosen as they register."

"Based on?"

"Based on size, speed, prior fight record, fight-suit data. Your partner is ice cold when she fights, by the way. Staff around here are bitter about the abrupt end of War Project Seven. Lost a lot of jobs. She might have been targeted because of being from Asattha."

With a flick of his index finger, he opened the video of Mara in the Box with Gunder and the Queen's now-dead champion. Both males watched in silence as Mara took the blow to her shoulder and rose up to punish the man as he shouted at the crowd about weakness and pride. The last blow to his temple was vicious, knocking the huge man into unconsciousness. Dalin couldn't look away as she turned and ran, jumping to the top of the wall and pulling herself over with one hand.

Sometimes she teased him about how good he looked in a uniform, but watching the recording drew Dalin's attention to Mara's lean build and the soft, subtle curves of her figure revealed by the skintight fight suit. Both beautiful and deadly, his partner was the stuff of fantasy.

"After that performance, they're going to target her, study her, make an example of her." Kucala shook his head.

After that performance, Mara would star in a lot more fantasies than just his.

"What if it was Wren?" Dalin resisted the urge to hammer the guy's shiny black dome. "She's like Wren to me." Well, obviously not like a sister, but he wasn't going to share that with Kook. "Precious to me. I dug into the data because I had to find out what they did to her. But now—"

"Now I'm giving you the bad news. This was only the beginning."

Dalin took a ten count to breathe and check his mental shields. "What do you mean?"

"This girl, Mara De La Luz? She's landing in the tournament, mark my words. And from now on she's an active research site. They're going to drag her out of wherever she's hiding and put her in a lab or a situation that will essentially be a test. She responded far too well to the new drug dosage for them to let it go."

Kucala waved a hand toward the hall. "I'd say you might get lucky and," he paused to crack his knuckles, "and the Queen doesn't know yet. But since Mara's the one who brought down that ass, the former champion, Vanora probably knows everything about her by now."

Chapter 7

Rafiq found Mara staring into the closet the next morning. He handed over the fight suit, folded and secured with its straps. "The tracking's live on this so we need to move out."

In her mind's eye, Mara saw the closet in her room at her aunt and uncle's house. That brief taste of life with Elana and Jameson was her most treasured memory. "How long would it take me to earn passage to Asattha?" Just thinking about ignoring the Mother Tree's compulsion and returning home shot a stab of pain through the back of her skull.

Her host raked his dark eyes from her head to her feet, no humor in his expression. "Depends on what you're willing to do."

A sharp buzzer sounded two short bursts. Rafiq raised an eyebrow and rested his right hand on the weapons belt he wore slung over a longer tunic and thick canvas trousers. "Early for company," he said. "Too fast to be that *antika* suit."

He brushed past Mara and shoved the hanging clothes to either side, reaching for the back of a middle shelf. With a click, the entire shelf wall swung open. "Geraldo will handle it. Let's move."

Slipping into the tight space between the inner and outer walls of the structure, he tugged Mara behind him and closed the shelf. In the space of one breath the oppressive morning heat filled her lungs and added an invisible layer to her clothes. After a few short steps they popped into an alley. Unfiltered sun burned her eyes until Rafiq handed over a shiny pair of sunglasses. They cut the glare but did nothing to stop the hot press of the sun. He wrapped a black-and-white checkered scarf around his head and neck, settling the cowl into place with practiced speed.

Rusted metal containers crowded the narrow alley along with crates and empty burlap sacks piled in a hodgepodge of large and small, new and old. The door they'd used had disappeared into the corrugated metal wall. Old stone masonry stained with urine, refuse, and time formed the other wall of the alley.

"Is this where—?"

"Nah, you were a bit closer to the spaceport. I saw you spill on that scum and stayed to watch the fight." Rafiq chuckled. "Best entertainment of the night."

"Mara De La Luz." The voice was in her mind, but also audible. "Leave is over. You are hereby ordered to return to the Queen's Military Skills and Strategy School along with the valuable property in your possession."

She clutched the tightly packed fight suit to her chest, squinting through the sunglasses as Dalin appeared at one end of the alley. Two Commonwealth soldiers blocked the other end.

He signaled to the pair to hold their positions and moved closer to Mara and Rafiq. The sun gilded his light hair and brightened his crisp, already whiter-than-white uniform. Yanking off his sunglasses, Dalin leaned in close with an expression that promised extra push-ups and laps around the palace.

"I'm yelling at you. You've taken refuge in a disreputable part of town and borrowed valuable equipment without permission." His conspiratorial tone was a sharp contrast to his expression and posture.

She took a half step forward. "Dalin, what—"

"When I heard the head of school was sending a party to retrieve you, I volunteered." He tilted his chin toward Rafiq. "Plan on putting up a fight? Or do you yield to our superior numbers?" The second question came out much louder for the benefit of the other soldiers.

"Youngster, you can shove your superior numbers. Mara goes where she wants, when she wants. I'm just a humble citizen here to help an injured soldier of the Queen. You should be offering me a reward, matter of fact." Rafiq smiled then, as though a brawl in an alley might be the best way to get the day started.

Geraldo appeared behind the two extra guards holding a wickedly sharp kitchen knife, though his bulk alone was enough to give anyone pause. "Boss?" he said.

Dalin spared a quick glance at the cook and shook his head. "Mara inspires loyalty wherever she goes."

"They rescued me, cared for me when I was sick. These men gave me food and shelter." Her voice cracked with indignation.

"Understood, but the escort and the show were deemed necessary." He lowered his chin and stared straight into her eyes.

"Mara," his soft voice sounded in her brain.

She took a deep breath, nodded in acceptance, wanting nothing more than to hug him and rumple the starched uniform.

Geraldo lowered the knife and shuffled forward, putting himself in front of the additional men. "Hey, you know this guy?"

"He's a friend from home," she said and gave the cook a reassuring smile. She kept her focus on Dalin, certain he wouldn't want her to say more. "And he knows I was safe here and intended to return on my own." She fought the urge to lean into his side and take reassurance from his steadiness and strength.

"He volunteered to protect me." As she spoke, Mara's voice dropped until this last was barely audible for anyone farther away than Rafiq to hear.

"Of course," Dalin said, with a flash of his trademark grin.

Rafiq nodded once and tugged the cowl from his head. "We've got a business to open. Been a pleasure serving the Queen's own."

"Come and wait tables anytime," Geraldo said. "The spacers will be asking for ya." He clapped Mara's uninjured shoulder and slipped past Dalin toward the commercial side of the eating house.

Dalin took her by the arm, making the hold look more painful than it was. "Don't speak out loud," he said. "You've just been chastised." To the two guards he said, "She's coming without a fight. Please clear a path through the crowd and we will follow."

The twin desires to punch Dalin and kiss him were as familiar as breathing. He kept a hand clamped around her bicep, and the contact made mental rapport as clear and easy as it had been at home. She could have closed her eyes and walked safely using Dalin's senses instead of her own.

"There was a scientist disguised as a healer. She's the one who drugged you. Do you remember someone with yellow braids?"

"Yes." She responded with an image of the woman who kept forcing her to drink water.

"Must have been in the water. Nothing tasted wrong?"

She licked her dry lips. *"A faint bitterness maybe. I think I'd know if I tasted it again."*

Ahead of them the two soldiers pushed and steered the market day shoppers out of their path. Curious glances assessed Mara's disheveled, ill-fitting clothes and the large bundle she carried.

She stumbled over a loose section of paving in the road, her feet slipping inside the borrowed boots. As Dalin's thoughts, at least the ones he let her see, worked over the idea of a nearly tasteless drug, soluble in water that turned a soldier into a superhuman fighter, Mara took in their surroundings, memorizing the route back to the eating house.

Lower Town was both residential and commercial with families living in, behind, and/or above their shops. Categories of commerce, such as weapons, tanners, and herbalists, grouped together in clusters of stands and stores. Market Square in Satri was a slow, orderly procession compared to the noise and chaos bursting from Lower Town as the sun rose higher in the sky.

As they marched farther and the ground began to slope subtly upward, order reasserted itself. The shops grew into larger, more permanent structures and the smells grew more pleasant. Cleaner, less-harried families moved at a slower pace, their clothes and jewelry proclaiming affluence. As the hot spots on both her heels began to pinch like blisters, their group entered the neighborhood of mini-palaces.

"*About ten minutes more*," Dalin assured her. She had kept herself open and he was aware of her discomfort. "*I'm taking you straight to the infirmary*."

"*Can't*," Mara sent. "*Boots need to be returned, have to log in suit, get my uniform from my locker*."

"*I'll deal with it. Do you trust anyone enough to draw blood? Run tests?*"

She conjured an image of the healer with the long Iloel tattoo curving around her ear. "*Sangita knows about the Tree and my connection to Her. My eyes went black during the fights and I could shield. Do you think that means a Tree is near here after all?*"

The hill was much steeper now and her feet kept sliding backward. She stumbled again and in a few staggering steps found a place to sit in the shade of a fruit tree with feathery leaves. Thinking about shielding reminded her of— "*Gunder? Is he all right?*"

Dalin called out to the two soldiers. "I'll take it from here, men. This soldier is not a danger and likely needs medical attention." The guards saluted and marched off.

He sat down next to her and leaned in to smooth a few damp strands of hair from her face. As he lifted her borrowed sunglasses, his earnest gray eyes locked on hers. "Blue now, blue as the summer sky over Satri." Never in the last few months had Mara wanted more than to crawl in his lap and kiss him until they both ran out of air.

Pulling the thought from her mind, Dalin smiled as he whispered, "Me too." "Soon. For now, let's get you to the infirmary. Gunder's there, recovering nicely." He stood and brushed off his uniform then reached out a hand. "You can see for yourself."

Her head spun when she was fully upright, memories of the fight, blurred impressions washing around in her brain. "I didn't kill that fighter."

"No, you forced him to yield and then you knocked him out in front of everyone."

"But he died? His funeral is today?" She had to get these questions answered before they entered the school grounds.

"The *official* story is that he took his own life out of shame." Dalin shook his head and shrugged.

Mara concentrated on walking as they turned the next curve and saw the gates in the distance. "Why send the Queen's Champion into the box with me?"

"He may have volunteered. I'm still checking into it," he said. "I was sitting with some of the instructors and we didn't see him come from the royal box."

"The soldier who stabbed Gunder, his main duty is to protect the Queen?"

"Was his duty, yes."

She stopped and put her hands on her hips, squinting up at the palace. Her heart was speeding up and she couldn't get a deep breath.

Dalin put his hand on her shoulder and leaned in close. He smelled like *gontra* trees and home. "Almost there," he said.

The final stretch of road snaked back and forth as the hill was far too steep to walk straight up. Small one-person service vehicles passed at regular intervals. Finally they reached a black gate. Dalin's wrist unit buzzed them through.

Mara dropped onto the first bench inside the blissfully cool lower hallway. "Got to get out of these boots," she said, drawing up one knee and reaching for the laces.

Dalin knelt in front of her, running a warm hand up the back of her calf, fingers kneading the tight muscle. Quickly, he unlaced the boot and pulled it off, revealing an angry blister across the back of that heel. Bending his head, he reached for the other boot, his short golden hair catching stray shafts of morning sun coming through the high windows.

With both blistered heels exposed, Mara bit back a groan. She wouldn't be able to wear her own boots now either. But Dalin wrapped a hand around each heel and poured energy into the injuries. In seconds, the pain receded to a slight throb.

He glanced around for cameras before standing and pulling Mara up against him. "I'm going to hack the feed anyway," he muttered then brushed her lips with his own. "I was worried," he whispered, his arms tightening around her as he dipped in for a short but hard kiss.

When his lips touched hers again, Mara pulled him closer, rising up on her toes to fit her mouth against his. Fatigue, confusion, worry melted in the heat of the kiss until only Dalin was left, rock solid at the core of her consciousness.

He kissed the shell of her ear. "When I saw that monster walk into the box... I knew he could kill you—"

A door slammed down the hall and the pair sprang apart.

Eyes now a dark smoky gray, Dalin took deep breath and rubbed a hand over his hair. It was hard not to stare at his mouth. "How you tempt me." His words a gravelly whisper.

Through his eyes, she saw her own face: kiss-reddened lips, long tousled dark hair, blue eyes hazed with passion. Powerful to know that was how he saw her.

"*I wish we were alone,*" she sent, taking a step away. "*I want to touch your skin.*" She could almost feel the warm tan expanse of his chest. She'd seen him without a shirt once so she sent that image back to him.

He closed the distance between them in one stride and pushed Mara against the interior wall, pressing his body against hers. He nibbled and tasted her lips before his tongue slid in her mouth, tangling with hers, igniting her from head to toe. She threaded her fingers in his hair and urged him closer.

"I'll find a way," he rasped before he broke away. He grabbed the fight suit from the bench and marched toward the locker rooms.

Mara sagged against the wall, head spinning, bare feet cold on the tile floor. She touched her sensitive, swollen lips and took a deep breath, then another, trying to get her bearings. Next step was to get to her locker and change into her uniform.

Due to mass attendance at the funeral, she made it to the locker room without notice. After a quick press of her thumb, the lock clicked open and released the door. Her day uniform was wrinkled and far from clean, but it would have to suffice for the walk back to the dorm. She shrugged and rotated her injured shoulder, feeling the tug of the stitches. Another thing to owe Rafiq for, something he hadn't even mentioned.

* * *

A few hours later, Annelise caught up with Mara in line at the Mess Mess.

"Mara," Annelise squealed. "That fight was amazing. And you saved Gunder. They say no fatalities but everyone thought he was going to kill Gunder and—"

"Have you seen him today?" Mara interrupted quietly, ducking closer to her friend.

"They're going to release him tonight. He lost so much blood he had to get a transfusion, but he's much better already."

They got their food, green mush with white squares, rice, and white meat with red spices, and looked for a place to eat. The Mess Mess was full at peak time for the evening meal but the normally boisterous crowd was more subdued, groups huddling in closer together than usual. Some pairs and trios ate quietly without talking at all.

The two Protectors grabbed chairs at a central table. Annelise went back for utensils and Mara nabbed two tall glasses of water.

"Quiet tonight."

"The funeral," Annelise spoke around a mouthful of rice. "He'd been the Queen's Champion for five years. I think she really," she ducked her head and whispered, "I think she loved him. She was so broken up, she couldn't hardly give her speech."

The *saag paneer* tasted great, but Mara wished her plate was loaded with green chile and potatoes. "How did someone that important end up in the Box with me and Gunder?" She kept her voice quiet as she wondered aloud.

"No one knows, or if they know, they're not sayin'. Friday fights is cancelled for this week 'cause they're gonna announce cuts Friday morning."

"How many?"

Annelise shrugged. "Not us, that's all I care about."

When she stood to get another piece of fruit, Mara casually scanned the room for Fentress and the girls in her squad. It was the first she'd heard of an all-female group being allowed. Grabbing a banana, she walked to one of the corners and looked along the far wall. In the opposite corner, a white-blonde head bobbed among a crew of braids and close-cropped dark hair. Fentress turned and caught Mara's gaze. She nodded once. Mara nodded back.

A few minutes later, Fentress appeared behind Annelise. "Got good use out of those boots, yeah?" As Annelise turned and stared, another fighter, just as tall and deadly looking as Fentress, leaned in and whispered something in the blonde's ear. Her nose stud flashed as she dipped her head and nodded in agreement.

"You girls have some fighting skills," Fentress said. "And the Furies, we're always looking for fresh talent."

"The Furies? I've heard of you." Annelise started to bounce on her chair, then visibly stilled herself. "Yeah, you have this leader who almost became Queen's champion, right?"

"Daphne," the black-haired girl said. She slipped her arm through Fentress's and pulled closer. "Daphne founded the Furies and now we have fighting groups across the Commonwealth."

Where Fentress was tall and broad-shouldered, uniform molding to her arm and leg muscles, her companion was slim and straight, but equally toned. Different fighters for different fights. One could imagine Fentress handling a weapon, but her friend *was* a weapon, no accessories needed.

"It was an open tournament, like the one her majesty will be announcing shortly. Daphne showed our strength and honored every one of us. A Fury will win this time," Fentress said and when she smiled, it wasn't so much friendly as it was ferocious.

"Kailer here wanted to meet you." The blonde indicated her companion. "And I wanted to tell you to bring my boots to the morning workout. Can't wait to hear about your adventures in Lower Town." She winked.

"Nice to meet you," Mara said to Kailer.

Kailer stuck out a lean, dark tan hand and clasped her forearm. "I'm looking forward to going a few practice rounds with you," she said, her voice surprisingly light. "You too, little one," she said to Annelise. "Saw a few of those vicious kicks and takedowns on Friday. No prisoners. I like your style."

"*Hasta mañana*," Fentress said and tugged Kailer toward the exit.

Annelise's blue eyes rounded with excitement. She fanned her face with one hand. "Oh my, the Furies are interested in us."

Mara nodded, excited and flattered in spite of herself. "Fentress helped me run the other night."

"I wasn't going to ask, but you were in Lower Town this whole time?"

"Yeah," she said and began an abbreviated version of the past two days, leaving out most of the key details about Geraldo and Rafiq.

* * *

While it might be romantic to tell himself he'd never doubted that Mara was the one for him, Dalin had his doubts during the years they'd been apart. Until she'd dropped him and put a knife to his throat their first night outside the war project, and then the certainty returned. He'd wanted to kiss her right then.

What he'd said to Kucala wasn't untrue. He cared for Mara beyond reason, and he'd sacrifice anything to keep her safe and happy. But the physical longing was short-circuiting the logical part of his mind. She'd been drugged and injured, had to run away from school, and he just wanted to get her naked.

When they'd been on Asattha, the Tree had been wise to place the pain blocks in his mind. It was *almost* too bad the effects weren't sustained once they left.

As he logged Mara's fight suit and dropped it into the cleaning chute, Dalin continued lecturing himself, interspersed with fantasies about being alone with Mara at the wayhouse, in a tent, anywhere but the Mess. Problem was, the more time they were alone together, the more ties that would bind them together as a pair and the worse for them if something bad happened to either one of them.

Dalin had to make sure nothing bad happened. Ever again.

The healer Mara trusted, who knew about the Tree and Mara's connection to her, had an office between the locker rooms and the Box. He passed individuals and groups of students on the way, a few from his combat classes calling out greetings.

Each of the healers had a small digital sign showing name, specialty, and office hours to the left of his or her door. Near the far end of the hall, much closer to the Box, Dalin found Sangita's door closed. Glancing at the posted hours, he knocked.

Soft light spilled onto the syncrete floor when a stocky woman opened the door. Tilting her head to the side, she said, "Yes?"

"I'm here about follow-up care for a student you treated on Friday," he said.

She glanced into the empty hall behind him and motioned him inside. "Which student?" she inquired, expression politely neutral. She stood in front of a simple, bare wooden desk, a matching chair with colorful cushions pushed back. The room held a high training table for massages and other healing work, and one stool.

The woman was shielded, but it was light, easy to penetrate. Dalin thrust a picture of Mara into her mind as he closed the door behind him.

Sangita gasped and staggered back to her cushioned chair. Dalin gave her a series of images—Mara as a child, Mara leading the young Protectors, Mara sparring one of the militiamen from Satri. "She's my partner," he said.

The older woman sat still, fingers brushing her right temple. "I'll forgive you that transgression, this once." Her shield tripled in strength and she severed Dalin's connection. "You're distraught. As am I. Do you know where the Daughter is now?"

His stomach dropped at the word "daughter." When he glanced away he saw the huge image of the Tree covering the entire wall to the right of the door. That didn't help.

Trying to recover his equilibrium, he said, "Mara found refuge in Lower Town but she's back at the Mess as of now. She says she trusts only you to take her blood. We'll need samples to analyze what the drug is doing to her system."

Muttering under her breath, the healer activated a shield in the room. It felt more organic than the one in Kucala's lab, but equally strong. "Sit," she commanded and pointed at the table.

Dalin swallowed. He'd been too hasty, too forceful. Disrespectful. "Forgive me the intrusion," he said. "The room didn't feel safe and I needed you to know I'm not, I would never—"

"You are bound to the Daughter. You would never betray her," Sangita said, her brown eyes bright as she stared at him.

His mental senses told him this woman was far more powerful than she seemed, though in every visible way she was merely a healer from Iloel, working at the Mess.

"Quit pecking and pushing and just ask. Is this how you treat your elders at home?"

"No, ma'am. No, I… Please accept my apology. The preliminary reports about the drug they used on her are…" Awful. Terrifying. Inhumane. "More than concerning."

Sangita moved forward and brushed her fingers across his forehead, her irritated expression softening. "You bound yourself to her long ago. And the Tree Mother, she strengthened the bond."

"Yes."

"I am pledged in service to the Daughter. But to love her, be bound to her, that is a different sort of service altogether."

Dalin's posture sagged for a moment and he scrubbed a hand across his hair. "Yes."

With a clap on his shoulder, Sangita said, "Well, that makes us allies, does it not? When the Daughter comes, I will take the samples. Some I will give to you—" Dalin opened his mouth to argue and snapped it closed again at her glare. "Some I will give to you," she repeated. "And some I will have analyzed by my people, as you say."

Stepping down from the table, Dalin executed a deep bow, in the style most favored on Iloel. "My gratitude is yours."

She caught his arm as he reached for the door. "The Mess is not a place to be hasty. Take care."

Chapter 8

The next morning, Mara threw the borrowed boots in a backpack and let them bounce against her shoulders as she ran through the quiet halls. Fitful sleep left her tired, and the assessing looks of her bunkmates as they'd crossed paths kept her wary. In Lower Town she'd felt pressed to return to school; now she felt tempted to run out the door and back down Palace Hill.

Breathing hard, she came to a stop just inside the large gym. The weight machines and mats were empty except for Fentress and another female.

The tall blonde waved her over. "Hey," she said. "What's your worst weapon?"

Mara shrugged out of the small pack and handed over the boots. She took a long drink from a water bottle she had scrubbed out and refilled, just in case, and thought about the question.

"I don't know. Haven't tried them all."

"Ha, see, that's a true answer," Fentress said to a short, thick woman with large defined biceps doing heavy reps on the bench press.

"You get into any of the live fire simulations yet?" asked the woman from the bench press.

Mara stretched out on the mat and reached for her toes. "Like energy weapons? No. Do we get to learn that here?"

The thick woman sat up and wiped her face on the hem of her shirt, revealing a large intricate tattoo in heavy black lines across her stomach. "You should. That's what we're facing in almost every conflict except Asattha."

One of Mara's favorite stretches was to cross one leg, knee bent, over the other and reach around the other way, like a hug. "You've been in action besides on your home world?" She asked, genuinely interested now in the woman and her tattoo.

"Yeah, grew up on Dorado, but just got back from Tian. It's all energy weapons and distance fighting. Doesn't matter how much I can lift," she gestured to the weight bench. "Or how far you can run," she pointed at Mara. "Everything depends on your equipment, timing, and aim."

A few machines over, Fentress worked her triceps. "Lupe, this is Mara, the one who knocked out Mr. Fancy Pants. We're thinking she might be Fury material."

Lupe grinned, dark brown eyes sparkling under long black lashes. "I cannot believe I missed your fight. Saw the recording, but Darkness take me I wish I'd been there. That man was the most narcissistic piece of sh—" She stopped herself and self-consciously fingered her stubby black ponytail. "Sorry, you get used to speaking a little too freely away from this place."

Usually Dalin was here by now, but only two other students had appeared and they were busy on one of the training mats, working some kind of fight combination. "I grew up inside the Protector Project," Mara said as she stood. "I probably couldn't speak freely if someone paid me."

Fentress laughed. "You Asatthans are a quiet bunch. Doesn't matter to us as long as you get the job done. ¿Estás de acuerdo, Lupe?"

Lupe offered her hand to Mara. Standing, she was eye level with Mara's collarbone. "You keep fighting like that and the Furies would be proud to call you one of our own. Stick with Fentress here, she'll keep you right."

"Thanks," Mara said, shaking the woman's small hand.

"I may have orders waiting when I get back to quarters," Lupe said to Fentress. "If not, I'll catch you and the other zorritas at dinner." She rolled the r and showed her teeth.

Both Fentress and Mara watched the seasoned soldier walking away.

Fentress switched to the bench press. "Spot me for a few?"

"Sure." Mara couldn't get into her routine anyway, not without Dalin.

"Lupe was the leader of the Furies when I got here. She's been deployed the better part of two years." Fentress motioned Mara close enough to whisper in her ear. "She and her whole platoon got recalled because the fight on Iloel is completely squigged. Gonna be shipping out hundreds of fresh hands to get it squared away."

Fentress let the bar clang back into the holder and sat up. "The girls and me would love to get in on that, but technically we don't graduate until spring."

Dropping into the tricep machine, Mara asked a question that had been bothering her for a while. "Once you finish your fifth year, how do you get deployed? Are there terms, contracts for years of service?"

The older girl moved to the mat and started a set of fast sit-ups. "Yes and no," she said, breathing out with each rep. "Part of how you pay for the privilege of attending this school, her majesty feeding and training you, is to fight for the Commonwealth in whatever manner, in whatever location they see fit. Minimum payment is three years." The older girl got out a few words each time she sat up to her knees.

Finishing triceps, Mara checked the door and scanned the entire gym again.

"Looking for your hometown honey?"

Fentress had flipped to her stomach and was holding a high plank position.

"What?"

Breathing shallowly, the Fury said, "Your guy, the one you work out with in the mornings. The instructor from Asattha. He's your *novio, sí?*"

Mara blushed and looked away, her eyes landing on the "No Relationships" sign.

Adjusting her position, Fentress shifted her weight to her forearms and flattened out her back. "You don't have to say anything. Good for you, he's *pivonazo.*"

One corner of Mara's mouth turned up when she met the blonde's knowing smile full of shared appreciation.

* * *

On Friday after classes ended, all of the first-year students were summoned to the Box. Their point totals hung in the air, visible from all four sides. The bottom twenty-five percent lit up in red, and a lead instructor asked those soldiers to stand. He launched into a speech about service and the elite task of serving Queen and Commonwealth at the highest levels. The departing students were thanked and then dismissed.

"Some of the figures aren't right," a fully recovered Gunder muttered on Mara's left.

"What do you mean?" she whispered, feeling mildly jealous as she watched her former classmates depart.

"I was doing totals in my head over and over on Friday night, partly 'cause I was worried about you." He smiled a little. "And partly because I was so nervous. Anyway, I had a bunch of the bottom memorized. And that ain't it. Looks like all of them lost points for losing, you know? Every single fighter who lost two outta three or three outta three rounds is going home, even if they was out of the danger range before. And plus this is two months early. Cuts wasn't supposed to happen yet."

Annelise elbowed Gunder and shushed him, pointing to the middle of the box.

Mara's wrist unit pulsed, but just as she touched it, the figure in the center of the empty fighting floor began to speak.

"It is my privilege to announce to all of you who have already given so much to the Commonwealth a rare opportunity to do even more, something incredibly special. It is the best reward for good work, as they say, the opportunity to do more." The speaker paused and chuckled at her own joke. "My name is Emily bin Haribin and I work in the Ministry of Information."

Bin Haribin wore a sheer blue headscarf over long, braided auburn hair. Her semi-fitted blue and gold *djellaba* masked nearly every detail of her physique, but her lips were painted a bright scarlet. Clearly not a fighter, not even ex-military, she swayed and gestured with both hands as she continued.

"When the King's or Queen's Champion is lost, as happened so tragically only one week ago, it has become tradition to hold an open tournament to replace him."

"Or her," someone shouted from the stands.

Emily bin Haribin smiled. "Well, that's up to you, my dear."

The students rustled and muttered. But no one else shouted.

"As I was saying, the official announcement of the tournament is today, though some groups, internal to the school only, were informed earlier in the week. The details of events, categories, requirements, etc., have been sent to each of you to peruse at your leisure. You must submit your intent to enter within the next two weeks, but the tournament itself will not take place for at least a month or more."

Mumbling and whispers grew louder again.

"In a break with tradition, the Queen is opening the tournament to every citizen of the Commonwealth. Her majesty wonders if perhaps she might have cast a wider net for the last contest. And in a gesture of goodwill, spectators from every home world will be invited. Distance viewing will be provided to each capital using holoprojectors as well."

Mara pushed back in her seat and slouched down so the people behind her had a better view. From the excited whispers of the two boys over her left shoulder, it sounded like they both wanted to enter.

She had an appointment with the Iloellian healer, Sangita, in ten minutes so she hoped the announcements wouldn't last much longer.

"You are highly encouraged to read the entire list of qualifications and, most particularly, the entire list of tournament rules before committing yourself to enter. Some of the, ah, *expectations* increase as the number of contestants decreases." Ms. bin Haribin straightened her headscarf as she turned in a tight circle to reach each student with her gaze. "Please direct any questions to my office using my com codes. Dismissed."

A lot of the first years talked and postured boisterously after the meeting ended, but only a few would be a match for older students at the Mess let alone any trained fighter in the Commonwealth.

Mara picked her way through the seats and down a set of back stairs until she could walk freely to the training rooms. The healers worked on strained muscles and recovery from more serious injuries. She had made the appointment, if anyone asked, because of her healing shoulder. But only to herself, Mara admitted she wanted to find out more about what this woman knew.

The door was slightly ajar so Mara knocked and then pushed it open.

"Tree's Daughter, you do me honor." The Iloellian healer bowed deeply. The saffron yellow of her uniform set off her light brown skin. As she straightened, the beads in her braids clicked softly together. She gestured toward her massage and exam table. "Please, sit."

She slipped past Mara to close the door, snapped her fingers, and said, "*Bodhi*." Instantly, the energy in the room shifted, lightened, the air became easier to breathe somehow.

"Did you just shield this room?"

The woman smiled. "Old Sangita knows a few tricks. I wish to help your shoulder, but I wish to speak with you also."

All of the training rooms were small, but Sangita's space felt less crowded. The syncrete floors were covered in thick brown rugs, and the healer's chair had a red and gold patterned cushion. On the wall opposite the table she'd fixed a gorgeous holo of a *gontra* tree, almost as large as the Great Tree herself. The depth of the holo made it appear as though Mara could walk into it and lay her cheek against the bark. She inhaled, almost expecting to smell the *gontra* sap. The image had been captured in a warm season with thick grass growing at the base of the tree and golden light filtering through the branches.

"The Great Tree of Iloel, as she once was," Sangita said and bowed her head briefly.

"Iloel does have a Tree." Mara's voice rose with surprise and hope.

"Yes, she is far away from the cities and was not discovered until the first rebels sought to create far more than a base for operations. She appeared once they sought to create a new home for themselves and their families."

"My Tree said she had sisters who needed care," the words slipped out, and Mara couldn't take them back. She swallowed as she unfastened her jacket and slipped it off with only a small wince. Stepping out of her boots, she tucked them beneath the table.

Sangita made a hmming sound in her throat as she laid a cool hand across Mara's partially healed cut. "I'm sorry I could not serve you better after your fight with the *dharm wirodhi*. But we will fix this now so that you may continue your work on behalf of the Tree Mother. Your partner came to see me, did you know?"

Turning to look at her face, Mara said, "He mentioned something about blood samples."

"Your bond is strong," Sangita replied. "And so I will trust him. May I?" She held out two quick extraction kits.

After the blood draw, the healer helped Mara to lie on her stomach on the table, left arm extended to the side.

"Do you know what's happening on Iloel? Some people are saying the fight's even more out of hand."

"My brothers and sisters wish to be a self-governing people living in a home free from conflict and the tyranny of the Queen's oppression. We have more than sufficient resources to support ourselves and will not tolerate any further experimentation on or drafting of our people." The words came out in a quietly fierce tone as Sangita's hands kept an even pressure on the injury, knitting and soothing the layers of the deep cut.

"Who is fighting who? How did the problem start?"

Sangita hummed as she kneaded and worked Mara's arm, shoulder, and back muscles. "The first man to call himself King of the Commonwealth came from a region on the Origin that had seen many wars fought on the basis of beliefs. The most dangerous wars, the ones that never ended were those." The healer tucked Mara's left arm against her side and walked around the table to work on the right arm.

"So that King, he thought, 'How about I build a force that believes in nothing, rejects all spiritual teachings as evil. In case we're ever invaded by crusaders on a mission, these soldiers, they will be conversion-proof.' And that's what he did. So we're fighting our own people, same as you on Asattha. The conflict had all but burned out, with the rebels living peacefully far from the soldiers and the nonbelievers, when the Tree Mother found us. That was my grandmother's generation."

With her eyes closed Mara could see the villages, see the soldiers and the fighting across both desert and dry grasslands. "Did something change? Something recent? Word is they're pulling troops from other deployments to be sent down there." It was challenging to think about tactics on the soft table with the soothing energy flowing into her shoulder.

Sangita sighed. "I am blessed to see this day. The capital city fell to rebel forces and the puppet Parliament has been disbanded. And now you have come."

Mara pushed herself upright, needing to see the healer's face. "Say that again."

Patting her shoulder, Sangita dropped onto a stool. "The Tree's gifts are somewhat different on Iloel. We do not gain the mental rapport, nor do we grow taller, as you do on your home world. But some develop prescience and some develop...other talents." She fingered one of her braids, her young-old face thoughtful.

"Two years ago, an *ombiasi*, a future seer, came to me and said I must travel to the Queen's Mess. She said I must find work and wait for a Daughter of the Tree to arrive, and now here you are."

Mara was unable to suppress the memory of Ponapali, the former head of the King's Men, telling her he had been searching for the Daughter of the Tree. Dread settled on her heart, even as her eyes drifted back to the beautiful tree in the holo.

The older woman nodded, eyes narrowed. "You know a little of your destiny, no?"

Mara couldn't deny it. "Others have recognized me. Said they recognized me," she amended. "When I was young, I was taken from my parents and my memories were blocked. I know who I am, where I come from, but the rest is mostly jumble. I'm not special. I just want to learn something beyond fighting, so maybe I can also live a life free from conflict and the Queen's tyranny." She guessed that's what the Tree wanted also, for herself and her sisters.

The older woman appraised her for a long moment but then her entire expression softened with compassion. "You think you can control your fate?" She clicked her tongue and shook her head. "Come off the table and sit here, daughter." She indicated the chair. "Let me braid that hair."

Chapter 9

The following Saturday morning, Mara recorded a short holo message to Elana explaining that she had stayed off the cut list and wouldn't be coming home for a visit as soon as she hoped. Mara swallowed her sadness. "I'm learning a lot, and...I made some new friends." The blank glass panel showed her own face back, but she tried to imagine Elana nodding encouragement. "Send a message if you can."

The post center had ten booths for recording and sending holo messages. A student's account allowed for one message a month; additional messages cost money. There was also a counter with a scale, a place to weigh packages needing to be sent. The opposite counter was where students picked up packages mailed in to them. A message had pinged her yesterday because a package was waiting. The clerk scanned her wrist and then went to the lower shelves beneath him, digging for a moment before coming up with a small, wrapped parcel.

"Wrist unit for receipt," the clerk said, shoving a small, lighted box across the counter.

She waved her wrist over the box and tucked the parcel under her arm. About a month ago, Jameson had sent a canteen and new sunglasses. Elana had included two pairs of earrings and a soft black leather hair tie. The package tucked under her arm was smaller and less rumpled, as though it hadn't traveled quite as far.

Walking briskly to the main library, Mara pushed through the thick oak and glass doors into the heavy, carpeted silence. Her favorite study cube was tucked along the far wall of the fiction section. Glancing around to double-check she was alone, she carefully unwrapped the paper and pulled out *Dark Deception*. She stifled a laugh at the cheerfully shocking cover, so out of place in the stately collection of great written works. Inside the first page was a scrap of paper with a few looping swirls of writing. "Hope all is well. Come by for a shift sometime. –R"

Mara glanced at her wrist and then the skylights. She had studying and workouts to log, but no appointments, technically, until Monday. It took less than thirty minutes to gather necessities in a small pack, ping Dalin and Annelise, and file a quick off-campus notice.

First years who survived the initial cuts had four off-campus days a month now. They didn't roll over though; it was a use-or-lose privilege. With a job that earned money, if she couldn't go home as a washout, she could go home as a paying passenger—eventually. As she strolled down the hill, she actually whistled a tune Elias, her old stable master, used to sing.

By the time she reached Lower Town, Mara was a little lost. The walk was a lot longer than she remembered, but she kept moving toward the sounds of the space transports launching and eventually found the alley behind Rafiq's place. The front entrance was marked by the standard Lower Town symbol for tavern, the flowing tap, and a small sign flashing alternately in Origin English and script she recognized as Origin Hindi, "Cousins."

She stepped over the ledge of the door seal and looked around.

"Not open for another hour—" Geraldo stuck his head into the dining room to yell. "Hey, *prima*, lookin' better, you. Come on in the kitchen, help me out."

Mara hurried over, surprised by the urge to hug the large, friendly cook. "Hey, Geraldo, thought I might pick up a shift if you've got one."

The kitchen smelled fantastic, even better than she remembered. Garlic, onions, spices, cooking meat—her mouth watered just from the ingredients she recognized.

Geraldo pointed toward a huge metal kettle of potatoes. "Got anything against peeling?"

She shrugged. "No, because I like to eat."

The cook laughed, a deep rolling sound. "Knew I liked you. Got another reason now."

"You talking to yourself, big man?" Rafiq's shout carried through the swinging door.

"Yeah, *jefe*, the crazier the cook, the better the food." He grinned at Mara as he stirred the contents of two cast-iron pans.

She settled onto a stool against one cabinet, content to review coursework in her mind while she peeled the multiple kilos of potatoes in the kettle. Geraldo rattled around, slicing and throwing things in bowls. He muttered to himself, mostly in what sounded like Origin Spanish, the words blending with the rest of the kitchen noise.

At about the halfway point of the potato pile, the cook came over and took a close look at her peeler hand. He tsked over the wet, wrinkled skin.

"Time to do somethin' else for a while, yeah?"

Standing and stretching, Mara reached for the ceiling above one of the pan racks. The top of her shirt pulled away from the waist of her pants and at the height of her stretch, Rafiq banged through the door.

"Darkness take you, Geraldo, I don't care how much cabbage we have. Throw it out. The stink is hanging over the dining room like a shuttle cloud—" His expression shifted from annoyance to flirtatious with a long, smooth smile.

"Weh-hell," he drawled. "Look what the camel dragged in."

She gave a half-wave, not sure how the owner of the eating house would respond to her presence. Geraldo hadn't required an explanation, but she was sure Rafiq would want a reason.

"I, uh…" She let out a breath, started again. "I'm not training for the tournament, and I already studied, so I came by, like you said. To work." She wanted to ask if there might be other work, beside the tables and the kitchen, to earn money more quickly. She'd replayed his comment about the money depending on what she was willing to do a dozen times.

Rafiq, in a black t-shirt and gray linen vest with matching trousers, sized her up. "Saturday's the busiest night of the week. You want to earn more tips, you might want to wear something more appealing."

Frowning, she looked down at her clothes. "This is all I have, besides uniforms and exercise gear." She'd left all her good clothes at her aunt and uncle's house in Satri.

"Probably have something in the back," he said and motioned for her to follow.

Alone in the quiet hallway behind the dining room, Mara said, "Thank you for the book. I've never had one of my own."

Rafiq grunted. "It's got a special message, that one. Thought you might want a break from the history of the Commonwealth and mathematics for military maneuvers." He shoved clothes across the hanging bar in the guest room closet and reached to the far side, fishing out a blue dress.

He held it out. "Give this a try. Might be the right fit."

In the washroom, Mara shucked her clothes and wiggled into the dress. The soft linen hung above her knees, the perfect shade of blue to darken her eyes to the color of a stormy summer sky. The sleeveless bodice was loose but when she moved, still managed to cling to her curves in a way that left little to the imagination. Her only dresses had been intended for serious occasions or at least for warmth. This dress was...fun and left more skin exposed than anything she'd ever worn except undergarments. Dalin would like it.

She found Rafiq in his quarters, rifling through a stack of papers. His appraising stare was harder to withstand than a senior Protector's. Refusing to look nervous, she resorted to the never-fail technique of staring at his ear and thinking about sword drills.

At last he said, "I guess I forgot how tall you are. Does the length of the skirt make you uncomfortable?"

Looking down at her scarred, brown knees, Mara shrugged. "No."

He scooped up the stack and gave it one precise tap on the desk. All papers in place, Rafiq motioned toward the door. "After you."

In the hallway, Mara's wrist unit pinged. A virtual note unfolded in the air just above her arm. "Iloel mission details at 0600, room 42A." No signature, no time stamp or department mark. If she wanted to add to her ticket fund, she'd better get to work.

* * *

He'd adjusted to their mostly separate schedules at the Mess, but Dalin was still surprised Mara had left campus for Lower Town. A part of him was glad she'd made some friends. And Cousins was a well-respected eating house, which only meant no students had been thrown out or gotten ill eating there. Her life had been too narrow before, was too narrow now. For the thousandth time he second-guessed the choices, hasty choices, they'd made to end up at the Mess.

Mara's first move had been to take on the mission from the Tree as though it was hers alone. That was unacceptable. He'd said they could work on the human side of the problem if they got closer to the Queen. Mara reminded him about his opportunity to choose something for himself. Dalin had countered with a series of images from the Satri University campus, the pair of them studying and working side by side. And then she kissed him, ending the conversation.

The healer from Iloel was right about him. He should be less hasty, especially for his partner's sake. If he'd stopped to think, if he hadn't been so focused on the Queen, they could have found passage to a different part of the Commonwealth and worked on the Tree and human problems there. Now they seemed stuck on the path they'd taken, and everything about the Mess screamed danger, which made Dalin unhappy, wary, and frightened for Mara.

His wrist unit vibrated once and a virtual envelope appeared, a notice that the coded data from his father had arrived. He turned toward the library and walked straight into a fourth-year student from his edged weapons class.

The male was tall and broad, with a nose so prominent he was teased about his beak.

"Halifax, sorry about that," Dalin said.

"No problem," the student said, a smile creasing his deeply tanned skin. "Glad I, well, you ran into me." Halifax leaned closer, lowering his voice to a conspiratorial whisper. "I'm getting assigned to a mission."

Frowning in surprise, Dalin said, "Aren't you in your fourth year?"

"Yeah, exactly, but they're sending a student team. I heard it's a mixed group of years, maybe even one first year. We can only take a single weapon. Only supposed to observe." Halifax shrugged. "So, since you're an expert, which weapon would you take?"

Intuition prickling, Dalin asked, "Where are you going?"

"Iloel. Command's sending down a bunch of troops due to the unrest lately."

Unrest was a tidy way to describe the overthrow of Parliament and the occupying of the capital by unsanctioned forces. Dalin searched his memory. "What's the official word on energy weapons? They've been deployed on the ground in at least some areas."

Halifax approached fighting with the same intellectual drive to understand and to master as Dalin did. Halifax's recall for factual information got him teased nearly as much as his nose, but he was a valuable asset, a valuable person.

"Unofficially, I'd say stash at least one energy weapon somewhere deep; if you can lay hands on extra charges, pack those too," Dalin said. It was the same advice he'd give a friend.

The large fourth year tilted his head, looking even more like a bird for an instant.

Dalin continued before he could interrupt. "Officially, I'd recommend a long knife with some weight to it, like a kukri."

"It can be a tool or a weapon." Halifax grinned. "I have just the one. Thanks. I'll look forward to reading the class notes and watching the recordings when I get back." With a brief salute, he continued on his way.

* * *

Just before 0600, Mara found the briefing room listed on her summons. It was in a hallway that branched out from the school wing and led to the palace. A man with a small data tablet took her wrist and tapped the band with his stylus.

"Miss De La Luz, part of the student observation team, right down front." He waved toward the bottom tier of seats arranged in semicircular rows. Mara made her way down the steps, glancing at the uniformed soldiers already occupying most of the approximately one hundred seats. She was surprised to see Dr. Elsebet Iskindar manipulating a floating image of Iloel.

The other students wore fourth- and fifth-year insignias on their uniforms but were otherwise the same mix of gender, coloring, language background, and planetary origin that the first-year group was. Fentress and Kailer slipped into the seats next to her just as the man with the data tablet closed the upper door with a clang.

Elsebet Iskindar glanced at Mara and away again. She tapped a continental mass on the planetary sphere and it lit up with a bright yellow glow.

Dr. Iskindar cleared her throat. "Good morning."

The assembled group murmured, "Good morning," back to her.

"The first part of your briefing is from the civilian side. By a show of hands, how many here today have been to the surface of Iloel?"

Mara twisted to look at the rows of soldiers and saw fewer than ten hands. Fentress caught her eye and shrugged.

"Thank you," Dr. Iskindar said. "And again by show of hands, how many in this room were raised on Iloel?"

A quick look showed one hand in the air, a girl in the row of students.

The teacher nodded. "Yes, so few left to recruit, you see." She sketched a circle and highlighted a series of dots on the floating continent. "Because of its resources, Iloel was the first planet investigated in our system. Our founding King deployed the terraforming technology he'd helped fund on the Origin. Although the largest land mass is primarily desert," she tapped a different mass on the floating map, "a true atmosphere, one that could sustain human life, wrapped around the planet. The King's explorer corps eventually found grasslands and rain forest, minerals, gems, spices— a veritable treasure chest of wonders. Settlements grew as workers arrived." She touched the colored dots and each glowed briefly in turn.

"For the first five or six decades of our Commonwealth, Iloel had by far the largest population of any planet. Life was hard, but for many, it was prosperous. Workers' families came over from other systems, and cultures jostled against one another."

A series of still images began to scroll where the planet had been: people working in mines, a large crowded outdoor bazaar, a city with tall slender buildings, children playing in fields, children sitting in a classroom. Mara wondered again about the professor and why she'd chosen to visit Satri. It was even more odd that for a time, Dr. Iskindar had pretended to be learning Origin English and joined Mara's class.

"Some historians believe the seeds for the first of the war projects grew in this fertile mix of cultures, languages, and beliefs. Certainly on the Origin itself, the longest-lasting wars were rooted in a conflict of beliefs." Dr. Iskindar's expression held regret as she touched the image of Iloel.

"The red dots represent the population density of Iloel one hundred fifty years ago." Her next touch was a light brush of her fingers. "These green dots represent the population density today. This is real data taken from monitoring stations yesterday."

Fentress rocked back in her chair and let out a low whistle. Well over three quarters of the population dots were gone. Low murmurs replaced the silence.

"These are the consequences of a holy war," the teacher murmured almost to herself.

Mara leaned forward, searching for the southern settlement where the Tree's sister was located, according to Sangita. The teacher caught her eye. "The green dots represent a group of twenty-five or more; the larger the dot, the larger the group. Parts of the eastern hemisphere are settled but in such a scattered way that the data is much more difficult to capture."

"Thank you, Dr. Iskindar," a deep voice boomed from the top of the stairs. A lean, muscular man with cropped hair and dark copper skin bounded down the stairs to stand next to the teacher.

The newcomer was dressed in a black shirt and desert fatigues tucked into the tops of combat boots. No insignias, nothing to indicate rank, just the air of authority and sharp blue eyes raking over the assembled group.

"Here's your military briefing." He tapped his wrist once and new images appeared.

"We've lost contact with everyone on the ground. Rebels have taken the capital, the Parliament building, and every other structure in city center. Just before this latest assault, intel from the field reported rumors of a new weapon coming into play. But we're blind right now."

His bright gaze fell on the group of students and his movements stilled. "We serve the interests of the Commonwealth and the Queen. The Iloellians want to govern themselves? Fine. I don't give a dog's breakfast about that. But what does push my hurry-up button is knowing our soldiers are trapped down there. Good men and women. Our mission is to get them out."

"It's 0620 now. Orders have been sent to all of you. Spaceport at 1100. Dismissed." He took a step forward and said much more quietly, "Student observer group, hold please."

In less than a minute the room was empty except for the ten students.

"I'm Colonel Mannus Naran. Don't waste your breath telling me you can fight. I know all about each of you. Unfortunately, I didn't earn the privilege of leading by disagreeing with my orders. So, I choose to interpret the role of observer in its strictest sense. You will not speak. You will not walk, think, touch, handle, or interact with any object or person without my express permission." Naran took a menacing step forward. He glared down at Fentress, Kailer, and Mara.

"That means you, ladies. We clear?"

"Yes, sir." Mara gave a short sharp nod.

All of the students answered with *sir* or *yes, sir* in a staccato chorus of agreement.

Naran crossed his thick arms over his chest. "I went to school here and I know the routine. As of now, your teachers have been notified of your impending absence."

The setup was all wrong. The students were strangers to Mara and to each other for the most part. Anyone with a rudimentary understanding of military tactics knew that teams needed training and time to work well. Unless they were expected to fail, like the Protectors had been.

Naran continued answering questions in short, impatient bursts.

Following her own logic, Mara realized that if, probably *since*, the student observation squad was meant to fail, they'd chosen students who were too good to wash out of the Mess for lack of points. Troublesome students who were too smart and asked too many questions like they were doing now.

This injustice, this complete devaluing of young human lives was why she and Dalin had come to this Light-forsaken school in the first place. He would want in on this mission, she was sure of it.

From the brief look at the map, Mara couldn't guess where the Iloellian Tree might be. But she knew she and Dalin would bring themselves and the squad back alive whether they helped the Tree or not.

"Sir, Colonel Naran, sir," said a boy about the same build as Gunder. "Did we get chosen, were we chosen—" He tried again. "Is this some sort of project or something? For a grade?"

It was a question most of them had to have been wondering.

The colonel's eyes narrowed and he took a long breath in through his nose. "Mr. O'Kelley, is that right? Patrick O'Kelley?"

"Yes, sir."

"You're in your fifth year at the Mess, correct?"

"Yes, sir." O'Kelley's pink face reddened under the officer's glare.

"So then you know already that every minute of every camel-humped day is an evaluation here. What you're asking me is if this will be a holiday jaunt? Time off from being graded?"

O'Kelley shook his head. "No, sir."

"Two things." The colonel flipped his palm up and jabbed two fingers forward in a strike at O'Kelley's throat. The student did not flinch.

"And I'm repeating myself, which I hate, so pay attention this time. One, we've lost contact with our people. That is the reason we are going. The only evaluation, therefore, will be the real kind. The kind that asks, did you get the job done or not?"

Naran dropped his hand from O'Kelley's throat and paced a few tight steps down the row of students, sweeping them with sharp appraisal.

"Two, I was given your files and told to take you lot. No combat, just observation. That's all I need to know."

"This is going to be the holiday jaunt I've been dreaming about. Joy."

The mental voice was crystal clear in Mara's head. She tucked a loose strand of hair behind her ear, controlling the urge to look around. Surely the other students saw how odd their inclusion in this mission was? The whole situation reminded her of the briefings at Northwest Protector compound, the ones where she'd asked pointed questions and been whipped for lack of obedience.

Raising one black eyebrow, Colonel Naran said, "O'Kelley, you're senior here among these people."

O'Kelley nodded once.

"This is your squad now. If any one of these soldiers is not at the spaceport, hangar twenty-seven fifty-five, by eleven hundred, I'll take it out of your hide. Dismissed." Naran bounded up the stairs.

Leaping to her feet, Fentress said, "Wait. Introductions first. We won't get a chance to talk later and I need to know who I'm *observing* with. Kailer, you start."

Kailer stood and met the eyes of the rest of the group. "I'm Kailer. Fifth year. Specialty is hand-to-hand, but I'm also a sharpshooter."

Fentress nodded to a male sitting in the second row. He cleared his throat and stood. "Raymundo, fourth year, my specialty is languages."

"In a fight you're going to translate?" Fentress said.

A wide grin spread across the soldier's face, transforming it from attractive to truly handsome, like the men on Rafiq's book covers. "Don't worry about me in a fight, *rubia.*"

The soldier next to Raymundo gave a quick laugh and slapped hands with him. "I'm Angelo. Fourth year. Specialty is demolition." Angelo had the same dark brown hair as Raymundo and the same beautifully symmetrical features. They looked like brothers.

Introductions went quickly. All of the students were fourth or fifth years. Combat and strategic skills ran the gamut. Every single person was confident and skilled, a potential asset to any military posting. And yet they were going to be thrown away on a suicide mission? When Mara's turn came, she stood, reining in her anger to speak.

"I'm Mara. First year. My specialty is the sword—"

"She's the one who beat the Queen's Champion. Don't judge." Fentress jumped in, responding to the expressions of consternation among the group.

Mara pressed her lips together as she faced her fellow student observers. From the change in posture and the nods, her right to observe with the rest of them wouldn't be disputed. *"I've seen more combat hours than the rest of you put together,"* she added in her mind.

"Good to know."

The mental voice was female. The girl on the far right, Sritha, stared hard at Mara and raised one eyebrow. She was lean, medium-height, with a round face and large round eyes.

Fentress dropped her hand on Mara's shoulder. "I'm Fentress. I'm the head of the Furies and I'm good at everything. Fifth year. Squad leader?" She turned to O'Kelley.

The redhead shook himself. "O'Kelley, from Kels. Fifth year, due to graduate next month. My specialty is tactics, deployment. Otherwise it's ground fighting."

Kels produced wrestlers. Jameson had talked about that when he talked about his brothers.

"Plan on being at the hangar by ten forty-five, people. We're the O Squad unless anyone objects to that name. Given the skills in this group, I doubt any of us was chosen at random. You're gonna want to get in on the action. Talk yourselves out of that right now." O'Kelley's face was serious, belying the smile lines around his mouth and his ruddy cheeks. "I'll arrange a transport from the Mess to depart the main gate at ten thirty. Be there if you need a ride. Dismissed."

* * *

After a brief stop at her dorm to collect gear, Mara met Dalin coming from the other direction holding a bundle under his arm.

"Hey," she began.

Dalin shook his head. *"Rapport,"* he sent. *"Just turn and walk along as though we happen to be heading to the same destination."*

"I need to get my sword from the weapons check—"

"Got it. And I'm also loaning you a knife. Spent all night following up on the rumors about Iloel and trying to get myself assigned to the mission. Before I became unreasonable, I was told you were 'especially chosen to go as befits your top rank within your class.' But no one will tell me who chose you. Especially not now."

Dalin's shoulders were tight, his strides long and fast. She could scarcely keep up with him without looking ridiculous. The connection to his mind felt as cold and stiff as an ice-fishing line.

"Where are we going?"

"My rooms. I need to pack some things into your gear." He glanced over his shoulder, gray eyes glittering silver.

Dalin was so far past his usual collected self, even his mental voice had deepened and roughened with fury.

She had to ask. "What did you do trying to get assigned to the Iloel mission?"

The hall split, taking them to the left and down a half-flight of stairs. They passed a pair and two individuals going the opposite direction. In the Mess, both students and teachers tended to move at a brisk pace with an underlying sense of urgency.

"First I offered bribes, then I tried blackmail with some of the data I found. I challenged a member of the Queen's Council to a fight. I was...out of my head, and I think he was about to shoot me until Dr. Iskindar intervened."

At the next corner Dalin pulled up short and she bumped into his back. A lock clicked when he waved his wrist unit, and Dalin dragged them both through the door. He hurried into the second room while Mara turned in a slow circle.

The time they'd stolen together was always in common spaces like the library or the Mess Mess but now that she saw how he was living, she knew Dalin had kept her away to prevent her from seeing his living conditions.

His quarters and the meager furnishings were nothing like his house in Satri. Instead of deep-cushioned high-backed couches, a narrow flat bench and two chairs were the main furnishings. Gray paint covered the walls and thin gray carpet covered the floors. No art hung on the walls, and only textbooks filled one shelf of the otherwise empty bookcase. He had sacrificed every nice thing, every comfort, to join her.

Mara's fingers tightened on the backpack's straps. Dalin should be with his parents and his sister. He should be leading his men in the transition away from the Protector Project. Fatigue from the previous night coupled with guilt pushed her to one of the chairs. She perched on the edge, leaning forward to accommodate the weight on her back.

Strong hands lifted the pack away, easing the padded straps from her shoulders. Dalin put the bag on the floor and emptied the contents in one neat row. He drew a tiny cut down one of the seams along the bottom of the bag and slid a flat knife into the gap. A small heating tool helped close the self-repairing fabric. He looked up from his work without smiling.

"One weapon is practically unarmed for the situation on the ground. Naran knows it. You're going to take a lot of blades, as many as we can strap on your body or hide in your pack."

She rested one palm over his left hand, thinking to soothe. Instead the depth of Dalin's concern flowed into her consciousness.

"You found notes about the drug they gave me?" Her empty stomach rolled and her mouth suddenly went dry. This was about more than her deploying without him.

He kept his attention on the bundle containing her sword, her beautiful deadly sword from Jameson, as well as two throwing knives and arm sheaths.

"Take off your shirt." He looked up then quickly back down.

"Tell me about the notes," she said.

"Take off your shirt," Dalin repeated, his expression serious as any field commander's.

She locked eyes with her partner before drawing her shirt's light black fabric over her head. Dalin didn't mind her scars just as she didn't mind his. But part of her wanted this moment of undressing for him to be less about weapons and more about mutual attraction.

He knelt before her chair and brushed her left arm with his fingertips.

She shivered in her thin tank top.

Dalin's silver eyes had darkened to a smoky gray and his breathing quickened. "I found the notes in the researcher's log. It took me longer to get a copy of the original studies and the drug formulas." He cleared his throat and reached for the first arm sheath, wrapping the straps with care around her forearm.

"She was pleased with your response, especially your increased strength and speed. The compound was originally designed for laborers in the most challenging projects. More specifically, the miners in the deserts of Iloel. But it had pronounced side effects on the levels of aggression in the men, so the trials were stopped."

He slid a flat-bladed throwing knife into the sheath and moved to her right arm.

"What else?" Mara asked. That wasn't enough information to get her calm, logical partner to this level of anger.

Taking a deep breath, Dalin slid the second knife home and reached for her shirt. "Eight men died in the first trial. Thirty men died in the second round, although five of those were because of injuries from fighting, not the drug itself." He tugged the shirt back over her head and adjusted the sleeves until the knives were hidden.

"This was the right top to choose," he said. "The spare shirts you brought are the same?"

She traced one of his eyebrows and let her thumb graze his rough jawline. The information he'd found was terrifying. But there was more; the worst was still untold. Her partner looked torn between kissing her and searching for more places to hide weapons.

"What else did you learn?" she whispered, more interested in being alone with Dalin and not for conversation. But if they kissed, he would hold back the information, be thinking of her more as a girl and less as a fellow fighter.

One corner of Dalin's mouth turned up as he followed her thoughts. He pushed up from the floor and sat next to her in the other chair.

"The men who survived changed. Some of the effects became permanent."

Mara shivered again, in no way comforted by the cool metal knives hidden along her arms. "After one dose?"

"The handful of survivors who became permanently altered had each received no fewer than three rounds of increasing dosage. Most had received five or more administrations of the drug."

She nodded, waiting. She had to be the calm one so Dalin would share his concerns.

"Based on the next steps in the healer's report, I think they're planning to field test this new version of the drug on you again, during whatever action occurs. But what she put in your water was super-concentrated, the equivalent of three doses of the original compound." He traced the outline of the arm sheaths, taking measured breaths.

"Only eat food that's prepared and given to everyone in your group. Only drink water from a running source. Don't take *anything*, ingest *anything*, that's given to only you or only a few. You might be hungry, but there's food, fresh food in the markets if you can get there. I'll put Iloellian currency in your socks with your other money…"

When Dalin finally met her eyes, the worry had gone and the fury had returned. She took the hand tracing the pattern on her arm and kissed his knuckles. Leaning forward, she tipped her head up and touched his lips with her own. She inhaled the smell of his skin, breathing in home, filling her mind with it. They hadn't been apart since Dalin made contact on the battlefield over a year ago. She trusted their connection and willed him to do the same.

"Thank you." Mara stood and reached for her pack and sword, glancing at her wrist unit.

He stood as well and tugged her close, scrutinizing the straps on her pack.

"The pack, my gear, it's all more than fine, thanks to you," she said. "Thank you for getting my sword. We won't be gone long." The words sounded like a false promise. She tried a different kind of promise, based on her commitment to him and their mission. "I fully intend to return in one piece and bring all the other students back with me."

"Nothing is more important. Your safety is—" He stopped himself. "You are my priority."

"Would you be willing to send a message for me? To Rafiq? It doesn't have to do with my safety but—"

Dalin's face registered surprise and then suspicion. "The guy in the eating house?"

"Right, he needs, well, they've been shorthanded and I was supposed to pick up some shifts…" She trailed off, feeling stupid for bringing it up. "Just let him know I won't be around for a while. Please." She buckled the sword belt around her hips, the weight at her side a small comfort, a reminder of her Uncle Jameson and her family.

"Are you in too much trouble to stay on mission?" she asked. "Did you lose your instructor status?"

Leaning down until they were nose to nose, Dalin said, "Don't die."

She cupped his cheek and whispered, "Understood," her lips brushing his with the shape of the word.

Chapter 10

Ten minutes of walking took her to a part of the Mess she'd never seen. Corrugated metal siding gradually replaced brick walls, and the smooth tiled floors became textured, molded plastic. Her boots thudded dully as she passed soldiers in a variety of Commonwealth uniforms moving with purpose through connecting and perpendicular hallways lit by bright overhead fixtures. Without the soft chimes from her wrist unit dictating her route, Mara would have been utterly lost; and the culture of the Mess was never to ask for help.

That was one of the biggest things about the Mess she hated the most: never feeling part of a team, as though no one cared about her success or failure. Instead she had to depend on tech.

Without a connection to people or purpose, she was hard-pressed to find a reason for students to succeed or fail. Yes, the Protectors had been divided into compounds in different regions on Asattha, and within the compounds into cohorts. But she always felt a part of something bigger, something important, and most significantly, something that made life better for others. Not once had "make life better for others" been expressed as a value at the Mess.

The layout of the school from the gates to the classrooms to the gym was not designed with teamwork and community in mind. Why found a Commonwealth? Why build a school to teach leaders to serve the Commonwealth that in no way focused on the common good?

The philosophical seething did nothing to dispel the true reasons for her anger and worry. Dalin would be alone and so would she. No partner, no fellow Protectors, and here she was, heading into an unknown combat situation. Some people would quit, run away from the danger, but she was the only one on the student squad with enough experience to bring everyone back alive.

Sudden light ahead caused her to stumble, and she nearly tripped into O'Kelley. He caught her arm with his free hand. "Easy there, you can slow down now. Got about ten minutes until we move out." His hazel eyes were fringed with nearly white lashes, and his eyebrows were several shades lighter orange than his hair. In stark contrast to the dark gray of his fifth-year uniform, his fair skin stood out like a beacon. Like all of them, he still had the look of a soldier even if he didn't cause instant panic like Fentress might.

Mara tugged her arm away gently and looked around the courtyard. The east gate was much smaller, less ornate, and more functional-looking than the main gate. Five autos, the most efficient single-person vehicles, more sleek than the boxy uprights on Asattha, were parked against one external wall and another had a short row of the single-seat mini transport trucks. In the middle, a personnel van idled, much like the one they'd taken from the spaceport when they'd first arrived.

Two of the male students leaned against it, deep in conversation. One was Fusao, a lightly-built boy from Hépíng Xīng, who claimed to specialize in all bladed weapons, especially throwing knives. The other was Halifax, who like Fentress could probably stop a fight or argument with a look. With his high cheekbones and arched nose, along with his broad shoulders and defined muscles, he could have been an ancient warrior from a history text. Mara hadn't been the only one trying to hide surprise when he'd told the group his specialty was probability and statistics.

A smaller figure, skin even darker than Halifax's, flipped gracefully from the roof of the van. She tagged Fusao and said, "Gotcha."

Fusao captured the girl's bare wrist and threw her, but she landed on her feet with a grin.

"Van's clear," she said with a smile. "Road's clear, gate's clear, no one is here but us poor suckers."

Fusao rolled his eyes at Halifax. "Dom's the most paranoid student in the fourth-year group."

"Call me Dominique," the girl said, sticking her hand out to Halifax. "And don't listen to Fusao." She drew out the syllables Foo-saa-oh. "He's just sore because I won our class challenge last month." She reached up and back over her head, bending her body, then dropped onto her hands and kicked Fusao's knapsack as she flipped back to her feet. Dominique's hair was in hundreds of tiny braids all gathered into a single ponytail. Her long-sleeved black shirt and long pants fit like a second skin, shimmering and stretching with every movement.

"What was the challenge?" Mara asked, walking over to join the group. As far as she knew, the first years hadn't had any challenges separate from the Friday fights and tests in various classes.

Dominique dusted her hands across her thighs. "Capture the flag, with a twist. You're Mara, right? The first year?"

Mara nodded. "That's me." She was saved from having to answer for her membership on the O Squad when Halifax interrupted, directing his question to Dominique. "How did you win?"

"Fusao likes to be first, but I like to be right."

Sritha jogged into the courtyard, followed closely by Raymundo and Angelo. Raymundo tapped O'Kelley's clipboard and said, "Kailer told me she and Fentress have their own way down the hill. They'll see us at the spaceport."

Chapter 11

No one said much during the jouncing van ride down to the spaceport. As they all piled out, Mara took in the massive series of buildings, struck again, not only by the skills needed to construct something so huge, but also the expertise to pilot a craft between planets. Each building rose at least twice the height of the tallest house in Satri, six or more floors, but was entirely open on the inside, rising up to a peaked roofline latticed with metal girders and catwalks.

"The best place to service the equipment on top of the spacecraft is up there," Sritha said. "Can't be worried about your own balance or stability when you're installing a com array or tuning a star drive."

Several student fighters looked at the workers in the rafters and then back at Sritha.

"Both my parents are spacers, space craft techs, in the main s'port on Iloel. We might see them when we land."

"We're set to dock just outside of Samradhi," O'Kelley said.

"That's the one," she agreed.

O'Kelley led the group through a checkpoint and deeper into the military side of the spaceport. Shiny, dark stains in irregular patterns covered the rough, syncrete floor. A pervasive smoky stench hung in the air. The hangar bays, while still immense, grew smaller as they walked, as did the craft.

Mara, Dalin, Annelise, and Gunder had come from Asattha on a gigantic, multipurpose transport. The ship resting in Hangar 2755 was much smaller, in length maybe five or six Satri houses and in height, maybe two houses.

The snub nose of the craft and its roughly triangular shape gave it the look of a bird. Mara tilted her head, trying to imagine where one hundred fifty soldiers would sit. Smooth, dark gray metal covered the visible exterior. Light seemed to slide away from the hull, creating the impression of an immense shadow. Energy weapons were made of metal like that, but to use it for an object this large staggered her imagination.

"This ship is about ninety meters long and thirty meters high at its tallest point. Since you were wondering."

Mara looked down at Sritha, who shrugged. "Houses aren't an accurate unit of measure. This craft is a newer model, a beauty, my *ummi*...my mom would say. Probably been modified inside, but the basic design is good, has a good balance between principles of flight and comfort."

"I'm a telepath," the girl added as she stood next to Mara and looked at the ship while spacers and soldiers bustled around them. *"But you're not, not a born one anyway, in my head you sound—"*

"Everyone front and center," Colonel Naran's voice rose above the bangs and crashes. "Squad leaders report in."

Fourteen squad leaders reported all members accounted for. The last to speak was O'Kelley.

"Sir, O Squad—all present, sir." Fentress and Kailer flanked him, both dressed in black fifth-year uniforms, backpacks bulging.

"Listen up, boys and girls. Sergeant Bogdanovich is going to get you loaded. We depart in thirty." He strode off and flagged down one of the spacers.

The woman Fentress had introduced as Lupe stepped over a series of hoses and positioned herself where Naran had been standing a moment before. She looked the same as she had in the gym, but uniformed and serious now. Mara raised her eyebrows at Fentress, who flashed a smile and a tiny wink.

"If you get sick on planet jumps, we need to know ahead of time; there's meds for that. Tell your squad leader before you board." Lupe, Sergeant Bogdanovich, took a step closer to avoid another hose snaking past. "Embarkation and debarkation go through me only. You sit when and where I tell you. We don't know if hostiles control the s'port so the landing might get rough. Updates will be provided to squad leaders as needed. Questions?"

Since she'd been at the Mess, Mara had come to understand that no one asked questions when a person in power offered to answer them.

The O Squad was the last to board. Mara filed in behind Raymundo, all of them following O'Kelley down a long central aisle past compartments filled with the Queen's soldiers. Their leader stopped at the last compartment and stepped to the side to usher them in. Twelve semi-reclined chairs in an open U shape all pointing toward the center filled most of the space.

"Everyone drop your gear on a seat and use the latrine if you need to," O'Kelley said.

Mara shrugged off her pack and placed it on the seat between Fentress and Halifax. The wall between their compartment and the next one shimmered and she blinked, but the shimmer remained.

"It's an opaque energy wall," Halifax said, his voice a low, pleasant baritone. "Human factors engineers calculated the relative sense of security in a smaller compartment versus a larger, keeps passengers forty percent more relaxed. But also, command can snap those walls tight or drop them depending on if they need to clear this deck for action or an emergency response. It's in the top three percent most efficient designs in the fleet."

Kailer rolled her eyes. "Halifax, what's the probability that you could lecture us on the design features of this spacecraft all the way to Iloel?"

The soldier ran a finger down his nose and gave her a good-natured half smile. "While the probability for an initial lecture, stemming from my own enthusiasm, is high, I would run out of information approximately midway through our journey."

Fentress laughed and O'Kelley grinned and shook his head. "Fax, since you're so keen on design features, would you please demonstrate the stowage capacity of these flight chairs and also how the harnesses work?"

Each seat was fixed on its base but opened on one side to reveal a space large enough to hold two medium packs or one large one, as Halifax quickly showed them. He popped open a door behind O'Kelley's chair and pointed out a fire extinguisher and emergency medical kit.

"If we get the signal to clear the deck, everything can be stowed in the floor." O'Kelley touched a button on his chair and it folded and rotated into a shallow opening revealed by the rotation.

Halifax moved Mara's pack to the floor and gestured for her to lie back in the seat. It wasn't a test of bravery; she guessed it was just a little joke on the new girl. Avoiding eye contact with the rest of the squad, she stretched her full length on the cushioned surface.

"First step is harness," Halifax said, tapping a tiny screen on the armrest. A black web snaked across Mara's torso and a second web wrapped her legs. The webbing wasn't uncomfortably tight but her movements were completely restricted. Her heart rate sped up. They hadn't been confined like this on the trip between Asattha and Laska.

"The second step is energy shield," the broad-shouldered soldier continued. "On a shorter hop, the shields are necessary on both liftoff and landing. Helps absorb the excess turbulence. I could explain the physics of gravity and acceleration but—"

"Better to show you," Fentress interrupted. She tapped the screen on the armrest and a blue glow arched over Mara, dulling all her senses. She couldn't move to test it from the inside, but Fentress jumped and dropped toward the shield, elbow down, aiming for a body slam. The tall blonde bounced lightly above Mara and grinned down at her. "Knew you could handle it." With two taps, she released Mara from both the shield and the harness.

A heavy thud shook the floor of the ship. "Just shut the cargo door," Sritha said. "Crew door will be next." The sounds of increased activity came only through the one compartment door. Just like a physical wall, the shimmering wall kept their conversation in and everyone else's out.

Amid the bustle of the squad getting settled, Mara checked her wrist sheaths and the weapons hidden in her knapsack. Although she couldn't be prepared completely for an unknown situation, it made her feel better. The ship vibrated with another loud thud.

"Crew door, the one we used, just shut and sealed," Sritha said, settling into her flight chair.

"Since this is your regular trek, Sritha, would you take us through the timing?" O'Kelley stood in the center of the chair formation, watching to make sure all harnesses fastened correctly over the squad members.

"Sir," Sritha said. "This is a good ship, not flashy 'cause it's meant to work. We'll be port to port in just under two days. Same distance took the first explorers almost six months, but they traveled by the space equivalent of a camel. And this," she patted her armrest with affection, "this is a racer."

"Wrist units won't work for coms or anything else once we're off-planet. Stow 'em somewhere deep," O'Kelley said, tucking away his pack.

Mara used the stowing of her wrist unit as an excuse to check the contents and placement of her pack one more time. With reluctance, she settled into her chair and triggered the harness.

On her only other journey between planets, she had been in an upright seat with a single shoulder-to-waist harness. The gigantic starship, a mixed civilian and military transport, moved so slowly a crewman stood upright without any support and lectured on flight safety for several minutes before strapping in. Asattha to Laska had been a two-week trip, and this one would take two days.

O'Kelley tugged on Mara's torso and leg webs. With a genuine smile, he asked, "All set?"

"Yes, sir." Mara nodded, too nervous to smile back.

A buzzing in the floor and walls grew into a whining drone. The entire ship jolted and O'Kelley almost went over.

"*Trasero en una silla*, squad leader. *Siéntate*," Fentress called.

"Hey, boss," Raymundo said. "Before you sit down, Angelo needs those meds for not getting sick on jumps." His cousin punched him hard on the arm.

O'Kelley turned, one hand on his seat. "*¿Verdad?* True, Angelo?"

Angelo shook his head as a loud buzzer began to sound in short bursts repeating over and over.

"That's sixty seconds to launch, everyone confirm harnesses and shields now. I need to double-check my optical interface." The squad leader triggered his web and shield as the engine noise increased to a higher pitch. The remaining nine members of the observation squad shouted verbal confirmation one at a time.

The overhead lights flickered and dimmed as the great ship shuddered and picked up speed. To Mara it felt like the muscles of a horse bunching and gathering before jumping a creek. The launch threw her back in her seat with sudden violence. An immense force, like an invisible hand, pressed down on her lungs and her mind until everything went black.

* * *

"Hey, chica, we're up." A hand shook her shoulder. "Don't let anyone make a joke about first years and jumps. C'mon. Pilot even turned gravity on for you." The shake was a little rougher this time.

Mara opened her eyes and, at first, saw only blurs of movement in the dim light. Up. She was…up?

"Leave her alone, Fentress." It was Halifax's voice. "Only half the squad is awake."

She rubbed her eyes, realizing her harness must have been disengaged, and sat up. Her head throbbed and her stomach felt wrong, definitely sour. Fentress handed Mara a plastic bottle of water.

"Drink up and then suit up. It's cold in space."

Although they were probably a quarter of the way to Iloel already, Mara gave a mental shout for Dalin. She didn't expect an answer, just hoped that somehow the rapport could reach across the vast distance. But even though she couldn't reach her partner, the light and energy of the Tree smoldered inside her, ready to ignite with a breath.

The rest of the O Squad came awake within minutes. The compartment became crowded with soldiers in jumpsuits digging through their gear and talking.

"I want everything squared away in five, got it?" O'Kelley's voice penetrated the din. Some responded with "sir," and some responses were more grumbled, but in five minutes, the student soldiers were back in or near their flight chairs.

"Couple of things," the squad leader said. He stood, one hand in a pocket. "First, I was conscious throughout the launch. Some of you expressed concern regarding our vulnerability. So I want you to know my chair has a continual vid and audio feed from command. To put some of our more vigilant minds at ease—"

Fusao coughed, "Dominique." She stomped on his foot.

O'Kelley stared them both down, his expression bordering on annoyed. "We're going to run a twenty-four-hour watch, three-hour shifts. Should stagger out about right by the time we land."

Kailer raised a hand. "What's the chow situation?" After a nearly disrespectful pause, she added, "Sir."

"It's strictly protein and water, synths to keep the vitamins on." O'Kelley scratched his neck and looked at the floor as several soldiers groaned. "It's only two days, people. I thought this squad was full of fighters, not royalty."

"We thought observers might get better *tabemono* is all," Fusao said.

"*You* thought," said Dominique. "No one else thinks they're special."

A crewman in an orange jumpsuit pushed a hovering cart of stacked bottles and boxes into their doorway. "Squad leader?"

"Here." O'Kelley shifted to meet the cart.

"One bottle, one tube per person. It's all the same." Fentress helped the squad leader quickly unload and helped hand around one sealed bottle and one tube to everyone.

The bottle was a thin, single-use water bottle, much like the ones they'd been given at wake-up. The gray tube carried only a single label with the words "meal replacement" and several number sequences. It weighed about half as much as the water bottle.

"Not these," groaned Fusao, frowning at his tube. "I thought they'd upgraded, added more sugars and carbs, a few flavor choices. Those people from R & D said—"

"You forget the urgent nature of this mission, soldier. We're working with what's on hand." Sergeant Bogdanovich spoke from the doorway.

"Attention!" Fentress ordered.

The squad snapped into standing positions, arm tight to their sides, eyes straight ahead.

"As you were," the sergeant said.

The soldiers dropped back onto their seats and Angelo flicked Fusao on the ear. "*No dices palabras más dulce, no comerías. ¿Comprendes?*"

Mara didn't know much Origin Spanish, but from the look on Angelo's face, she got the message—be nice or you won't eat.

The sergeant shot Angelo a quick smile before gesturing for the two senior students to follow her into the corridor.

Fusao muttered something in Origin Japanese that made Raymundo hoot before he slapped a hand over his own mouth.

"The first couple of hours are easy," Sritha said quietly, scooting onto the lower part of Mara's chair. Due to the ever-present background hum of the ship, it was possible to speak so that only one person could hear, even in close quarters. "It's the last few hours before landing that take forever." She seemed friendly and genuine enough, but Mara kept her mental shield smooth and strong.

"Anyway this stuff, it takes the edge off, but no one ever asks for seconds." She looked at Mara for acknowledgment so Mara shrugged. "The best thing to do is alternate a mouthful from the tube with a drink of water." The telepath demonstrated with her rations, grimacing a little as the first mouthful went down. With a nod, Sritha ambled back to her chair.

Halifax leaned over and said, "I'm going to read until our watch. If you doze off, I'll wake you, don't worry."

"Read today, weapons check tomorrow?" Mara responded.

"Sure," said Halifax with an easy grin. "You brought a book?"

She slid from her seat and opened the panel in the side, rummaging until she produced the treasure from Rafiq.

"Looks a lot more interesting than mine." Halifax held up a much larger volume bound in plain brown plastic. "It's the history of Asattha," he offered and flipped to the table of contents, missing Mara's flinch. "It's got everything from the first explorers, to the Great Tree, the family lines, and a lot about the project. Published before everything went down though."

"I'm..." Mara licked her lips, tasting paste residue. She would have to trust Halifax in combat. In a way, he reminded her of Dalin's father, Jin, a scholar and a fighter. She took a breath and started again. "I'm from Asattha."

His warm brown eyes practically glowed. "We just... I've never met...only a few from Asattha at the school." Grinning with a touch of embarrassment, Halifax wiped a hand over his face and then patted the heavy brown book. "Fourth years have to do a research project and I picked War Project Seven. This book is for background, but if you know anything about the project, maybe you might answer some questions during watch?"

* * *

Dark Deception was the tale of a young woman, raised in the home of a wealthy merchant until she was fifteen, and then kidnapped and apprenticed to a master assassin. The target of her first solo kill was intended to be the son of a rival merchant, a youth destined to inherit his mother's shipping empire. But the young assassin, Lusani, fell in love with her mark. The pair was about to share true love's first kiss when Halifax shook Mara's shoulder.

"Must be a good story, eh? Didn't hear me talking at all."

She flushed, glancing down and committing the page number to memory. "Sorry I—"

Her watch partner waved away the apology. "Happens to me all the time. Here's the sitrep. Fentress and Kailer are in the latrine. Everyone else is bunking down for sleep. Once they get back, we've got three hours in the doorway."

"Did they have anything to report?"

"Sergeant Bogdanovich came by to chat, but that was strictly social. She used to be head of the Furies."

"I heard," Mara said.

"The compartment closest to the pilot is a special group of Queen's assassins. They do almost everything through mental attacks. More dangerous than anything else on the ship."

Fentress and Kailer came back together, dropping into their flight chairs without further comment.

With a glance at the pair, Halifax grabbed his book and settled himself comfortably on one side of the energy boundary. Mara took the other so that she was facing down the long stretch of corridor.

Boots or knees hung a fraction onto the walkway from several doorways; otherwise, it appeared empty. No sounds rose above the engine noise. The floor was colder than the chairs, however, and she shivered.

"The chairs can be heated or cooled," Halifax said. "Lot to be said for a warm bottom in the right conditions." He stroked the cover of the book and then opened to the table of contents, running his large hand along the tiny text. If the calluses and scars were any indication, Halifax had been fighting most of his life, just like her.

On the long spaceflight between Asattha and Laska, she and Dalin had agreed that, if questioned, they would talk about the war project but not much else. The gifts of the Great Tree and their encounters with her needed to be kept secret.

"Only a few groups your age receive extensive military training on Asattha. I saw you beat the Queen's Champion. Fangald might have been an arrogant propaganda tool, but he was also a crafty fighter."

It was impossible to look away from Halifax's keen eyes.

"You didn't show any fear and you fought to win, so I'm pegging you as a Protector, not one of those in costume fighting on the research side."

"I'm—" Mara cleared her throat. "I was a Protector."

* * *

Dalin followed his schedule—teaching, going to the Mess, and returning to his quarters at the same intervals. He felt empty without the constant awareness, however small, of Mara's state of being. Her absence was a distraction, because her presence grounded him. They'd never properly tested the full distance of their mental bond. But clearly it couldn't stretch between planets.

On a modified version of house arrest after his out-of-line behavior, Dalin could not get out of his head. The constant cycle of worry and recrimination prevented anything resembling healthy levels of eating or sleeping. Occasionally something would remind him how capable Mara was, remind him that one of the many reasons he loved her was *because* she was such a strong fighter and leader. But soon after would come another round of imagining Mara's death in countless combat or poisoning scenarios. He'd calculated the time frame for when her ship would land on Iloel. Accessing the mission reports and status updates was beyond his skill, for the moment, but he'd have all the intel soon enough.

Two days after her departure, the first of the monsoon storms hit Crown City. The previously unremitting sunlight now barely penetrated the heavy clouds. In classrooms and common rooms, windows were unsealed to allow the breath of fresh moisture in. Long-dormant smells bloomed, until the scents of old wood, old brick, and the living smells of humanity for once dominated the plain syncrete and plastic scents in the newer parts of the Mess.

He'd taken to passing Dr. Iskindar's office during her posted office hours in hopes of catching her alone. While going about his routine, he'd scripted several possible conversation paths, depending on if she was willing to speak with him at all, and if so, which subjects they might broach.

As he turned the corner, one hand in his pocket and eyes on the rain-spattered windows, a student exited the office and left the door ajar. Dalin continued his casual walk to her door. He didn't hear voices so he knocked.

"Enter," Dr. Iskindar called.

She looked up and nodded when he slipped inside. With a hint of a frown, she said, "I've been expecting you, young master de Forest." She gestured to the two chairs facing her plain dark wood desk. "Please sit."

Given the layout of this particular hallway, and the woman's status, he'd expected her office to be larger. Two overflowing bookcases filled the only available wall, floor to ceiling. Certificates, diplomas, and awards scrolled through a mini holoframe to the right of the desk.

With a swipe through the air, Dr. Iskindar pulled down the documents she been reading and dumped them back to the portable screen nearly hidden amid the piles of paper and plastic covering two-thirds of her desk.

"You've been expecting me?" Dalin repeated, not able to hide his curiosity. And, despite himself, he felt relieved his academic idol knew of his existence beyond the trouble he'd caused.

The professor took a sip from a handmade-looking stoneware mug, eyeing him over the rim. "Not everyone, very few in fact, orders permacopies of my original research."

Dalin swallowed as the back of his neck went hot. "I admire the structure of—"

"Not everyone, very few in fact, foils an operation of the King's Men," she interrupted. "And not everyone, only you in fact, is partnered with the Tree's Daughter."

Skin tingling, Dalin held perfectly still. He shields were smooth, unbroken, and yet how…?

Dark eyes as sharp as any predator's, Dr. Iskindar leaned forward. "Are you an ally to the cause?"

He couldn't look away didn't sense any shields protecting the room. Words of agreement formed in his mind but he kept silent.

Turning to the portable screen, the professor threw a virtual folder into the air between them. Semi-transparent images of faces opened—his parents, Jameson and Elana, his sister, sketches of the Tree in both her forms, the recently deceased leader of the King's Men, Ponapalli, Annelise and Gunder, Twyla and Chris Puente.

He allowed himself a deep breath and then another. Dr. Iskindar stared at him through the faces, waiting for a response. The normal contrast between silver threaded braids and the sharp angles of her face was gone today, all that hair pulled back in a single knot. The sleeves of her tunic were pushed up past her elbows, dark midnight forearms textured with muscle and ropy veins.

Finally he said, "The Daughter is my cause."

Her expression did not change, but Dr. Iskindar walked around the desk to close the door and hit the switch that turned off her office hours sign. She moved past the chairs, the long layers of her skirt brushing the floor, and gave the second bookcase a light tug. The entire thing swung back, revealing a passage beyond.

"This way," she said, gesturing for him to precede her.

Reaching out with all of his senses, Dalin could not detect any other mental signatures. He stooped to walk past the professor and into the tight passage. He couldn't help his surprise, though his parents' house had several hidden passages, as did their wayhouse. He didn't expect to see this type of thing here, although the cobbled-together design of the palace and school was perfect for irregularities in blueprints.

The bookcase clicked shut and Dr. Iskindar said, "Approximately one hundred meters straight ahead."

As he walked, his eyes adjusted until he could make out a dim rectangle of light in the near distance. The passage smelled like wood and plaster, slightly damp, just like the rest of the school. The less rational and nervous part of his mind wanted to make a joke about getting a cleaning crew back here. After all, some of the servants did clean the hidden hallways at the de Forest home. But Dalin kept silent, glad for the silent traction of his light-duty boots.

The rectangle was the entrance to a relatively large chamber lit by skylights. The rain poured down, the patter of drops against the glass both strange and welcome after so many months on Laska.

As Dalin turned in a slow circle, Dr. Iskindar triggered a few suspended overhead lights that grew brighter after a few seconds. The room was a rough oval, with nooks for chairs and desks as well as antique-looking storage cabinets. In the center was equipment as new as that in Bryant Kucala's lab.

"Before we continue our conversation, Mr. de Forest," Dr. Iskindar said. "You must swear to hold this place and its secrets as dear as your own life." She held out an old book, its flyleaf scrawled with signatures.

Dalin glanced toward the nearest desk for a writing tool, but she turned the first page to reveal a working palm scanner. "What is this place? Whose secrets does it keep?"

The professor smiled slowly with a hint of pride. "It is the base of operations for the King's Men. It holds the secrets we have kept, the secrets we keep in the name of the first king."

"And you are the head of the King's...Men?"

Instead of answering, she held out the scanner. He placed his right palm on the scanner and said, "I swear." The scanner buzzed an electric jolt into the center of his palm.

Dr. Iskindar pulled the scanner away, tapped a few lit buttons, and nodded. "I am the head, yes. For more than a decade. And you are our newest member. Welcome."

She returned the old book to a drawer in one of the desks and said, "While the historian and scholar in you would be intrigued by the list of names in that book, today is about the future, not the past."

Without a doubt Dalin wanted to read and research the names on the flyleaf. He also wanted to open every drawer in every desk and cabinet and read every file, every record, every document. It took some effort, but he maintained eye contact with the professor, hands open and still at his sides.

His cause was the Daughter. It felt uncomfortable to be allied with the group that had hurt so many people on Asattha. And yet, he knew without question he would hurt or kill to keep Mara from harm.

"Do you have current intel on the situation on Iloel?" he asked, deciding to get straight to the most important question.

"Yes. Come." Dr. Iskindar motioned him to a screen placed high on the wall and behind a hinged painting of a woman in ancient British court dress.

"The Iloellians have used their self-sustaining war project as camouflage for decades. The smokescreen of revolution served as their excuse not to export any of the planet's precious resources and provided them with an excuse for eliminating contact with the Commonwealth. No governmental contact means no diplomacy. The accepted narrative is that Iloel is a worthless mess and will continue to be a waste of the crown's time and personnel."

"So why send troops now?" Dalin asked.

"Resources." She increased the magnification on the screen showing Iloel until only one continent showed. "Many, many reports were filed indicating the mines were played out. But then a few too many smugglers were caught with ships full of rare planetary metals." She paused and tilted her head, the classic pose of a teacher waiting for the student to catch up.

"The local leaders decided they'd rather make their government public and attempt to gain independence, but they kept the war ruse going as long as they could to discourage interference," Dalin said.

Dr. Iskindar nodded and pointed to the screen. "They'll try to keep the Commonwealth troops here." A black dot popped on the central continent. "Near the capital."

She gestured again and a second black dot appeared, larger than the first. "Though the people of Iloel, my people, are generally united in their faith and in their opposition to Commonwealth rule, not everyone agrees how to proceed."

Needing a moment to think through the information, Dalin looked away and rubbed his tired eyes. He'd planned questions, but he hadn't really expected answers. As much as he wanted to know more about the situation on Iloel, this woman possessed information about Dalin's personal cause. "Do you know who took Mara from her parents and hid her in the war project? Is that information somewhere in this room?"

Dr. Iskindar dimmed the wall screen and swung the painting back into place. "For nearly a full two centuries, archives were divided across the Commonwealth so that no one repository contained the full history or full scope of our work." She tapped the central worktable with her index finger, her smile holding a touch of regret. "Connection and access have been a gift, but the risk of access by outsiders reminds us all of the validity of the first king's paranoia."

Dalin narrowed his eyes. In his limited experience with Elsebet Iskindar, she tended to answer questions in a direct, precise manner.

"Who kidnapped Mara? Why would the Kings' Men sanction such an action?"

"Are you certain that is the answer you seek today? Information more than a decade old?"

Yes, but no. He wanted to know about Iloel. "Do you know who assigned Mara to the student observation squad?"

"I did."

Chapter 12

"Here's the word." O'Kelley met each soldier's eyes in turn. "Communication started coming through about oh six hundred, but it's patchy. Plan A is go in business as usual, land in the spaceport. Plan B is go in firing and clear a place to land. The colonel makes the decision in about an hour, once we're close enough for the special corps to do their version of recon."

Several people spoke into the stunned silence. Sritha waited and then said, "If command is relying on special corps, does that mean the city is gone? The rebels have the whole infrastructure?"

The squad leader shook his head. "Unknown. History from the Origin would dictate that a takeover is not complete without control of all major transport. I'm sorry, Sritha, if I knew I would tell you."

Raymundo said, "I thought they were trying diplomacy, trying to co-exist."

"During the cease-fire and peace summit two weeks ago, Commonwealth fighters staged an offensive on a key town to the south while most of their leaders were up in Samradhi."

"They don't want peace?" Angelo muttered, almost to himself.

"They want control," Kailer said.

Into the silence, O'Kelley ordered a weapons check. Most everyone had gone over their weapons during the flight, but it kept their hands busy and their minds on routine.

Not a single member of the O Squad had followed the "only one weapon" rule. Multiple knives, throwing stars, and swords came out for sharpening and oiling. The average was closer to three or four weapons per person, not counting what else was hidden in the packs and in arm or leg sheaths.

Next Fentress had everyone check their boots—seams, laces, soles—making the case that they would be on their feet and in motion for an unknown length of time. "No one on this team will go down for equipment," she said.

Packs were checked next, and as they were doing so, the last round of meal tubes appeared. Their squad leader asked for extra and made each student tuck away at least one tube of the nutrient paste.

As Mara went through her pack and surreptitiously checked the hidden knives she considered the situation on Iloel. It wasn't right to fight people who just wanted freedom from the Crown. What were the proposed terms of the peace treaty? She lowered a section of her shield and sent, *"What was it like when you left? The situation between the rebels and the Commonwealth forces?"*

Sritha looked up from folding and rolling her spare clothes. *"Tense, but stable. We were used to it, like the weather. Sometimes sunny, sometimes cloudy."*

"And your war experiment? War Project One?"

"That ended before I was born, when my parents were young. That's when those in the experiment, the Iloellian side, I guess, separated completely and went to live on the southern half of the continent." The girl sealed her pack and scooted over to speak quietly. "That's considered common knowledge, but you wouldn't have had any of the war project classes yet, since you're in the first year."

It was spoken with kindness, but Mara barely suppressed the automatic flinch. Ignorance had been punishment of the worst kind, a part of her past she could not shake.

Interpreting Mara's expression a different way, Sritha said, "Told you. The last few hours are the longest—"

Booted feet pounded down the walkway. A soldier motioned for O'Kelley to follow and both hurried away.

"All right, people, finish with your gear." Fentress smacked the side of her chair. "Command will be calling for strap down in less than thirty. Ready or not."

Going into the Box for the Friday fights, Mara had felt only a fraction of full battle anticipation. As her heart picked up speed now, it was all she could do to keep her energy shield down and her motions smooth. Every instinct said the student squad would be fighting as much as observing. For an uneasy moment, she wondered how the drug in her system would react with the adrenaline. But the part of her that loved the puzzle and the challenge of the Gaishan month after month itched for a new enemy to fight.

O'Kelley appeared in the doorway. "It's Plan A," he said. "Going into the spaceport. No shooting yet."

"Anything else?" his self-appointed second, Fentress, asked.

His eyes flicked to the only Iloellian on their squad. "No," he said. "Strap in. We picked up a little speed coming around the planet. Time to land."

"Wait." Halifax took a step forward. "What exactly are we supposed to observe? Naran never got specific."

The redhead took a deep breath in through his nose. "Anything that will help you personally become a better soldier for the Commonwealth. That's a direct quote." He matched his posture to the other boy's—chin up, chest out, eyes narrowed. "Repeat. Observe, not investigate. Clear?"

Halifax raised his eyebrows and shrugged. "Clear."

With a quick jab to her friend's ribs, Dominique said, "Yeah, Fusao. No investigating."

"Stealth ninjas aren't supposed to talk," Fusao replied, catching her elbow and putting her in an arm lock. "Gives away your position."

"You heard the boss," Fentress said. "Strap in, *niños*."

* * *

O Squad was the last team out of the ship. The hangar was nearly empty, quiet except for the hot, dry wind. Unlike the spaceport in Crown City, no hoses snaked across the syncrete and the catwalks were empty of personnel. The students pulled into a tight formation without being told, weapons at hand.

"Where's the crew?" Sritha asked. "The deckhands and spacers should be here, checking the ship."

"We came in with the automated beacon," O'Kelley replied. "When our pilot locked on, the colonel chose Plan A. Two of the other squads are here, one's clearing the interior. The other has the perimeter. The rest are moving out to Samradhi. We've got the interior for the next hour as well. I thought you might know where we should look for clues about what happened." This last was directly to Sritha.

The girl nodded and adjusted her pack. "I speak only two of the local dialects, so I'd like Raymundo to come with me, for translating purposes."

Fentress spoke quietly to their squad leader. He grimaced and scrubbed a hand over his face. "All right. Stick with your watch partners for now. Swap Dominique and Angelo. Fan out and cover the immediate area. Be cautious and *observe*. Report in thirty."

* * *

Dalin left Dr. Iskindar's office and walked for a while, not certain of his destination.

His wrist unit chimed, reminding him his next class began in fifteen minutes. He brushed at the grit on his uniform and picked up his pace. He made it through a hasty clothes change and back to the training floor with less than a minute to spare.

The Mess had several large gymnasiums all connected to the locker rooms by a long hallway. This one was divided into five padded areas large enough for approximately twenty people each. Built with both a flexible wooden floor and a bamboo subfloor, beginners typically took class here where drops and falls had less painful consequences. Noise bounced off the ceilings and echoed across the large space, however. When all five areas were in use, it could get loud. Teachers often had to yell to be heard.

His beginning hand-to-hand class needed work on anticipating what the next move might be and also on improvising and feeling confident about which moves to choose.

Walking through the groups, he noted how little contact anyone made or, if they made contact, how light it was. That tall blonde had told him he'd been pulling punches for too long and she was right. His practice fights might look better than these beginners, but no one feared for his or her life.

When was the last time he'd been afraid for his own life?

As the class neared its end, Dalin told the group, "In a real fight, your opponent is looking to disable or kill you. Let's be clear about that. Going forward, every class is full gear and every class is full contact. Dismissed."

Watching the last students file out, movement on a far mat caught his eye. A bare-knuckle brawl between two students, one female, one male, watched by a group of ten, all in their fourth or fifth years.

The male fighter saw Dalin's approach and held up both hands to his opponent. "Hold," he said through his mouth guard.

"What's this?" Dalin asked, posture relaxed and conveying no judgment or urgency.

"Tournament training, sir," one of the spectators replied.

"Open to all comers?"

The female fighter spit her mouth guard into her hand and grinned. "You're looking for a fight? We'd love to practice on you, wouldn't we?" She opened her arms, palms up to invite comment from the group.

Most nodded but one student called, "You outrank us."

"Won't be ranks in the tournament," Dalin said. "Someone recently told me I'd been pulling my punches for too long. I need the practice as much as you, if not more."

"Fair enough," said the female. "Get your helmet and mouth guard. You're up next."

When Dalin arrived at his door later that night, he was too tired to go through his routine checks. It was hard enough to prop himself against the metal frame while opening the locks.

The past few hours of fighting had allowed Dalin to lose himself in the moment. None of the matches made him fear for his life, but he got hit and returned punches and kicks harder than he had in a long time.

At first he attributed his sense of wrongness to his rapidly swelling left eye. Vision blurring and head aching, he took a few steps to the tiny kitchen area. The chairs were wrong. The sink faucet was wrong. Turning in a sloppy circle, he surveyed the larger part of the room. Tiny shifts in the furniture, the books, made his bruised stomach lurch. He returned to the door and confirmed the fresh rust dust under the hinges. He lumbered into the bedroom where his bed covers were pulled not quite tight enough.

Grabbing a cooling pack from his first aid kit, he pressed it to the side of his face and checked all the places where he kept additional weapons. They'd been disturbed, but not taken.

Because of snooping through electronic records? Because of his insane actions prior to the departure of the Iloel mission? His meeting with Bryant Kucala or Elsebet Iskindar?

His rooms being searched brought all of the larger worries crashing back into his battered body.

Chapter 13

The student observers didn't have much to report. O'Kelley and Fusao had worked the commercial side of the spaceport, where travelers and traders would have checked in, waited, and departed. It was empty, but undisturbed. The log Fusao found indicated declining numbers of flights over the past six months until this port was handling as few as two per week. Nothing in the log gave reason for the decline.

Dominique reported that the private crew lounges were also empty and undisturbed.

"Your parents weren't on the schedule or signed in for the past week, Sritha, as far as we could tell." Angelo gave her a reassuring smile. "You should look for yourself and double-check, but that's how I read it."

"Orders are to follow the road toward Samrahdi and regroup with the other teams from Crown City. Time to head out."

"Wait." Kailer looked at the head of the Furies and back to their squad leader. "We found food stores. Not fresh stuff, but good dried fruit and noodles ready to make. We...I...think it would be worth ten minutes to add a little to everyone's packs."

Several squad members nodded at the mention of food. O'Kelley said, "Ten minutes, that's it. Then we're marching double time."

During the short pack restock, Mara tested the running water, emptied three bottles, and re-filled them in a sink. Once the group reunited with the rest of the platoon from Crown City, she couldn't be sure of the availability of liquid supplies. She was hungry too, glad the dusty food packages most likely had not been tainted with experimental drugs.

The first stars shone in the darkening sky as the ten student soldiers marched double time toward the capital of Iloel. Mara hadn't had a run in over two days and despite the additional supplies, the weight of her pack felt great. Away from the spaceport, the cool night air carried only a slight acrid tinge.

Sometimes a particular spot on the plateau back home would get more sun than rain if they had a hot spell in the summer, though the northwest section of the Protected territory didn't get hot much. But when it did, what she smelled now reminded her of her home: trees and grass lashed by the sun.

The nearly bare landscape left nowhere for an enemy to hide. When the sentry for the camp appeared on the road, the person was visible for nearly a hundred meters. O'Kelley went ahead for a quick conference and then jogged back to update the team.

"Two tent pads, one for males, one for females. They've got a watch schedule already. My preference is we keep our own, but in two-hour shifts instead of three. Even if she was inclined, the sergeant is too busy to do us any favors. Someone from our squad needs to be alert to changes throughout the night."

The students received the last scrapings of the camp dinner. A few tents were already up, but some teams had chosen to sleep on pallets in the open.

"O'Kelley wants us behind the tents, upwind of the latrine pits," Halifax said as they prepared to begin the first watch.

Mara followed him about twenty paces up a gentle rise. At the top, she checked the draw of her sword from the shoulder harness and the knives in her arm sheaths. Halifax checked his own weapons and then they both turned to take in the view.

Tents ringed each of the two fires in concentric, semicircular rows. Wood smoke drifted up and swirled on the light breeze. Armed sentries patrolled the rows on either side, and a few more sentries walked the outer perimeter, though not as far as their spot.

"Have to admit," Halifax said, "since I started at the Mess, this is the oddest assignment yet. And there've been some odd ones."

It didn't seem much different than any other small troops exercise to Mara. Except for the part where they'd be marching into a city larger than Satri tomorrow, a city reported to be occupied by hostile forces.

"You ever fought in a city before? Do you know what kind of weapons this conflict uses?" she asked. After so much time with Dalin, it felt strange to voice her thinking and then listen to a response out loud, to create pictures with Halifax's words herself, instead of receiving images.

The war experiment on his home world, Hépíng Xīng, was contained in a specific location, just like on Asattha. The nickname for War Project Six was "Terrain Train" because so much of the fight data was collected while the soldiers tested new equipment in the foothills and mountains of his homeworld. The brawny scholar rattled off facts and figures that Mara tried to absorb. She lost track until he said, "…increased casualty rate from twenty-five percent to forty percent."

It was about an hour into their watch and the camp was quieting down. Looking directly at Halifax's sharp profile, she asked, "What was the time frame for the casualty increase?"

Her tone caught his attention. "First spike was about eight years ago, according to the data. Second spike was just this year, approximately six months ago. My cousin is part of the Science Corps and she said the increases were ordered, straight from the Queen and the Queen's Council. If reports showed the casualties weren't increasing, the variables got changed to make things worse on the experimental side. Like how they decreased the Protector food supply and took away academic classes. And let sickness spread in the settlements."

Clenching her back teeth together so she didn't scream, Mara walked a few paces away. The poison started with a tingle of ice at the base of her spine and spread quickly through her arms and legs. Without conscious effort, the energy of the Tree, Iloel's Tree, flowed into her. It twined through the Darkness in her mind, tugging at the roots of her anger and sorrow. The surge of alien energy dropped her to her knees and forward onto her hands, the gritty, sandy thatch cutting into her palms.

"Hey, are you sick?" Halifax's voice was low, but full of concern. He patted Mara's shoulder.

Breathing through her nose, she closed her eyes and tried to be glad the Tree had made contact so quickly. But the shame of knowing so little about the Protector Project and the nausea from the dark drug reactivating in her system were almost overwhelming. No matter what else happened, ignorance would always be her worst enemy.

"We only have about twenty minutes left. Why don't you turn in?"

Mara swallowed hard, avoiding eye contact as she pushed off from the ground and stood. "No, I'm okay, I…didn't know the Queen brought the sickness to the settlements, that's all."

A long breath escaped her watch partner. "I figured the more I learned, the more I could help." He walked soundlessly back toward their post, pounding one clenched fist against his thigh. "But how are empty facts going to keep families and children safe? Long time ago, I stopped wanting the war projects to make sense. Stopped caring if they did, I mean. But here? These people?"

Even on an unsettled plain, Mara couldn't shake the habit of looking around for recording devices. Halifax could get dismissed or worse for expressing such ideas out loud.

"We'll be helping our fellow soldiers," she offered.

"Are they the ones who need help?" He folded his brawny arms across his chest and turned to stare at the camp spread out below.

* * *

The tent was stifling hot as the early morning sun poured down into the camp. As quietly as possible, Mara repacked her gear and ducked outside. The slight breeze carrying the last tinge of the night's chill dried her sweat in an instant. Fentress motioned her over to join a small portion of the O Squad.

For a few minutes, the squad ate and observed the rest of the teams eating and packing.

Scraping his plate for a last bite, Halifax turned to Sritha. "Something I heard has been bothering me. It was a recording of one of the Iloellian leaders shouting at Commonwealth troops. She said, 'The daughter comes and we make the way clear for her.' I feel like I once ran across legends about a daughter of something." He shook his head. "That bring up anything local for you? Local legends?"

"Fax not remembering something? Not an auspicious start to our day," Fusao joked.

"Leave the man alone," Angelo said. "He knows more than you'll forget in a lifetime."

After a deep swig of water, Sritha said, "War Project One was about faith. The original battle lines were between those who had no faith, well, or faith in humans, faith in tech, and those who were taught to draw strength and energy from the natural world. That was in the textbooks." Everyone in O Squad nodded except Mara.

Mara kept silent, certain she'd felt the energy of this planet's Tree the previous night.

"Sometimes we would hear rumors of a Great Tree on Iloel, a tree that provided energy and enlightenment to those near Her, who chose mothers and daughters to share her wisdom. But no one's ever found it or been able to separate religious doctrine from fact. It's possible, of course, that other planets in this system have Trees of their own. But so far, the only one is on Asattha." Sritha shifted her gaze to Mara and then back to the group.

Raymundo kicked his cousin's foot. Angelo kicked him back. "What?"

"We should tell about tío Escobar." The translator's face was serious. "Maybe it would help?"

"He was crazy—" Angelo broke off and looked around at the team. With a sideways glower at Raymundo he said, "We have this crazy uncle who says his dad was part of the King's Men."

Everything in Mara had gone still at Halifax's original question. Now she raised her eyes slowly, anxious to hear the rest.

Some of the O Squad were scraping the last bits of egg from their trays, but Dominique and Kailer were both staring at the two cousins. "Your uncle's dad?" the scout said.

"Yeah." Angelo rubbed the back of his neck and looked down. "So, Escobar, he was in the local regiment, but sometimes when he was off-duty, he'd tell me and 'Mundo stories about his dad, traveling the commonwealth on a great quest for the Tree's Daughter."

"She's this legendary warrior, just a story, but—"

"Supposed to be beautiful, hotter than tía Linda's *salsa del diablo*." Both laughed at that.

Dominique leaned forward, her entire body intent on the story. "The best surveyor in my settlement was a retired scout, and when we'd go out on a job, sometimes he told stories about the quest for the Daughter of the Tree."

"Was he part of the King's Men?" Kailer asked, her tone more brittle than usual.

The smaller girl shrugged. "He didn't say. I didn't know to ask. Thought it was just a story until now."

The whole O Squad was listening, but also showing the tiny signs they were ready to strike camp. Unable to handle the discomfort a moment longer, Mara stood and left the circle. If the conversation continued, she missed it in her haste to withdraw.

Mara already knew the legend and prophecy. The Tree's Daughter returned the Light to the Commonwealth.

Despite her encounter with the leader of the King's Men the previous year, Mara didn't believe the legend was about a real person. Certainly it wasn't about her. But part of her wished for the power of the mythical figure so that she could strike down Queen Vanora and erase her dark shadow forever.

Chapter 14

Dalin decided to take his own advice. He ate only from the busiest food stations in the Mess Mess, making sure to rotate without a discernible pattern. It was inviting sabotage to leave his water bottle out during classes so he started carrying sealed extras and immediately switching if his container appeared moved in any way.

Despite his small injuries, Dalin went back to the fight group the next day after his classes ended. Some of the students nodded to him, some ignored him. He'd won his three practice fights, but not by as wide a margin as he might have a year ago.

The female in charge took him aside as the bouts began. "You know who Fentress is, right?"

He shook his head and shrugged.

"She's the head of the Furies at the Mess? Tall, blonde hair, pierced nose?"

The one who helped Mara. "Yes, we met but I didn't get her name. She's the reason I'm here, actually."

The female's mouth twisted down at the corners. She was slim but muscular, a yellow-green bruise spreading across the dark golden tan of her throat. "Sorry to hear that. Fentress is the one who set up this group and the rules. The thing is, you can train with us today, but after that, you need to find a more advanced group. Fighting you yesterday was bad for morale."

Before he could catch it, anger surged. It was the story of his life, classes weren't a good fit; he'd have to move up or study on his own. "Aren't you training for the tournament? Who do you think you'll be up against? And anyway, I didn't walk away unscathed."

"True. What you say is true." The female folded her arms across her fitted black tank top. She turned to watch the two fights in progress. "Are you training for the tournament?"

He wasn't. But he asked, "Why?"

"Some of the others, a few fifth years, they found a place to train in Crown City, in Lower Town. Getting ready for all the fight styles we don't learn here."

"And you're suggesting that's my next step?" Despite himself, Dalin was intrigued. He'd been exposed to plenty of styles at university, but hadn't much access to teachers outside of Jameson and his father since then.

As if to emphasize his thoughts, one of the pairs on the mat dropped to the ground, one fighter reaching for a submission hold. "Roll out!" the female yelled at the fighter being held. Looking up at Dalin, she said, "You're welcome to hang around and let us beat on you. But if you fight back as hard as you did yesterday, I'll lose students."

"Can you give me a contact?" He didn't want to agree with her. Yesterday's fighting had felt really good. But if the rest of the students perceived him to be that much better, he needed to find a different group.

She tapped her wrist unit and a virtual note appeared. "These two are part of the group training in Lower Town." She flicked the note toward Dalin and he caught it with his own wrist unit, like a virtual soap bubble. The holos weren't necessary, but they were fun, a rare thing at the Mess.

"Thanks," he said. He had time right now, might as well keep looking for the next fight.

Dalin stopped by his quarters to fill a pack with supplies and suit up in rain gear. At the checkpoint, he signed himself out, extending the notice until curfew.

The walk down the hill reminded him of the last time he'd been this way in the bright sunlight with Mara by his side. He missed her. His days were built around time with Mara, organized around her class schedule, as much as his own. The past two days of waiting for updated information on Mara's health and safety had been mental and emotional torture. When he wasn't worrying about his partner being dropped into a smoldering revolution, he would worry about the drug in her system instead. The only moments of peace had been in the midst of the fights yesterday.

He kicked a loose rock and tried to shake off his growing anger by looking outward instead of inward, as his father used to say.

The rain had softened the afternoon into near dusk. Without shadows, the houses and trees merged into a muted landscape. He forced himself to wonder how his favorite artist from Satri might capture this scene on canvas. The rain released smells in the Mess, bringing life into the building. But out here on Palace Hill he couldn't smell much beyond the damp foliage, except maybe a hint of flowers.

Long ago he'd taken a survey course covering the ecosystems and biomes across the Commonwealth, too long ago to remember which flowers bloomed during the monsoons on Laska. Planetary engineering had been in its infancy when the Commonwealth was founded. Somehow, whoever worked on this planet had nudged the seeds of the environmental template into a climate not unlike the first king's home, India, on the Origin.

The address he was looking for was deep in the heart of Lower Town, not too far from Cousins, the eating house where Mara had taken shelter. Where she'd made friends, converts really. As she did everywhere she went. And from this unlikely place, she now had a standing offer to work when she was available.

Without making a conscious decision, Dalin found himself at the door. Today was about intel more than training, and it wouldn't hurt to verify the reputation of the fight school with a local source before suiting up and taking punches.

An alley was to his right. Behind him, across from Cousins's door, was a trio of shops specializing in gear for the s'port workers, specialty tools, coveralls, different types of calibrated and tinted eyewear. No wonder so many spacers ate here - it was a good business model, grab some gear and a bite in the same trip.

"You coming inside? Or just taking in the atmosphere?"

The question startled Dalin, his hand tightening on his bag. He turned to greet Rafiq, the owner of the place.

"Looking for you actually," he said.

"That so?" The man scratched his perfectly trimmed and sculpted beard, the sharp look in his dark eyes belying the casual gesture. "Well, this isn't a neighborhood where loitering goes unnoticed, so why don't you come on in, get out of the rain?" He opened the door, an exceptionally thick door, and motioned for Dalin to go in first.

The main room of the eating house featured heavy plastic tables and chairs resting on pitted and stained syncrete floors. Yet it smelled as though everything had been recently cleaned. The interior was no less dim than the rainy afternoon outside; industrial-looking lights housed in metal cages ranged across the corrugated metal ceiling.

The ceiling was thicker than just one layer of metal roofing. Dalin squinted at a corner, certain it was actually two metal layers with one or more layers of insulation in between. The owner of the eating house, Mara's rescuer, was the same. Easy to dismiss if you just accepted the obvious, but more functional and more complex if you spent some time looking.

"It's a lovely ceiling," Rafiq said following Dalin's gaze. "Tourists come by just to see it."

Dalin pressed his lips together, but couldn't entirely suppress a smile. This guy was giving him a tough time and he deserved it. "Is there somewhere we could talk?"

With a shrug, the owner of the eating house gestured to a table next to the kitchen door. "You here to eat?"

"Maybe later." Dalin chose the chair that faced the main entrance and dropped his bag at his feet.

Rafiq poked his head into the kitchen and yelled something, before turning back to Dalin. "Water?"

"I'm fine," Dalin said.

Sliding into the chair closest to the kitchen so that they could both see the main door, Rafiq leaned back and spread his hands in the air, palms up. "I admit, I'm curious. Last time you were here, you were starched within an inch of your life, as my mother would say."

"I was on official business," Dalin said, shrugging. "I didn't want anyone else from the Mess to make first contact with Mara after her...absence."

The man nodded. "And now you're," he waved a hand from Dalin's head to the tabletop, "out of uniform. Although still exceeding the cleanliness standards for Lower Town."

"I'm looking for a fight," Dalin began, unzipping his jacket.

"Plenty of those around here," Rafiq said. "But before you get to the details, I should inform you that nothing is free in Lower Town, especially information."

Dalin had currency in one of his pockets, but the casual request for payment was a first. "You charged Mara for your help?" He couldn't keep the accusation out of his voice.

Rafiq's grin flashed, even white teeth bright against his dark skin and beard. "I don't reveal the details of my *arrangements*."

One hand curled into a fist and the other tapped the most available knife, just under Dalin's shirt at his hip. The innuendo was another first. *No one* talked about Mara like that.

The owner of the eating house looked like an easy target. His shirt wasn't even properly buttoned and his loose sandals were an obvious weakness. But the way the man looked at Dalin, both lazy and menacing, like one of the great hunting cats, kept him in his chair.

For the moment.

The massive cook banged open the kitchen door and dropped a plate of food in front of Rafiq without ceremony. He glanced at Dalin, expression hardening with recognition.

"Hey, you're that *cabrón* came down here and hassled our—"

"New waitress," Rafiq said. "This young man says he's looking for a fight—"

The cook folded his arms across his massive chest. "Yeah? I know some people who feel the same way."

Despite his flushed face and weight, Dalin suspected the cook would be a formidable adversary at close quarters. He moved with balance and coordination that signaled some kind of training.

"I was just explaining to this guest that nothing is free in Lower Town. Sometimes I accept money for my extremely valuable help, and on even more rare occasions, individuals choose to work off their debts. But I prefer information."

These men had helped Mara, had been ready to defend her. And she liked them, chose to be here during her free time. "What kind of information?" Dalin was willing to hear Rafiq out, for her sake.

"Well, what about your story?"

"And if I give you my extremely valuable story," with certain parts deleted, "you'll set me up with a fight trainer or a gym or someplace I can work out, learn—"

"You're entering the tournament *de locos*?" the cook asked.

He wasn't. But maybe he'd get better help if he said he was. Dalin shrugged and gave a small grin. "Maybe. Might as well try, right? Get knocked out in the early rounds?"

* * *

The heat of the morning and the pace of the march had the whole squad sweating by the time the tall towers of Samrahdi appeared beyond the low yellow hills. At first it didn't seem that much different from Crown City, just built from darker materials, but as they drew closer, the height of the buildings continued to grow, taller than any structure Mara had ever seen, easily ten times the height of the palace.

Colonel Naran called a halt about two hundred meters from the nearest outbuildings, huts, and falling-down structures, all slumped over and abandoned, not unlike some of the worst sections of Lower Town.

For the past kilometer, the main road had grown darker and slightly spongy underfoot but remained completely empty of foot traffic or vehicles traveling either direction. It didn't take tracking skills to see no one had used this road, not regularly, in a long while. "Eight-minute break. Squad leaders with me," Naran barked and strode a few paces away.

Immediately postures relaxed as packs were unslung and water gulped. Before she drank, Mara checked the draw on her arm sheaths, worried about the slickness of her sweat under the long sleeves. Wearing sunglasses helped with the sun glare, but distracted her whenever she looked down or tried to manipulate her own things.

"Ever seen anything like it?" Halifax asked, wiping his mouth with his hand and pointing to the silent city. "I've seen plenty of images, and intellectually I understood the scale and the design principles, but to see the oldest industrial center in the Commonwealth, it's so much bigger than I imagined."

The O Squad stood in a circle, half facing in and half facing out. Fentress kept her eyes on O'Kelley and the group with the Colonel, but over her shoulder she said, "It was modeled on the last big cities on the Origin. Populations were so dense they had to pile people on top of each other."

"The engineers and the techs, the first ones after the explorers, they built this and moved in. As the miners acquired wealth, they moved in as well." Sritha picked up the story now. "But after a few generations, the knowledge to run these huge towers was lost, partly due to the drain on energy resources and attempts to find alternatives. Trying to cool those monsters down during the hottest months was nearly impossible. No one lives there now, and bits fall off, especially if it's windy."

"Where are the people now?" Fusao asked, just as O'Kelley stepped into the circle.

Their pink-faced leader looked first at Fentress and then scanned the faces of his team. "None of Naran's scouts have returned."

Dominique snorted and kicked the road with the toe of her boot.

The two Furies made eye contact and Fentress asked, "Nothing from the sergeant?"

"Not that he said. I'm guessing no." O'Kelley took a drink of water. "Sitrep is this. Last reports had the fighting on the far side of the towers, near the main government building."

"Parliament Hall?" Sritha offered.

Nodding, O'Kelley removed his sunglasses and began polishing the lenses on his shirt. "He didn't say, but that sounds right. Two sets of scouts, one last night and one this morning, haven't reported back."

"We need to get out of the sun before midday hits, but taking shelter in the towers puts us at risk. The best option would be to split and shelter in smaller groups, but that poses another level of risk." O'Kelley accepted Sritha's assessment with a nod.

Side conversations erupted in sharp whispers from several of the pairs. Looking at the ruined towers ahead, Mara imagined all the places for fighters who knew the territory to hide. She couldn't think of the Iloellian soldiers as the enemy even though her student uniform was as good as a Gaishan mask to them.

"Where are all the people?" Fusao repeated his question.

"Well, the section of the city we can see has been abandoned for multiple decades. People live closer to where they work, the spaceport, the mines, I mean, the fields. Government workers live on the other side, based on the population maps." Sritha nodded.

"But all the metal, the tech, in those towers—" Kailer began.

"Oh, they stripped the lower floors long ago, but the higher you go, the higher the risk, and no one's figured out how to bring down one of those monsters safely. Not yet, anyway." The Iloellian girl shrugged and glanced at her wrist. "We heading out?"

The squad all looked toward Naran, still deep in conversation with officers from the other groups.

"Take the time to hydrate, people," Fentress warned. "The heat'll kill you sure as a sword."

After a few more minutes, the colonel gave the signal to move out. O Squad fell in to the center of the column, their pre-assigned position among the veterans. Only Mara had been part of ongoing action and apparently that didn't count for much. When she'd been a leader in her Protector cohort, she'd made sure to help the newest, the youngest find their strengths and emphasize them. What was the point of acting like no one knew anything prior to arriving on your team?

The heat kept her from thinking about anything for too long until finally, the first of the shadow tunnels opened before them.

* * *

Dalin had studied lying with the same diligence he applied to other important skills. It had been an offshoot of his larger study of human communication. What he'd found was that an individual would often indicate, however subtly, what he or she was hoping "the truth" was. He had practiced letting the conversation lead the lie until his delivery was as smooth as a knife throw.

"I'll tell you the first part today," he said to the owner of the eating house, "and then you'll walk me to the fighting gym, introduce me around."

"Half today," Rafiq countered. "Half tomorrow. You've really got to start training if you want to make it past the first round."

Dalin kept his smirk on the inside. "True." If he was going to talk, he needed some water. With reluctance, he reached into his small pack and drew out one of his sealed containers.

His host raised an eyebrow. "Didn't I offer you water?"

"You did," Dalin agreed.

"Afraid of being drugged?"

"Discretion is the better part of valor," Dalin offered the quote as an explanation.

If Rafiq recognized the reference, he gave no indication. Just took a bite of his meal and chewed, eyes focused on a point past Dalin's head. "That might get noticed, never eating or drinking at the gym. Plenty of fighters bring their own stuff, but everyone uses the bubbler at some point."

"A source that's used frequently and by a lot of people isn't a problem," Dalin said. "Just when the preparation or pouring takes place out of my sight."

His stomach growled; he hoped the other man didn't hear. The food smelled delicious, and watching Rafiq eat reminded him of the small, nutritious but bland meal he'd eaten earlier. If Mara was going to work the tables here, maybe the giant cook would let him work in the kitchen?

The metal fans in the ceiling moved the humid air and kept the cooking smells fresh. Even the oil smell was light, only a part of the entire bouquet, not the dominant note like in so many of Crown City's eating establishments.

Allowing himself one more sip of water, Dalin began his story. "I was born on Asattha. My mother's line goes back to the first scientists to land on C-7. My father is from Tian."

His host nodded. This was why skillful liars opened with something entirely true.

"I was very fortunate to learn Origin Chinese from my father while also learning Origin English from my mother and at school."

Rafiq agreed, "Very fortunate." All that was left on the man's plate was what looked like scrambled eggs and the remainder of the sauce. Rafiq tore a piece of tortilla from those in a basket near his right hand, rolled a little egg inside, and swiped the whole thing in the sauce.

Dalin's mouth watered a little. He looked down at his hands spread flat and still on the scarred heavy-duty plastic tabletop. He hadn't cooked his own food in months.

"Sure you're not hungry?"

"I've been hungry since I started growing," Dalin said. "But I'm fine right now." He hesitated. "Is that green chile?"

"One of the specialties of the house," Rafiq said as he fixed himself another egg and tortilla bite.

"My education was accelerated because I learned so quickly," Dalin resumed his recitation. "I entered the University of Asattha at thirteen." *The year Jameson found Mara was the year Dalin began planning his life around keeping her safe.* "Earned my first diploma in military history at sixteen. My parents sent me to Hépíng Xīng because we thought I might take after my mother and choose a career in diplomacy. But that didn't work out."

Actually, it might have worked out, but they'd gotten word Mara would be on the Protector lines in a year. Dalin couldn't let her fight alone. He could watch, help shape the battle plans. Keep her safe, since it was his failure that allowed her kidnapping in the first place.

"I decided to join the Satri militia instead."

A pair of spaceport workers strolled in. One nodded at Rafiq and he nodded back. Just as the pair settled into chairs across the room, the cook banged through the kitchen door, carrying two glasses of water.

With a sigh, Rafiq pushed his plate to one side. "As stories go, yours is on the short side." He drew his fingertips down one side of his sculpted beard and then the other, considering Dalin with sharp brown eyes.

"One of the key problems in using information as currency is that I can't exactly bite into it, like you would a counterfeit coin, to prove if something is false. But you're leaving out everything important. On purpose," the owner of the eating house spoke with mild disappointment. "That choice changes our terms—" When Dalin began to protest, Rafiq folded his arms across his chest. "I get three questions. You will answer with truth or no deal."

From his loose linen pants pocket, he produced a scrap of paper and a pencil. After quickly scribbling three questions, he shoved the paper across the table and walked away, taking his dishes with him.

1. What is your interest in/relationship to Mara?
2. Why are you entering the tournament?
3. What are the properties of the *gontra* seed?

Dalin's wrist unit pinged and a note opened. "The O Squad is on the ground. Moving out to Samradhi." Since no one was looking, Dalin squeezed his eyes shut and pinched the bridge of his nose. Fury at his inability to manipulate his way onto that squad rose like the aftermath of a bad meal.

Meanwhile Mara was marching into the most volatile conflict in the Commonwealth with a drug in her system that could kill her if her survival required that she fight full out.

Dalin glanced at Rafiq's questions. *What was his interest in Mara?* The obvious: keep her safe, protect her. It was the first thing he remembered his parents asking him to do. "Look after Mara. Just like she was your sister." When the Protector had stormed into the De La Luz family home and snatched her from the dinner table, Dalin had only been a child himself, but the memory and the guilt haunted him still. The rest of what he felt for Mara was nobody's business but theirs.

A loaded plate slid in front of him, the delicious-smelling steam promising an even more delicious taste. "You gotta eat, kid." The big cook's voice was kind. "You're so thin, makes me want to cry. No friend of Mara's gonna be starving in my place. Plus, what will the customers think when *el hombre más flaco* don't eat?" The big man wiped his hands down his stained white apron, round face creasing into smile lines like the Buddha statue in Jin's arboretum. "*Jefe* can be hard, but he's a good guy—"

"I can cook," Dalin interrupted. "Mara worked for you and maybe on the days I'm down here training, I could come by and cook after. Be your *sous* chef." The words flowed out without consideration, but he didn't want to take them back.

Rafiq pushed open the front door and ushered in two groups of people, one clad in the same orange jumpsuits as the first group, the other a family group of men wearing turbans and women wearing headscarves. Once the customers were seated, he ambled over, his sandals flapping.

"What's this?" he said to Geraldo. "This man hasn't paid a thing."

"Boss, you forget that's how it works in eating houses. *First* people eat *then* they pay. Plus, look at him. Those new fighters coming in from Dorado will break him in half." The cook mimed eating at Dalin and glided away to talk with the new guests.

Muttering under his breath, Rafiq dropped back into his chair. "If I really wanted an answer, I'd take your fork and let you sit there smelling the food. But it's better hot. House guarantee against poison. That's the same breakfast burrito I ate."

Dalin lifted his fork, held it midair. "Any of those three questions is worth more than a simple introduction to a fight club."

The other man tilted his head in acknowledgment. "Humor me and tell me about your interest in the tournament. To cover your meal."

Taking three slow bites, Dalin savored the thick, spicy green chile and the tender *puercotro*. He couldn't help the huge grin spreading across his face as he said, "I'm in love."

"You're entering the tournament because you're in love. That's classic."

Palate singing with the spice and the complex flavors brought into the mix by the eggs, potatoes, cheese, and beans, Dalin grinned again. "I'm in love with this chile. I'm entering the tournament because I can't find the level of fight that I need up at the Mess. My training has fallen off since we got to Crown City."

Rafiq rocked back onto the rear legs of his chair. "We've had customers propose marriage to Geraldo over that chile. Am I understanding you correctly? You can outfight anyone at the Mess?"

Dalin took another swig from his water bottle and eyed the too-rapidly diminishing food. His mother and etiquette teachers would be horrified, but he was seriously considering licking the plate. With food this good, no wonder Mara wanted to keep coming back.

"Got kicked out of the most advanced training group today," he said. "I'm a junior instructor, so I can't fight the other instructors and I can't show weakness by asking for instruction. That's why I ended up here. A fourth-year student, one of the Furies, gave me some referrals in Lower Town, but—"

"You wanted to check them with me."

Dalin shrugged and reached for a tortilla to dip in the remainders of the burrito. "You sheltered my partner. She trusts you." He sighed as he finished the last bite. Mara loved to eat. He felt closer to her for a fleeting moment, knowing she would have enjoyed this meal with him.

With a metallic rattle, Rafiq dropped his chair back down onto four legs. He stood and clapped Dalin on the shoulder. "All right, drop that plate in the kitchen and let's check out the clubs. I think I know just the one."

Chapter 15

Raymundo had stopped to look up, and Mara bumped right into him. Mumbling an apology, she followed his gaze upward, impossibly high. Even tipping her head straight up, the tops of the nearest towers remained out of view. Cool, dusty wind buffeted them, kicking a metal window frame down the walkway.

"Move," Sritha shouted as she pushed both squad mates out of the road. A split second later, a heavy chunk of something, almost half as tall as the girl, hit the spot where they'd been standing.

"When the wind gusts like that, you look up, and then you run." She balled her fists and glared at her team. "Get me?"

Still shocked by the near miss, Mara stared at her, the rest of the squad in similar states of surprise. "Thank you," she said.

Sritha rolled her eyes as the leading soldier from the next group caught up with them. "Saw that debris come down. Everyone okay?"

"We're good," O'Kelley replied.

"Double time it to catch up then," the soldier replied. "Can't fall behind." He punched Sritha's shoulder and said, "I'll pass the message to keep eyes on the sky."

Around the next corner, the street fell completely in the shadow of the towering high-rise buildings and the wind blew surprisingly hard. Within moments, Mara's sweat had dried and goose bumps prickled her skin.

The farther into the deserted forest of structures they marched, the deeper the shadows, until they passed into an unbroken twilight. Eerie clanging and groaning accompanied the ever-present breeze, the air stale and metallic.

Bits of scrap and glass continued to patter down, but nothing as huge as the first chunk. The sound of marching feet echoed off every artificial surface, announcing their presence to any waiting fighters.

Behind the gaping walls and broken glass, empty floors, devoid of furnishings or embellishment, stretched out for blocks at a time. An energy weapon aimed at one of the central towers could bring down a significant portion of the abandoned district.

Far ahead, sunlight glimmered off the odd black road surface. The colonel called a halt. "Use your own scouts and choose a location to wait out the heat. Post watches and check in with my staff in three hours."

With barely a nod from O'Kelley, Dominique handed off her pack and darted out of sight.

"We're not going to waste the gift of a local guide," the squad leader said. "Sritha, do you know a safe place to rest?"

"The closer we get to the mouth of the river, the safer we'll be," the Iloellian said. "City engineers managed to take down or reinforce the structures around the water."

Flipping out a compass, she led the group south and west for over a kilometer until she stopped at a building with an unusual brick and wood exterior. All of the walls appeared intact, as did the door. The top of the building was easily visible, less than twice the height of the palace. No signs or images indicated the mouth of the river was near, but their guide checked the door and nodded to herself.

"Door's locked. Means we're in the right place. Across the street should be a good spot." Sritha turned and jogged to the facing building, its open, metal framing reinforced with additional struts and supports. A wall, a meter and half high, wrapped around one corner and was topped with wire mesh. The small blind provided cover from the street, but visibility also.

"Wait, we can't get down to the water?" Kailer asked.

"We could, if we broke through the lock. Over here is better and keeps us out of the way in case anyone else decides to go for the water."

"Forty local fighters are hidden near the water facility," Dominique said, arriving a few minutes later. "But I think they're meeting more. My languages aren't great, but what I could catch gave me the impression they're going through that door for people as much as for water. The first thing I'm doing when we get back is change my schedule to include language intensives."

Fusao raised a brow.

"What?" Dominique scowled.

"Scouting isn't just terrain?" Fusao brushed a thumb over the back of her hand and twined his fingers with hers for the briefest millisecond. Their eyes met and Dominique pulled away. She took a few light steps to Sritha who was rummaging in her pack.

"Can you get into the abandoned part of the city, this part I mean, by following the river to the source?"

Sritha said, "Yes, well, you could follow the river up, but it goes underground... Wait, it doesn't go underground. I mean, there's a waterfall fed by the river just outside the Parliament building. Always wanted to dive in there when I was young." She sipped water and swished it in her mouth. "Why?"

Mara reached out with her senses. She could focus the direction and strength of her search, but tuning it, gleaning more information, that was supposed to come from practice with Dalin. Practice they never had time or privacy for. Frowning, she reached again and found a crowd of mental energy, at least the forty Dominique reported, but maybe double that number.

"Was the water cut off somewhere downstream?" she asked. "Are they trying to take the source for their families, or crops?" She spoke quietly, almost to herself.

Halifax's low voice rumbled in her ear. "Remember we're here to observe. Her majesty does not care about anyone's family or crops."

Raymundo and Angelo joined them by the edge of the wall. "Hey, 'Fax, water source would be a strategic asset, right?" Angelo said.

The scholar nodded. "It's hard to find an example of a conflict that wasn't over resources. Even here, the King set up Iloel's war project to be about ideology, but in the end, it was about the mines."

"Both sides felt like they got what they wanted," Sritha said. "My *jadati,* my grandmother, used to say that the people who went to the south and east, who made their own way, they were the winners because not only did they get land, they got freedom."

"Giving up all the profit from those mines though." It was Raymundo who spoke, but the cousins from Dorado shook their heads in unison.

Shrugging, the Iloellian girl said, "They stopped dying, in the war and in the mines. Now they have life, freedom, grow their own food, and whatever they can't produce themselves, they trade for."

"Lot of persistent rumors, legends almost, of the free capital way out east. Depending on whom you believe, it's the richest trade city in the Commonwealth. Maybe part of this fight is the Queen wanting a piece of that action." Halifax was rubbing his hands together, showing signs of launching into full lecture mode.

Only Mara saw the door to the water facility burst open. "Look!"

Shoving in next to her, Fentress muttered, "Where in the Darkness of Nix is the squad leader?"

A sharp whistle echoed through the deserted street. At first Mara thought it was a signal to the hidden fighters, but the lock breaker and his or her partner turned sharply. One gave a barking call into the door and they both dove for the nearest alley. Fighters in ragged gray and black hurried out of the water facility. A few swords and knives were visible, but not much else. Mara had counted fourteen when the first shots from energy weapons sizzled against the doorframe.

About a dozen of Naran's troops fanned out around the alley and the door, shooting blast after blast. Off to the side and slightly behind them stood O'Kelley, not fighting, but not hiding either. An unexpected pang of betrayal rolled through Mara's gut.

If these people just wanted water for their families, interfering was wrong. The settlers on Asattha might have had water, but the Queen kept them from adequate food and medicine. If she had known the truth back then, she would have led a raid just like this.

As if conjured by her anger, dozens of rebels burst from hiding, yelling and running to defend the door to the river's source. Few of these fighters wore the ragged robes of their comrades pinned down in the alley. Their uniforms shimmered dusky brown, gray, and black, appearing to absorb or deflect the few flashes of light that penetrated the shadow tunnel.

Not that Mara wanted them to win exactly, but it pleased her to see female shapes in the thick of the skirmish.

Three gray-clad fighters swarmed O'Kelley. He struggled, got in a few strikes and kicks, but they pinned his arms before he could draw any of his weapons. One had a knife to his throat and another had an oddly shaped energy weapon that molded around the firing hand. With Iloellians outnumbering Commonwealth troops five to one it was no contest to drag the student leader away.

Fentress was three steps into the street before the other Fury caught her. "Wait," Kailer said. "He's already gone. All the rebels are falling back and the door's about to close."

The nine remaining students pressed against the edges of the broken building. Of the original dozen Commonwealth soldiers, only three remained standing on the street below. O'Kelley was gone and the others lay dead or critically wounded.

"Listen," Fentress said. "One of ours is missing and the troops need assistance. I'm ready to lead us out of here and ignore our orders. Help with rescue and support and break cover before scheduled rendezvous. Any issues?" She scanned each face.

"I want to go after O'Kelley." Mara surprised herself by speaking the words aloud.

"That won't be sanctioned—" Fentress shrugged into her pack.

"There's precedent," Halifax interrupted her. "I looked up actions by student squads before we left and—"

Pinning him with an icy glare, the tall blonde said, "Did you hear me say no? Sanctioned is permission from the higher-ups, that's all."

As the rest of the squad hurried into their gear, Fentress ambled over to Mara. "You taking anyone with you?"

Swallowing hard, Mara asked the group, "Anyone with me?"

Sritha, Halifax, and Raymundo all raised their hands.

Chapter 16

Dalin spent several hours being visible and available at the Mess all afternoon, first in the gym, stretching out his sore spots, and later in the data center. He wanted to cross-reference the fighting styles list and weapons list for the tournament with the limited research he could access without hacking. He also wanted to cross-reference the lists with the extensive rules they'd received.

He'd bring the tournament rules down to the fight school, La Kill, tonight, in case the head trainers hadn't seen them yet. Rafiq would like a copy as well. Maybe it could be payment of some kind.

No one approached him, so once class hours were over, Dalin considered his work day over and logged himself out. He placed additional shin and forearm pads in his bag along with several energy bars and sealed water bottles. Rafiq had been right about the bubbler. Everyone used it at some point. The large circular fountain sat in the middle of the first courtyard of La Kill, in sight of students and instructors at all times.

On the walk down the hill, Dalin's thoughts centered on Mara, who was doing the Light knew what somewhere on Iloel. It seemed foolish to hope the student observation squad would avoid combat. And though she saw herself as peaceful, even reluctant to fight, Mara wouldn't hesitate to jump into the fray if one of the other students, or even an adult soldier, needed assistance.

In a fight, the drug would likely reactivate in Mara's body though it was hard to know how powerful the berserker state would be without a fresh dose. The drug in her system stemmed from the same irresponsible, lethal practices that elevated the value of experimentation over the value of human life: the key factor in all of the original war projects. If that drug ever got into the general population…

Dalin lurched to a stop on the uneven stone street. The smells had begun to change and the shadows deepened as the residential neighborhood gave way to commerce. Not *if* the drug got out, *when*.

The timing was not a coincidence. Drugging Mara hadn't been about her being a Protector or her role in bringing down the project on Asattha. Or maybe those things had been a bonus, but it had been about her height and weight and getting the drug ready for use in the tournament.

His contracted training time began in thirty minutes, but he needed to see Rafiq.

The owner of the eating house was not at Cousins. Dalin asked Geraldo to let Rafiq know he'd stopped by and hurried to La Kill. Fight masters Shanshan and Bahran took the Protector rule of preparation to new extremes. Dalin had better be warmed up, in his gear, and ready to fight at the appointed time or someone would jump him anyway, ready or not.

His first night had been a revelation of how sheltered his fight instruction had been. The two masters had kept him on the edges of the ring, blocking and parrying as though his life depended on it. His forearms and shins wore a line of solid bruises from a lack of padding. By the end, he'd managed fewer than five offensive strikes. Maybe two landed, but he suspected that was because they'd taken pity on him near the end.

The entrance to La Kill was a heavy iron door, decorated with irregular patches of rust and set in a brick wall in an alley. A view port in the door slid back after his knock. "What?" said the guard.

"Lifeblood," Dalin replied.

The guard grunted and slid the view port closed. A series of clicks sounded, and then a loud bang as the main bolt slid back. The heavy door swung open just enough to allow him entry. The rust on the front of the door was just camouflage. Everything moved smoothly and silently in La Kill, even the door.

The foyer was a combination yoga studio and teahouse, complete with floor mats and carved bamboo screens. Despite it all being contained inside a large, high-ceilinged building, the design created a sense that the real entry was through the teahouse, an authentic-looking replica brought from Tian.

A small group of mixed ages and flexibility levels practiced yoga poses off to the side. A few of the teahouse tables were occupied by individuals or pairs. Should the uninitiated gain entry to La Kill through this main door, they would be immediately disoriented by the peaceful nature of this first room.

Dalin hadn't time yesterday, nor had he been inclined to do ritual in front of anyone. But today he went to the far side of the teahouse and knelt to light a stick of incense as his father had taught him. Nostrils tingling with the familiar heavy floral and spice scents, Dalin bowed his head and asked his ancestors to watch over Mara, to keep her safe, and to bring her home to him quickly.

As an afterthought, he also asked for their blessings on his fight endeavors.

With a quick glance around, he stood and walked onto the teahouse porch, his heavy bag brushing the delicate railing and several rocking chairs.

Planter boxes of red and yellow flowers graced the edges at precise intervals. The swinging shutter doors opened onto the large training courtyard. Four small rings, one in each corner, surrounded a stretching area where the bubbler circulated water through multiple drink spigots. A fully leafed cluster of potted ferns hung from the ceiling. Though the mats were scrubbed daily, according to Rafiq, old brown stains formed dappled patterns on each ring's floor and the smell of sweat hung in the humid air.

On each side of the room was a door to the men's and women's locker rooms. Shanshan and Bahran had tested him in this main room yesterday, but today his training would start in the next room, in one of the smaller rings. Despite the pain he knew was coming, fighting was the only activity that kept his worries at bay.

Chapter 17

The door to the water facility was wedged crookedly in the partly melted frame. With a mighty shove, Halifax popped open the door and ushered them through. In the chaos of the after-action on the street, none of the Commonwealth troops called for them to halt.

Mara took point, leading their foursome down a set of metalwork stairs. Behind them the door clanged almost all the way shut, leaving just a narrow bar of light cutting down into the dim interior.

Mist hung in the air and every handhold was slippery, despite being reinforced with textured rubber. She sensed a group of people hiding nearby and another group moving slowly away from their position. As they descended the second flight, the dark increased, but faint lights penetrated the fog of moisture.

"Fascinating," Halifax murmured.

"So much water," Sritha said. "I never knew it was like this. We thought the waterfall and fountains were for show."

By the bottom of the third set of stairs, they'd adjusted to the dim light that just penetrated the thick water vapor. First-year students did not participate in any of the action or team exercises, but Mara used the Protector hand signals to indicate enemy nearby and hoped for understanding.

In her mind, Sritha asked, *"How many?"*

"Not sure. At least ten. A larger group is in motion along the river, based on the speed," Mara answered.

The smaller girl turned and signaled to Halifax and Raymundo, who both nodded. *"I'll teach you our signals the next time we have watch."*

That promise seemed a bit optimistic given their current situation, especially as she led the group away from the staircase in the direction of the traveling enemy. Asking to go after O'Kelley had been an offer made in haste, but Mara couldn't let a member of their squad get taken. One more life lost to the Queen's pointless war was one life too many. Unlike other leaders, Mara never thought in terms of acceptable losses. To her, no loss was acceptable.

It was likely the group on the move had their squad leader. The ones hiding here, well, it only made sense they were waiting for fighters from the street, either to subdue the enemy or to reunite with their own people.

Sure enough, a challenge call came out of the mist about five meters from their position. The four students shifted into a tight circle, facing outward, weapons drawn.

"I can answer with 'friend' or 'friendly,'" Raymundo offered. "Might help."

"Depends what this group is waiting for, if they're covering the retreat or waiting for something," Halifax muttered. His shoulder touched Mara's on one side, heavier and warmer than the other male's.

The challenge call came again and this time their translator answered. They were only a few paces from the water's edge, and several floating platforms bobbed in the current, visible as the water vapor shifted.

"Water travel," Mara said, low in her throat as a second call came, slightly closer.

"Asking my name," the translator said.

"Give them my family name," Sritha said. She rattled off more than a dozen syllables, which Raymundo repeated, his voice echoing in the subterranean cavern. The foursome edged toward the water and the rafts.

Mara wrapped her fingers around a heavy steel ladder bolted into the wall of the channel. Sliding her sword into its harness, she climbed down four rungs and reached one boot onto the nearest conveyance. Not exactly a boat, not exactly a raft, up close it had about a meter of raised edge around the perimeter and came to a narrow point at the bow. The platform only dipped slightly under her weight and she motioned for the other three to follow. Waist high, wooden side rails set about two steps from the edge provided a place to brace her hips, as first Sritha, and then Raymundo dropped onto the deck. The students' boots squeaked across the texturized rubber deck, but the rushing water covered most of the noise.

The whole thing dipped and bobbed as Halifax came aboard. Raymundo worked on the mooring knot and Sritha lifted the steering oar at the back. An angry yell from the top of the ladder froze them all. Two gray clad Iloellians yelled and gestured with swords for them to leave the raft.

Mara pulled enough energy from the Iloellian Tree to shield her small team. *"We don't want to fight you,"* she sent, broadcasting as loudly as she could. *"We just want our friend back."* She added an image of O'Kelley to the message. They were moving toward the Tree on this planet, she could feel it.

One of the two grabbed his forehead and staggered back just as the knot came free. The little river craft jumped forward into the current, just as a different call came out of the mist. "Daughter?" shouted a voice in Origin English.

The boat raft picked up speed and carried them swiftly into a broad tunnel. Mara dropped the shield and sagged against the railing. No orders, and now no leader. If they didn't retrieve O'Kelley and rejoin the Commonwealth force quickly, they were in for a serious reprimand, if not dismissal. She felt a little sick about the risks they were taking, though that could have been from the irregular rocking motion of the deck.

"Deep breaths in through your nose," their translator patted her shoulder. "You ever been on water before?"

"No," Mara said, wonder overcoming discomfort for a split second.

"We grew up on the beach. A beautiful protected bay with white sand and good waves for body surfing." Raymundo's voice was low and easy. "If we weren't in a tunnel, I'd tell you to look at the horizon. But just take deep breaths. We'll pop out of here soon."

The tunnel smelled like marsh and the mud flats that sometimes developed after a flood rather than the clean wet odors that perfumed the air after a rain. Mara closed her eyes and thought about her favorite clearing, the one where she met Dalin in rapport. Thinking of her partner centered her at the same time it reignited her longing for him. When she breathed in, her mind embraced a fresh cool breeze and the damp resin of evergreens and needles underfoot.

Opening her eyes, she gritted her teeth into a smile. "Thanks."

"Machisma," he said. "I like it."

Small lights and steel ladders winked in the gloom as they floated past. Gradually, the tunnel began to lighten and the vapor to diminish. Soon the smooth ceiling came into view, too regular to have been carved from rock.

"I think we're nearing the plaza," Sritha said. "Up there is the channel that feeds the fountains and the waterfall. But this continues on. Have they stopped, Mara?"

Energy from the local Tree amplified her sense of the other humans. Her small group continued to travel at roughly the same pace as the rebels' team. "No, and we're not exactly gaining on them. Wait." She turned to look past the Sritha. "A group is following us now, same pace."

"Is this skill something all Protectors have?" Halifax clung tightly to the little railing, but his expression was eager.

Glancing at Raymundo before she answered, Mara said, "No, not many."

The waterway narrowed and the current pushed faster, splashing over the deck and up the tunnel walls. About twenty meters later, they passed a large platform similar to the one where they'd taken the raft. Low lights illuminated the open space and metal stairs.

"Was that a control booth?" Halifax asked.

"Probably," Sritha said. "They can turn the fountains on and off, program the water jets in different patterns for celebrations."

Turning to look back as the platform and lights faded behind them, Halifax said, "Is there a sluice gate or dam or anything like that we need to worry about?"

The girl shrugged, one hand on the steering oar, her mouth tight with strain. "No idea. As of now, we know more about this waterway than anyone in my family. Sorry."

On Asattha, the energy flowing from the Tree, through all of the *gontra* trees, was easier to reach when the density of the root network was high. But here on Iloel, once Mara touched their Tree's source, it surrounded her. The energy wasn't the same, wasn't as bright. It was impossible to tell if that difference was a result of the drug in her system or a true difference in the energy.

Either way, keeping track of two groups at once was no more tiring than watching two practice fights at once.

The river dipped and their raft slid down a meter or two. Bright light appeared ahead and then they popped into open water, sun streaming down through thin trees laced with vines.

"Shouldn't we still be in the capital, if we just passed the plaza?" Raymundo voiced the question they all had to be wondering.

Halifax shook himself, still clutching to the small railing. "They've been fighting near the Parliament building precisely because it is on the edge of the city. So few people live in this direction, it's great cover. S-sorry, I knew that before...but it was a lot...my cognition—"

"Up ahead, they're slowing down," Mara interrupted. "Anything we—"

"All this does is steer." Sritha tugged at the wooden handle in frustration.

The current swept the four students forward. Straining to hear any sounds ahead or behind, Mara closed her eyes. The water gurgled and bubbled along the rocky banks, birds twittered, and a gentle breeze rustled through the overhanging branches.

Her lungs full of fresh air, she was once again vigilant and in charge of a group. Mara felt as close to her real self as she had since she left the northwest Protector compound.

"Did anyone see if O'Kelley was injured?" Sritha asked.

"I've been thinking about that," Halifax said. "We have no tactical advantage. And even if we can stop before they see us, how can we get him back to base if he's hurt?"

"What I don't comprehend is why grab the squad leader in the first place? He's a good enough guy and a great wrestler, but what use is he to them?" Raymundo shook his head.

A low rumbling started coming from the east bank of the river, slightly south of their position.

"It's an engine," Sritha murmured.

Motioning to the steering oar, Raymundo said, "Let me steer us into the shallows. It'll be bumpy but that's the only way we can slow down without coming up right on top of the enemy."

Sritha and Raymundo switched places with care and soon the little raft was bumping and splashing over water-worn rocks near the left bank. Halifax and Mara reached for tree branches overhead, trying to slow them even further. The humming whine of the engine grew louder as they finally drifted to a standstill, wedging into a sandy pool between the roots of several thicker trees. The river curved to the east, so they were hidden from those just ahead, but their view was blocked as well.

She had to get closer and confirm O'Kelley's location. Mara shouldered her pack and scrambled up the bank, steadying herself with the long grasses and slender trees. Following the engine sounds, she stayed under cover but moved downriver about twenty-five meters, Halifax and the other two behind her.

Glad for the drab Commonwealth uniform, she stayed in the shadows and watched as the Iloellians tied up two rafts and humped the last of their gear up a short, steep flight of stairs set into the riverbank. Three long vehicles idled at the top and the group of soldiers appeared busy arranging gear and themselves. One handed clear containers around, and then bent down to tip liquid into the mouth of a soldier slumped against a rock. Though matted with sweat and grime, O'Kelley's orange hair was unmistakable, as was his pale white skin.

"*It's him,*" Sritha's mental voice whispered. "*Solar-powered personnel carriers. I had no idea the rebels had this kind of vehicle.*"

"How many people can one of those carry?" Mara directed the question at Halifax, but the translator answered instead.

"You can pull out all the seats and fit twelve small soldiers or ten large ones. With the seats bench-style, it'll fit more like six to eight, depending on the gear."

The student rescue party clung to the steep bank, only partly covered by trees and scrub plants. A rebel soldier stood guard at the top of the stairs, her gaze intent on the rafts and the dock.

Only eleven Iloellians were visible, but it would be stupid to ignore the possibility of more soldiers in the personnel carriers. But why send three?

Turning to her companions, Mara said, "We've got to get him now. Otherwise, who knows where they'll take him."

"Their rafts have engines." Raymundo nodded down to the dock. "Water takes us east, away from the rally point, but that's the only escape route I see."

"Three to one." When Halifax smiled, all traces of his scholarly demeanor vanished. Instead, the battle grin pulled his face tight against the sharp slashes of his cheekbones. "I like those odds."

Belly tight, mouth dry, Mara stared at her team. It had been a long time since she'd risked anyone but herself. And despite the other three being older and seasoned fighters, the responsibility weighed heavy. "I can't shield all four of us in a mobile fight. But if they pull energy weapons, get behind me. My shield slows down the blasts."

"Command at the Mess has no idea," Halifax muttered, adjusting his grip on a tree root.

"Five steps up and over," she said. "'Fax, you grab O'Kelley. We'll engage with the guards. 'Mundo or Sritha, who wants the sentry?"

The Iloellian girl spit into her hands and rubbed them together. "I do."

With a massive tug, Mara channeled as much of the Tree's energy as she could. Her shield flared, temporarily surrounding all four students. If the drugs activated in her system, she'd be that much closer to dead, and so would their opponents, people who weren't even the real enemy. But they had the squad leader. And the dark Queen wouldn't try to get him back.

"On my signal," she said. Eyes locked on the troops at the top, she charged up and over the bank.

Chapter 18

Dalin's body hurt more this morning than it had in years. Moving so as not to call attention to his injuries took a great deal of concentration. That along with the energy maintaining his mental shield, and he was already spent when he took a seat in one of the larger lecture halls. According to the list at the top of the briefing, today's session included more people from more levels at the Mess, including more of the Queen's personnel. His best hope for getting top-tier classified information was Kucala, but today he might at least get names or faces for members of the Queen's Council.

He had to have progress on that part of their mission before Mara returned. Knowing who signed the orders to increase casualties would be a big step forward.

This room was in the oldest part of the Mess. The hinged seats of the chairs folded down, some with squeaks and groans. The material of the chairs was either a wood-plastic hybrid or plastic weighted, colored, and grooved to imitate wood. The walls were hung with plain tan fabric frames for sound insulation and the floor was bare syncrete.

A thin brown carpet runner went up the stairs on either side of the main seating area. In front of the first row of chairs a single podium stood, decorated with the Queen's emblem on a bright gold and black banner.

Dalin glanced around for Bryant Kucala and found him on the right side of the podium about five rows back. At two minutes until the designated start time, Professor Iskindar slipped into the unoccupied seat next to Dalin, her bracelets jingling, the fabric of her skirt and tunic making a soft rustling sound.

He nodded. "Dr. Iskindar."

The leader of the King's Men nodded in reply just as the lights went out.

A glow brightened above the podium and then burst to life with a fully dimensional image of the Queen, crimson lips curved in a hint of a smile, black hair in a heavy braided twist at the back of her neck. Next flashed the braided knot symbol for the Commonwealth. A recorded voice began to speak in Origin English about the history of the royal family and the glory of the champion's role. The information ended with a few ringing bars of the Commonwealth anthem.

The overhead lights flicked on as abruptly as they'd gone out. At the podium stood an auburn-haired woman in a pink and yellow *djellaba*. She smiled with lips painted a pale shiny pink, taking a moment to gaze at the assembly seated before her.

"I see many familiar faces in this room today," she began. "It's both a sad and happy occasion that brings us here." The woman bowed her head.

After a showy, deep breath the woman looked up. "In case we have not yet met, my name is Emily bin Haribin. I have the privilege of serving in the Ministry of Information. What you just saw was the visual package sent out to every planet, specifically every combat center in the Laskan Commonwealth." Her gaze landed on Professor Iskindar and flicked away.

"That package went out in all of the main Origin languages along with the details of how to register for the tournament. For the first time, we had to charge an entry fee in order to cover the costs. One issue was the construction of barracks, but we needed additional training and healing staff, additional kitchen staff, additional food stuffs, and so on. You understand, I'm sure. And of course, that was all explained through the attached information."

Wrist units chimed in imperfect unison around the room. Professor Iskindar sat as still as Dalin, not glancing around, not shifting in her chair. He surreptitiously stretched his legs into the aisle and angled his body. Professor Iskindar was not a small woman, she was surely feeling crowded in these seats.

"Our purpose today is to go through the roles and responsibilities of the Military Skills and Strategy School staff during the tournament. As we go along, I will continue to send information that you might find useful." Ms. bin Haribin glanced over as a half dozen of the *vishakanya* entered the room and clustered near the door.

"Vanora is en route," Professor Iskindar murmured so quietly it was almost sub-vocal.

"First," bin Haribin continued, "is the data about the fighters who have registered. This chart shows the distribution across the seven planets." A graph appeared in front of the group.

"As you can see, the majority of entries, just over fifty-one percent, came from Laska, with Tian, Dorado, and Iloel sending the next largest numbers in that order." When she named each planet, a section of the floating graph brightened. "We have only a few each from Hépíng Xīng, Kels, and Asattha, but that may be a result of limited communication systems and comparatively smaller populations as much as anything else."

After a brief pause, a new graph appeared. "This table shows the distribution by age and gender of our entrants. As you can see, most of the entrants are between the ages of eighteen and thirty, with about sixty percent identifying as male."

Bin Haribin gave a frank nod to the group. "In our history, we have never had a female champion for the sitting monarch. But," she turned and acknowledged the *vishakanya*, "our beloved Queen Vanora is well protected by her all-female guard and is therefore quite open to the idea of a female champion."

Quiet cheering erupted from several rows behind him. A contingent of the Furies, most likely.

Dalin furtively touched his wrist and pulled up the full tournament roster. Mara was off-planet and would certainly never register for this insanity, but she'd ended up on the O Squad without any action or request on her part. He breathed an internal sigh of thanks when he didn't see her name or recognize any of the nine names from Asattha.

Prior to being contaminated with a lethal drug, Mara would've been an excellent candidate for the first female champion. She was strong, smart, and versatile with weapons and techniques. And she picked up anything new with only a single repetition, most of the time.

They'd been talking about math, about the numbers of casualties across all seven war experiments. And Mara had said people weren't numbers. People had value that couldn't be calculated with paper

154

and pencil. Their commonwealth deserved a ruler that understood this. But if a person wanted to use numbers, Mara had added with a small smile, for this equation to balance they needed to subtract the "q."

Professor Iskindar glanced away from the door to look at Dalin. Her left hand now rested palm up on her left knee, a round silver sphere cradled in the center. "Be ready to run," she said, again speaking in the softest murmur.

Cold air began pouring from the vents under their seats and around the top of the walls. In less than a minute, the room temperature started dropping.

From their seats, he couldn't see the inside of the podium, but Ms. Bin Haribin tapped something and frowned. "Excuse me," she said to the group, before glancing at the *vishakanya*. Another few taps and a series of blueprints lit in front of them.

"The first rounds will take place in the new stadium and in the Box. Tickets to these rounds have already sold out and the various forms of visual transmission are in high demand. Through a grant of funds from the royal treasury, her majesty has graciously offered to erect viewing areas throughout Crown City."

The Mess was generally cold, but the room had become winter-storm-on-Asattha cold. Some of the staff had gone rigid, facing the door like Professor Iskindar. They looked around, shrugging at each other and surreptitiously rubbing bare arms or blowing into their hands.

A small figure clad in black appeared in the doorway. The light from the hall was brighter than the light in the auditorium, casting the person in shadow. More *vishakanya* filled in the space behind the figure, while those in front snapped into a wedge formation.

"Too much information can be poisonous," said the figure, moving into the room. Her voice was high-pitched, almost childlike. "The monarchs of this commonwealth learned their lessons from the Origin, destroyed by people with too much information yet lacking the wisdom or experience to use it."

Emily bin Haribin bowed low and backed away from the podium until she hit the wall, crouching, but visible in her bright clothes.

Murmurs of "your majesty" and "the Queen" rippled through the room, and though they were crowded into the auditorium chairs, people folded themselves as best they could in supplication.

Dalin tucked his chin to his chest and out of the corner of his eye saw Professor Iskindar do the same.

"Please," said Queen Vanora. "As you were."

With unfortunate squeals and creaks from some of the chairs, the assembled staff sat up and looked forward once again. The room was silent, as though people had stopped breathing.

Deep grooves etched either side of the Queen's mouth, her lips pressing together in a thin line as she surveyed the room. Two more deep vertical creases split her forehead between her black brows. She wore a sleeveless black linen tunic over black leggings. Her tiny feet were encased in flat black slippers, nearly identical to dance slippers, and she wore elbow-length black gloves that sheathed her hands and forearms. The skin at her ankles, upper arms, and throat was a pale brown, the color of sand dunes at night, her face sharply boned and an even paler shade of brown.

The only similarity between the living Queen in front of them and the one portrayed in the holo-information was the heavy black braid coiled at the base of her neck. A black cape hung down her back from clasps at each shoulder, emphasizing the straight lines of her body.

As she began to pace in front of them, the cape billowed like smoke. "This tournament means everything to me," she said. "My champion is not only a physical guard but a symbol of our strength."

She raised one thin arm and shook her fist. "Data is not our purpose here." Her voice swelled into a shriek. "Too much time is being spent on information, and not enough on gathering the best fighters, the fiercest combatants who will stand, not only for your Queen, but for all of you."

Each time the Queen turned, the *vishakanya* rearranged their formation to keep her covered from all sides.

She glared at the woman from the information ministry now cowering with her head tucked under a transparent yellow headscarf. "You. Have we not discussed these priorities at length? And on multiple occasions?"

Emily bin Haribin stood and reached out one shaking hand. "My deepest apologies, majesty, but I do not recall those discussions." She hiccupped and a single tear tracked down her cheek.

Vanora sighed and folded her gloved fingers together. "And this is why necessity forced me to join this meeting today. We cannot continue in the wrong direction. So little time is left before the tournament begins." Her voice took on a crooning lilt.

The silver sphere in Professor Iskindar's hand had elongated into a thick cylinder.

"'Those at the pinnacle of responsibility must work together as one seamless unit. Like a carpet, like a tapestry, knotted together into one beautiful creation.' This was a saying of my late and beloved grandfather. Many of you heard him say it, yes?"

Heads nodded with a quiet rumble of assent.

The Queen paced a few steps away from the assistant information minister and the woman's shoulders slumped.

"So I ask you, the leaders of my school, what is the purpose of this tournament?"

Heavy silence lay over the group until Elsebet Iskindar said, in her clear, deep voice, "To gather the best fighters and fiercest combatants, who will not only stand for you as your champion, Majesty, but for all of us."

Squinting up into the rows, Vanora swallowed and licked her lips. "Just so, Doctor Iskindar. Well said." After a deep breath that she let out on a sigh, the Queen stalked back toward the woman huddling against the wall. She tugged lightly at the fingers of one glove until it slid off, eliciting a gasp from Emily bin Haribin as well as several of the assembled teachers.

With the Queen's attention focused elsewhere, Professor Iskindar said, "If she loses control, you will run. Everyone will run. A door behind the top row of seats will get you clear."

Months ago, Dalin had told Mara she might need to run from a fight and he now felt the same surprised affront to his honor at the command from Professor Iskindar. Even in his earliest years in school, he'd never walked away from a conflict.

Despite his shields, the fear in the room was a perceptible, growing entity. His pulse rate picked up speed and his muscles tensed for action as he took in the micro-cues of the people around him.

"Your mistakes are forgiven," Vanora said, reaching out to stroke the woman's cheek.

A frightened squeak bubbled from bin Harbin's throat and her muscles spasmed at the touch.

The Queen's smile revealed two rows of tiny white pearl-like teeth. "But mistakes must be swiftly removed from public view lest the citizens of our commonwealth become misled." She now placed the flat of her palm against the woman's face, cradling it.

Sharp breaths stuttered from the woman's mouth and her body jerked, braced now by two of the *vishakanya*, their hands also bare on bin Haribin's arms, their smiles reflecting their leader's. The stricken woman's eyes snapped wide open and then drifted closed, her body crumpling.

The Queen tugged off her other glove and tucked the pair into her waistband. "It is understandable that some would lose the heart for this challenging work." She tittered, as did some of her guards. "That is why only the strongest are fit to serve." This last on a keening wail as the door closed and the lights dimmed.

Professor Iskindar leapt into the aisle, her silver weapon more than a meter long now. She shoved Dalin behind her and said, "Run."

He fled up the stairs, injuries forgotten, feeling his way along the wall until his hands found first hinges and then a recessed handle. He pushed the few teachers who'd run up the stairs with him through the opening into the dark passage. With several short trips up and down the aisle he tugged and pulled as many as he could to safety, even as the sounds of terror rose from the front of the room.

Everyone fled, ranks forgotten, as another door opened at the top of the other aisle. Down below, Dr. Iskindar did not engage Vanora in combat. The professor stood in the aisle three rows up from the floor, flow baton twirling in a blurring figure eight, protecting the retreat. Either she was shielding or the weapon gave off a faint glow. As *vishakanya* lunged for the teachers behind her, she struck out, her baton delivering blows as well as intense pulses of energy.

Dalin took one last look at the carnage unfolding in the classroom below, shoved the last few people into the escape passage, and slammed the door shut.

* * *

At the top of the incline, Mara got close enough to hit O'Kelley's guard with the butt of her sword before something cold wrapped around her arm. Energy drained from her shield into the ground more quickly than cider spilling from a glass. Sritha managed to throw the sentry down the bank, but no one else landed a blow. Twelve soldiers piled out of the resting vehicles. Four held nets.

A sleekly uniformed older woman patted the length of sticky vine coiled around Mara's forearm. "Don't waste the Tree's blessing on this fight, Daughter. The *auriculata* vine will keep you here with us and out of the Darkness." Smile lines fanned around the woman's dark eyes. "Do you and your team need the nets? Or will you come along?"

Halifax grunted against the tight arm holds of the two men on either side of him, but he watched Mara, waiting for her signal. The other two students were restrained equally well. Every sense blunted except her direct vision, Mara felt almost fogged, incapable of making a decision for herself, let alone others. She tried to reach out to Sritha's mind and discovered that ability had gone. With a slight shake of her head, she communicated surrender to her team.

"What is this?" she asked, tugging at the vine with weak fingers, sword arm trembling.

Sun glinted from the woman's steely gray hair as she turned and gave a sharp two-part whistle. The Iloellians swiftly began boarding the transport vehicles, placing O'Kelley in one car, Raymundo and Halifax in another, and piling in behind the prisoners until Mara stood alone with Sritha and her captor.

Dark eyes locked on Mara's. "You have much to learn. Won't you sheath your weapon and come with us in peace?"

"You took…" She tried to form the accusation before she spoke. "O'Kelley. You took him and he's done nothing—"

"We knew you would follow the ginger one. What is he to you?" A smile curved the older woman's mouth. "A lover?"

Shock cleared Mara's mind. These people knew more than they should, but not the most critical things. She lowered her sword into the harness. Cool knives braced each of her forearms and, thanks to Dalin, she had the means to sever the connection to the vine if the head of this ambush relaxed her guard.

Mara mumbled, "He's our leader and a fellow soldier." Rubbing at the coils of vine moved the lengths a millimeter or two. They were tight, but not eating into her skin.

After the last clatter of boots and gear faded, it was just the three of them standing outside the vehicles. The leader laid one brown hand on the *auriculata* vine and stared hard into Mara's eyes. "You don't want to hurt us. And you don't believe in the Commonwealth mission."

"True."

Unwrapping the vine, the woman tucked it into a green mesh pouch. "I'm Ylas. Our objective was to subdue you and your party by any means necessary. But you didn't use your power as a weapon, only to defend the others."

Gravel and dust scraped under Mara's boots as she shifted her stance. Her senses began to work again, the smell of Ylas's sweat coming through first, then sounds of rushing water and the tiny puffs of breeze. Even in the grasp of the *auriculata*, the Tree's energy touched her, but with the blunted penetration of sunlight through a curtain, rather than a sharp beam. Her chest loosened and she took a deep breath.

"That's enough for now." Ylas bent to kiss Sritha on the forehead. "*Ahsanti.*"

With a slight bow the girl said, "Thank you, my duty is my pleasure."

The leader gestured for Mara to precede her into the dark interior of the vehicle, taking the opposite side with Sritha. Both watched as Mara slid awkwardly across the seat, unhooking her shoulder harness as she scooted. The weapon reassured her, steadied her faith in herself and her family. She laid the sword and harness across her knees and met her captor's eyes as the transport shifted into motion.

The shock of Sritha's betrayal started as a slow burn in the back of Mara's throat. Some might say she was lucky to have lived so long without a fellow soldier turning against her. But this felt like the opposite of luck.

"We have a little more than an hour before we get to landmarks that might give away our location. When we hit the perimeter you and your friends will be blindfolded for the duration, about thirty additional minutes."

"How long did you have this planned?" Mara asked Sritha, her attention riveted on the girl's face.

"Aw, Mara, I'm a student, same as you. Except for this one extra duty. My commitment to my people outweighs any commitment to the pampered, sadistic *banouteh* some call Queen."

The transports had fallen into a single line with their car in the center of the formation.

"How long have you been conspiring to betray us?" Mara pressed, anger rising.

The girl crossed her arms tightly and glared at her. "They made contact at the spaceport. It's not betrayal." She jerked her chin toward Ylas. "You sympathize with our cause. I know you do, whether you're the precious Daughter or not."

Disgusted, Mara looked away. Through the heavily tinted windows, low hills rolled by, crowned with more of the low, stunted trees. When they didn't make it to the rally point with Colonel Naran and Sergeant Bogdanovich, what would happen? None of the students on the O Squad knew the mission parameters. Except maybe O'Kelley?

The commonwealth ship was her only ride back to the crown world and Dalin.

Dalin.

Laska was too far, but she reached anyway. He'd been captured before. He'd studied this conflict. Just as quickly as hope flared, disappointment followed. It was too far for her mind to reach.

She took a deep breath and let it out quietly, reviewing the locations of her hidden weapons. Hiding so many knives on her person and in her pack was one of the many ways Dalin showed how much he cared. The roots of their connection were deep, if not yet balanced. Once she returned to her partner, she would try to measure up to the promise that was Dalin.

Leaning back against the smooth seat, she let her hands fall open on her knees. The interior of the transport smelled new, and the floor was clean, marred only by the dirt and dust from the current trip. With slow deliberate movements, she shifted her pack between her feet and pulled out a water bottle. The seal released with an audible pop. The cool water eased the last of the dizziness from the contact with the vine. She hoped the rest of her team was comfortable.

Finally, she gave in and asked the question bothering her the most. "You knew Commonwealth soldiers would try to retrieve O'Kelley? Or you knew *I* would try to retrieve him?"

"The people have been waiting for the Daughter to appear. We made sure you were on the mission to Iloel and captured the pale solider to lure you away." The older woman rubbed her fingers across her eyebrows, heavy lines of disappointment settling around her mouth. "Why don't you use the power to attack? The Daughter is supposed to be stronger than any of us. A weapon for peace."

Chapter 19

Dalin was in the Mess Mess eating lunch alone when his wrist unit chimed and a note popped up. It was an anonymous summons to lab D-1 at his earliest convenience. He had fight training later, so he forced himself to slurp down the rest of the noodle bowl rather than drop everything and rush to meet Kucala. After placing his tray in a slightly dirtier, but updated version of the kitchen window at the Northwest Protector compound, Dalin hurried through the maze of hallways until he reached the restricted lab corridor.

Once again he showed the summons to the guards and made his way down to the Kook's lab. Kucala waved him in and Dalin braced for the intense transition through the room's shield.

"Long legs make a significant difference in walking time," Bryant Kucala said by way of greeting. "You were in the Mess Mess six point five minutes ago."

"I'm glad you made it out of the briefing yesterday," Dalin replied.

Kucala rocked back on his stool and tapped his worktable with one index finger. "Yes. The records don't really do her justice."

"The Queen?"

"Well, yes." Kucala rolled to the edge of the table and flicked open a holographic file. "But I meant Dr. Iskindar. That flow baton is a mere footnote in her history. Whereas, Vanora being poisonous is common knowledge."

Typical that he would define "common knowledge" as something only he found obvious. Whereas, Dalin *had* known about the flow baton because he'd read all the footnotes about Dr. Iskindar. On any other day, he wouldn't give Kucala the satisfaction of asking. But he had to know.

"Did Vanora kill that woman, Emily bin Haribin?"

The overhead light reflected off Kucala's dark, shaved head as he bent toward one of the many open screens floating above his table. "Yes, and two others. Our beloved monarch secretes a neurotoxin. Causes cardiac arrest. Before you leave, I'll give you a file summary to read."

He held up a hand as Dalin took a breath to speak.

"I'll tag it with an auto-phage code. You're still a fast reader, right? Extra muscles not interfering with your brain? No recent concussions?"

"You still swim?" Dalin asked. He'd been hit hard the night before. Hard enough to alter his vision for a few blinks. But not enough to cause swelling inside the cranium. None of the Kook's business, either way.

"I do." Kucala rolled his head to crack his neck. "It's the only thing to get the kinks out. And the pool here is tragically underutilized. Have it to myself more than fifty percent of the time."

The data wizard tilted his head and assessed Dalin for an extended pause. "Look. I—" Restless fingers tapped across the massive table until only a single plain text communication hung in the air. "You said that girl who…that girl is important to you, your partner. This is what I thought you needed to see."

He waved Dalin over. "Can't touch it much beyond opening and closing because it's top level. This went to Queen's Council eyes only."

The missive simply read:

```
Iloel mission status: Yellow

Multiple attacks

Abandoned sector of Samradhi.

Commonwealth forces: 29 KIA and 17 MIA

Student observation squad: 5 MIA
```

Dalin rubbed one hand over his heart as he read and re-read the lines. Finally, he asked, "The names of the missing students?"

Kucala nodded, his expression somber. "That was in a separate communiqué. It's—" He typed for a split second. "Here."

The list scrolled in the same plain text as the message. The first was the official Killed in Action and Missing in Action list for the Commonwealth troops. The second list was five names, including Mara De La Luz.

Rocking just a fraction onto the balls of his feet and back, Dalin clenched his fists at his sides. *Mara.* He'd failed to save her *again.* The noodles sat cold and gooey in his stomach and as extra saliva began to pool in his mouth, he knew he was going to vomit.

Lunging for the lined trashcan next to the cooling unit, Dalin heaved until his stomach was empty.

Kucala offered him a handful of tissues, his expression concerned. "They don't have her body, de Forest. You were in War Project Seven. No body means probably not dead."

Darkness settled over Dalin's mind, blanketing the fear, sadness, and frustration. A colder, deeper fury welled until it filled him with a desperate need for action.

"This girl. She's a great fighter. Bested the best guy and—"

"And she's carrying a drug in her spinal fluid that will burn out her nervous system if she has to fight at that level. If she's fighting for her life, she's ending it."

* * *

The capture and transport suddenly felt like an important exam. Why didn't she use her gifts to attack? Why wasn't she a weapon of immense power?

Mara had no idea how much to tell, how much to hide. At the Mess, third-year students and older could take an elective class on being captured and captivity, but the subject had not been broached at all for the first years. Not being able to trust a fellow soldier, at least someone her own age, was even farther beyond her experience.

With a deep breath, she opted for a part of the truth. "I was a Protector on Asattha." This got a visible reaction from both Iloellians.

"We heard that experiment imploded last year," said Sritha.

Mara nodded and licked her lips. "It did."

"Our experiment ended decades ago, and still we cannot banish the Darkness from our world. False differences became true differences and the fight never ends." Ylas gazed out the window as she spoke.

"My team—" Mara began.

"All fine, no one needed the nets. The time for covering your eyes draws near, however. Tell me again, you have no training in harnessing the energy of the Tree as a weapon?" Her captor's gaze sharpened as did her probes against Mara's mental shield.

Wiggling her toes in her boots, she thought about Fentress and her insistence that no one would go down for equipment issues, just in case the probes could pick up her thoughts. She had to get away from her captors and free her team, but they were moving closer to Iloel's Tree. Adding to her immediate problems, the compulsion from the Mother Tree bloomed in her mind in response to her sister's promixity.

If she couldn't go toward Dalin right now, she had to go to the Tree. These people weren't the enemy. They didn't wear masks and they didn't serve the Queen. Mara needed to get her team out, unharmed, as soon as possible. As always, the weight of others' lives sat heavily on her shoulders.

She gripped her sword and raised the harness a centimeter from her knees. "I'm trained with this weapon, and other types of blades, as well as staffs and sticks. That's all." It wasn't really all. She was trained to care and trained to lead with honor, unlike the two people facing her.

Lips twisting in disappointment, Ylas nodded at Sritha.

She shook out a shallow head covering and leaned forward to wrap Mara's head and eyes.

When they stopped at last, someone opened the door from the outside and removed the hood. Blinking against the bright artificial light, Mara shouldered her sword harness and pack and hurried over to the other students.

Halifax and Raymundo had their packs and weapons as well, though Halifax's bottom lip was swollen and Raymundo's left knuckles were crusted with blood. Still pale, O'Kelley wavered on his feet between two soldiers and looked around, confusion deepening when he saw them.

"Some kind of underground garage," Raymundo murmured.

166

"Smells like new tires and expensive fuel," Halifax said.

Dark streaks crisscrossed the stained, gray syncrete floor where their four transports parked. The students huddled within parallel stripes of yellow paint, arrows pointing toward a metal staircase and a large double door. What they could see of the facility made it a near relative of the s'port attached to the Mess.

"You were expecting huts, weren't you?" Sritha said.

Mara shrugged. "I wasn't expecting anything. Listen, is everyone unharmed? Quick sitrep before they move us."

"What happened when we engaged?" Halifax asked, dark eyes flaring with concern. "That woman wrapped something around your arm?"

"It blocked my ability to shield. I couldn't move, couldn't think." An involuntary shudder ran up Mara's spine. "I didn't know such a plant existed, I was responsible for our team and—"

Raymundo frowned as he lifted his pack. "Does anyone have a guess why we retained all our gear and weapons?"

Ylas pushed through the door and yelled something over her shoulder at the guards from the other transports. She tossed a few other commands over her shoulder in Origin Arabic and Sritha responded affirmatively.

"I told them you wouldn't resist," Sritha said with an apologetic shrug. "Can you help get O'Kelley to medical?" she asked Halifax and Raymundo. "And then we can all eat." The three stared at her while all but the two soldiers supporting O'Kelley filed out of the garage.

"You betrayed us." Raymundo shook his head in disgust.

Halifax tilted his head, lips parted but not speaking.

The girl raised her chin. "I'm pledged to serve my people. They wanted Mara." To Mara she said, "For the record, I don't think you're holding out or holding back some secret power. I think everyone is so desperate for a miracle, they'll latch on to any sign."

As her explanation spilled out, Halifax and Raymundo had shifted to flank Mara. All three faced the lone girl now.

"We're still a team," Sritha began.

"No." Halifax spoke with quiet calm. "We're not."

* * *

Dalin had money, plenty of money to buy passage to Iloel. But all transport to the planet was blocked. The s'port in town only allowed sanctioned trade and transport ships. Even though he was out of uniform, even though he was handing out currency like it was candy, not a single spacer would tell Dalin which s'port the smugglers used. "No smuggling here," they would insist.

Was it his military-short hair? Was he too clean? Too desperate? The more forcefully he asked, the more roadblocks he encountered until every door he pounded on remained closed, every window dark.

Tired of asking, his thoughts went to hijacking. He could hide in the bays of the s'port and stow away on a ship headed for Tian or Dorado. Once in transit, he could attack the pilot and demand they change course. But security was tripled, maybe even quadrupled at the s'port. A full painstaking hour of scouting confirmed that for once, the Commonwealth guards were doing something by the book.

Why hadn't he demanded pilot lessons as a child? Darkness knew he'd been forced into nearly every other type of lesson. He'd always prided himself on being prepared. Ha. Not prepared with the one skill set he needed most right now. If he could fly, he would find a way to steal a ship.

When he made his way back to Cousins, it was as dark and locked as every other place he'd tried in Lower Town. Out of options for the moment, Dalin turned to La Kill, needing to numb himself in the violence and immediacy of a real fight. Just a few quick rounds to burn off the frustration of the past few hours and then he'd track down the owner of the eating house and force Rafiq to get Dalin on a ship to Iloel. Before dawn he'd be on his way to Mara.

Two moves into his first training bout of the night and Shanshan called a halt. After a long look into Dalin's eyes, she'd ordered him into all his pads and sent him to the yoga mats to meditate.

"Many people come here looking to break something and end up broken," was all she said.

Finally released from his meditation corner, Dalin hefted the long, heavy bo staff and watched his opponent step back into the ready stance. Breathing even, the cool dark mist in his mind obscured every feeling except the anger.

Bahran bent his knees and turned his wrists to lift his staff to shoulder height, looking more or less like a batter stepping up to the plate in cricket. But instead of swinging at Dalin's midsection, he flipped forward, landed in a crouch, and slammed the staff against the back of Dalin's legs, just under his knees. The hard sweep unbalanced him and Dalin toppled backward, landing awkwardly on one wrist.

The fight trainer threw down his staff and, using a quick-float step, brought up one leg to stomp on Dalin's face. Dalin grabbed the man's foot and wrenched it hard to the left, spinning him to the ground.

Rather than waste the energy to stand, Dalin threw a leg over his opponent's body and followed with his full weight. He kneed Bahran in the chest, then used the man's own momentum to double him over into a tight submission hold.

Bahran laughed and tapped the mat twice.

Dalin heard the laugh and the tap, but the Darkness in his mind urged him to squeeze, to punish.

"Boy." Bahran grabbed Dalin's thumb and bent it into a painful joint lock that extended into his freshly hurt wrist. Nerves firing up his arm, Dalin released his hold and the fight trainer did the same.

With the ease of much practice, Bahran sprang to his feet and extended a hand to help Dalin stand. "You mixed three styles and one weapon," he said. "Better."

Ignoring the comment, Dalin walked to the far wall and fished in his bag for water. He took a long drink and then asked, "Does everyone know Vanora is poisonous?"

"This is fight training, not revolutionary training," Bahran said with a cautioning shake of his head.

"Yesterday I saw her touch someone, and as a result of that touch, the person died. Will there be opponents in the tournament who can do that?" Dalin asked.

Bahran's expression shifted to neutral, his normally expressive dark eyes going flat. And without the warmth in his eyes, his face transformed from approachable teacher to pitiless thug.

The man was covered in scars, especially on his face, hands, and arms. His nose was a misshapen lump, probably the result of breaking and improper healing over the years. "Wait here," he said. "If you want to keep training with us, don't move until I return."

The pain in Dalin's wrist lit up then disappeared into the recesses of his mind. Pain was irrelevant. If the next fight didn't start soon, worry would consume him. The Kook had been right to reinforce the fact that no one had found Mara's body, to reiterate that she was only missing in action right now, not on the official kill list.

For more than ten years, Dalin had worked to always have control, to cultivate the power to make situations better. If he was honest with himself, every choice he'd ever made about school, where to go, what to study, his career with the militia, all went back to one night and the overwhelming helplessness of a small boy watching his best friend, a girl he loved, kidnapped by a terrifying stranger.

He had to move, but he kept himself to pacing in a tight circle. Bahran might have meant "don't move" literally, but staying near the bench was the best Dalin could do. His body demanded motion.

Shanshan entered the training room and stood just a few steps inside the door, hands on her hips. Tall and slender, she was an elegant, lethal foil to her business partner's brawler physique. Her black hair was pulled back in a high ponytail, black eyes marked with dark cosmetics, and her short nails painted a matching black. In the few days of their acquaintance Dalin hadn't seen her in any color except black. Her features were the most ethnically Chinese he'd seen in Crown City and even in a tough fight, looking at her reminded him of his father and sister.

"Though we do not speak of poison here," she said. "It is possible one of the *vishakanya* or someone who has learned their ways will enter the tournament. Skin contact is lethal. It's impossible to hide though, so everyone would know after the poisonous fighter won his or her first match."

Bowing deeply from the waist, Dalin straightened and said, "Thank you for the information."

Shanshan took a few steps closer and tapped his helmet with one black fingernail. "You have one more round tonight. No pads, no weapons."

Perfect. Rafiq would have to return to Cousins to sleep. After this fight, Dalin would go to the eating house and wait. He gave a tiny bow and hurried to strip off everything except his long-sleeved t-shirt and close-fitting cargo pants. He stashed the gear quickly and neatly in his bag and returned to the center of the training floor. "Who will I fight?"

"Me," she replied with a fractional shift in her stance. Her hand flashed out and chopped down hard on his collarbone. Dalin blocked her next strike but missed the sharp kick to his inner thigh. Embracing the pain-free oblivion, Dalin emptied his mind and launched himself into battle.

The exchange of blows was rhythmic, a beautiful ritual marking his skin. Practice fights with Mara had gotten to this level of speed and skill the longer they worked together at the Protector compound. The *thing* missing with Shanshan was the rapport and the split second of communication that let the fight flow even faster. And that *thing* between him and Mara was everything.

Shanshan punched him in the face, the force snapping his head back. Blood rushed from his nose and his right eye blurred. "Your mind must not travel. This is not a dance. Our fighters do not bleed. We take the blood of our opponents."

The Darkness filling Dalin's mind accepted the challenge, spurred on by thoughts of Mara.

An unknown time later, every physical alarm that he'd suppressed began ringing at once. Vision narrowing to a gray tunnel, Dalin dropped to his knees, joints and muscles screaming.

"All right, kid, looks like you get tomorrow off for bad behavior." A steady hand hooked under his armpit and pulled him back up. "Deep breaths through your mouth. Clamp that flow." The same person shoved a snowy white handkerchief into Dalin's hand.

Blinking at the drops of blood on the floor mat, Dalin tried to remember where he was.

"Let's go. It's a short walk. Say thank you to your teachers."

"Than oo," Dalin managed, clumsily lifting his head. His upper lip had begun to swell. Shanshan had the most devastating straight jab of any opponent he'd ever fought.

Shanshan.

La Kill.

"They called me when you got sent to meditate. Been here for a while," Rafiq said, still holding him under the arm.

Dalin nodded, the mere motion sending pain lashing through his face and neck.

"Don't know you well," Rafiq said, moving them a few steps at a time through the series of training rooms. "But I can guess you're not someone who turns into a sloppy mess very often. I don't figure you for a pain junkie either." He paused to motion for the guard to hold the door.

"Thanks, Xiao," he said.

Dalin stumbled over the threshold, caught himself, and forced his body upright. He focused on the solid weight of the equipment bag in his good hand and putting one foot in front of the other.

"Take you back to my place, get you some food, some ice for your pretty face, and then you'll tell me what got you into this state."

"I have to get to Iloel," Dalin tried to say, the sounds emerging too garbled to form words.

"Um hmm," said Rafiq, still keeping one light hand on his arm. "Almost there."

Dalin landed with a soft thud in a fabric-covered chair in a tiny room dominated by a bed, the dresser crammed into a closet without doors. He still clutched the now blood-soaked handkerchief, but he also had a bag of ice pressed to his face.

"Stupid *baheem* medicine…backwater…inexcusable…*ahmak* science," Rafiq muttered as he shoved Dalin's gear on the far side of the bed. "Need a medically trained professional, need a sterile med suite…not this *antika* emergency bag."

Rummaging through a large orange duffel, Rafiq pulled out a roll of tape and a roll of gauze. With care, he placed both of the rolls and a pair of scissors on the side of the bed closest to Dalin.

"Kid, you are a holy mess. What set you off? Bahran said something about the Queen? Poisoning someone?" He wrapped his fingers loosely around Dalin's swollen wrist and carefully tested the range of motion.

Closing his good eye, Dalin forced his thoughts into a line. His wrist hurt, but it wasn't broken. His nose was probably broken. Rafiq had been summoned to La Kill, witnessed his meltdown, and walked him here. The man's accent had changed. Or was that his hearing? "Mara," he pronounced her name slowly and carefully through his swollen lips.

Rafiq squatted down to look at him. "What about her?"

He looked into the blurry face of the eating house owner. "Missing," he slurred. "MIA."

"Missing," Rafiq repeated.

"Missing," Dalin said, the dark anger rising again, feeding off the pain.

With a pronounced grimace, as though he'd eaten something rotten, Rafiq dropped the orange bag and hit the wall. The corrugated metal rang and he pounded it again, cursing in an impressive mix of Origin Arabic, Origin Hindi, and Origin English.

Geraldo's voice came from the doorway, "*¿Jefe? ¿Que paso?*"

"Problem one is Prince Charming got a little too invested in the facial reconstruction services provided by our fine friends at La Kill. We need to call a healer. Problem two." Rafiq's shoulders slumped. "Problem two is our new waitress is MIA on Iloel."

"Last known location?" Geraldo asked with complete calm.

Dalin raised the hem of his shirt to his mouth and wiped away bloody drool. "Outside of Samrahdi."

"Any other intel?" the cook asked.

"No." He forced himself to add, "Not at this time. That's why I need to get on a ship. You have to get me on a ship. Right. Now." Dalin put the bag of ice on the bed and pushed at the arms of the chair, attempting to stand.

Dropping a meaty hand on his shoulder, Geraldo stepped fully into Dalin's line of sight and said, "Stay."

Chapter 20

Mara stared for a moment at the girl she'd just been getting to know. Her curly hair frizzed out of her tight ponytail, her eyes a light, clear brown. Sritha bounced nervously on her toes. "Do your parents really work at the s'port?"

"Well, yeah, when it's in use," Sritha said, shoving hands deep in her pockets.

With a nod to her companions, Mara said, "Time to find an exit." She reached for the Iloellian Tree and ran in that direction.

Through the double doors and to the left was a long stretch of rooms, some occupied, some empty. She passed a washroom and kept going until the hall stopped at a t-junction. Dead ahead was a door marked with a picture of stairs. With a deep breath, she pushed open the door and started climbing.

After about four flights of their boots echoing much too loudly in the narrow stairwell, the quality of the light began to change from artificial to natural. The higher they climbed, the more the ceiling lightened, bright with afternoon sun. The final turn revealed a single door. With a quick push they were out, breathing the warm, dusty air. No alarm sounded.

From the outside, the buildings looked like the last bastion of advanced goat husbandry. Grit and dirt billowed across worn syncrete pathways between weathered buildings in assorted sizes and configurations. Dozens of goats roamed the immediate area. Everything smelled old and run-down, tinged with manure. People not in uniform hurried from one place to the next, heads covered by large scarves.

After a quick pause to check for the Tree, she led her team toward a gate at the end of a short road.

"Stop." Sritha threw a handful of loose rocks toward the gate. At the top of its arc, the pebbles bounced and the dirt sizzled, dropping straight down.

Slowing to a skid, but unable to resist, Halifax crept forward hand outstretched.

"No," Mara said, grabbing one of the scholar's arms, while Raymundo grabbed the other. " 'Fax, I've seen massive shields in use before; this is, it's more like an electrical wall. Without shielding of your own, the current will kill you."

"Not quite." Sritha shrugged. "But the pain will make you wish you died."

Swallowing down bile, Mara narrowed her eyes against the bright afternoon sunlight. "Why stop us? Do you actually care?" Nothing was visible or audible from the high-powered shield, but she was certain it stretched above them as well.

"What I care about is my family, our Tree Mother, and making all of Iloel free from Commonwealth rule. Seers of great power predicted you, Mara. And I was born into your timeline. My soul would be consigned to Darkness forever if I let you die by running into the barrier." The Iloellian girl crouched and opened a panel in the gatepost. "Look."

Mara bent down and squinted into the narrow space. Inside was a tiny, slender *gontra* tree. Despite its size, it bore *gontra* pods, as a mature specimen would. Her fingers reached to stroke a leaf; it had been so long since she'd touched a part of the Tree.

Shouts sounded from behind them.

"Be careful," Sritha warned.

As her fingers closed on the fragile plant, the powerful snare of connection caught Mara by surprise, like a sudden kick to the head in a sword fight. When she fell, both boys lunged for her, catching her before she hit her head. The gentle pressure of their hands barely registered as Mara's consciousness spiraled deep into the planet, joining the living root network underneath them.

* * *

Dalin woke in the chair, head lolling to one side. Speaking with a healer was a vague memory, but when he touched his face, he felt the glue and tape on his temple, more tape on his nose. No wonder his brain had gone off line. Someone had landed a perfectly targeted knockout blow.

One side of his nose was still clogged with blood, but through the other side, he smelled the spicy frying odors of the eating house. A light blanket had been pulled up to his chin. He shivered, realizing someone had cut through his shirt. To check his collarbone? Maybe his ribs?

The room had no windows, but his internal clock told him it was between the middle of the night and early morning. His first class didn't convene until ten, but he'd need to sign back in to the Mess and adjust the logs as early as possible.

His wrist unit confirmed it was 03:17. He'd been out for more than five hours. Standing slowly, Dalin shook the blanket and folded it. He bent with care and hefted his gear bag onto the bed as his collarbone, shoulder, and wrist protested. Luckily, even though they should have, they hadn't put his right arm in a sling. An arm sling would be even harder to explain than the damage to his face.

Using his left hand, he dug to the bottom of the bag and pulled out a clean shirt and a plain, hooded jacket. The room carried the chill of the desert at night, which meant outside would be cold. Not midwinter cold, but cold and probably raining.

Donning the clean clothes was a painful ordeal that took far too long. Compounding the lack of rigor in his fight training, he hadn't worked out his nondominant hand with weapons in months. "No time like the present," he muttered.

Dalin tried to move quietly, but the furniture in the tiny room was so crowded and his equilibrium was still compromised. Every awkward motion bumped him into the chair or the dresser that in turn hit one of the walls.

Rafiq appeared in the doorway looking clean and alert. He carried two heavy mugs, offering one to Dalin.

The steam hinted at a soothing mint and chamomile blend of tea. After a deep breath Dalin took a small sip, grateful to rinse his mouth. "Thank you for the intervention last night. I needed, I wanted other pain to distract me."

He tapped the warm ceramic mug against his chin as he organized his thoughts. "I have to get to Iloel. This whole mission smelled wrong from the beginning. It's reverse logic. Who sends students into an active conflict? Her majesty. Why? The higher the death toll, the better." Despite his upbringing and extensive training to care for the greater good of humanity, Mara's one life meant more than every other death combined. "You were gone yesterday, so I tried to leave on my own, but I couldn't get any of the spacers to help me, even for cash."

He was not proud of his choices, but at least he'd taken the pain on himself rather than hurting other people. "When I'm fighting, I can relax." No, that wasn't it. He tried again, as much to explain the problem to himself as to Rafiq. "When I'm fighting, it's the only time I can handle the worry, the frustration that I'm not doing something to help Mara."

"Kid, half the fighters in there were watching you by the end. You would not stay down. Can't think of a time I saw someone take a worse beating than you did and keep asking for more."

Dalin switched the mug to his left hand and gingerly touched his right fingers to his bandaged temple. "I don't remember it like that, but—"

"But you blacked out on your feet, like a drunk, still moving. Healer ran a tox screen on you. You're clean." Rafiq shrugged and scratched his chest. "You'd get a lot of supporters if you entered the tournament."

Taking a larger sip of tea, Dalin placed the mug on the dresser and finished packing his bag. As far as he could tell, all his gear was there. He tossed the ruined shirt into the trash.

"I owe you," Dalin said, looking directly into the man's face. "I'll cook. Help in the kitchen on the busy nights to work off my debt. But Mara is first."

Rafiq raised his eyebrows. "Well, my *cocinero* would need to try you out, but that's a handsome offer. I have access to a ship, but the Iloellian conflict ranges over more than half a continent. Not gonna file a flight plan without more information. For now, I'm gonna escort you back to the school. While we walk, you can answer another of my questions. Think of it as a goodwill gesture to the friend who rescued you from yourself."

"I told you her last known location was outside Samradhi," Dalin said. "What other information do you need?" He hated having to ask for help. This situation called for swift and decisive action. Mara was missing in a combat situation with more variables than the best computer models could handle.

"Ever hear the expression about how hard it is to find a needle in a haystack?"

"No. And how is that relevant?" Dalin stumbled as he pushed past Rafiq and marched into the main dining room. He could get a map from Kucala, get a tracker for Mara's wrist unit. Rafiq said he had a ship—Dalin bounced off the wall of Geraldo's chest and dropped his bag.

"Stop," the cook said.

Dalin raised his hands. "You gonna make me?" Though his vision blurred, adrenaline and frustration kept him on his feet.

Instead of throwing a punch, the cook laughed. "My *abuela* could stop you. You're not any good to anyone right now." He dropped a heavy hand on Dalin's shoulder, almost knocking him to his knees. "It's like you have to hit your target but you only have one bullet."

Rafiq cleared his throat.

"One arrow, one arrow I mean. So you can't shoot all over the place, you have to hit the target on the first try 'cause it's your only try. Or she's done. Give Rafe just a little more time to figure out where's the right place to shoot. It's a big planet, yeah?"

"More time could mean the difference between life and death." Dalin fumbled for his bag and got all the way to the door before Rafiq's voice stopped him.

"What's more important, your need to rescue her or her survival?"

Dalin slammed through the door determined to get the necessary data and tools from Kucala. Walking hurt his knees and ankles, but he moved as quickly as he could.

"The news that Mara is MIA, that's what set you on this suicide course?" Rafiq asked in a low, quiet tone.

Dalin clenched his teeth, sending pain shooting up both sides of his face. Son of Darkness, the man was persistent. How could he begin to explain the depth of his connection to her? "I've known Mara since she was born. Our families were friends, are friends." He swallowed down the sudden longing for a family dinner with his parents, sister, Mara, Jameson, and Elana.

"When we were young children we were close. I'm older than her, and I was given the job to look after her, to protect her. And I failed." Abysmally failed and more than once.

Rafiq didn't respond for a few minutes. As they passed the last of the shops and entered the first section of residential housing, he said, "That's all? You're her protector? Like a bodyguard or a big brother?"

No one knew about the depth of his feelings for Mara. Not his family or friends back home. He'd only shown Mara some facets of how he felt.

Dalin cleared his throat. "We were separated for more than ten years. When I saw her again, it was on the battlefield. She was—" Magnificent, beautiful, awe-inspiring. "She was everything I hoped to find in a partner." He cleared his throat again. "She *is* everything I want in a partner."

"Oh yeah?"

"Have you seen the recording of her fight against the Queen's Champion?" Dalin asked.

"I have."

"Well, think of her, that natural, instinctive fighter you saw, leading more than five hundred teenagers in a losing fight against a better skilled, better armed force of adults. She's an even more skilled leader than fighter. Sometimes those kids came close to winning. Because of her."

"So…you have a charge to protect Mara and you also admire her because she's so capable." Rafiq's tone was flat, nonjudgmental.

Dalin shrugged, which also hurt. The street grew smoother and steeper the farther into the residential area they walked. A light drizzle sent tiny freezing drops inside his collar. Dalin pulled up his hood and sniffed, his nose beginning to run on the non-bloody side.

"Pretty girl like that, skilled, comfortable with herself, she could write her own ticket where I come from. Instinct tells me she's just fine."

"She's more than pretty," Dalin said unable to hold back the argument. He could see Mara's face, feel the heavy softness of her unbound hair running through his hands. In a few minutes he'd be walking through the entrance to the Mess where they'd come back from the eating house together, where they'd kissed.

"Look, you need to take a break from La Kill for a bit or you're not going to make the travel team. In the past few hours we've already started running down information from Iloel. I've reached out to our mutual associate. Not all the sources match, but so far no reports of student bloodshed. Don't bother the nice people at the spaceport anymore either. They just work there." The smuggler pointed down the hill. Just beyond the dim lights of Lower Town stood the massive series of hangars and warehouses that made up the spaceport.

"Come find me before you fight again." Rafiq brandished a finger at him. "We'll pool our resources and go get her. Even though she's part time, Mara is part of my crew. I take care of my crew."

"How long?" Dalin gripped the man's arm.

"Might be a day—"

"No, that's too long—"

"Might be longer." Rafiq pulled Dalin's fingers back until he released his hold. "You don't get rested and healed, you're not going anywhere."

Chapter 21

In the Iloellian Tree's home pinpricks of light, tiny stars in the vast heavens above, penetrated the dusk. Mara stepped forward, bare toes curling on the smooth dirt floor, a white linen dress floating around her legs. She'd been wearing the arm sheaths for so long that her arms felt lighter, naked without them.

Other women, some younger, some older, walked in and out of doorways, traveling down the dim corridors in a twining, weaving pattern. At least she thought it was a pattern. Maybe the women were dancing? Certainly the movements were graceful, and the swirling white linen looked like flowers or snowflakes.

A tug on her hand turned Mara around. The Tree smiled. *"Welcome, daughter. Your sisters and I welcome you to your new home."* Much taller than her sister on Asattha, the Iloellian Tree towered over Mara. In the dim light, her skin was silvery pale, shadowed and gnarled with ropey muscles and veins. She too wore a simple white linen dress, cinched high and falling in strait pleats down past her ankles.

Mara struggled to reorder her mind. One part felt glad to be welcomed to this new home, so obviously peaceful and free of struggle. Another part challenged the notion this was home. Home was Dalin and her family on Asattha. Thinking hurt. She pushed past the pain, mentally smoothing the walls of her consciousness as she pushed.

This was what distance rapport felt like, she reminded herself. Her body was at the gate-post. "Where can I find you?" she asked, trying not to worry for her friends. Maybe a minute more to get a location; any information to help her quest.

But the Iloellian Tree was already fading, the link gone. Mara pushed to her hands and knees, gagging and spitting. A bruised and sweating Halifax crouched over her. Raymundo brandished a sword.

"Get back," he shouted at the people in uniforms inching closer. Sritha was to his left, attention bouncing between the three students and the advancing soldiers. She hadn't drawn a weapon.

Anger and frustration surged through Mara. Wiping her mouth with the back of her hand, she struggled to her feet.

"He said get back," she yelled and pushed energy out in a shock wave, knocking out every human standing between them and the main building.

Mara's head pounded as she struggled for balance. "We've got to go. Now."

"They wanted to take you," Halifax said, following her as she sprinted away. "Sritha was going to drug you while you were unconscious." His voice held both outrage and shock that they could be betrayed further.

Mara shook her head and spit again. Anything would be better than the bitter taste coating her tongue, even a tube meal. "Sritha was dedicated to their Tree as a child. It is her first loyalty."

Raymundo muttered something in Origin Spanish and kept running, his expression grim.

It wasn't altogether surprising Sritha hadn't sounded the alarm yet. She'd want to check all the fallen people for injuries. No one else could explain what had happened because they'd all have the amnesia, the fogging, that accompanied Mara's power.

She took a breath and let it out, counting to ten. Mentally checking for humans inside the stairwell, she motioned the other two students forward. They crept back through the building, retracing their steps to the underground garage.

Halifax took the walls and Raymundo took the vehicles, frantically searching for keys, sensors, anything to open the heavy door to the outside. Mara used a precious minute to adjust her sword, knives, and pack.

Sritha appeared, alone, empty hands raised in supplication.

The girl reached for Mara and dropped to one knee when Mara shifted to avoid the contact. "Lady," she said, head bowed. "Forgive me, I did not believe." Tears dripped down the girl's face and she sniffled.

Fighting the urge to shake the traitor, she said, "Sritha, we have to go. Who did you alert? How long do we have?"

"You can bring the Light," the girl said, looking up, brown eyes shiny and wet. "Our Tree. You can help her but not as a servant. I—I didn't alert anyone. You must be free so you can lift Her from the Darkness." She fumbled with a buttoned pocket and produced a small card with a printed string of characters. "Take this. It's a code for the hovercars."

When Mara reached for it, Sritha hesitated. "The Light Bringer is honest. She does not trick or lie," she said.

"We will work to bring the Tree out of Darkness. That's my mission here. But you must protect O'Kelley." Instead of taking the card, Mara cupped the girl's elbow and helped her stand.

Raymundo gently plucked the card from the Iloellian girl's limp fingers.

"I promise," she said. "I'll keep watch over the squad leader, get him back to Laska. I promise."

The translator slipped into the driver's seat of the hovercar nearest the door and tapped in the code. The engine whirred to life. "How long on a charge?"

"A thousand kilometers, give or take," Sritha said. She bit her lip. "Good luck."

"Until the next fight," Mara said, grasping the girl's forearm.

"Until the next fight, my lady," she replied with a small bow. She hurried to a wall panel, which slid open in response to her palm scan. A few quick taps and the massive door began to lift.

Halifax slid into the front passenger seat and Mara slid into the back. "I'll take nav."

"Yeah, I better drive 'cause I'm the only one who can read the displays," Raymundo said with a grin, smoothly nudging the hovercar onto the road.

* * *

Dalin hurried down the hall, keeping to the shadows. This time of the morning, only a few lights illuminated the areas around the healers' rooms. Sangita's door was closed and dark, but he would try again before class.

In one far corner of the men's locker room, in the back of a rarely used equipment closet, Dalin had hidden a basic holoscreen and keyboard. From there he could erase or change the recorded surveillance and the entrance/exit logs. The first month or so, he'd just explored the rudimentary systems at the Mess. He'd tried a small change to see if it triggered any response, either inside the system or externally, like a changing of passcodes. Nothing happened.

Both Dr. Iskindar and Bryant Kucala manipulated the internal micro data for the Mess with no repercussions. Dalin had grown increasingly confident in doing the same. The only recordings that were truly monitored were the fights, and the only student data that was mined or analyzed was the fight data.

After erasing his most recent departure and arrival and replacing everything in the equipment closet just as it should be, Dalin stripped down and took a long, hot shower. Though his shins were still bruised from fighting, most of his new injuries were concentrated on his upper body and face.

With a touch of regret, he turned off the water and dried himself with one of the rough towels. The cool quiet of the locker room was almost peaceful, dawn light streaming in through high windows on the lone outside wall. He threw the wet towel around his shoulders and wrapped a dry one around his hips before padding barefoot to the mirror to check out his face.

The healer must have set his nose the night before. It was taped and still swollen, but otherwise in its original configuration. Thin medical tape also ran across his eyebrow and the lid of his right eye. His upper lip had a partially healed cut inside, up near the gum line, but the lower lip was no longer swollen.

"Mara likes scars," he told his reflection and then frowned at his stubble. Shaving was not going to happen today. Luckily, his facial hair was light-colored enough to grow another day without violating dress code.

He dressed quickly in the spare uniform he always kept in his locker, making a mental note to replace it. Still keeping to the shadows in the hall, he made his way back to the healer's hall. Much to his relief, Sangita's door had a light on underneath.

The Iloellian healer opened the door at his knock. Her surprise shifted to dismay as she got a good look at his face.

"Come in, young master." She gestured for him to sit on the healing/massage table. "I can work on these injuries. You have more under your clothes, I assume?"

When the healer reached out to touch his face, Dalin moved back a fraction.

"Wait, thank you, but first, I…" He faltered, not wanting to hear the words again, let alone be the one to say them, "Mara is missing on Iloel. Taken by rebels outside of Samradhi."

Sangita pressed her palms together in the center of her chest. She closed her eyes and nodded. "Do you know which rebels? Which group?"

The woman's lack of concern was confusing, but also hopeful. Clearly of the two of them, she knew far more about Iloel. "No, not yet," Dalin said. "One person I know is working on information coming in through the s'port. There's another individual I'll be speaking with soon." Dr. Iskindar could surely find information about Mara through her networks.

"The Daughter will go on a journey across Iloel. It is foretold. The Tree Mother is far from the capital, so let us hope that Mara is quite well and on the way to fulfilling her destiny."

Mara's destiny? The idea that Mara had taken action herself, separated from the student squad and Commonwealth troops intentionally to seek out the Tree on Iloel, changed the possible scenarios. For the first time since he'd gotten the message from the Kook, some of Dalin's tension ebbed away. He hadn't been able to see past the shock and worry. The news of Mara being missing had triggered his old childhood guilt. It left him unable to reason or see her as a capable soldier.

"Let us work on you now. Lie back."

Dalin couldn't avoid the wince when he jarred his collarbone and shoulder. His feet dangled off the end of the table and he felt momentary regret for not removing his boots.

The healer clicked her tongue, making a tsking sound. "You have a shoulder separation. We start with this, then your nose."

Dalin closed his eyes and let the warmth flow into the injured joint and surrounding tendons.

More than an hour later he could breathe through his nostrils, and his jaw and neck pain were gone, as was the pain in his right wrist, elbow, and shoulder. Sitting up felt almost easy. Without the pain, his mind was more limber too. His wrist unit read 09:45. Just enough time to get to class. He offered Sangita his gratitude and left her room with something akin to hope.

As he walked into his rooms, a message chimed.

With a flick above his wrist unit, Dalin opened it.

```
Young master, we will finish your healing this
                    evening.
         Meet me an hour before curfew.
```

Between his first class and lunch, an announcement came across the running boards in the halls, as well as pinging across the coms. Just under three hundred of the registrants for the tournament had been eliminated as duplicates or disqualified for rules violations. Registration would reopen that evening and close again once a total of fifteen hundred entries was reached.

Interest sparked and buzzed through Dalin's students during the afternoon classes. One even asked him, with an admiring glance, if "any of the teachers" would be vying to become the Queen's Champion. He recalled Rafiq's remarks about the supporters he would have if he entered and then shook off the thought. He just wanted to train to be that good, not actually prove his merits in front of an interplanetary audience.

After class, he stopped by his rooms to change his clothes and look for a gift for Sangita. Currency did not change hands at the Mess for instruction, healing services, laundry, food, or drink. Bartering was lively though, and his mother had helped him pack several bins of items that might be valuable in trade.

In the middle of the second bin, he found what he hoped was a worthy gift for the healer—a large colorful square of textured and patterned fabric, just the right size to be sewn into a pillow cover. The Light praise his mother and her forethought. The bright hues reminded him of Market Square in Satri, and when he pressed the linen to his nose, he caught the faintest trace of *gontra* seed. With a quick glance at his hinges and the tiny pile of rust dust, Dalin hurried off to the healers' hall.

Sangita opened the door as he raised his hand to knock. She motioned him through and, when the door closed, waved her hand in a downward motion. A shield snapped into place with a perceptible pop.

"Did you shield the room this morning?" Dalin asked, the gift in his hand temporarily forgotten.

With a warm smile, the healer brushed one hand over his recently healed shoulder. "Oh yes. It's a good habit for when dangerous students come through." Soft fingers moved up to his nose and temple. "That healing took well," Sangita said. "But see that you sleep extra hours the next few days, let your body continue to heal."

Dalin held out the fabric. "I have a small gift to show my gratitude for your help. It's not much—"

"Thank you." The healer's face lit up. "A thoughtful gesture. You were thinking of my pillows?" She laid the fabric across the top of the larger chair, next to the other two pillows. "Yes, lovely."

He bobbed his head, glad the gift had been well-received.

Sangita's smile faltered. "I'm sorry to say I have a dark reason for asking you back here tonight. A place I found that I need to show you."

Immediately Dalin thought of the passage from Dr. Iskindar's office into the headquarters of the King's Men.

"Walk with me?" she said and held out her hand.

The Iloellian healer said nothing as she led the way to an outer door. Head held high, she walked out through a tiled courtyard, past a small ornamental garden, and around a steeply angled corner. This part of the building showed clearly how much of the foundation had been dug into the rocky hillside. A humid breeze carried the reminder of the week's monsoon rains, but at the moment, the clouds brought no additional moisture. A stand of several column-shaped, leafy bushes screened their next turn and suddenly, they stood in front of a door.

No recording devices were in evidence. Dalin didn't recall seeing any images of this area when he first began sifting through the visual recordings of the Mess. As far as he could tell, after a quick mental scan of the area, they were alone. But human energy signatures were definitely inside the door.

Instead of using her own wrist unit, Sangita pulled a different unit from a pocket and waved it past the tiny sensor in the doorframe. With an audible click, the lock disengaged and she pulled open the thick metal door.

Dalin reached above her head to pull it open a bit more, then ducked inside the narrow passageway. Crisp filtered air blew past them, bearing a strong astringent smell. Small light globes, too dim to fully penetrate the gloom, sprouted from the ceiling about every ten meters down the long corridor. Closed windowless doors appeared at slightly smaller intervals, more like every five meters. He sensed those rooms were empty, but people were certainly ahead.

He raised his eyebrows at Sangita.

She leaned forward and spoke in a quiet voice. "Most of the staff rotates out between dinner and curfew. After curfew, only a few nurses are in the ward. They don't circulate much, as far as I've been able to see."

"The ward?" Dalin said, matching her quiet tone.

With a nod, she tugged him forward.

They moved slowly toward a set of double doors on the right side of the corridor, a room even deeper under the foundation of the Mess. Pale light spilled from square windows as the pair drew close.

"Let me check first and then I'll bring you in," Sangita said.

"But—" Dalin began.

"I wrote myself some orders to be here, so at least I have a reason if nurses are in there." She turned and moved through the swinging doors with purpose, just as any staff member walked through the halls above.

Uneasy, Dalin listened for voices raised in challenge. But Sangita was back in under thirty seconds. "This way. Hurry."

He followed her through the door and stopped after a full step inside. Rows of narrow, metal-framed beds filled the large space. And nearly every bed held a prone human, many with visible bandages on arms, legs, and heads.

The astringent smell was much stronger here, burning into his nose. But underneath were the smells of any injured group—vomit, blood, urine, and infection. A small black clipboard was attached at the top of every bed frame. Sangita lifted one and flipped through the pages. She motioned Dalin over.

"Do you recognize this name?" she asked.

He licked dry lips and scanned the few lines. "No."

"This is the girl Mara fought in the first round of the Friday Fights just before the mission to Iloel."

The person in the bed had a heavily bandaged face, but some dark tangled hair was visible on one side.

"She was dismissed for having too low of a point count," Sangita added, gesturing to the girl.

Dalin scanned the room more slowly this time, counting the occupied beds. "This is what happens when students wash out? They end up here?"

The healer looked as ill as he felt. "Maybe so. I've been checking a few more names each time and so far they've all had low points and dismissal in common. One difference is the time of it." She shook her head and flapped one of her hands. "What I mean is that some were dismissed with this most recent group, but some of the children in these beds were to have been dismissed a year or more ago."

Dalin walked along the closest row of beds, alternating his gaze between the prone forms and the walls and ceiling. The absence of visible recording devices was almost more concerning than the extensive security. Patient data kept on paper attached to the beds signaled methodology from twentieth-century medical practices on the Origin.

What those two choices indicated was that the architect of this ward was far more cunning, and had a much better understanding of data and data security, than the staff in charge of basic security around the Mess. It also meant he wouldn't necessarily be able to obtain more information without physically returning to this place.

As he reached the far side of the room, a patient whose feet came right to the end of the bed caught his attention. The beds looked to be the same standard length as in the dorms, meaning anyone over the standard height didn't fit comfortably. The shape of the patient was female, her eyes bandaged, but clearly tall with long black hair. Dalin's heart seized in his chest and he took two running steps to grab the clipboard. With shaking hands, he flipped the first page over to check the patient's name. Woo. Ouyan Woo. Blinking, he rubbed his eyes and read the name five more times.

Not Mara.

It could have easily been her, if she hadn't been drugged and earned so many useless, darkness-cursed points.

He let the clipboard clatter back into place, staring at the girl in the bed, her limp feet just at the edge of the thin mattress. Unable to resist the compulsion, he tucked the bottom blankets tight and then tugged the sheet covering her until it was smooth and up to her chin. Just as he reached to brush a lock of hair from her forehead and the heavy gauze around the female patient's eyes, Sangita walked up behind him.

"According to the charts I've read so far, they're all sedated, some in chemically induced comas," she said.

"Someone needs to help these people." For the rest of his life, Dalin would not forget this room.

Mara might be the Daughter of the Tree, but the Prophecy cast her as half a pair. The Commonwealth had another species besides the Great Tree. Humans. If he was the other half of that pair, maybe it was his purpose to be the champion of the people while Mara took care of the Tree and her sisters.

Too concerned with what he had seen to think clearly, Dalin followed Sangita back the way they'd entered, down the hall, and out the door.

"How did you find that place?"

Sangita shook her head as they hurried through the cold rain back toward the Mess doors. "We were nearly out of sheets, just plain white sheets for the tables we use in our healers' rooms. I saw a man pushing a cart full of sheets going out the door. This door, actually," she grunted as she pulled it open. "I didn't want to call out because it was nearly curfew, but I thought if I caught up to him, he might give me a few to get through the next day."

Shaking her arms and legs to get rid of the raindrops on her yellow uniform, Sangita said, "I believe the Tree Mother guided me to follow him. As he came to those doors and opened them, the wrongness billowed out like a swarm of black flies. A vision that night told me I needed to discover what was hidden. The next day, the same laundry worker dropped a wrist unit as he was stocking our closet."

Dalin had felt the wrongness too; he smelled it still, the taint in his mind as much as in his nose and lungs. He nodded as Sangita continued to speak.

"And I believe the Tree Mother guided me to you also," she said, reaching up to press his arm. "The *ombiasi* from my village spoke of the *Santulan*, the balance, for the Daughter. I am just an old healer. But you, young man, if you are the *Santulan*, your work will be *with* her, but *for* all of us."

Chapter 22

Every time Dalin closed his eyes, and even when they were open, he saw the tall girl in the hospital bed. And given the Queen was comfortable murdering her employees in public, that the hospital was even slightly hidden gave him cause for greater concern.

He paced in his two small rooms, forcing himself to picture Mara, healthy and sitting on his chair. The morning before she left she'd been shaken from the drug, worried because he was so worried. But she'd been her beautiful, intelligent self. Calm and poised, despite the insane order that placed her on a student away team deploying to the middle of an active conflict. And he'd been an idiot, giving her weapons instead of convincing her not to go. Time and time again, he failed to keep her from harm.

Various teachers had spoken of the preciousness of time, of life. And certainly the great poets from the Origin wrote on those topics. Mara had been right here. He paused and brushed the arm of the chair with his fingers. And he'd been so angry about the drug in her system that he hadn't, they hadn't... Dalin looked into his starkly plain sleeping room.

And now she was MIA, kidnapped, or gone on a quest. The Mara who sought answers, who prepared unskilled children for battle, had embarked on her mission to help the Mother Tree of Iloel.

He hoped the rebels hadn't taken her weapons.

He hoped she wasn't alone.

Why wasn't he on Iloel with her? He needed answers from Rafiq and he needed transport on any ship that would get him to his partner's side.

Sangita had seen Mara's eyes when she'd been drugged, had recognized Mara enough to call her Tree's Daughter... So if those "signs" were obvious to any Tree servant on Iloel, they would have kidnapped Mara or convinced her to go with them for her "destiny."

Dalin was not one for tricking himself with false hope. But given Sangita's calm, and Mara's propensity to ignore mission parameters in favor of protecting someone or something, he had to also consider the possibility that she was merely MIA in service to the greater cause of the Tree and not in some anonymous medical facility.

Darkness. His oldest fight was against the Darkness in his mind, against the part of himself that had wanted to admire a wily and poisonous Queen, a regime that all but announced, "It's not a school, it's another experiment."

Some ancient history texts absolved the evil of rulers long dead, instead placing the blame for their atrocities on advisors, or other powers behind the throne.

Not this Queen.

She made no apologies for being truly evil.

Restless and uninterested in sleep, Dalin took a wrapped protein bar from one of his cabinets.

Rather than think about Vanora, Dalin forced himself to first eat and then sit and encode a message to Jameson. It was a complex and difficult code created for their work on Asattha, smuggling food and medicines into and people out of the war project zone. Just the sort of mental puzzle he needed to shift the majority of the worrying to his unconscious mind, since fighting was out of the question for the moment.

Message finished and neatly folded, Dalin tucked it into a pocket and stretched out on his bed. He fell into a light doze, fully dressed on top of the covers. His busy brain kept turning the current situation over and over, digging, pushing, shaping. How close could he get to the Queen, how much of his Darkness would he need to reveal to convince her to accept him?

"Know your enemy" was an early, early lesson from Jameson. And the closer Dalin was to the power in the commonwealth, the more Light he could bring to those in shadow. It was a much larger scale version of what they'd done on Asattha—and the risk was much greater.

When Dalin's wrist unit woke him at 0500, the moment curfew lifted each morning, the best option for completing his side of their mission presented itself with perfect clarity. Sparing a few moments for hygiene and personal needs, Dalin ate another energy bar and hurried to the nearest tournament registration kiosk.

* * *

For the first part of the first hour, Mara stared out the window while the two other students piloted them away from the Iloellian training base. Tinted glass deepened the twilight, but tiny glow panels kept the interior bright enough to see. The seats were a soft tanned finish, not leather, but something similar. She was so deeply lost in thought it took a few minutes before she realized Halifax was talking to her.

"Light Bringer? Do you know what Sritha was talking about?" he asked.

"Some random first year at the Mess turns out to be the *one* the King's Men have been searching for, my *tío* will turn into a frog," Raymundo added.

"What?" Halifax half laughed.

"It's an expression, means he'll turn green with jealousy and start jumping around, *cómo una rana.*"

"If you'd rather, you could tell us about this power to channel energy and knock out more than a dozen people at once," Halifax said, voice gentle and joking, eyes serious.

Shifting on the seat to face him, she reached out with her mind and brushed gently against the scholar's consciousness. Unshielded, his keen curiosity and basic goodwill came through over layer after layer of information. Multiple questions processed at different levels, appearing to her like storm systems around a planet. She wondered if this was what Dalin's mind was like once, before discipline molded it into a stone fortress.

Raymundo's mind was different. The thoughts flowed through deeper channels, each one translated into multiple languages. But like Halifax, his curiosity was entirely friendly and positive.

"Does the map show any settlements along this road?" Mara's hunger and thirst were beginning to build. "I don't want to eat or drink anything from that place."

Tapping his nose, Halifax frowned at the map displayed across his half of the front panel. "Wait. Where is this? Looks like we left O'Kelley at a university. It's the goat place."

When neither Mara nor Raymundo responded, he said, "University of Alexander de Badji Mokhtar? They specialize in goats." The scholar sighed and adjusted the magnification

"Good to know but where are we headed?" Raymundo asked, nodding toward the map.

"A big city." Halfax touched a huge irregularly shaped mass colored bright green on the display and surrounded by smaller dots on the eastern edge of the continent. "This is too big to go unmarked. But I know it wasn't on any of the Iloel maps we studied en route."

"Alandalus?" Raymundo said. "The smuggler city?"

"It's the right location for a massive trade center, in theory," Halifax agreed.

The two male students glanced at each other.

"This hovercar might be conspicuous depending on where we stopped. But if we see a town where we won't stand out, I'll let you know." He rotated and scrolled across the floating display. "Looks like there might be something in sixty, maybe ninety minutes."

She nodded and dumped out her pack on the long, low seat. She hadn't searched to the bottom since Dalin repacked it. Had only four or five days passed?

Like the hovercar she'd been transported in, this one had a slightly new smell to it. Pressing one of her spare shirts to her nose, she inhaled, imagining Dalin's sandalwood *gontra* scent. The neatly rolled socks reminded her of her partner as well. As promised, a large amount of Iloellian currency was hidden in each pair, along with a smaller pile of Laskan bills.

Halifax glanced at her piles and did a double take. "How much shopping did you plan for this mission?"

Mara raised one eyebrow. "I don't shop. This is for emergencies, specifically food and water emergencies." She ignored the questions in his eyes and went back to sorting. It was hard not to linger on the weapons, especially since two of the knives were Dalin's, but her sword was clean and ready, as was the rest of her gear. The search did not turn up any additional food.

Thirsty, light-headed, and drained from the energy pulse back at the gate, Mara tried to fight off fatigue.

"Big town coming up in about twenty minutes," Halifax reported. "Nice flying, by the way, 'Mundo. Any sign of pursuit?"

"Radar's engaged, and energy scans are running, but if their tech can hide a massive city, they can hide a few cars," the translator replied. "You should fly with Angelo sometime. That boy, his moves are smooth."

"They may think we'll run north," Mara said.

"Tactically, if resources aren't an issue, they should dispatch two teams, one toward Samradhi and one toward Alandalus." Raymundo tapped his console and adjusted the perspective.

Facing into the rear of the car, Halifax nodded to her. "Brings us back to you, Mara. Are you worth a full-out pursuit?"

"Yeah, are you the one the King's Men have been searching for? Because that would be *fantástico*."

She wanted to deny it. She was just a soldier, just another student at the Mess. Sure, she had a few extra gifts, but so did every student on the O Squad. Conscious of her own ignorance, she closed her eyes and took a breath.

"'Fax, have you ever heard of someone who can do what I did back there?" She rushed on before he could answer. "I'm asking because all of the Protectors can shield, most quite well. So that was normal and expected for us. But at the Mess, no one can shield, even people who have that skill, because they can't find an energy source." Her hands twisted together and she forced them apart, forced herself to be still. "Do you understand what I'm asking?"

Nodding slowly, the scholar rubbed his chin. "You're asking if it's hypothetically possible that others with the ability to channel energy and create shields can do what you did. And if I've heard of such a phenomenon or people with those talents."

She relaxed a fraction. "Yes."

"Despite the pride I take in knowing a lot of information—"

Raymundo snorted.

Lips quirked, he continued, "Knowing a lot makes me the most aware of how much I don't know. Like what you just said about the Protectors all being able to shield; that's news to me. Nothing of that nature is in the official documentation."

"I thought the Browns, I mean the Science Corps, recorded everything. Weren't they required to?" She couldn't fathom a scientist leaving out such an important detail of the Protector training.

"The experiment's been down less than a year. Reports will be redacted for a good long while, at least for those of us without a high level of access." On a sigh, he said, "If we accept that it's possible for others to do what you can do, we have to accept the opposite as also possible."

Mara shook her head at him, distracted by the road signs and shapes ahead, indicating a settlement or, hopefully, a city. "What do you mean?"

"That you're the only one."

Chapter 23

"The second day the bruises always look worse," Dalin reassured one of the younger students at the end of his class. This particular girl stayed after with a question or comment most classes, but today he had even less time for a chat. A summons from Dr. Iskindar was something he did not want to delay, especially if she had news about Mara.

The girl scrubbed a towel over her short black curls and threw it in her bag. "Well, it's not exactly an inspiration when you're teaching self-defense and show up looking like the losing end of a serious fight."

Surprised by her tone, Dalin glanced up from packing his gear. "Did you need inspiration?" The student reminded him of Annelise, or how Annelise used to be, with an open face and a kind smile. She was small and curvy with dark, dark skin.

"Tournament starts soon, doesn't it? 'Course I need inspiration."

"You…you entered?" Dalin didn't want to hurt her feelings by expressing doubt, but this student was no killer.

"I'm a second-year," the girl said. Dalin realized he didn't know her name, which wasn't like him. "And word went around that the best way to avoid washing out was to enter the tournament. Might even get a point bonus if we make it to the second round." She jammed her feet into her boots and looked back up at him. "So yeah, I, *we*, might need a little inspiration."

"I'll keep that in mind," Dalin said. But a few steps outside the gym, the conversation was forgotten as he took the shortest route to Dr. Iskindar's office.

"Enter," she called in response to his knock. Dalin glanced back at the empty corridor before slipping into the crowded office and pulling the door closed.

It didn't seem possible and yet more books and papers were piled on the professor's desk as well as on the other, already full, surfaces. The cloudburst had been brief the previous night, and the Mess was drier, leaving the professor's office smelling less like books and plaster than it had on his previous visit.

"Thank you for the other day, I wouldn't have—" Survived.

"I have news," Dr. Iskindar said without preamble.

Dalin felt compelled to thank her for protecting him and the others from the Queen, but she stood and walked directly to the passage leading to the hub of the King's Men. Once inside, she activated the central holocell and brought Iloel into focus in three dimensions hovering in front of them. Today she wore an uncharacteristically plain, dark gray sari and only a few bracelets. The somber attire matched her expression.

Like most of the planets in the Commonwealth, terraforming had produced one giant supercontinent on Iloel with only a few minor landmasses in the vast ocean. The professor tapped and shaped the image until several layers were visible. Dalin leaned forward, interested in both the geography and the man-made features coming into sharp relief.

"The force of two hundred landed here." Dr. Iskindar touched a structure outside a large city. "And they marched to here." She tapped the city and zoomed in.

"That's Samradhi," Dalin said half to himself. The view rushed past huge, immensely tall buildings in an empty area. "Where are the people? Is this real time? Can you track their wrist units?"

"No, this is a map. People haven't occupied the commerce center in nearly fifty years. It was built using some truly innovative and efficient tech to convert the area's abundant solar energy. But with the focus on mining and then the distraction of the ongoing civil war, the skills and knowledge to maintain the tech were lost until pieces of buildings were falling into the street like coconuts from a tree. As for the wrist units..." Dr. Iskindar shook her head. "Those are toys, worthless outside a ten-kilometer radius of the Mess. Pre-Commonwealth tech."

She continued to manipulate the controls, zooming down a street and pausing the view in front of a shorter brick-and-stone building. "This is a key water facility. A group attacked the Commonwealth forces in the commerce center and kidnapped the five currently listed as missing members of the student observation squad. My people have a few mobile links between them to upload messages. That's where this information comes from."

Dalin leaned forward into the holographic projection as though he could transport himself there through sheer will. His fingers curled on the edge of the desk, his mouth dry with fear.

"But the Light protects its own and Mara De La Luz is alive and well. For a brief time she was a prisoner at one of the rebel facilities in the south, a training base hidden in a university." The professor gave a half smile and a shrug, acknowledging the congruence with their situation at the Mess. "She and at least two members of the student squad are now at large. It is presumed they are unharmed."

His knees locked with the effort of controlling his outward emotions, and Dalin swayed a little. Mara was alive. Of course she was.

"Breathe, Mr. de Forest," Dr. Iskindar advised.

* * *

Dust particles mixed with the barrier surrounding Alandalus, smudging and shadowing the students' first view of the city. From their vantage point about a kilometer outside the barrier, houses and low buildings formed the outskirts and surrounded slightly taller, larger structures at the center. Halifax drove and Raymundo translated road signs as they got closer. Though morning was just touching the sky, vehicles of all sizes traveled along the road in both directions.

"We'll be stopped outside the barrier. Right at the guardhouse," Raymundo said. "At least that's my guess. They're going to ask us if we have anything to trade, which we don't. And they're going to ask what's our business in the city."

Halifax slowed the hovercar and pulled to the side of the road. "They've already seen us, but we can stall for a few minutes, pretend we've got a tire jam. What's our story?"

"Let's stay close to the truth," Raymundo said. "We're students. We're sightseeing."

"And we're not related but we go to the same school. And we're training to be…" he trailed off. To Mara he said, "What else can you do?"

Closing her eyes in frustration, Mara said, "Horses. I can buy, train, and trade horses. Do they even have horses on Iloel?" She glared at the floor. She hated it when people asked her what she could do.

Raymundo shrugged but Halifax frowned and tapped the console, steering them back to the line outside the guardhouse. "Yeah, just like on Laska, the wealthy people do. The first King loved polo, so all the courtiers learned to play, passed the sport down through their families." He shook his head. "Guess you've never been to the stables at the palace?"

"Focus, 'Fax—we're all here to study the goats. *¿Me entiendes?*"

"Understood," 'Fax replied. He guided the hovercar forward at a slow roll.

"And I have a friend who was supposed to be dropping off a shipment in Alandalus. He's our ride back to Laska," Mara said.

Raymundo looked at her, twisting around in the front seat to stare.

"I can say it with conviction because I really wish it to be true," she said as they pulled up to the gate.

A surprisingly young guard tapped his weapon on the hovercar's window, gesturing that they should shut down and step out.

"*Salaam alaikum,*" he said. Every inch of his jewel-green uniform was pressed, clean, and precise, including the small brimmed cap sitting perfectly straight on his head.

Both Halifax and Raymundo responded, "*Wa alaikum salaam.*"

"State your business," the guard said, holding his weapon loose and ready. Another vehicle rolled to a stop next to the other guardhouse.

"We're students," Raymundo said, first in Origin Arabic and then in Origin English. "Just finished up a tour of the goat facilities out at University of Alexander de Badji Mokhtar."

The guard smoothed his collar and looked them over, his gaze lingering on Mara. He asked, "Do you plan to trade while you're here?"

"No, just taking in the sights," Raymundo said. He gave the guard a one-man-to-the-other smile.

With a glance, the guard checked in with another uniformed person in the gatehouse. He nodded. "Scan's clean. How long do you intend to stay?"

"Two or three days, no more," Raymundo said. "Anything we shouldn't miss?"

"The *souks*, down in the *medina*. Really old down there. Lots of visitors say they've never seen anything like it." The guard waved at the next vehicle to begin pulling forward.

The three students piled into the hovercar and rolled onward.

Another fifty meters and they drove through the barrier. The energy made Mara's head spin; it was so imbued with the signature elements of the Iloellian Tree—protectiveness, anger, loneliness.

Fighting back nausea, she closed her eyes and reached out. Although no gateposts were visible along the northern and southern horizon, she guessed the creation of the dome shared some things in common with the boundary at the university. In her mind's eye, she saw the underground nodes pulsing out from the Mother Tree, leading back to the center of the city.

For a millisecond she caught something else, a more familiar energy signature. Dalin? She bit her bottom lip and sighed. As gifted as he was, even Dalin wouldn't be able to track her through this wreck of a mission. With Dalin she felt balanced. And their complementary strengths made them such a strong fighting pair. Missing her partner, Mara wondered what he would think about Alandalus.

As they moved into the city, the first housing areas appeared. Most were small, impeccably clean homes with large gardens between them. A midsize park appeared, half of the space covered by a fruit orchard. Though it was still early morning, families walked along the sidewalk, children and parents, apparently carefree and heading in the same direction.

"School?" Raymundo murmured.

"Wouldn't know," Halifax said with a shrug.

A large building occupied most of the next block, its open construction and many windows giving it an inviting look. A play park and more gardens, both flower and vegetable, graced the visible corners. The breeze coming in through the window vents held the promise of a steamy tropical afternoon, and it also carried the rich smell of growing things. None of the stink of people living close together, or of unmanaged trash and waste like in Lower Town.

Too soon, Halifax drove through a series of turns and into a tunnel. The traffic in the tunnel was denser than outside the guard post. The energy of the Tree pulsed in the walls when Mara could no longer see sunlight in either direction. She found it harder to draw a deep breath. Sweat prickled under her braid and she shifted in her seat, wiping damp palms on her heavy uniform pants.

Yellow lights affixed to the ceiling of the tunnel cast a dim, sickly glow over the never-ending stretch. When she shifted again in her seat, Halifax took his gaze away from the nav display to glance back.

"It's a long tunnel," he said. "Approximately twenty kilometers. Some large portion of the city might be underground, but I'm not sure how to read that. Even in three dimensions, it's confusing."

Mara licked her dry lips. "How far have we driven in the tunnel?"

"Not quite halfway," Raymundo said. "Have to say, I'm both sorry and glad this is bothering you. After that display of power back there, I was starting to worry you were the one my uncle always talked about. That's a lot of responsibility for 'Fax and me."

"Why don't you tell us about your smuggler friend?" Halifax said. The low light left most of his face in shadow, white teeth glinting in his smile.

The image reminded her of the first time she met Rafiq and that helped her start the story. She sketched out the details of her illness and rescue by the owner of the eating house.

"Cousins? I've heard of that place," Raymundo chimed in. "Bad part of town though. Rumor is they hate Mess students down there."

"The food is delicious," Mara said. "I would pick up shifts just so I could eat Geraldo's cooking afterward. No one's started a fight with me. Except for the first night."

She left out the story of her negotiations with Rafiq, and concluded that when she filed for off campus time, she was at Cousins, waiting tables.

"He doesn't hide the fact that he has outside means of moving merchandise from one place to another, but it mostly seems harmless, like old books. It's a long shot he's here, but I thought we'd listen for ships and traders heading back to Laska, in case Rafiq's been around lately or is scheduled." Finally, a sliver of light glimmered through the windshield.

Giving an exaggerated shrug and then rolling his shoulders to release tension, Raymundo said, "I can't catch a different ride back to Laska. My priority is to get back to Angelo here on Iloel. Problem is our hovercar is about out of charge. We've got maybe two hundred kilometers if we push it, but we've come so far east, that won't get us to Samradhi. Not even halfway."

Before either Mara or Halifax could respond, the tunnel opened into a vast cavern. They took the left fork of the main road, gawking at the collection of buildings that ranged in height from low to towering. Above them hovercars zipped onto and out of mid-rise landing pads, some cruising forward to roads leading away on that level, some soaring higher to the top levels of buildings and roads. The enormous cave was easily as high and as long as five or six times that of the Queen's palace on Laska.

Light sources dotted the walls and the lower street had lamps, like the ones in Satri. The air was much cooler, but still humid.

The Tree was close.

People walked along the streets, most moving quickly, like any other city on a business day in the morning. The gift of the Tree on Iloel did not appear to be height. What had Sangita said? Something about gifts being rare...rare and unpredictable.

Halifax drove them toward the center of the underground city, Raymundo navigating by the posted signs.

"You ever seen anything like this? Heard about anything like this?" the translator asked.

"Stories. Fables and myths from the Origin. Fiction," Halifax said.

A sudden and urgent mental shout pierced the shield around Mara's mind. She winced and leaned forward to tap Halifax's shoulder. "Turn right, we have to get to the Tree."

She directed him for a tense few minutes. As they wound deeper into the city, the gloom thickened as did the walls of the structures. Some of the buildings were rough-cut stone, as though the cave had been dug out around them. The crowds increased, bustling along despite the low light, moving with the focus of any Satri folk on the way to the main square. They were stopped at a gate with a sign proclaiming "Pedestrians only" in all the standard Origin languages.

Raymundo tapped and rotated his display. "Here." He pointed at a blue outline. "This is a place to park the car. Go back one street and turn right."

Tires crunching on the uneven brick street, Halifax turned the hovercar around, taking care to avoid the pedestrians. A flashing light directed them into a hive-shaped structure with an internal circular ramp. Mara handed over Iloellian cash to the woman on duty. The attendant wore clothes similar to many of the women on the street—long skirt, sandals, long sleeveless shirt, hair wrapped in a colorful scarf.

"Is there a Tree ceremony today?" Mara asked. It was something she'd seen in the brief moments of rapport she'd had with the lady in the white dress.

The woman considered the question while rolling her tongue up and over her front teeth. She narrowed her eyes. "Tree ceremony every day. She looks—" Frowning, the attendant muttered something in Origin Hindi.

Replying in the same language, Raymundo asked the question again. With an agitated flap of her bare brown arms, a torrent of explanation poured forth. She slapped a flat blue metal disk into his hand and stalked away.

The three students stared after her for a surprised moment. Raymundo drove onto the ramp and parked two levels down. "The blue coin is to get us back in later. Parking closes at sunset. Curfew."

"Best take everything with, just in case," Halifax said, shouldering his pack. Both Mara and Raymundo followed suit, slipping into their plain black Mess-issued packs. "We're going to stand out as tourists. But we really are students, so sticking with the story is best."

Before he entered the locking sequence, Raymundo took a moment to show the other two how to unlock the hovercar and access the controls.

"Listen." He reluctantly looked at Mara. "The Tree has been on some kind of rampage the past five days. She's left her..." He paused and took a shallow breath. "Her home and she's popping in and out of stores, houses, everywhere, *como una diábola*, searching for the Daughter."

Both boys looked at Mara now. She stared back, refusing to shift her weight, bite her lower lip, or make any other movement that would show concern. "The Tree is an indigenous life form. This one's been poisoned." Just like her. "I have to go to her grotto, or whatever her home is called. It's a promise I made before I left home. I also told Sritha I would try."

The light of the parking ramp emphasized the sharpness of Halifax's cheekbones and nose. He pressed his lips shut, clearly holding back his thoughts on the matter.

"It makes sense to split up here," Mara said. "I'll be fine with the Tree on my own. You should look for a ride back to Samrahdi. Get news about the rest of our squad. I'll meet you here before curfew."

"Gonna hold you to that," Raymundo said, exchanging a look with Halifax.

What she hadn't been able to see from within the hovercar was that the buildings grew down from the ceiling, as well as up from the floor. High above, it was just possible to make out the stalactite shapes, with multiple levels running in no obvious pattern across the center of the cavern. Another reason for hovercars? Or modified hovercars that could truly fly?

As her companions walked away, Mara buckled her sword belt around her hips. She did not know this city, did not know this Tree. But she had food and water from their earlier stop, boots, and her sword. If she didn't return, Halifax and Raymundo would come looking.

Mara took a deep breath and started walking.

Down a small hill lay what had to be the oldest part of the city. Low stone buildings, crumbling at the corners, lined the narrow street. The Tree energy pulsed in the thick, stale air.

People, mostly very young or very old, lounged in some of the doorways of the row houses, but other homes had an air of abandonment, a tattered fabric curtain pulled over the space where a door might have been, broken front steps, gaping windows.

The noises of the city above formed a muted backdrop, the sounds of voices, feet, and transport trucks blending together. The closer she got to the *medina*, the more the noises of the market dominated, shouts of protest or excitement in several languages, as well as the scrapes and creaks of heavy materials moving across stone.

As she turned the next corner, the warm smell of baking bread wrapped around her like an unexpected hug. A cluster of food stalls welcomed visitors into the small, ancient market square.

This market had no obvious arrangement or order like the one in Satri, or even the one in Lower Town, the variation in people and goods much more intense. The Tree was so close now her dark aura permeated the entire area like a fog.

Mara's pace slowed as her heart sped up, every instinct on high alert. A display of sparkling new throwing knives caught her attention. Laid out on white cloth, the freshness of the booth and the merchandise was extremely attractive. Moving close enough to heft one of the blades, she let her fingers curl around the handle, the smooth grip a perfect fit for her hand. "It's so light," she muttered, weighing the small knife in her palm.

"It be a new alloy from Kels," said the female merchant, a tall woman with orange curls tucked under a patterned scarf. "Try it for yerself." She gestured to the back wall of the stall and the targets painted there.

Ignoring the pull of the Tree, Mara shifted to put her left shoulder toward the target. She picked the smallest painted object, a white and yellow flower, and sunk the tip of the knife in its center with a tight flick of her wrist.

"Best throw this week," the merchant said with a genuine smile. "You thinking to buy?"

In her entire life, Mara had never been at a market with money of her own to spend. As a child, and as a soldier, she'd accepted this without complaint. She might have felt the occasional wishful twinge on the inside, but many useful things could be gained through an exchange of work or trade.

Dalin always had extra weapons, and in this entirely unknown situation, one more knife wouldn't hurt. She fingered her trousers, wondering if the knife would be best in a pocket or on a belt sheath.

"The sheath comes with it, no charge," the merchant said, retrieving the knife from the back wall and laying it in front of Mara.

"Why no charge?" Mara asked.

The woman looked around and then leaned over the table. "You know about the Tree, right?" Without waiting for an answer she rushed on, Origin English accent sounding more like Jameson's now. "Well, yesterday she pops in here and starts touchin' all me merchandise. And she's huge, right? Waving her hands around." The merchant demonstrated. "And she says, 'The Daughter comes, the Daughter comes and you will give her what she desires.'"

Glancing to the center of the market, Mara couldn't suppress a tiny shudder. She took a step away from the table.

"You've heard about her eyes? They say she can copy every other bit of a human's look, but not the eyes. So hers are empty. And black as the deepest grave."

Mara took another step away.

"It's been good tradin' here for a number of seasons. But I'm wantin' to get home. I'll give you a deal—"

"No, thank you. I'd best be about my business," Mara said.

Right hand gripping the pommel of her sword, she squared her shoulders and went to meet the Tree of Iloel.

Chapter 24

Dalin wasn't sure how to contact Bryant Kucala without revealing their acquaintance. When they were in school together, Kucala's sister, Wren, had taught Dalin the best way to annoy her brother was to rearrange his things. Kucala kept a pristine room, especially his desk. Wren would move three to five items and replace them in equally logical spots. Upon discovery of the prank, her brother would explode and then spend up to an hour returning the room to his specifications.

Choosing a different tech lab, Dalin went back through his research strings looking for new details. As the time grew later and the lab cleared out, he initiated his hiding protocols and went deeper. Long into the night, he struck a particularly rich vein of research around the use of mental rapport, not to communicate but to kill. The only notes were from several dozen subjects on Kels, and one team currently deployed to Iloel.

Suddenly, all the text was replaced with an image of a giant tree. It changed into a lurid red skull and crossbones. With a quick glance around, Dalin confirmed that he was alone in the lab. Those two images flashed back and forth three times and then a door with an arrow appeared. The arrow moved toward the door, reset and moved toward the door again.

"Message received," Dalin said aloud. He took his time erasing his data path as he pulled back, closing each virtual door and erasing his presence. He changed the timestamp on his entry and exit into the lab and left.

His wrist unit chimed and a single line of text appeared: "Transport Bay 2358." The transport hub was on the opposite side of the Mess. And it was long past curfew. His status as a junior instructor allowed slightly less restricted movement, but Dalin still didn't want to meet anyone in authority along the way.

At this hour, the Mess was uncomfortably silent, the only sound the humming of climate control fans circulating the air. On the rubberized syncrete floors, his boots didn't make enough noise to attract attention.

Many people he'd met felt uneasy outdoors at night, particularly in the woods. The woods made sense to Dalin; he'd learned to see and hear the signals indicating potential threats. Here at the Mess, danger could be invisible, like the drug in Mara's water bottle, or silent, like the touch from the Queen.

Just as he entered the giant garage, fatigue hit him hard. Shouldn't he at least try to sleep?

Not until Mara was safe.

Whether she came back from Iloel—*when* she came back from Iloel, he wanted to have something of significance to report on his side of their mission.

Functionally the same layout as a stable, but for non-animate transports, the transport center smelled like machine parts and oil, with a lingering tang of combustion engine. Just like the s'port, the bays varied in size based on the type of vehicle stored.

And, like the halls above, the place was nearly silent. Activity would start at 0500, the supplies to keep the Mess running arriving in bulk. Dalin had been too involved in Mara's situation to wonder about all of the personnel necessary to keep the huge facility in decent condition. But as he walked though the cavernous interior, vehicles no more than vague shapes in the gloom, he wondered where all the workers were housed and how they were paid.

Bay 2358 was at the end of a long row. Inside Bryant Kucala polished a two-wheeled vehicle with a single leather saddle fitted over the center of the horizontal body. Rather than an overhead light, several bendable lamps lit the workspace.

"I told you to stay out of the research," Kucala said.

"I needed to talk to you and I didn't know how else to get your attention," Dalin replied.

Kucala grunted and continued polishing the shiny metal bars that led up to leather handgrips. As he moved, shadows played across his face and shaved head.

"How do you ride this?" Dalin asked.

"Like a horse," Kucala said. He swung one leg over and sat on the saddle, the tips of his boots just touching the ground on either side. "Vanora's grandfather imbedded solar cells in the roads to the city. This *otobai* uses modified solar power but it has a backup electrical engine."

"Do you...?"

"Even I have to leave the lab sometimes," Kucala said, answering Dalin's truncated question, then swung his leg awkwardly back over the *otobai*. "The former Queen's Champion, may he rot in peace, rode one like this. I...I was tempted."

The computer genius squeezed one of the handgrips, his expression hardening. "Saw your tournament entry form. What in the name of the great mother of darkness were you thinking?"

"Know your enemy, mostly. We came here to get close enough to plant seeds of destruction. For your sister and my sister to grow into adulthood without fear, this regime has to fall. Mara went to war as a child, fought beside children, and watched them die. She expects me to continue our mission. And that means getting close to the great mother of darkness."

Kucala opened a tiny chiller in the far corner and took out a bottle. Silently, he offered it to Dalin.

"What is it?"

"Carbonated stimulants and sugar," Kucala said with a rare smile. "It's my other vice. Source says it's from the Origin."

"After you," Dalin said.

He shrugged and pried the lid from the bottle with an audible pop. After his first swig, he poured about half the bottle into a metal cup. He offered the remainder of the bottle to Dalin with a smirk, eyebrows raised in challenge.

Kook was an ally Dalin really needed. If drinking carbonated stimulants mixed with sugar was his way of bonding, so be it. "Cheers," Dalin said and chugged down a huge swallow. His eyes watered and his throat constricted as he coughed and spluttered. The sweet taste was overwhelming, the sugar zinging through his bloodstream.

"Delicious, yeah?" Kucala prompted.

"Never tasted anything like it," Dalin agreed.

"Tell me a little more about this mission you assigned yourself."

He gave Kucala a basic outline of their plan, leaving out the part about the Great Tree of Asattha putting a compulsion on Mara to help her sisters. Without that salient fact, the rest of it sounded kind of thin.

"That's it? I expected more from you, Tree."

"What would you do if you were me?" Dalin took another sip of the bubbling drink and forced a smile.

"Do you remember Wren's final Applied Science project her first year?"

Closing his eyes and hoping the sugar would power up his tired brain cells, Dalin squeezed the bridge of his nose. "Something to do with algae. A water sealant? A water purifier." He snapped his fingers. "A live bioactive water purifier."

"Right. But the problem was testing it. Had to fill a huge tank and let it all run through."

Dalin remembered now. Because he was so much larger than Wren, she'd asked him to maneuver the huge rectangular tank out into a common area.

"The information networks across the Commonwealth have never been loaded, not even halfway. Millions of kilometers of communication network tech were built, and easily millions of communication nodes were built during the foundation, but only the military uses it." He shrugged and tilted his chin up as though contemplating the popcorn texture of the gray ceiling. "And a few of us who piggyback on that signal. Two hundred and fifty years old, but most of it still works." Taking a long sip of his drink, Kucala waved his free hand. "A lot of information dumped into that system would prevent the purifier from working."

"Just like too much water in Wren's tank overwhelmed the algae filter."

"The financial specs of the war experiments alone should cause significant concern, should those be made available to the citizens of the Commonwealth. Science experiments cost money. I remember thinking about that when we were in school. All that equipment, and the personnel, hardware, and software to support the data mining. And yet, in the basic war project survey course, what's the one thing left out of the textbook? The cost."

"Holoprojectors are going up all over the city—" Dalin began.

"And network capacity is being increased along with direct feeds to every planetary capital and major city," Kucala interjected.

"What else would get dumped into the system and shared?" Dalin asked.

"Recordings of you know who doing her thing."

"Killing?"

"Yeah, the crazy stuff. Enough to counteract every minute of propaganda ever distributed. Maybe even a propaganda counter, point-by-point style."

"But what about Wren, I thought she—"

"She's in a secure location. The other party wants in on this. They're willing to take public credit, which points far away from us and my sister."

Kucala fired up his machine. "Not going to let all those charged roads go to waste," he said, raising his voice over the engine noise.

Watching him drive away, Dalin felt a touch of envy. The *otobai* was a far more stylish method for travel than the wheeled upright boxes in Satri, if a person didn't have access to a horse.

The way the brackets were laid out, the winners spent increasing amounts of time with the Queen as they progressed. For the plan to work with Kucala's additions, he'd need to stay in the tournament for as long as possible.

* * *

At the bottom of the market, a tall tower rose. Made of mud, brick, and stone in alternating layers, it reached up and connected to the roof of the cave city. At least that was Mara's guess; even with her head tilted all the way back, she couldn't make out much of the roof.

The ground was more uneven here, the stones broken and in many places cracked wide enough to show hard packed dirt. Around the tower, semicircular wooden benches fanned out in at least a dozen concentric rows.

The benches were nearly full of people all chanting in a low murmur. Occasionally a person would shout and raise his or her hands toward the top of the tower; the voices would rise in pitch and then subside. Some rocked as they chanted but most were still, huddled forward over their knees, even the children.

Circulating through the crowd were tall, slender women in white robes. They carried baskets into which currency and small food items were placed. Engrossed in the scene before her, Mara tripped and stumbled hard enough to tweak her ankle. The pain sparked an answering flare of energy in the base of her spine. The crowd had left a space just behind the benches so Mara crouched down to unlace the top of her boot. With careful fingers, she probed the tendons and her ankle, more to confirm all was well rather than from any true concern.

Inhaling and exhaling, she was about to stand up and resume her slow approach when she caught the unexpected smell of *gontra*. A tiny sprig with a few silver green leaves poked up from a mound of dirt and broken stone just to her left. Mara leaned forward to touch the leaves, brushing at the dirt around the sprig. A massive root, nearly as big around as her waist, twisted up through the broken place in the road. Keeping her connection with the root, she turned her gaze back to the tower.

This was the place she'd seen in the vision, the Tree's prison.

Startled gasps and a few shrieks rose from the people nearby. Mara straightened and stood, coming face-to-face with the Iloellian Tree.

"Daughter," the Tree roared, her voice carrying an eerie multi-tone echo with pitches from low to high. "You come to free me. At last."

Standing a half-meter taller than Mara, the Tree's curly hair was a coiling mass of silver green, with only a few strands of brown and black showing through. Her bare gray-brown arms were corded with deep lines of muscle and her feet were bare under the drape of her white dress.

"Did you buy the knife?" the Tree asked.

Raising her gaze to the ancient face of the Tree, Mara repeated, "Did I buy the knife?"

A dark frown deepened all the lines and creases on the Tree's face. "Sometimes you buy it, sometimes you don't." She vanished.

More shrieks reminded Mara she was not alone. The people on the back benches had turned to watch, their expressions a mix of puzzlement, fear, and wonder.

As abruptly as she had vanished, the Tree reappeared, laying one heavy hand on Mara's shoulder. "Here. You'll need this." In the other hand lay the little throwing knife in a belt sheath.

"Thank you, Mother," Mara said. "May we speak alone?" This close to the Tree, the wrongness swirled around them both, a thick, nauseating miasma of taint and rot. She tucked the knife into a side pocket and pressed one hand to her stomach, breathing through her mouth.

The Tree nodded. "We do not fight," she said. "You never fight me. You are here to help."

"Yes." Mara patted one dry hand. "Please show me your home."

"It's a prison," the Tree bellowed in her eerie multi-voice wail. She jerked her hand free and waved over the people nearest them. "They can't understand my speech. They bring offerings to placate me so I'll maintain the shield. Only a few." She started walking toward the women with baskets. "A very few can understand."

The most senior-looking of the women in white blew into a delicate silver whistle hanging from a chain around her neck. At this signal, not only did the other women move quickly toward the center of the benches, but the crowd began to disperse as well.

At the base of the amphitheater were the archways Mara had seen in the brief rapport. The Tree stormed through, and Mara and the other women followed her into the tower. The senior acolyte blew her whistle again and the women hurried, no graceful pattern now, through four of the six visible doorways. Within moments, Mara and the Tree stood alone in the center of the dirt floor.

"Your sister sent me," Mara said.

The giantess's rough features looked as though they'd been carved by an inexperienced sculptor using a hunting knife. With her slash of a mouth, crooked nose, and empty eyes, she appeared much more alien than the Asatthan Tree. And yet, she also reminded Mara of a neighbor from the settlement where she spent time with Elias and his wife, an elderly woman who crabbed and yelled about her aches and her illnesses, but would gentle and smile when a kindness was repeated.

"Do your branches touch the ceiling of this cave?"

An angry sob tore through the Tree before she said, "Yes, but the keepers cut my branches, keep them short, shorn, within this tower. It's my roots that wrap around the whole city."

Mara wanted to ask about the weakest point in the prison. But she also needed to know how or if the cave city depended on the tower for protection in any way. Instead she said, "Can you tell me how you came to be in this place?"

The Tree shrugged her massive shoulders. "I've been searching for you, using this form so I may move among all the humans."

A woman with a silver braid past her waist stood, head bowed, in one of the doorways. Instead of a dress, she wore a tunic and leggings in white linen, her feet covered in thin, one-strap sandals. "Great Mother, while you rest I will speak with the Daughter, bring her to understanding about our home."

Wavering, the Tree again dropped a heavy hand on Mara's shoulder. "Daughter, you will not leave."

"Not until you are free," Mara said and swallowed hard. It was the promise she needed to give, compulsion or not.

The Tree disappeared, leaving Mara alone with the other woman.

"May I offer you some refreshment?" the woman asked. "Some tea or water? Perhaps a room where you might wash?"

She remained at the far side of the room but angled her face toward Mara. "The others will want to meet you. But you can take a few moments to refresh yourself."

"Thank you, yes. I'd be grateful," Mara said.

"This way." The woman gestured for Mara to follow her into an archway on the far right of the room. "We have guest quarters for pilgrims. A bit austere, but clean and comfortable."

"How long have you served, been with, uh, the Tree, here in Alandalus?" Mara's question tumbled out as awkward as she felt, her pack and sword clanking softly in the plain stone hallway. Up ahead, doors appeared at regular intervals on the right, the hall following a broad curve.

The woman moved slowly with a slight limp, as though she had pain in her hip or leg. She glanced back at Mara's question but didn't answer right away. After a few more steps she said, "More than fifty years. I was a young dendrologist then, and I'd also been taking classes in xenobiology. I journeyed here to study and to learn."

After a few more steps, the woman stopped and opened a door. "This is the room She chose for you. When you're ready, I'll be in the common room."

"Thank you," Mara said. "I'm Mara."

216

"We know." The woman gave a small smile and continued down the hall.

Dropping heavily into a chair, Mara unlaced her boots and removed them, socks too. The air in the room was cool but pleasant, with an earthy, underground smell. The bed looked inviting, a pale tan woven coverlet pulled back at the top to show white sheets and pillowcases. Woven reed mats, or some synthetic version of reed mats, covered the floor wall-to-wall. They shifted slightly as Mara stood and walked over to the bed to empty her pack. Just as well she dump her belongings over most of the surface, or she'd give in to temptation and lie down for a nap. Even without the weight of the pack, her shoulders felt tight and heavy.

Instead of a window, a large glowing square provided light. It reminded her of the wall in Sangita's office, where she displayed the giant image of a Tree. Two wooden chairs with plain cushions flanked a small table.

Mara propped her sword against the other chair. To the left of the doorway, and sharing an outside wall with the hall, was a small washroom with a sink, toilet, and shower. She could resist sleeping a while longer, but Mara couldn't resist the option of a quick shower.

Refreshed but hungry, Mara dressed in her cleanest clothes, a spare O Squad uniform. It was rumpled from being in her pack, but only worn once. Thinking of the other women she'd seen, Mara left her hair down, put her boots back on, added the new knife to her belt, and went in search of her hostess.

True to her word, the veteran dendrologist waited in the common room at a round table laid with food and drink. Two of the other women waited with her.

"Mara," she called, "please join us."

The light was dim at the edges of the room but slightly brighter in the center over the table. Mara walked slowly, assessing the room for threats. No one was visibly armed except for herself, and only three other people were in the room, eating at a table near the edge of the light.

"I trust your room is acceptable," the woman said as Mara hesitated behind the open chair. She just didn't want to take off her sword. Something wasn't right. So she sat a bit awkwardly, on the edge of the seat.

"Yes, it's fine, thank you."

"You've come to free the Tree Mother then?" the woman directly to the left asked. She had bright, pale blue eyes in a thin face, her dark hair pulled back with a single headband.

The other new face nodded. Her tan cheeks were round as were her brown eyes. But her expression was strangely unanimated and unfocused.

Mara looked at the hostess. "What do you prefer to be called?"

With a deep sigh, the older woman smoothed her braid and shifted in her chair. "Those of us who were called to this work or given to it," she smiled at the two other women, "we are called Daughter or, in my case, Mother."

"On Iloel the call takes many forms, and females from every station are dedicated to serving the great Mother Tree. To serve in her home is to give your identity over to her and live only in unison, in harmony with your sisters."

When the other two nodded again, Mara asked, "Are you in some kind of rapport?"

The dendrologist's eyes widened in surprise. "What do you know of this?"

Like the first day in Professor Iskindar's class. Mara felt unsure of how to proceed or how to behave. She stalled by tearing a piece of brown bread from the loaf that the girl with round cheeks was eating from and took a tiny bite.

"I had a little communication with the Mother Tree on Asattha," Mara said. "Rapport is sometimes developed by those whose families have lived many generations on that planet. At least in the parts where the Tree has groves and seeds."

"Ah. We only know a little of the other Trees," the girl with round cheeks said. Her voice had a slightly hollow tone to it, but she did look at Mara when she spoke.

The bread was just a bit warm, chewy, and delicious. Mara tore off a larger hunk this time and added a smear of butter as the others had. Since the other women hadn't touched the tea at the center of the table, she washed the bite down with water from her own bottle.

"Could you tell me about the situation here?" Mara asked. Her need to help the Tree wasn't a secret, and it wasn't time bound either, despite her wish to be away from Iloel and back with Dalin.

"The situation, yes." The woman called Mother nodded and tilted her head, as though listening. "The Tree is not a deity, not all powerful, not a goddess. But she is one of only a few sentient species, truly sentient, outside of humans, that's been discovered."

The woman with pale blue eyes poured the tea into cups and handed them around.

"Oh the xenobiologists had such a field day when the Tree first made herself known on Asattha. My goodness, those articles make for wonderful reading." The Mother took a long sip of tea and nodded her thanks to the woman on her right.

Mara waited until both other women began drinking to take a tiny sip herself. The dark tea was both spicy and sweet but creamy, as though milk had already been added.

"The other Trees chose to remain hidden from humans for one reason or another. The Tree of Iloel waited more than a hundred years before she chose to communicate. This Tree liked the families who sought shade under her branches, who brought children to play around her roots. She sympathized with their plight, their desire to remain hidden from the monarch of the time, away from the mining and the fighting far to the north.

"She knew how to hide. It was a natural offer, made with only one caveat. That each generation dedicate daughters to the Tree's health and to preserving the human, the caretaking side that is, of the human bargain."

Mara had a lot of questions, many of them tactical, but what came out of her mouth was, "Why only daughters?"

The woman with the tea pitcher topped off her own cup and said, "The Tree does not identify as female in the human sense. But to her, the human producers of life are the females."

Queen Vanora was a destroyer of life. And taking down the energy shield would free the Tree but leave the city vulnerable to the Queen's forces.

The overhead light dimmed and brightened. All three women stood, pushing in their chairs. Mara followed suit, disappointed about leaving the bread and tea.

"The next group has gathered and it's time to receive offerings. Thank you, daughters." Mother dismissed the two women with a nod. "My apologies, Mara, that was not a full meal. We will gather, all of us together, after the final offerings of the day. For now, I should like to show you 'the situation,' as you requested."

She turned and walked quickly toward an arched doorway on the opposite side of the circle from where the sleeping quarters were. The lights dimmed and brightened again as over a dozen women in white robes poured through the common room and rushed toward the curtained doorway to the amphitheater. Like the two at the table, they walked in a coordinated way, a near-perfect unison.

Mara couldn't sense the minds of any of them, and given that her soldier's senses were still tingling with unease, she didn't want to enter rapport here.

They moved swiftly down another carved corridor, away from the center of activity. The hallway grew quieter as they moved and the space between doors increased. At the end, the woman opened a heavy wooden door and motioned Mara through. Pinpricks of light in the high ceiling revealed a curved wooden structure, so massive, it was hard to see even as Mara's eyes adjusted. The rotten smell was stronger here and grew even worse as she walked forward to place one hand on what appeared to be the hull of a huge boat.

The moment her hand connected, Mara whipped it away as though burned. She whirled to face her escort. "This is a root!"

"Yes."

"It's polluted, she can't—" Mara suppressed a gag. "She can't find clean nutrients here."

"Yes." The woman's eyes were shiny with tears. "You see the Tree's side of the problem. Come with me and I'll show you the human side as well."

She opened the far door, mostly rust with a few patches of painted metal, and motioned Mara into a completely different room.

"Some aspects of the Tree's tower are controlled from here," she said, gesturing to three rows of workstations and several large screens. The place looked like little in Mara's experience, except perhaps the research kiosks in the library of the Mess. Only a handful of the workstations were occupied, and none of the workers had a sword, at least from what she could see.

The mother tapped the nearest worker on the shoulder, a man wearing a blue turban. She spoke to him in what Mara thought was Origin Hindi until the man nodded and turned to tap at the keys on his workstation. In a moment, the air above him filled with a three-dimensional map. At the top right was an image of a Tree with red arrows flowing out from it, forming a circle that encompassed the perimeter. At even intervals around the circle of red arrows was a series of red circles.

"Those are the monitoring towers that make sure the shield stays whole." The man in the turban stood and rotated the map as he spoke, his Origin English clipped. "Take down one, the circle can compensate. Take down two or three, not consecutive"—he blinked and frowned—"not adjacent, and the whole thing collapses. Alandalus would be visible to satellite imaging for the first time in more than a century."

Visible meant exposure for the Tree and danger for all the families living in the city.

Chapter 25

In the dense late afternoon crowds of the Lower Town market, Dalin had to walk single file behind Geraldo. It had been a hard few nights of tracking data and poring over reports, followed by restless sleep and long days of teaching combat classes. Today was the day Rafiq said the ship would be ready. It was only seventy-two hours until the tournament, but they could make it.

"Look at that." The cook pointed above the people toward the nearly finished stadium. "How they gonna get that done in three days?"

"I've heard workers are coming in from all parts of Laska," Dalin said. "Coming in by train, mostly."

Geraldo grunted but didn't say anything until they reached a heavily stocked fruit and vegetable stand. "We'll see you after this craziness begins?"

Dalin came around to stand next to the cook. He brought what looked like a ripe, red tomato to his nose and inhaled. Perfect. Instead of answering Geraldo's question, he said, "I was thinking about a vegetable curry, with Thai flavors." He just wanted to create for a while, take a break from his nearly constant spying, teaching, and training schedule.

"Yeah? How spicy?" The cook was only a bit shorter than Dalin so he didn't really turn, so much as open up one shoulder in his direction.

Dalin hefted a green squash and examined the vertical ridges. Some variant of zucchini. "Depends on what you're making. If you're doing a spicy special, I can make this a milder, sweeter curry. If you're not going spicy tonight, I can turn up the heat."

Geraldo pursed his lips and nodded. "I've got coconut milk and lemongrass, that work for you?"

"Depending on how much you have, we could also use the coconut milk in a dessert option."

"Done," the cook said. "But I want to go down to the stand from Hépíng Xīng; they've got the best pan Asian vegetables and fresh herbs.

Dalin's eyes lit up. "Really? I didn't know Hépíng Xīng did much exporting."

"Lotta new folks in town, *cabrón.* Look around you." Waving his meaty hand, Geraldo indicated the flowing mass of people around them. "The stand went up last week. So I talked to the woman and she says a couple hundred visas were issued to merchants and important folks from their capital. Be staying through the tournament and beyond. If they want to establish a permanent stand, it's a different process, but I intend to be a steady customer for as long as it lasts."

As he spoke, Geraldo was pushing through the crowd, his bulk carving a wide path for Dalin. Now that his attention had been directed toward the newcomers, it was easy to spot the people in the crowd continually gawking and looking around or moving aimlessly, rather than with purpose like the residents.

Clouds heavy with rain were building to the east, and the renewed wind sent welcome gusts through the clusters of moving people. Many parts of Lower Town smelled like unwashed humans, but the market held too many spice stands, fruit stands, leather stands, meat stands, and grain stands to take on a stink. Instead it was the most glorious assault on his nose, the breeze enhancing the mix and bringing hints of mint, pungent *lorentos,* saffron, and *naan* fresh from the stone ovens in baker's alley.

After acquiring several interesting items from the Hépíng Xīng stand, the two chefs opted for a different route back to the eating house. Turning the corner and striding into the large open air heart of the market, Geraldo came to a sudden stop, so sudden that Dalin nearly walked right into his broad back.

The center space of the market, formerly occupied by dozens of food carts and cook stands, held instead a huge, circular holoplatform screened in by a dome of fine wire mesh. The structure emitted a low humming sound. When transmitting, the images generated through the holoplatform would be enormous, taller and wider than the entire dining room at Cousins.

As they watched, one of Queen Vanora's propaganda messages began. "Citizens," called a disembodied voice. "Citizens! Your Queen has heeded the call for more access to the upcoming tournament." A huge three-dimensional projection of Vanora's head appeared over the platform, causing most of the people across the open square to stop and watch. "This holoplatform and many more like it have been erected across Crown City for your viewing pleasure." While the words continued on, the image changed to a bird's-eye view zooming over Crown City.

The message ended with a ringing trill of music, and when the final image faded, the crowd broke into a cacophony of response in multiple languages. Dalin allowed himself to be pressed forward until he could touch the platform. Made from thin metal, it was probably flexible enough to handle the vibrations of holoprojection over time.

A guard wearing the Commonwealth colors tapped his shoulder. "That's close enough."

"C'mon, kid," Geraldo said with an annoyed huff. "Cousins is empty so we gotta get back."

Busy thinking about the holoplatform and what its power source might be, Dalin didn't process what the cook had said for a few minutes. But as they emerged into a quieter, less-crowded street and turned toward the eating house, he asked, "Empty? Where's Rafiq? We're supposed to—"

"Tell you when we get back."

They walked for a few more minutes, baskets full of produce, including a few leafy herbs Dalin had never used before. Geraldo's response was bothering him, his mind now replaying their whole interaction.

He waited as the cook unlocked the front door and trudged into the kitchen, flipping on the fan and the lights. Dalin placed his basket on what was now his work area and asked again, "*Cocinero*, where's Rafiq?"

The big man began laying out each of his purchases along the pristine counter. He sighed and, without looking at Dalin, tied a clean apron around his waist.

"I'm not supposed to tell you. But you're not gonna believe any story I pull out of the air. It's complicated, but Rafe, he, ah, he has a lot of revenue streams. One is hiring out his ship and pilot skills for, what you might call, business ventures." Sweat beaded on the cook's forehead, but he stared right into Dalin's face. "Rafe got himself hired for a mission to Iloel. The trick was he had to leave immediately, late last night. He's going to recover Mara. At least we hope so. And you had to stay here because they might not get back before…" He waved a hand in the direction of the palace.

"The tournament," Dalin finished the sentence. Taking one step and then another, he forced himself to walk away from the sharp knives and heavy pans. Grabbing one of the nearly broken chairs from the stack of extras in the dining room, he smashed it into the syncrete floor. Pieces broke off and flew.

He was supposed to be on that ship.

Smash.

Mara was his to protect.

Smash.

He never should have trusted Rafiq, even if he allegedly worked with Jameson.

Smash.

The chair broke at the rivets but the metal and plastic components didn't shatter.

Not for a while.

* * *

"Are the monitoring towers vulnerable?" Mara asked, trying to suppress her desire to knock the towers down and be done with this mess.

The woman who called herself "Mother" and the man in the turban exchanged a look.

"That depends," the man said. He blew his nose on a handkerchief. "Excuse me," he muttered. Clearing his throat, he rotated the map until one of the tower circles faced the three of them. With a few taps, he made the tower a visible three-dimensional image. "You can see here," he pointed to the tower's base, "the outside is part of a wall."

It was an unremarkable wall formed of round tan and white field stones, maybe two levels tall. Raised one level higher, the round edge of the tower protruded less than two meters beyond the curve of the wall.

"But on the other side is an access door. This area is patrolled, but not guarded specifically, if you take my meaning." The mother placed one hand on his shoulder and leaned in to whisper. He favored her with a warm, fond smile.

"Rasesh and I have spent many hours together thinking about this puzzle," she said.

As she spoke, Rasesh tapped a different section of the map, and the inside face of the monitoring tower became visible.

"The Tree is trapped in two ways, one is through the shield towers. The second is through the physical containment in the cave."

Mara hadn't been able to shake the deep sense of wrong she'd felt touching the massive root of the Iloellian Tree. "What about the poison?" she asked. "Is that another trap? Another way to prevent her growth?" The syncrete floor and windowless walls couldn't block the foul haze that hung in the air.

The mother nodded, bringing her hands together and folding them under her chin. "Despite consistent testing and upgrades to our water purification and sanitation efforts, we've wondered if the poison is some kind of slow sabotage. We might be invisible from orbiting satellites, but the Queen's agents know about Alandalus. We've never had an outright attack, but the citizens have an evacuation plan. The Tree's erratic behavior the past few weeks has been causing small seismic disturbances, enough to empty out at least one section of the cave."

"It was three sections of the top level, Arlet," Rasesh corrected her. "Those closest to her tower."

Mara pulled and prodded the map until the amphitheater and the Tree's tower appeared in front of her.

The huge structure sat just inside the southwestern edge of the cave. Although some homes and businesses were clustered near the amphitheater, much of the business district was in the direct center of the circle while the residences hugged the upper levels and the eastern perimeter.

"What is this material?" Mara asked, pointing to the irregular, patched substance of the tower wall.

"Sandstone, a little syncrete here and there, some brick," Arlet said. "The wall isn't thick as it was meant to conceal, not restrain."

"Does it support the ceiling?" Mara traced the top section with her finger where the tower appeared to attach to the roof of the cave.

Rasesh tapped a few keys and changed the map view. They looked down on a small, but sprawling, town built on a hilly piece of ground, a small stream flowing along the eastern edge. On the southwestern side, a small grove of bushes and trees grew in an open space of wild grasses. Rasesh touched that unremarkable space and said, "This is as high as the Tree is allowed to grow. The top of the tower is open to the camouflage town above."

Frowning, Mara moved closer. She couldn't wrap her mind around the scale of this new map. "How big is the opening?"

"Just over ten meters in diameter."

Mara's stomach folded in on itself as her lips parted in shock. The Asatthan Tree was easily three or four times that large at the base. And for more than a hundred years this Tree had been cut back and restrained. No wonder she was so ill, so crazed.

"Does she have…are there groves with *gontra* trees and *gontra* pods in this area or any other part of the continent?" She braced herself for another terrible answer even as she asked.

"A few," Arlet said and Rasesh nodded. "They are far from here, almost to the coast. And they are guarded, a close-kept secret."

"If the researchers come, the city is discovered. If the city is discovered, the distance and freedom Iloel has earned from the Commonwealth through our false front of civil war and fanaticism would be lost." Rasesh touched the top of his turban with both hands and then brought them, palms flat and pressed together under his chin. "Now that Asattha has shaken loose of the Commonwealth's teeth, it is Iloel's turn."

Staring at the leafy treetop disguised as a nonsentient landscaping feature, Mara's focus sharpened. Her mission right now was to liberate the Iloellian Tree, as she had promised.

"The falling debris will be dangerous when the tower comes down. How long until the necessary sections of the cave can be evacuated?" Mara asked.

With a few taps and twists of the controls, he returned the map to the wide-angle city view. "These three sections are empty." He indicated the top levels near the tower.

"With a properly structured and communicated alert, we could get everyone out in under two days," Arlet said. "We've been waiting for the Tree to be ready, but to have the prophecy of the Daughter in our time, that's a sign we must heed."

The mention of the prophecy brought Dalin instantly to mind. How many days had they been out of contact? Was he getting reports about the action on Iloel? And if so, would the disappearance of half the O Squad have been noted?

Chapter 26

A day in the numbing silence and isolation of the Mess hadn't diminished Dalin's fury with Rafiq for leaving him behind. He flexed his bandaged hands and thought about how good it would feel to slam Rafiq into the floor until he broke like the cheap furniture in the eating house.

Tonight was weapons training at La Kill, so he carried a full bag of blades along with sticks, nunchuks, and a fighting staff. His sword was belted at his hip, the pommel under the top of his shirt.

If he got ambushed in Lower Town, he'd switch to the new techniques he'd learned at the fight school. It wasn't entirely unlikely that one of his teachers would incite a street fight for training purposes.

Modified Commonwealth Wu Shu was more of a flow style then what Jin had trained him to use for ancient Taekwando. He also liked the energy of Aikido with its concern for keeping the opponent from harm. Not knowing who he'd be matched against in the tournament, Dalin worked with as many different instructors and partners at La Kill as Shanshan and Bahran allowed.

Along with technique, Dalin had been working on his breathing and really strengthening his mental shields. Someone at La Kill had strong push telepathy and had begun pushing distracting images, mainly from the Protector Project, at his mind during fights.

One of his first nights Dalin had asked about Iloel, wondering what Mara might be facing.

"Depends," Bahran had said. "Up in the capital, and near the mines, the groups like it dirty—punch-ya-face, kick-ya-ass type stuff. No weapons though. Down south, there's the energy weapons and some blades." He'd punched Dalin so quickly, he barely got a hand up to deflect it, and nearly simultaneously thrown a vicious kick to his inner thigh.

The memory sent a rush of adrenaline through his veins. He bounced on the balls of his feet, waiting for the heavy iron door to open after he gave the password. The tea room held eleven people, the first training room another nine. Every single person worked, stretched, or sat alone. La Kill was not a place to make friends and it wasn't a social club.

In the next room, Dalin stacked his weapons in one corner and quickly pulled off his boots and socks while keeping his back to the wall and watching some of the other fighters enter the training space. Round one of the tournament was rumored to be a melee of some sort and he thought he'd be fully dressed, including boots. But the official rounds for participants and final rules wouldn't be posted until the next day.

Stepping away from the wall, Dalin drew his sword and began a simple sword form. His legs were warm from the walk, but his arms needed to warm up as well. At La Kill standing in the middle of the mat was the same as announcing you were ready for the next fight. Class started in eight minutes, but anyone in the room could jump him if they wanted to right now and be within the club's rules.

He'd welcome the distraction of a quick fight, anything to keep him out of his own head and the endless string of worst-case scenarios for Mara his imagination kept producing.

"Ladies and gentlemen," said Shanshan. "We will begin tonight's session with a preview of the tournament's first-round rules. Join us in the fountain court in three minutes." The fight master walked out the door, her long black ponytail rippling down her back.

The water had stopped running, so the bubbler was quiet. Dalin brought everything with him to the larger room and found a wall to lean against. Bahran entered through the near door and stopped in the center of the room. He tapped his wrist and a notification appeared in the air.

"They're gonna run fifteen rounds, hundred people in each to start," he said. "No weapons."

Many students groaned at that part, and Bahran made a sharp cutting motion with one hand to stop them.

"How many times have I told you any weapon you have can be used against you? This is good, really good." He scanned the notification and cleared his throat.

"First round is just survival. No style points. They're rigging out the new stadium with colored flags around the top of the wall. Guards up there too. Contestants have to fight through the crowd, run the steps, and grab a flag before they're gone."

"How many—?" someone shouted.

"Hold please," Bahran said. "Mistress Shanshan, do you have a diagram for us?"

A small holo projector rose from the center of the now-dry bubbler. After several audible clicks, a glowing light resolved into a three-dimensional image of the new stadium. Many in the crowd of fighters shuffled forward, peering at the projection. Curiosity tempered some of Dalin's anger, but it was hard to keep focused when he was hoping for news about Mara.

The stadium had a high-low design running around its entire top perimeter. Each low spot was three bricks wide, the high spots were six bricks wide.

Crenellated, Dalin thought, wondering if anyone else in the room knew the word.

"Our sources say the flags will be at these intervals, though possibly not all of them." Shanshan said, pointing to the low spots. "Any registered contestant holding a flag at the end of the round will move on to the next round."

"Each round is timed. Nine minutes." Bahran continued summarizing the rules. "And rounds is split, eight on day one, seven on day two. Half between 0700 and 0900 in the morning. Half between 1700 and 1900, or thereabouts, at night."

Mutters sprung up among several clusters of fighters, the three in front of Dalin talking about fighting in the earlier part of the day versus the later part.

"Oh and they've got a thirty-minute break between each round. To reset the flags."

"Or to pick up the bodies," Shanshan added.

Dalin raised his hand.

"Yes?" Bahran asked.

"How many flags per round?"

"They're not sayin', but we think about twenty."

Shanshan nodded slowly, her dark eyes scanning the crowd.

"That would put three hundred forward into the next round." Bahran said. "Fifteen hundred is good to start, for goodwill and such. And no weapons means the twelve hundred going home do so in one piece."

"No guarantees," said one of the female fighters near the projector.

Dalin raised a hand again. When Bahran nodded at him, he said, "Do the rules mention what happens to contestants as they're eliminated?" Acid burned at the base of his throat as he pictured the hospital of "dismissed" students.

"Didn't you read the fine print when you registered?" a man sneered. "It's at the discretion of them that's running the tournament, some portion of the Queen's Council."

"I did read it, *then*." Dalin emphasized the word. "But nearly every other 'rules and requirements' document has changed since. I just wondered if this particular set of rules mentions anything about the losers."

Bahran shook his head. "Not in this one, no." He took a moment to look many of the fighters in the eyes, person by person. "If you don't get a flag in the first round, best keep your wits about you. That being said," he rocked back on his heels and pressed his palm against his chest, "I'm confident everyone in this room can make it through a little weaponless scuffle."

"Rounds will be grouped by contestant numbers. All of that will be posted and sent out tomorrow morning." Shanshan clapped her hands together loudly once and smiled, slow and menacing. "Change of plans, no weapons tonight. Get those stowed and back here in five."

As Dalin limped up the hill much later that night, his wrist unit buzzed. The message header said, "Lecture Notes."

He didn't open it right away, wanting a more secluded place to read. Few transports or autos were out this late, but his instincts said this was a message to read in private.

It hadn't rained in several days and the grasses and trees around the private residences had pulled back to themselves, making the scents of fruit and flowers harder to distinguish. When they'd first arrived in Crown City, Dalin could still remember the scents of Satri, the brine from the Gulf and the rich *gontra* permeating everything. But now these were the only smells his memory could furnish.

Still, the dry air felt fresh against his skin, especially after the sweat-soaked humidity of the group fights at the club. Lowering himself to sit on a retaining wall tucked around to one side of a fine residence, Dalin opened the message. It was an article, written by Dr. Elsebet Iskindar, about the first King of the Commonwealth, outlining his vision for security and describing in unflinching detail each of the seven war experiments. On his second read, Dalin noticed that the text was fuzzy in places, just certain letters and numbers scattered throughout the article.

With a little concentration, Dalin was able to assemble five words and a time from the fuzzy bits.

King's Men, sworn, loyalty, plan, 0530.

It was going to be another short night.

Chapter 27

Mara needed to see the wall and the perimeter for herself. In minutes, the two girls she'd met with Arlet presented themselves as escorts.

"Do you use a name here?" Mara asked, not wanting to place her trust in these strangers without at least knowing their names.

"I am called Dita and this is Gracyn." Dita pointed to the taller female with the pale face and smooth dark hair. Both girls hurried to keep up with Mara's long strides.

"And you're in some kind of rapport with each other, the acolytes, and the Tree?"

Gracyn blinked and tilted her head to one side. "Yes, it is a precious gift we receive for our service."

"Do you have any combat training?" Mara asked. "Is that part of your lives here?"

"It is a peaceful life," Gracyn said.

A peaceful life was deceiving and did not excuse a lack of preparation. Suddenly the lessons of the fights in the Box became real. Sometimes a soldier did enter a fight alone. The terrain would be uncertain and the rules of engagement liable to change. But at the Mess, Mara had never been asked to keep unarmed civilians safe while she engaged with an enemy. And she knew she was much more fierce with someone or something to protect. The late Queen's Champion had learned that the hard way.

As they raced out of the tunnel, Mara strained to glimpse the Tree's main prison. "Dita, can you point toward the physical trunk of the Tree?" Both women swung smoothly, like compass needles, to point southeast. Dry, knee-high grass covered the rolling swells and hills around them.

Mara led the two women closer to the wall, keeping it within less than a meter of her left shoulder. An enemy would need to come over the wall to get to them or approach through the high grass in the other three directions. The nearest cover was the tower in front of them, the shed behind them, and a stand of scrub trees more than one hundred meters to the right.

The late afternoon sun blazed above and though the air wasn't as hot as downtown Samradi, it was still warm.

"It's the dry season," Dita said, her footfalls crunching in the sharp grass. "This area hasn't seen rain in more than a month."

"The farther you get from the coast, the dryer it is," Gracyn agreed.

Mara wanted to ask about fire danger, but a shadow moving along the tower wall caught her attention. She squinted and leaned forward into a jog. A soft thud sounded ahead and Mara shifted into a full run. "Stay as close as you can," she called over her shoulder.

A louder boom came from within the tower as Mara rounded the edge, looking for the door. Just on the other side of the curve, the remains of the door dangled from broken hinges. She pulled up sharply, senses on high alert.

As Dita and Gracyn jogged up behind her, breath heaving loudly, a single figure wearing a form-fitting black and gray suit, face covered in a gray mask, bolted through the doorway. The figure jumped past Mara and landed a hard kick in Dita's stomach, swinging around to clothesline Gracyn across the neck. Both crumpled as Mara pulled her sword free and chased after the stranger. But the figure was up and over the wall before she could take two steps. Rage tingled and danced through her bloodstream, and Mara took deep breaths to bring herself down. Nothing would be gained by pursuit, not right now.

Instead the trio double-timed it back. Mara kept on high alert but saw no people or signs of people along their route. She left Gracyn and Dita to report the situation and went to meet Halifax and Raymundo.

The two guys waited at the hovercar, faces and bodies tense. "An evacuation message is being broadcast in at least ten languages," Raymundo burst out as Mara approached.

"We didn't want to leave without you, but we've got to go," Halifax said.

"I was with the team that triggered the message," Mara said, coming to a stop facing them. "But before we evacuate, I need your help."

Halifax tilted his head, squinting at her past his sharp nose. "Our help with what, exactly?"

"Do you remember the tiny tree in the gatepost? That's how they power the shield over Alandalus, by imprisoning parts of the Iloellian Tree. We need to disable two additional monitoring towers. Preferably now."

"Two *additional* towers?" Raymundo asked, eyebrows raised. He adjusted his pack and shifted his stance. "*Qué pasó, chica?*"

"Is the hovercar secured? Do you have all your gear? I'll brief you on the way." When they followed her with only slight hesitation, Mara breathed a sigh of relief.

"Why this mission?" Halifax asked as they walked away from the garage.

"I'll explain, but first, what's the sitrep?"

As they walked down the hill toward the amphitheater, Raymundo began by talking about how few families they'd encountered. "Seriously, almost no one under fifteen anywhere. It's strange."

"When people have children, they pool their money to move out of the cave and into those suburbs we saw," Halifax added. "Something about the air in the cave being unhealthy. It stinks even worse down here, by the way." He pulled the neck of his shirt up over his nose and took an exaggerated breath. "I'm going to be sorry we ate at that food stall."

"So this whole place is a massive trade center," Raymundo said, throwing one arm out wide. "It's like the docks where we grew up or the s'port in Crown City. People and goods in and out all the time. No news about the O Squad."

"Anyone who knows has evacuated or isn't telling," Halifax agreed. "But we did get a few referrals for transport out of here."

They slowed as they got closer to the empty benches of the amphitheater. None of the acolytes were visible and the curtains in the archways hung closed. Mara paused to tap the exposed tree root with the toe of her boot.

"This is one part of the root system of the Iloellian Tree," she said, pitching her voice low to prevent being overheard. The street was nearly deserted, just a few vendors packing away wares. "It's not like this in Satri, um, the capital of Asattha, where I'm from. The Great Tree of Satri is happy and benevolent. She is tended to, nurtured, and most decisions about the city are made with strong consideration for how the action, even something temporary like a festival, will impact her."

Mara moved just a little closer, motioning Halifax and Raymundo in. "Here, it's the opposite. The Tree has been imprisoned for more than one hundred years—"

"Before the official collapse of the war experiment?" Halifax interrupted. "So someone knew Iloel had a Tree and never reported it?"

Raymundo nodded slowly. "That makes sense with what we found. So many factions have a presence here. And not just from Iloel, other planets in the Commonwealth. I caught a hint of visitors from or at least those who have contact with people from the Origin system. From Earth or maybe Mars."

The Commonwealth had seven habitable planets, but Earth's system, the first system to support human life, only had two, three including Earth's moon. Mara had never once imagined contact outside the Commonwealth. Could that mean, was it possible, that a government, a leader from outside might have more power than Vanora?

"That's fascinating," Mara murmured, forcing her mind back to the mission. "We have the blessing and the help of the head Tree acolyte. Disabling the monitoring towers harms the Tree only slightly, but the pain and destruction are enough to violate the acolytes' vows. Otherwise they would have handled this themselves decades ago."

"So they picked you, the Daughter, to set her free," Raymundo said.

A protest died, half-formed on Mara's lips. Instead she said, "Whatever the people here think I might be, at the end of the day, I'm a soldier trained to protect."

Just then, Dita burst through one of the archways. "Mara," she called. "Please come quickly."

Chapter 28

At three minutes before the requested meeting time, Dalin knocked on Professor Iskindar's office door. Gazing down the empty corridor, he wondered about the location of the professor's living quarters.

"Come," Elsebet Iskindar's voice was deeper and huskier than usual this morning.

Dalin pushed through the door and closed it behind him. The professor's dark face had a faint gray tinge, the silver at her temples more pronounced. Her clothes were somber and plain again, no clattering bangles or bright ear hoops. What was new was the heavy silver cylinder worn openly at her waist. Without saying another word, she stalked to the secret entrance and pulled the bookcase aside.

Following behind, Dalin closed the first entrance and then the second as the professor activated the room's shields. In the early morning dark, the headquarters was cluttered but light enough from the automatic lamps. He hoped for a day when he could explore the mysteries in this room.

"Have you sustained a head injury?" Her expression was flat and without humor.

"No," Dalin said. The last time he'd been here it smelled strongly of plaster and old brick. Today he smelled leather.

"Do you owe somebody money, a lot of money?"

"No," Dalin said again. Some of the stray books had been re-shelved since his last visit. He wondered who else used this space, what other King's Men spent time at the Mess and the palace.

"Then why, in the name of the first King and all that is bright in the Universe, did you register for the tournament?" Elsebet

Iskindar's black eyes were gleaming now, her outrage filling the space between them.

His shoulders wanted to slump at the heavy censure, but he forced them to stay straight and didn't break eye contact, his own anger uncurling in his belly. "I found a hospital. A hidden hospital. The rows of beds were full of students that we were told washed out of training and got sent home."

The professor shifted her feet and gripped the table edge. "Go on."

"It's not far from the palace complex, but someone's taken pains to keep it out of the public eye. Given what the Queen will do in public, that alone is cause for concern. If Mara hadn't been drugged and beaten the champion, she might have ended up in that place—"

"It's not the only one," Dr. Iskindar said, a hint of sympathy flashing across her face, there and gone. She sighed, one hand straying to the weapon on her belt.

"The propaganda says that Laska never really had its own war project because the royal troops were quartered and trained here and that was action enough to dissuade aggression. But recruits from across the Commonwealth signed, not three years, but their entire lives away when they enrolled at the Mess."

"I read the contract," Dalin continued, his eyebrows pulling together in consternation. "Five years in school, three years' term of service with the option for renewal on either side."

"Do you remember when you arrived that the contracts for your group weren't in the alphabetical stack? That much of your paperwork had been misfiled?"

Realization dawned as the professor continued. "Rather than call attention by only changing two contracts, I forged three dozen new contracts for everyone on your recruiting shuttle with the fine print about lifetime servitude, at the Queen's discretion, removed."

"Thank you," Dalin said.

"Well, it doesn't matter now, you fool. You committed yourself to the end of your life when you signed the tournament forms."

Etiquette dictated that Dalin remain standing while a person, especially a woman of higher rank, stood. But like the hot pain of being kicked in the balls, the professor's words made him want to double over and retch. Instead he walked a bit unevenly to one of the burgundy leather wing chairs and dropped into the lumpy seat.

He'd been so frightened, so angry when he registered, he hadn't read as carefully as he should have. The words had seemed essentially the same as his first contract so he'd skimmed to the bottom and signed with a flourish. Mara was MIA, and it just as well could've been her in one of those beds. That was all he was thinking about, how he needed to continue the mission even if she was gone.

"The people need a champion," he said. "Mara is the champion of the Tree and her sisters. But the Commonwealth has two sentient species and the other one is us. Humans."

Curiosity came over the professor's face and she gave a slight nod. She tapped her index finger against her lips. "Keep talking," she said. "I'm going to check something in one of the reference texts."

Dalin slumped forward, his elbows on his knees, face in his hands. He took a deep breath, willing his empty stomach to settle. When he looked up, the professor had pulled up a virtual folder and was flicking through the table of contents.

"What is that?" he asked.

"You were telling me about the temporary insanity that led you to register for the tournament," she said, instead of answering.

"We chose our mission. We wanted to get close to the center of it all, find out who was signing the orders to increase casualties in the other war experiments. Get every last one closed down somehow. Mara feels…we feel responsible for the increases since War Project Seven ended." He closed his eyes, visualizing the night Mara came to his room at NW Protector House to talk about her idea, trying to find a way to work with the compulsion from the Tree.

That night, she'd worn her hair down and he'd just wanted to touch her without the Tree interfering with his brain. He wouldn't admit it out loud, but he'd hoped if they left Asattha together, both their compulsions would disappear.

Well, Dalin had gotten his wish. And Mara was in mortal danger because of it.

"We let them recruit us to get ourselves closer to the Queen and her Council. When I thought she was… When she disappeared on Iloel, I couldn't think what to do, how to go on except to continue what we'd started. As a junior instructor, I have no access to the council or decisions being made. But the Queen's Champion does. So I entered the tournament."

The professor looked at him then back to the text in front of her. "The conversations with the Great Tree about a champion or pair of champions who would shift the balance of the Commonwealth back to the Light were a bit strange. In some things, she was clear about that time period and who or what was significant. Here." She tapped the page and it enlarged. "Here she says, 'Darkness enfolds the champions but can't extinguish their Light.' And here." She tapped a paragraph farther down. "The Tree says 'champions for us all.'"

Her frown deepened and Dalin recognized the signs of scholarly intensity when the quest for an answer was elusive. "The references to a champion, female, born on Asattha, are much more clear and much more frequent in the texts."

"Hence the King's Men tracking Mara to the Protector Project and wreaking havoc on innocent people," Dalin said.

"Ponapali ran that operation," Professor Iskindar said, looking back to the text. She highlighted the two sections she'd referenced, her eyes narrowed and angry again. "We work in independent cells for the most part. Which you would have learned, had you not committed suicide."

"You came to Satri, enrolled in a language class—"

"I wanted to meet her." The anger lines in her forehead softened. "When she was a child, she, we… Well, no one knew for sure."

"Ponapali took orders from you. Innocent lives were lost—"

"You said the Daughter is your cause. As she is mine, because she will bring peace." The professor flipped virtual pages until she stopped and jabbed a finger at a specific passage. "Some lives will be lost, yes. But how many more will live?"

They stood in silence, the thin morning light filtering through the high windows. Months ago, Dalin wouldn't have dreamed of facing off against his idol, the greatest historian of the age. But he was bruised and tired and needed to go about his day, his last day before the tournament began.

"In the first round get a red flag," Professor Iskindar said.

"A red flag," Dalin repeated.

"Stay alive," she ordered.

He couldn't help grinning at that, and slowly she smiled in return. "That's the plan."

* * *

Dita leapt into the aisle and was halfway up before stopping short at the sight of the two other soldiers with Mara.

"Dita, this is Halifax and Raymundo. We're a team. You can trust them."

The acolyte's body twitched then swayed, the layers of her white dress shifting as she moved. Her eyes closed, her soft brown cheeks warming to a rosy pink. "Yes." She nodded sharply before opening her eyes. "Come with me."

In a low voice to her companions, Mara said, "This facility is entirely female but they do have visitors' quarters—"

Halifax said, "All female? The matriarchal culture surrounding the Tree species is fascinating. Do you think they might—"

"Unless you speak Tree, they won't talk to you 'Fax," Raymundo said. "Me on the other hand, I speak many languages." He grinned broadly and puffed out his chest.

From the archway on the far right, Dita motioned frantically for them to follow. The trio caught up to her in a few steps, following closely as she led them down one of the halls to the darkened roots room and into the data center.

Rasesh and Arlet stood in nearly the same places where she'd left them hours earlier.

"Gentlemen," Arlet said without preamble. "Do you have any experience with explosives?"

The center of Mara's chest went cold. They didn't need explosives to disable the two monitoring towers, just an axe.

Raymundo said, "My cousin is a demolition expert. I know some of what he knows from working with him."

"Do you know what this is?" Rasesh asked, tapping a section of the holographic display and enlarging it to show an object about the size of a dinner plate.

While Raymundo stepped into the display to take the shape into his hands and manipulate it, Halifax asked, "Why? What makes you think this will cause an explosion?"

Rasesh moved to a different console and brought up the image of the camouflage town with the opening for the top of the Tree. "If we're going to free the Tree from the shield, we will also need to widen this opening so that she has more access to fresh air and sunlight. We've been monitoring the integrity of the cave dome in this area." He drew a red circle around the branches.

"At almost the exact moment you encountered the intruder at the nearest tower," Arlet said, picking up the story, "our visual sweeps detected a circle of these on the underside of the dome, a loose ring around where the opening would eventually need to be widened."

"It's not an explosive," Raymundo said, "as far as I can tell. See?" He flipped the image upside down and touched the flat surface. "No room for much of a payload. Did you run an image search yet? I'm thinking it's an emitter, probably sonic."

Halifax stepped into the image while Rasesh typed at the console. "I think I saw something like this when I was looking at the old mining files." He tapped his nose and looked down. When he looked up, his eyes were bright with concern. "It might help to narrow the image search to sonic mining tools. The miners had something like this on a remote trigger because it pulverized the solid matter around it to dust. That was great at first, but they found what wasn't pulverized was weakened, destabilized. Caused accidents. I don't know what happened after that. Miners moved onto some other tool or strategy most likely."

"What's the status of the evacuation?" Mara asked.

Arlet let out a breath as though she'd been holding it. "Good. Over fifty percent."

"Does the shield keep people in?" Mara looked at Rasesh. "We've only entered and exited through designated points. If people are in a mad rush—"

"It shouldn't keep them in, but—"

"Let's move," Mara said to Halifax and Raymundo. Driven by a need for action, she led the way up the stairs. Outside the door, she half expected to see more dark camouflage saboteurs, but it was the same empty expanse of wild, sharp grass spread out in both directions.

She wanted to disable the tower closest to the little town above the dome, and then see the cave opening for herself. "How far to the opening?"

"Every new initiate makes that trek," Dita said, coming up behind them. "It's about two hours' walk to the monitoring station in that direction and then you cut toward the center of the circle. It's about another hour's walk from there."

"Fifteen clicks," Halifax said.

"No way we can stay together and get this done," Raymundo said. "That dome's comin' down, *sí*? And even if it's just pulverized dust raining down, people gonna want to get out."

A heavy rumbling broke through the natural sounds around them. In the middle distance a large craft, metal glinting dully in the waning evening light, rose and blasted toward the sky.

"That's one way to get out," Halifax said.

Another rumble, this time much closer, vibrated through the soles of Mara's boots. "How close is the s'port?" she started to ask.

"It's the dome," Dita shrieked. "One of those, those emitters just went live and the others are lighting up." She clutched her head, eyelids fluttering.

The three soldiers exchanged a silent look. "I'll take her," Raymundo said. "See you back inside—"

"Back here," Mara interrupted. "By moonrise. If we don't make it, take your best transport option and go." She unslung her pack to dig out a wad of currency. Pressing the money into Raymundo's hand she said, "Good luck."

"You can get us there, right?" Halifax asked as they lurched into a fast jog.

Instead of opening herself to full rapport, Mara sent out just a tendril, picturing one tiny root pushing into the earth. After a few minutes she felt a pulse off to the southeast. She corrected their course to be more easterly and felt for the pulse again.

"I can sense the Tree. The monitoring tower has to be east, a little south, but mostly east of her."

As they ran, Mara relaxed, breathing slow and deep. It was a relief to have a clear objective. Once the shield went down, all the smugglers, thieves, their families, and anyone else who wanted or needed to could get out of Alandalus. If the sonic emitters were the devices Halifax thought they were, the cave city might never be safe again.

The Iloellian Tree would be exposed, but free.

That's what the Asatthan Mother Tree had asked of her. Free her sisters.

"I'm glad to be part of an evacuation effort," Halifax said, his breathing steady and even. "It's a far superior mission than multi-front urban combat in Samrahdi. But I really can't get a fix on who or which group is about what or trying to do what on this crazy planet. Ever since we got here, I keep recalibrating my thinking. Between the twining of the factions and the twisting of the politics, the history, it's stunning how much the Commonwealth didn't know."

As they jogged through the waist-high yellow grass, the ground began to slope gently upward. The last of the sunset dimmed behind them, their shadows skimming out across the open field.

"Someone knew," Mara said.

A deep crack split the air and the ground shuddered, throwing them to their knees. The dry earth hurt nearly as much as slapping her hands into rock. The blades of grass scored scratches on her palms as well as one cheek.

Far ahead a cloud of dust puffed high into the air.

"How much closer do you want to get?" Halifax asked regaining his feet and rubbing his hands on his pants.

"Closer than this." Mara wasn't sure if it was her imagination, or the proximity to the Tree, but as they ran, it felt like the ground was faintly trembling with every step.

The next concussion blasted up a section of the ground in front of them, opening a fissure and sending a plume of dust straight into the air.

"Monitoring tower," Mara shouted, changing course. Any human with sense would be evacuating the area, but the people below might be trapped by the shield unless they disabled it.

Sweat soaked through the long sleeves and waistband of her uniform pants. More sweat trickled down her neck, her damp braid slapping rhythmically as she ran. A slight breeze carried the rotten scent of the caged Tree. The grass crunched and snapped under their feet.

Halifax jogged along beside her, hands on the straps of his heavy pack. A long knife hung from one hip, a war axe from the other.

"If the Commonwealth is watching this area, since the extra troops were sent to Iloel..." He paused and ran for a few breaths. "When we take down this shield, the whole city will be exposed. Thermal imaging, whatever. But exposed."

"The citizens," Mara said. "They say they're ready to fight, if it comes to that."

Halifax grunted and staggered to a stop, his breath heavy and shallow. He pointed and said, "Is that it?"

Mara stopped as well, pulse thundering in her ears. Thank the Light. The tower stood alone and intact. "First ones here, I hope."

"Looks that way, but between that first tower and the dome above the Tree, some other team is—"

The tower door blew outward, the explosion sending wood fragments and debris thirty meters or more.

Both soldiers dropped to the ground, the grass waving above them the only available cover.

On her second deep breath Mara's ears popped and her stomach lurched as though she were falling.

"Did you feel that?" she whispered. "The shield is gone."

Chapter 29

Vanora stood on a raised platform in the middle of the barely finished stadium. Candidates filled the seats of the entire half that faced her. In the sand, directly in front of the platform, portable chairs had been arranged in two shallow semicircles, providing seating for forty. Ten *vishakanya* stood on the platform around their monarch, another six stood along the aisle between chairs.

The Queen wore a traditional gold sari decorated with black trim and tiny black faceted stones. Her dark hair was piled high, but even that, along with higher heels, did not create an impression of size. The *vishakanya* wore their uniforms of sleeveless, fitted black tunics over leggings with polished black boots. Only the ones in the aisle wore the elbow-length gloves. Vanora and the bodyguards around her had bare arms today.

Trumpets blared and Dalin, along with most of the others in his section, turned to watch the ambassadors file in. Names flashed across the score clock as each was introduced to Queen Vanora, bowed deeply, and was escorted to his or her seat by a *vishakanya*.

Familiar faces composed the group from Asattha, members of the Satri council, two of the highest ranking militia leaders, and the president of the largest university. Despite missing his parents, Dalin was glad they weren't part of the Asatthan delegation. It wasn't safe. Nothing and no one at the Mess was safe.

Most of the candidates clapped and cheered for each of the dignitaries, some cheering only for their home worlds, and a few sitting quiet, like Dalin.

When all were seated, Vanora raised her hands for silence. "Welcome candidates, valued guests, and ambassadors from across our Commonwealth. It is my great pleasure to welcome you to

Crown City. Your presence here signals a new era of communication and celebration across our seven worlds."

She took a breath and a few people clapped, probably thinking the Queen had uttered an applause line. And maybe she had, but she continued speaking, reading her lines in her high-pitched, breathy voice like someone unaccustomed to public speaking.

"Thank you for sending these brave warriors to me. Their competition has an ultimate goal: to provide us with a new champion. But through this competition, their unique talents and skills, representing the diversity of training and opportunities available to all in our Commonwealth, will also be on display."

The Queen paused again, and a few more uncertain claps began. She waited, looking up at the assembly and back down at a screen or projection or paper. Dalin was too far away to see. Applause built until the candidates were roaring and stomping and the ambassadors clapping with big, enthusiastic motions.

Vanora nodded and pressed her thin, red lips together. "Thank you." She nodded again. "In a moment, our tournament director," the Queen opened her palm to a man in the front row, "will give you a preview of the events planned over the next ten days—"

A beam from an energy weapon hit the platform directly in front of Vanora's feet. The next shot caught her bare arm as she dove for cover, shrieking. The *vishakanya* on the platform moved as a unit to swarm over their ruler, their small bodies shielding her as they pulled the crouching Queen off the platform and toward the far wall. Shots tracked their retreat, hitting two *vishakanya* square in the back. Both girls crumpled, their bodies dragging along for a moment, linked to the group, before falling to the sand.

The two militia leaders from Asattha, along with other military guests, were urgently directing the distracted and upset guests back to the entrance they'd used only a few minutes before.

Flames ate at the temporary platform, the ticking and crackling audible through the sound amplifier, as Vanora disappeared through an exit on the Mess side of the stadium.

Tiny lights glowed on the recording devices hovering over the stadium, transmitting the attack across the Commonwealth. "We should go," Dalin said quietly to the people on either side of him and stood. Other candidates straightened from their seats, talking in hushed tones. Once in the aisle, he craned his neck back and forth, trying to pinpoint where the shooter's position might have been.

The candidate next to him said, "Should've jumped down there and saved the Queen. That would've got me the job."

A female candidate turned around and said, "I had the same idea but it happened so fast."

That's the only way an assassination could happen, Dalin wanted to say. But he kept that treasonous thought to himself.

Dalin made his way back to the Mess, thinking about assassination, both the historical attempts and the successes on the Origin. If other attempts had been made on Vanora's life, that news hadn't traveled to Asattha.

At first he didn't process the military jangle of gear and thump of running boots. But as he looked up at the huge campus of brick and stone buildings, a squad of uniformed Commonwealth soldiers jogged past, heading out of the Mess and down the hill. Not ten steps later, another squad jogged by, going in the same general direction.

By the time Dalin entered the locked gate below the healers' hallway, five squads had passed him, all moving toward the city.

The curfew bell sounded and he frowned at his wrist unit. No new messages. Mid-afternoon call to quarters? The thought of enforced detainment in his barren rooms was enough to have him reversing course and walking back through the gate.

Once he reached the lush estates and rolling green hills of the mini-mansions, Dalin slowed to look for Commonwealth soldiers. A rational search for the assassin would require door-to-door inquiries in all neighborhoods. Picking up his own pace to a jog, Dalin continued toward Lower Town, concern growing about adrenalized soldiers mucking up the delicate ecosystem of families, tradespeople, spacers, and criminals.

Shouting and the heavy clang of metal shutters drifted up from the nicest edge of Lower Town. An older woman yelled in Origin Chinese at a helmeted soldier. She did not want to close her shop in the middle of the day. Plenty of customers want the good silk at good prices, she argued.

Dalin took two steps past and turned around. He stopped next to the woman and waited until she finished her tirade about how much revenue they gave to the royal treasury in taxes.

"What's going on?" Dalin asked the soldier. It was disconcerting to speak to someone in a heavy mask wearing at least three visible weapons. The soldier was average size and his gloved hands were open and loose. This wasn't going to be a fight, yet.

"An attempt was made on the Queen's life. Orders are to secure Lower Town."

"You're closing down all the shops and stalls?"

"Yes, that's the order."

"Until when?" From her face, Dalin was certain the older woman followed the exchange. Merchants had the most obvious reason to acquire many languages.

"An all-clear will sound from the palace when the traitor is caught."

This elicited a shriek from the woman who threw up her hands and yelled in a combination of Origin Chinese and Origin English. They'd never been shut down. This was a good and honorable business. Great ladies and important men buy fine silk from her store.

With a polite touch on her shoulder, Dalin addressed her in Origin Chinese, "Grandmother, peace."

To the soldier he said, "All of the customers and shoppers will be cleared from Lower Town for the day?"

"Yes, all citizens are required to return to their homes. Visitors must return to their lodging."

The soldier shifted, looking down the hill, ready to leave this confrontation and move on.

"There will be no customers today, grandmother," Dalin continued in Origin Chinese. "It will not harm the reputation of the best silk store to be closed when all other merchants have shut their doors and customers are gone away."

Just then a second helmeted soldier walked past the first and shoved the store owner hard enough to send her stumbling into the door of her shop. Her head snapped back and she crumpled to the ground. "Get inside and stay there," the second soldier shouted.

He shoved the first soldier away from the store, yelling, "We don't have time for this. The whole area needs to be cleared."

Dalin placed himself between the old woman and the angry soldier. Hands in fists, he set his feet and took a deep breath.

"We gonna have a problem?"

"Not today," Dalin said.

As he made his way toward Cousins, similar scenes played out across both the established merchant areas and the less-respectable, more temporary market areas in Lower Town. La Kill appeared closed all the time, so they were left alone. Geraldo had turned off the eating house's sign but left the door unlocked.

"Depends on how many uniforms they leave to enforce the order," the cook said. "Otherwise, we'll be back to business as usual by dark. That would be the smart thing to do," he added. "Riling up the locals seems like bad form with all the folks visiting from around the Commonwealth."

And still, no news from Rafiq.

To comfort himself, Dalin thought of an old saying from the Origin. No news was good news.

* * *

Mara took a slow, deliberate step toward the tower. On the second step she drew her sword and reached for the energy of the Tree. Halifax followed, unclipping his axe and hefting it in his right hand.

A smallish man clutching a bag to his chest suddenly ran through the doorway, stumbled and regained his footing. Behind him came a pair of women and a child. A stream of people began pouring from the tower door. As they hit sunlight some stopped short only to be pushed by the person coming behind. They hurried away from the center in small groups.

A ship zoomed overhead, banked and came about. The silver metal craft had open sides, soldiers within visible as it came lower.

"Commonwealth gunship," Halifax said. He glanced down at the small insignia on his uniform. "What side are we on?"

Energy weapons opened up in short bursts, targeting the people fleeing.

Yes, these people had hidden from the Commonwealth, but they weren't criminals. Not all of them. Not the children.

Blasts hit the ground, sending clumps of grass and dirt flying. The evacuating people bent and ran in weaving patterns.

"These people should live," Mara said as much to herself as to Halifax. "They can be tried later, if her highness so desires, but right now, I'm on the side of life." She sprinted to the door, calling for the evacuees to slow down and take cover.

Halifax was on her heels. "Is that your shield?" he said. "I never thought I'd see one. You'll have to teach me."

Mara glared at him, her sword coming around to point at his throat. "First we have to get these people safe."

"Who's in charge, is anyone assigned to this group?" she asked the next woman to emerge.

"No," the woman said, her face and hair covered in sooty dust. "We just ran for it, a lot of families still trying to evacuate, the alarms are going and the ceiling of the cave is…crumbling…"

An older man stumbled up behind her, a bloody wound splitting the top of his ear. "Haven't done an evacuation drill in more than ten years, but— Darkness, is that the Commonwealth?"

"Away from the city." Halifax was pointing and guiding people in the right direction.

"The Commonwealth? Is Vanora blowing us up?" an older woman asked, her eyes red-rimmed and wide.

The shooting had stopped and the gunship settled heavily onto the grass about fifty meters closer to the dome. Troops began jumping free and running toward the tower, the one in the lead calling, "Halt in the name of the Queen."

"Go," Mara hissed and shoved the people toward Halifax. "Keep running." She darted into the small room and hauled the next person up, a tiny teenage girl, only a few years younger than herself. "How many behind you?"

"More than a hundred," the girl said. "The top of the dome, it's exploding into dust a section at a time. We have a bunch of families in our neighborhood because it's on the far perimeter and our house," she paused and coughed with her mouth open, a deep wet sound. "Our house is covered in—"

A man jumped from the ladder and grabbed the girl. "You've got to run, they're shooting out there. Can you make it?"

The girl coughed again and it was only as the man turned, pulling the girl behind him, that Mara noticed his camouflage uniform.

"See that soldier out there, with the axe?" The man in camouflage pointed and the girl nodded. "Run to him. I'm sending your family to you. Keep everyone moving."

The girl coughed, then nodded. Another man in camouflage, followed by a woman in the same uniform, emerged from the ladder.

"Go," the first man ordered and pulled an energy weapon from his belt, opening fire on the Commonwealth troops.

"Who are you?" Mara asked as the woman pulled an energy weapon from her belt, clearly intending to follow her comrade.

The woman gave her a huge grin. "Friends of freedom," she said, thumping the flat metal disk over her heart.

The ground rumbled again, the concussion lasting longer this time. Shrieks echoed from within the tower and shouts came from outside.

"You in the fight or on evac detail?" the woman asked, her Origin English carrying an unfamiliar accent. It wasn't clear if she was talking to the man or to Mara.

"I got this," the man said. He bent over and called down the ladder, "Oy! You down there. We'll get you out but you got to get the young ones up to me first. Just pass 'em up. Work together all nice like."

Halifax was out there with one ally and a lot of frightened and injured civilians. A shot hit just outside the doorway, spraying debris into the room. The woman leapt out the door, returning fire. Mara moved cautiously into the open space, the tainted energy in her shield like swimming in a fetid swamp.

"I'll hold position about fifteen meters out. Send the children to me and I'll get them to my squad mate," she said to the man at the top of the ladder.

"Roger that. Stand tall," he said.

The base of her spine tingled, anticipation of a fight singing through Mara's blood. The man's response distracted her as she ran three steps away from the tower. A shot penetrated her shield and grazed her left shoulder just as the first group of children tumbled out the door. Four of them, one a toddler, clung together, looking in horror at the gunship.

"Here," Mara yelled. "Run to me. Now!"

The man and woman in camouflage were either better shots or had superior weapons to the dozen Commonwealth fighters still upright and moving forward. Each step at least one was felled. But they kept coming.

The children hurried toward her, half-carrying the littlest one. She had to hold her position, couldn't extend her tainted shield any farther. Her heart pounded in her ears and her shoulder throbbed.

Another group of children emerged, slightly older, but dusty and bleeding. At least one had bare feet. What kind of troops shot at children? Who gave orders to shoot children?

Anger burned through Mara and she brandished her sword at the gunship. Energy leapt down her arm and onto the blade, lighting it with a bright white glow. A wave of energy swept outward from her sword and struck the Commonwealth craft, knocking it onto its side.

Just as the children reached her position, a portion of the gunship burst into flames.

She counted nine enemies targeting her. No new shots came from the two "friends of freedom." Maybe they'd gone down or needed new weapons?

With a deep breath, she drew more energy. Her eyes burned and the sounds of the battle muted. "Run, children," she ordered, her voice sounding strange. She pointed her free hand to Halifax. She wanted to run between them and the weapons, but more little ones emerged from the doorway, just a pair this time.

Seeing no alternative but to draw the fire to herself, Mara ran toward the enemy troops, her shield blocking most of their shots. She ran headlong into the first one and shoved the burning blade into the soldier's chest. Shifting to check the evacuation, Mara stumbled when another sustained explosion rocked the ground. As she fell, she swung her sword in a two-handed grip and took a Commonwealth soldier out at the knees.

As the rest converged on her position, Mara lost herself to the fight.

Chapter 30

Eating breakfast in his usual corner of the Mess Mess, Dalin's circling thoughts were interrupted by loud females. He looked up from his lentils to see a familiar tall blonde high-fiving and hugging a group of students. Fentress. She'd been on the away team. And her shadow, the thin, dark-haired one who was always near. She'd been on the student squad as well.

Dalin moved without thought, plowing through the line of people still waiting for food. If she knew anything about Mara...

"Dalin?" Annelise caught his arm just outside the circle of Furies. "Light be praised, I was starting to worry. Gunder and I were just saying how we haven't seen you in so long and—" She released his arm, taking in the mottled bruises running from wrist to elbow. Stretching on her toes, she peered at his face. "Who's been beating on you?"

"Did you talk to Fentress? Does she have any updates about Mara?" Dalin didn't even feel his injuries, he just needed to know *anything* about Mara.

The cheer in Annelise's eyes dimmed. "No, they just got back and the team that was MIA are still missing."

"Romeo." Fentress broke through the circle to clap him on the shoulder. "That's some girl you got. Listen up, ladies."

She paused to make sure the others were looking her direction. "You know how our rules talk about 'an act of sacrifice or extreme bravery'? Well, that first year, Mara De La Luz? She saw that the squad leader was being dragged into this water facility. Some group of *locos* bent on taking him hostage, we're not sure. But I'll tell you what I said in my debrief. That girl volunteered to take a team and go after O'Kelley. The other three stood up to follow her, no hesitation. She's got it, *zorritas mías*. And when..." She patted

Dalin's face. "Listen to me, Romeo, *when* she returns, we're inducting that girl into the Furies just like that." She snapped her fingers in his face before throwing back her head and howling. The others chimed in, howling, laughing, and whooping.

Throat and gut tight with disappointment, Dalin forced himself to walk back to his seat. He rubbed his hand over his hair, his mind fixed on an image of Mara leading the charge to save a teammate. Of course Mara had volunteered for something dangerous. That's how she ended up a prisoner. She never thought about her own safety.

"Mind if we join you?" Gunder dropped his tray down across from Dalin, and Annelise slipped in next to him.

Annelise reached over and patted his hand. "You heard what Fentress said. Mara volunteered to rescue the squad leader. She's off having an adventure." The last was said with a touch of jealousy.

"We was looking for you because your name's on the tournament roster. Did you sign up?" Gunder asked.

Dalin scrubbed his face with both hands. "I did."

"What kind of Darkness is strangling your brain right now? You're supposed to be the smartest guy on the planet," Annelise whisper-yelled, glancing over her shoulder. "Mara's gonna get back and find you what? Dead? Serving"—she grimaced as though she'd bitten into a rotten apple—"serving the Queen?" She leaned over the table and jabbed him in the chest.

"How can we help?" Gunder asked, patting Annelise's arm and tugging her back to her place.

Ignoring the question, Dalin's gaze strayed back to Fentress and the Furies. They looked so happy, brimming with the relief of a friend coming back from a fight alive.

What would he give to see Mara in that circle, safe and laughing? He closed his eyes and renewed his promise to protect her, to care for her, and to help her be free so that she could live the life that had been stolen from her so long ago.

* * *

The next morning the check-in process for the flag round involved being weighed and measured, a calculation of body mass index, a brief diet log, and a cataloging of personal effects.

This part of the fight complex smelled likely freshly poured syncrete, the edges of the walls and corners of the ceiling rough and un-sanded, bits of metal framing poking out in several places. Rather than actual desks or any purposefully constructed data station, the tournament officials stood behind plastic temporary tables, shuffling paper in and out of stiff plastic folders.

After more than thirty minutes of waiting, Dalin was assigned locker number 235 and sent to put his things away. His unpainted metal locker was full length and wider than some, and his bo staff just fit, wedged in at an angle. As he was stuffing in his gear, his hand brushed a stray piece of tape underneath the top shelf. He leaned down to investigate and found a tiny piece of paper. With a quick, casual motion, he removed it and shoved it in one pocket. No one was watching him, but large, visible cameras were mounted where the rough walls met the open beams of the ceiling. And although some crowd noise filtered in, the area was relatively quiet but for the loud blowing of several ineffective fans.

Not trusting the water fountains or sinks, Dalin sipped from his own water bottle and leaned against one wall. Just beyond the locker room was a rudimentary shower setup. Nozzles against the wall, one largish floor drain, tile floor, and towel hooks. Towel hooks, but no towels.

In addition to the handful of armed palace guards, two *vishakanya* stood by the entrance to the stadium. Dalin stayed near the wall, moving in a slow and nonthreatening way until he circled around to that entrance.

It was an open doorway leading to a large chamber with a grid on the floor. At the far side was a larger doorway, currently closed, but, presumably, the gate they would march through.

"*Oye*, Romeo, fancy meeting you here."

Dalin turned to see Fentress and her ever-present companion dropping equipment bags in front of the nearest lockers. He nodded and ambled over, well aware they still had nearly ninety minutes to wait.

"I'm Dalin," he said and stuck out his hand to the slim, quiet female. Her brown hair was too short to pull back in a ponytail, so she'd tucked it under a wide black headband. Like Fentress, she wore black shorts, a black tank top, and boots. Her tank bore the image of a winged trio of women brandishing swords.

"Kailer," she said, shaking his hand.

"You were on the student observation team," he said, his brain furnishing a copy of the list he'd read so many times.

She nodded and opened a locker.

"Why are you doing this?" Dalin couldn't help but ask. "You just returned from—"

"It wasn't combat," Fentress cut him off. "And we want a chance to serve the Queen, same as you." She jerked a thumb over her shoulder at the temporary table. "That's what you told 'em, right? Serve her majesty?" Something hot and angry flashed through her eyes.

"Vanora deserves someone special," Kailer muttered, bending down to wedge two different swords into the locker. "And the Furies are the best fighters in the Mess, as you know." She smirked and kicked her locker shut.

"Fentress mentioned it," Dalin agreed.

Kailer leaned up on her toes and kissed Fentress's cheek. Fentress shifted to kiss her lips and then pulled Kailer close to whisper in her ear. She nodded and reached down to link their fingers.

"You got any allies in this bunch?" She nodded to encompass the people either shoving gear into lockers, stretching, or milling around, her bright hair gleaming in the artificial light.

Taken aback, Dalin followed her gaze. Knowing the tournament would have a single winner, he hadn't considered that contestants would form alliances. "No," he said. "I've been training at La Kill, but the others who entered aren't in this round."

"We'll help you if we can," Fentress said. "For Mara. You do the same?"

"For Mara," Dalin said slowly, not surprised at the pang of hope he felt just hearing the Fury talk about his partner with the certainty she was still alive.

"Five o'clock group's all in," Kailer said. "Tildi and Mogen made it." She and Fentress slapped hands.

"A Fury is gonna win this," Fentress said, switching to the laces on her other boot. "*Lo siento*, Romeo."

Under the pretense of rearranging his gear, Dalin took time sizing up the opponents. He and Fentress were the tallest. From what he'd seen of yesterday's rounds, long limbs were a significant asset.

A few of the adult male candidates carried a lot of muscle bulk, some showing it off by going shirtless, others by wearing skintight clothes.

Dalin pulled the tiny paper from his pocket and unrolled it, reading the two printed words. "Red Flag."

Full of pent-up energy, he paced from one side of the locker room to the other twice and then made several circuits. A few fighters kept moving, as he was. Many others sat on the plain plastic benches talking and, in some cases, laughing. Didn't they know what was at stake? That failure might be a death sentence?

"All right, time to pay attention." The official with the folder had moved to the wide doorway. His black hair clung in thin strands to his scalp, allowing the shine of sweat to catch the light as he nodded. "Form up on the grid. You will not touch, brush, bump, shove, hit, flick, trip, or punch a person around you while marching into the stadium. You will not speak. Citizens from the entire Commonwealth are here as well as watching via a host of communication tools. This is the only round for many of you. As your stated intent in entering was to serve our great and glorious Queen, you will show her respect by following these orders."

"How do we—" someone shouted.

"You will line up by the second two digits of your assigned locker number. Zero one, you stand at the top left. Double zero, you stand at the bottom right. Can't remember your locker number, ask."

Thirty-five was right in the middle of the formation. The worst place to start. Dalin shuffled forward until his feet covered the painted number thirty-five inside the red painted one-meter square.

"The stadium reset is nearly complete. The gate will open and I will signal you. You will move as a group. You will stop in the center of the arena. After a few remarks, the nine-minute signal will sound. If you reach a flag, pull it and a door will open in the wall. Place your hand inside and a mark will be transferred to the skin."

Dalin's stomach twisted with nerves, a chill prickling along his arms and up his chest and neck. For the first time, he saw the magnitude of the risk. It was challenge enough to get a flag, but someone wanted him to get a red flag. And if he didn't get a flag at all, it was over.

If the unthinkable happened and Mara was gone forever, he *had to* carry on their mission for her. It would be his only reason for living if she were taken from him.

But first he had to survive this fight.

Swallowing hard and shoving that line of thinking into a dark box, Dalin turned and found Fentress and Kailer over his right shoulder, near the bottom right edge of the group in what looked like positions eighty-nine and ninety. Fentress winked and grinned like they were off to a fun and slightly naughty escapade.

The smile reminded him so much of Mara that Dalin had to look away. This was for her. She would understand the good he could do as the champion.

It might have been the power of his wishful imagination, but as he reached and thought of Mara, a tiny flicker answered his call. Startled, Dalin reached again, this time with a stronger pull. The flicker was there and then nothing.

As the gate opened and the group marched forward, he focused on the most important lessons from La Kill.

The opponent is an obstacle.

Focus on the win.

Inside the arena, the speaker's amplified voice was completely distorted. Like everyone else in the formation, he was counting flags.

Twenty-four flags.

Only two flags were red, both behind him. One was at the northwest corner, the other at the southwest corner.

Cool shadows slid over his mind, coloring his resolve. For the first time in his life, no one expected him to do the right thing. No one expected him to check his power or skills so that a lesser opponent might have a chance. For years he'd hidden his capacity for ruthless brutality, using the Light and the energy from the Tree to stay balanced.

Today that Darkness would keep him alive.

The buzzer sounded and he bolted to the left, elbows out, hands up. He slammed his elbow into someone's temple, chopped another across the windpipe. Both collapsed to the sand. Dalin dodged around a grappling pair and kicked the person in front of him in a perfect kidney shot.

He burst out of the formation, a snarl on his lips. As he sighted the red flag in the northwest corner someone kicked the back of his knees. Stumbling and catching himself, Dalin pulled one leg up and shot a punishing back kick to the center of the person's chest. Fighters on this side of the stadium were surging toward the stairs now and for a split second, he registered the screaming crowd.

Dodging the nearest runner, he missed her partner swinging for his head. Dalin ducked at the last minute but caught a significant portion of the blow on his right ear and right shoulder. Shock waves burned down his arm and his fingers twitched as the nerves misfired.

He planted his foot in the female's stomach, slipped around the male's next strike, and landed a hook punch on his jaw. With a shove, he dropped the male and stomped on the back of his neck.

Crowd noise surged, calling Dalin back to the task at hand. Get the flag. A red flag.

He sprinted for the northwest corner, momentarily relieved those stairs were unoccupied. Every sort of weaponless fight surged across the sand, more bodies down than he'd seen the previous day.

"Romeo." Fentress and Kailer, shoulder to shoulder, fought toward the northwest stairs. They held off a group of four, harrying them with short kicks and strikes.

Dalin used his momentum to crash into the center two, knocking their heads together. Kailer and Fentress each took one of the remaining fighters, nearly identical spin hook kicks slamming into opponent's faces.

Stomping the pair he'd felled an extra time to keep them down, Dalin licked his lips, tasting blood. Prickly sand coated part of his forearm and scratched at the top of his socks. Five flags remained on the near side of the stadium. The red flag in the southwest corner was gone.

"Two minutes, Romeo! ¡*Ándale*!"

Dalin ran ahead of the two Furies, catching and throwing slower runners into the stands. Three rows from the top, a spectator jumped to his feet and kicked Dalin in the face. He bit his tongue as his teeth slammed together, sending flashes of red across his vision. Someone, probably the same person, landed a blow on his sternum, but Dalin's sight was so blurry he couldn't block effectively.

A shriek from above. The next hit didn't land. Dalin's ears were ringing. As though underwater, he heard a garbled, "Romeo! Thirty seconds."

Dalin got to one knee and spit blood on the stairs, distracted by the other brown smears and clumps of reddish sand.

Mara wouldn't quit. She hadn't quit in the Box. And with that thought a surge of power swept through him, clearing his vision and buoying him to his feet.

"That's it, lad, go on and get the flag," a deep voice yelled in his undamaged ear.

Stumbling, he regained his footing and leaped up the last few steps. He snatched the flag stem and shoved his hand in the opening as the buzzer echoed around the stadium. After a brief, hot flash of pain, he pulled his hand free, a red triangle blazing bright from knuckles to wrist.

A few meters to his left, Fentress brandished an orange mark. Just past her, Kailer clenched her purple hand and shook the marked fist at the crowd.

"Be seeing you soon, youngster," the deep voice said.

Dalin whipped his head around so fast he almost fell again.

Jameson?

Chapter 31

By the time Dalin made it back to his room, the adrenaline had burned through his system, leaving him shaky and ill. All of the candidates with flag marks had been sent to on-site healers. A man he'd not seen before worked on his ribs and his wrist and closed up the cut on his face. Throughout the brief exam and healing session, his brain kept replaying moments in the fight, taking him from euphoria to self-loathing on a repeating cycle.

Pausing outside his door as he always did, Dalin took a deep breath. The rust shavings under his hinges had been disturbed. He checked the corridor before he opened the door and let it swing all the way open to hit the wall in case someone stood just inside.

Out of habit, Dalin reached with his mind, wanting his other sense to tell him if another human was nearby. The shock of the incoming information, the clarity and volume, sent him staggering over the threshold. No humans inside, but many in the hallways around him, more than twelve. He sensed gender, age, health, fatigue, and in many cases could read a current thought or two.

Dropping his gear on the floor, he grabbed his head with both hands and slammed the conduit shut. As though it would make a difference, he also shut and locked the door before stumbling to a chair.

Bile rose and he barely made it to the sink before the dry heaves and shudders started. He needed a shower. And to rest. The tournament schedule for days three and four would be sent out and posted at 0500.

But as he stood under the warm spray, bracing himself with his left arm, Dalin's memory jumped from the fight loop to the man he'd seen as he grabbed the red flag.

Although the spectator wore sunglasses and a black and gold shirt with a large image of Queen Vanora, Dalin was sure the man was his mentor, his aunt's husband, who had been standing there. The scarred, half-white, half-black eyebrow just visible from behind the rim of the dark glasses belonged to one man in the Commonwealth, and that man was Jon Jameson.

Dalin checked his bedroom, common room, tiny kitchen, and washroom. No signs of a search or of anything being disturbed except the hinges of his door. What if nothing was taken, but instead something was added? Could Jameson have snuck in here and left something?

Glad, so glad to have something else to think about, Dalin tore open packages of crackers and cheese and started eating. He drank several large glasses of water as he ate and searched everything again, this time with an eye for anything new.

As he was taking every book from the bookshelf and shaking it, a single folded sheet of rice paper fluttered to the floor. He smoothed it open and skimmed the coded response from Jameson written in the same personal code he'd used just a few days before.

Grabbing a pencil, Dalin brought the note to his narrow kitchen counter and decoded it in record time.

"Good fight. E is in town. New ID tomorrow. You don't know me."

* * *

The posted schedule required all candidates to report to the healers no later than 0630. Check-in at the fight complex, not the stadium, wasn't set until 1300. Before he slept, Dalin had triple-checked his decoding. This morning he shredded the delicate paper and then flushed it for good measure. The red mark on his hand hadn't changed in the shower the night before and, if anything, if was brighter and more distinct after his morning rinse. When Dalin rubbed it, the center of the mark tingled, the skin slightly raised and irritated.

It was only 0530 when he entered the Mess Mess, so the large hall was relatively empty. He loaded his plate with fruit, eggs, cheese, and plain bread and sat down with his back to the wall.

Some of the students drifting by ignored him. A few saw the mark and mumbled congratulations. Halfway through his meal, a newly installed holocell flickered to life. Words and columns of numbers started to scroll without sound.

Unaccustomed to any sort of communication or entertainment at the Mess, many of the students picked up their trays and moved closer to the holocell. It was the size of a large fish tank, about two meters long, one meter tall, and about ten centimeters deep. This kind of cell could handle all but the most detailed holoprojection, but it was more likely to be used for projecting text or flat images.

Dalin wished his father was with him to talk through the technical specifications of holoprojection, in general, and the devices as well. But Jin was far away and safe. Dalin hoped.

Following the other students, Dalin grabbed his tray and moved closer to the projection cell. Three columns scrolled in a continuous loop. The left column was names and the next two columns were numbers. Students were reacting to the information, groaning or slapping hands, as lines of text went by.

After a minute, the column headings appeared. Name, damage caused, damage received. Nothing about this had been in the morning's tournament information.

"That guy's a beast," said one of the students right in front of him to a friend.

"Brutal," the friend agreed.

Dalin de Forest was the top name on the list.

Though the darkest part of his competitive nature was pleased, Dalin, an otherwise rational, balanced human, dropped his tray on the closest table with a clatter.

When the first speaker glanced at him, Dalin said, "Do you know how the damage points were assigned?"

"Uh yes, it's about kills, critically wounded, maiming—" He broke off and hit his friend on the shoulder. "It's him!"

"*Lìhài!*" The second speaker put up his hands. "So awesome. You crushed out there, literally, all my friends from Tian are insane for you. Top of the board, man." He lifted his hand for Dalin to slap.

Dalin slapped the student's hand and nodded to the semicircle of students now staring at him.

As smoothly as he could manage, Dalin picked up his tray and began to walk back to the seat by the wall. How could he have done worse damage than the fighters on day one? So much worse than any other candidate?

Unfortunately, his two new fans didn't notice his silence. They followed him chattering about the fights.

"…And then when you smashed that guy in the throat?"

"Right, but you kicked that one female right in the small of her back, how did you know that was a kidney shot?"

"We were screaming for you to get to the flag but some *nǎo cán*, deficient brain, jumped out of the stands to—"

"Yeah, he only got in one good shot, and this other dude threw him back into the crowd. That's what I would've done if I'd been there."

"Yeah," the other student said, pulling up at the table with Dalin.

Both of them looked like first-year students to Dalin, but that meant they were only a year or two younger than he was. They resumed talking while he contemplated his tray.

His food wasn't warm now, but he forced himself to spoon down the eggs.

"…You teach here, right?" the first fan was saying. Both looked at him with hopeful anticipation. The first fan had a completely shaved head, the bones of his face sharp, his dark eyebrows and dark eyes the only punctuation marks in the tan skin.

The second fan carried more weight in his face and on his frame. He had close-cropped black hair with a bright streak of hot red along the side part.

Swallowing the last bite of egg, Dalin washed it down with a long gulp of water. "I teach here. Armed and unarmed combat."

"Yes. And you're Chinese." The two fans slapped hands again. They switched to Origin Chinese, words picking up so much speed, Dalin was hard-pressed to follow the exchange; Something about Tian and cheering for him today.

The first fan popped up from the seat and grinned at Dalin. "*Shàng dāo shān, xià yóu guō.*" The second fan added, "*Zhù nǐ hǎoyùn.*" Both gave him slight bows and hurried away.

A true friend will do anything for you, climb the knife mountain or get into a pot of boiling oil, Dalin translated as the students disappeared through the doors.

After mourning his lack of friends, here were two offering him limitless friendship and wishing him luck.

He didn't think Mara would be impressed.

* * *

The healer wouldn't touch the red flag mark on Dalin's hand. Every other part of him was adjusted, taped, or completely healed, but not the mark. Dalin explained that it not only itched, but pressed into the bones of his left hand. But the healer, the same man as the previous night, shook his head emphatically.

Dalin had been assigned one of the first appointments, so once it was complete, he'd been allowed to pick up his gear from the stadium locker room. At ten, all candidates were instructed to report to training. The flags on their hands designated which room.

Just as when the Friday Night Fights were going on, the cavernous hall had been divided into eight midsize spaces. Seven were marked with a colored flag at the door. The remaining room was set as an on-site clinic and reminded him uncomfortably of the secret hospital. It had fewer beds, privacy screens set up between them, but the basic equipment was all the same.

The candidates didn't talk to each other as they filed in, though several of the larger men and a few of the women gave him long assessing looks. His current rank at the top of the damage board wasn't likely to win him any allies among the contestants.

Hefting his gear bag and slinging his bo staff bag over his shoulder, Dalin walked toward the doorway with the red flag. Several other candidates with red flag marks were loitering just outside the door, probably waiting for someone else to enter first.

Expect to win. Another useful rule from La Kill.

Dalin walked into the training space as though he owned it, a technique his mother had actually made him practice years ago. The lone figure at the far end of the room looked up and scowled.

"Dump that gear in the corner," the man said, voice carrying across the makeshift room, though it was low and rough as tree bark. "This is a weapons-free zone for the time bein'."

The people walking in behind Dalin changed directions and started a pile of equipment. Dalin continued forward until he and the man were only two meters apart.

"You're that chancer who caused too much damage in the arena and called attention to himself," the man said. Gone was the shaggy hair and the tourist shirt from the previous day. Both eyebrows matched the military-short hair, black with a dusting of silver. He wore close-fitting pants and a short-sleeved shirt, all black.

"And you are?" Dalin replied, his heart picking up speed as he repressed a grin, trying to match the man's disapproving glower.

"Come a wee bit closer," said Jameson.

Dalin and a few of the others edged closer.

"C'mon now, everyone gather in. Are we all here?"

With a quick look over his shoulder, Dalin counted the people in the room. "All but two," he said.

"That's good enough for me," Jameson replied and lunged forward to plant his head in Dalin's sternum while wrapping one leg around his knees.

With an ungraceful "oof" Dalin dropped to the mat, his bags thudding next to him. He tucked his chin and didn't hit his head, but it was the opposite of cool, legs wrapped and arms spread to catch himself.

Leaning one elbow almost casually against Dalin's windpipe, Jameson said, "I'm the one who's charged with getting you lot ready to win this thing."

Dalin scissored his legs and, with a shove, rolled free of the hold.

Jameson nodded. "Good one. Don't get surprised next time." He settled into a seated position on the floor and motioned for the group to sit.

Ignoring the request, Dalin grabbed his bags and took them to the corner while the rest of the group settled in. He rubbed the new bruise forming in the center of his chest and allowed himself a tiny grin. Jameson hadn't dropped him like that in years. But it was a good dominance move and had hopefully made the correct impression on the others.

"First off, everyone comfortable with Origin English?" A few people glanced at each other, but no one protested. "Thanks for that. I can speak bits and pieces of all the languages in the Commonwealth, but probably not well enough to coach." He waited a beat before continuing. "You competed as individuals to get here and you grabbed the red flags. For the next four days, we compete as a team."

This announcement garnered sounds of surprise and many overt or surreptitious glances around the group. Dalin ambled forward and sat behind the person closest to the door.

"Now I'm from Kels originally, but for the better part of my life, I've made my home on Asattha." This produced more sounds of surprise.

Jameson ignored the responses and continued. "Her highness determined that fighting under the names of the planets in our great Commonwealth was a way not only to vary the tournament play, but also to engage the spectators around the worlds. Starting now, we are Team Asattha. Say it back to me."

"Team Asattha." Some mumbled and some spoke clearly. Several continued to look around the group with puzzled expressions.

"It's my understanding that each team has a coach from the planet they represent. Mostly I think that's someone's fancy idea. My first job, as I see it, is to keep you alive and second, to get you through the team competition and into the next phase."

"We have four different activities to complete this morning. All data will be recorded via the transmitters in your hands." Jameson grabbed the nearest person's hand and pointed at the red flag mark.

"The four categories are," Jameson paused for effect. It was incredibly strange to watch him behaving this way. "Speed trial, dexterity trial, food tasting, and chess."

Dalin folded his arms across his chest and let out a breath.

As startled groans and protests rose from the group, Jameson said, "Think about it. Bein' the Queen's Champion won't just be about smashing your way through a crowd."

Heads nodded in front of Dalin. That made sense but why chess? He hadn't played in at least two years. And it was hard to imagine many chess masters among the brawlers who won flags in the first round.

A woman off to one side raised her hand. When Jameson nodded at her, she said, "Is the food tasting to determine our palates? Or is it to find poison?"

Jameson shoved one hand in his pocket and looked down. "I believe it's to find poison."

"So we could get poisoned?" she said, sounding disconcerted but resigned.

"Yes, that's my understanding. We're not in mortal combat. Not yet. But death was a possible outcome for any of you the minute you signed those forms." Jameson shot Dalin a meaningful glare.

"Right then. Let's get warmed up and then we'll start with speed."

They stretched and jogged in place while Jameson moved through the crowd, introducing himself to each person. He asked names and ages only.

Someone had attempted to sanitize the mats, but they were the same ones used daily by the Mess students. By the time their group was ready to try the speed course, the old smells drifted around them. No changes had been made to the temporary walls used for the Friday fights. They were scarred and stained with broken bits along the bottom.

Jameson led them out of the fight complex and into one of the main halls. A gate of sorts had been erected. One small box had been attached to each of the gate poles. The boxes were metal and had only one visible open side on the front.

"We're going to jog the entire course, get you comfortable with the layout. Essentially, it's a giant loop around the palace and school. Any confusing turns are marked with these." He pointed at one of the metal poles.

"When we get back to the start, you shove your hand into a box." He demonstrated with his own hand. "And that records your start time. Go as fast as you can, safely, and then stop the timer by putting your hand back in the box when you finish. Clear?"

"Does it have to be the same box?" one of the older male competitors asked.

"No. Either will do." Jameson waved them through the gates and joined the middle of the pack as they jogged the metal, brick, and syncrete corridors of the Queen's Military Skills and Strategy School.

The halls were nearly empty. A message had appeared on Dalin's wrist unit about rerouting some of the main arteries of the campus, which would also account for the lack of students and Mess personnel on the route.

Around him, the other people with red flag marks jogged, most showing no discomfort. A few lagged behind, and one heavier-set fighter even stopped for a brief moment to bend over, deep breaths shuddering through his chest.

Back at the gate, Jameson motioned for the group to bunch together. "Let me stress that today and tomorrow are *team* competitions. I don't want to see anyone shoving or tripping. Plenty of chances to get hurt. Don't be the teammate causing damage to one of your own."

A few people glanced at Dalin in the back of the group. He cleared his throat and said, "Just to clarify, are you saying that no damage points can be earned or lost during the speed trial?"

"Yes, that's correct." Jameson rubbed the back of his neck. "Far as I know, damage doesn't apply until after the team trials are complete." It looked like he was muttering to himself, but then he straightened and addressed the group once more. "Any questions before you run?"

No one spoke up.

"All right then, give me two lines, one on each gate post here. Ten seconds between starts. Ready? Go."

At the back of the left-hand line, Dalin breathed deeply, trying to get his lungs and blood as oxygenated as possible. He estimated the course was about two and a half kilometers. The boots he wore had cushioned, flexible rubber soles and would be fine for a short distance, though not as good as shoes designed specifically for running. Given the turns in the hallway and the number of people, he estimated he could run the loop in under eight minutes.

Mara ran much more frequently than he did. Moving closer to the gate every ten seconds, he reflected that, as with fighting, running was something he hadn't really pushed himself to do full out for a long time. He grinned at Jameson as he placed his hand in the metal box. A tiny beep sounded and Dalin sprinted away.

With his long stride, he caught the middle of the group in under two minutes. Focusing on his breathing and his gait, the mental attack took him completely by surprise. Dalin stumbled and hit the wall, catching himself on one shoulder. Three people ran by, shooting questioning looks as they passed.

Blinking hard, Dalin picked up speed again and slammed down the extra mental barriers he'd been working on. The next salvo hit as he rounded the back side of the loop. But he was ready and it slid off without much impact this time.

He pushed his frustration into the run, stretching his steps and pumping his arms. Weaving around the other runners, Dalin finished third, but with the best personal time. He paced a short distance down the loop and back, shaking out his arms and legs as his breathing began to slow.

The mental attacks felt malicious, but not like attempted murder. The nature of the attacks reminded him of bullies or mid-tier predators, testing for weakness without full commitment to initiating harm.

Over the next few minutes, the remainder of Team Asattha ran through the gates. Jameson clapped and yelled for the last dozen and a few others ambled over to join him.

"Great job finishing, everyone," Jameson said. "Back to our room for a few."

They jogged back to their room in the fight complex at Jameson's moderate pace. No one had spoken to Dalin yet, but he didn't mind. He was just glad fights hadn't erupted during the run, especially when the mental attack knocked him into the wall.

Jameson glanced inside and stepped into the doorway, blocking it.

"Listen up. The training tools for the next challenge were set up while we were gone. Orient yourselves. Play with the games until you figure out the rules. And let me remind you again, this is a team. If you don't know what it is or how to use it, someone in this group likely does." He moved aside to let them enter.

Dalin paused at the door. "You helped me yesterday," he said, quietly enough that the competitors in front of him wouldn't hear.

"Ay, you great stupid lummox. I helped you." The anger on Jameson's face was real.

"And you got me on this team," Dalin said. "Put yourself as the coach."

Jameson leaned closer and jabbed Dalin's chest. "This monarchy is on the brink. Everything we've worked for is in motion toward the end we want. My hands were full before you joined this circus." His now-matching dark eyebrows pulled low over his pale eyes.

"But my bride, not to mention your parents, are wringing their hands over your stupid, impulsive—"

The force of Jameson's fury took him by surprise and Dalin stepped back, a matching frown on his face. "It was my decision. I knew the risks. But Mara—" Saying her name washed away the anger, leaving him empty.

Jameson's frown softened as well. He shook his head. "They're always goin' on about how smart ya are. But you've got to be patient, lad. Play the long game. Our girl isn't gone."

Excited shouts rose from the training room and with an admonishing glare, Jameson walked inside.

"How do you know?" Dalin whispered.

Chapter 32

"This is a deep burn, but there's another injury, barely healed, on the other side. Scars on her back, scars on her hands, arms, legs—"

The muffled voice was cut off by a low murmur.

"Right away."

Cocooned in a haze of pain, Mara reached for a better grip on consciousness and flinched at the much sharper pain her head. A groan escaped her lips.

"*Habibti*, so good to see you awake," a familiar voice murmured right next to her aching head.

Mara cracked open one gritty, swollen eye and closed it immediately. Hallucinating. Rafiq. She took a deep shuddering breath and tried to relax away from the pounding in her temples.

"You had my employers worried, little cousin. Sadly, I've seen you like this before. But how did they manage to drug you again?"

Rafiq was talking to her and she was not in the middle of an energy weapon fight outside a collapsing cave city on Iloel.

"Where?" she managed, opening both eyes this time.

"My ship," he said, immediately putting gentle but firm hands on both Mara's shoulders as she flinched and tried to sit up. "No. Nowhere to go. We're in transit from Iloel back to Laska. About halfway there. Nice work, by the way. You helped save a lot of lives, according to your friend Halifax."

"'Fax?" She struggled against Rafiq's hold until he sighed and helped her sit up.

The room was small and gray with one rounded wall. The opposite wall was floor-to-ceiling cabinets and shelves full of medical equipment. It smelled of disinfectant and something warmer, like cloves.

"He's fine. Scarcely worse for the wear and healthy as a horse. Where does the Queen find such specimens?" In response to Mara's stern look, he said, "I see your sense of humor was injured in the fight as well. Some of my clients admire her majesty's collection. That's all."

The chill in the room began to register and Mara rubbed her bare arms. She wore her tank top and uniform pants, a light silver blanket warm on her lap. Bare arms.

"My knives, the wrist sheaths?"

Rafiq patted her pack on the table next to the bed. "All present and accounted for. Listen, Mara, my client wants to speak with you. Their medic is interested in you as well. I'll be in the room, but I won't intervene unless it's necessary. Given that I'm only a smuggler and I'm just here to get paid." He smoothed his hands over his long, black linen tunic.

"And," he said, expression sobering, "there's a situation back in Crown City. Your boy, Dalin, is blazing toward the top spot in the tournament."

"What?" For a moment the room swam out of focus and bile rose, forcing saliva into her dry mouth. Shuddering, Mara pressed her palms together and touched the tips of her fingers to her forehead. As she asked, "How long?" the door opened and a man in the distinctive black uniform of the King's Men stepped over the raised threshold.

She shut her mouth and swallowed hard. A King's Man was Rafiq's client?

The man extended a deeply tanned and weathered hand. Mara shook it, looking into his pale green-gray eyes. Deep lines scored his forehead underneath thick, closely cropped gray hair. His firm grip drew attention to his lean, muscular build.

"Ms. De La Luz," he said with a broad smile. "My name is Colonel Dirk Van Fuuren. You put on quite a show outside Alandalus. I'm honored to have seen you in action." His Origin English had the same unfamiliar accent as the three fighters from the tower evacuation site.

"You were there?" she asked. Her memory had fragmented and blurred, just as it had after her fight in the Box.

"No, but monitoring through a live holo stream." His tone sounded wistful and his grin dimmed for a brief moment. "Forgive me, do you have a rank or title you prefer for address?"

Mara refused to be intimidated despite sitting on a cot in a medical room wearing only a tank top, dirty pants, and a blanket. "No. I'm just a student at the Mess."

"And before that, a Protector," Van Fuuren said.

Mara kept her face blank and looked at the man's mottled tan ear. "Yes."

"My organization appreciated your cooperation and support on Asattha. The Protector Project had to end."

Unable to disagree, Mara simply said, "Yes, it did." This didn't seem like the time to point out the King's Men who invaded Northwest Protector House had also ended several innocent lives in their efforts to bring down the experiment.

"I commissioned Mr. Malouf," he gestured toward Rafiq, "to help us find you, once our organization learned of your deployment to Iloel. You've been difficult to track, Ms. De La Luz."

Trying to ignore the pounding in her head, Mara said, "The mission deviated from plan and protocol within less than forty-eight hours."

Van Fuuren shrugged. "No plan survives first contact." He held her eyes in a long, assessing stare. "My medic has not yet cleared you for any length of conversation. So I'll leave you with this. The King's Men believe you are the Daughter of the Tree and the one foretold to help us restore peace to our Commonwealth. In order to make an unequivocal confirmation of your identity, we must bring you to our headquarters for testing and comparison with the original Tree scrolls."

The silence stretched thin. Finally Mara said, "You came to Iloel to find me?"

"We did," Van Fuuren replied.

That an otherwise competent and seasoned soldier would buy into a myth was a puzzle. But Ponapali, the first King's Man she'd met, was the same way: ruthless, competent, and devout.

She took a deep breath and let it out slowly. "I will participate in the identification tests."

Van Fuuren blinked rapidly and flexed the fingers of his right hand. "Well, that's—"

Mara held up her hand, palm out. "Not immediately. If you know the Tree Scrolls well, you know some stories feature a pair of champions, not the Daughter alone. My partner has entered the tournament in Crown City."

"Dalin de Forest."

"Yes," Mara agreed, her heart squeezing at the thought of Dalin coming to harm without her there to fight at his side. They'd been out of contact far too long. She missed his mind and his touch.

"I won't go through the tests without him," she said. "Further, Halifax must have safe passage back to the Mess. He should be free to choose his service, not forced into working for the King's Men by circumstance."

Shooting a triumphant look at Rafiq, Van Fuuren stuck out his hand again. "Very well, I agree to these terms." With a final nod to Mara, he left the room.

The medic entered a few minutes later. As soon as he spoke, she realized his was the voice she'd first heard as she regained consciousness.

"Hello, Ms. De La Luz, how are you feeling?"

Tired, hungry, thirsty, headache; the list went on and on. But Mara was reluctant to trust a stranger for anything beyond simple stitches or a cold compress.

"Do you have any sealed water?" she asked.

The medic rolled his lips together, pink in his dark face. "Mr. Malouf had only a little knowledge of the drug that has been introduced to your system. If you could tell me a little more, I could research it while you get hydrated, fed, and rested."

"It is believed to be a modified version of a drug used to increase the performance of the miners on Iloel, developed more than a century ago." She waited for him to ask how she knew this, but he just scribbled a note with his stylus.

"Um-hmm, and do you have any allergies?" the medic asked, glancing up at her. His dark gaze was penetrating but kind. Unlike Van Fuuren, this man had jowls and a bit of a paunch.

Mara wanted to pull the silver blanket over her head and sleep until she felt better. "I'm allergic to poison."

The medic jotted another note and nodded. "Well, yes, most of us are. Susceptible, anyway, if not allergic, strictly speaking." He turned his attention to Rafiq. "Mr. Malouf you had a dab hand with our patient yesterday. Are you comfortable assisting me in setting up a saline drip?"

Rafiq nodded. "Performed plenty of triage and field assists in my time."

"Splendid." The medic turned his attention back to Mara. "You're about to feel much better, my dear. And when you wake up in a few hours, I believe you'll be able to handle solid food."

Leaning close to her ear, Rafiq whispered, "Cooperate and trust me to watch this guy. You're gonna want to wake up ready to eat 'cause Geraldo sent something extra special. Got it vacuum sealed and waiting for you."

* * *

If his mentor was confident Mara was alive, Dalin wanted to believe him. But Jameson was a master of the nuanced truths that were the almost-lies of spy craft.

Another team, this one with purple marks on their hands, jogged past, likely on their way to the running trial. Kailer threw a salute as she went by. Fentress and Kailer had been there when Mara left to head an unsanctioned rescue. They were fully confident she was alive. Least likely to be killed in action, they said.

Dalin brushed a mental finger over the place in his mind where he'd felt the connection to Mara. When they were within a few kilometers, it was a warm, living beacon. Pretending not to notice the tiny spark of hope, he reached for her energy signature, shouting at the top of his rapport range. He held his breath.

Nothing.

Without Mara, he felt empty, but he could still execute their mission, if for no other reason than it was theirs. But he had to keep his head in the competition. His gaze landed on the far wall, the one his partner had climbed with a dislocated shoulder to escape the Queen's soldiers. She'd escaped. And if, no, *because* she was alive somewhere else, his duty was to make sure she stayed free.

Inside the training room, the mats had been stacked against one wall and the remaining floor space held over a dozen game stations, including an arrow-shooting game, a ball throwing game, a holocell fish catching game, and several complicated stacking and sorting games. Only a few had screens or holo tech. Most were physical and modeled on centuries-old entertainment.

When a space at the arrow-shooting game opened up, Dalin took it, interested despite himself. The game used a midsize bow with an easy draw. The arrows had sensor tips and the object was to shoot them into shifting holo targets down a narrow lane. Hefting the arrow, it was immediately obvious that they were unbalanced and would fall quickly without more velocity than the small bow could provide.

Dalin made an exaggerated search for posted rules, in case all of this was being recorded, and then dismantled one of the arrows to add weight and fletching to the other four. The smallest target was worth the most points. It also shimmered in and out of focus. His guess was that he had to hit it when it was in focus, like the catching-the-fish game.

He nocked the first arrow and took a deep breath, releasing the string as he breathed out. It wobbled a bit and hit the target next to the tiny one. A cheerful trumpet sounded along with a sparkly burst of yellow and red virtual confetti. Dalin adjusted his stance and waited for the cycle of targets to repeat, checking the timing. At the correct moment, he loosed the second arrow and hit the target on the other side of his goal. Again he received a sparkly burst of confetti.

"Great job," said someone behind him.

With a shake of his head, Dalin shifted his feet and this time remembered to adjust his shoulders as well. As the cycle repeated, he fired the third arrow straight through the target, just as it faded. Nothing happened.

"Went dark just before you hit it," said his spectator, a lanky guy about his age. "Just a millisecond sooner and it's yours. Where'd you learn to shoot a bow?"

"From my aunt's boyfriend," Dalin said, counting through the timing of the targets. Feet, shoulders, elbow, wrist all aligned, he pulled back and shot the arrow straight into the tiny glowing target. Louder trumpets blared and tiny animals, bears and dogs, jumped up and down in the sparkling rainbow-hued confetti.

"You got the high score with only four shots. Didn't this game have five arrows?" The spectator dropped to all fours, peering under the station table.

Dalin tapped the guy's shoulder. "I dismantled arrow five to make the other four fly true." He walked down the narrow shooting lane, through the holo targets, and grabbed the four arrows from the back wall, each tip stuck in some kind of foam board. "See?"

The guy took an arrow from Dalin, first hefting it and then checking the balance. "Destroy to create. I like it," he said, placing the arrow on the station along with the other three. "No wonder you fit in so well around here."

Destroy to create. No. That's not what he did, not who he was. But the simple statement gave life to the dark flower of doubt growing in his mind. As he stared unseeing at the games and people around him, the worst mental attack yet blasted his brain. Excruciating pain lit up every nerve, he endured agony beyond a concussion, a fall from a horse, a punch to the face. His eyes burned and blood dripped from his nose.

Someone had been throwing sucker punches, and this time Dalin wanted to hit back. Though he had never been trained to use his mental ability as a weapon, he dampened down his own pain and "saw" its point of origin. He lashed out, imagining a mental arrow flying true.

Just outside the door, Dalin's spectator swayed and fell, his head bouncing on the floor. Jameson was there in a few steps, barking for a towel to put under the man's head as his body arched into a *grand mal* seizure, feet drumming and neck straining. Jameson rolled him to his side, but the seizure continued on for another half minute. By then, despite the noise from some of the automated games, most of the team had gathered around.

Jameson yelled for a healer but sent two people from Team Asattha to the eighth room, the mini hospital, as well.

"Anyone see anything? Know anything?" Jameson asked, staring at the gathering crowd. Candidates looked at each other and back to the man on the floor. The seizure had passed, the body lying in a slack, awkward tangle of limbs. On the other side of the group, Dalin didn't see much in the expressions around him except indifference or, at the most, mild concern. He wiped his bloody nose on his sleeve and kept quiet.

"Is he dead?" a girl just behind Jameson asked.

"Still got a pulse. Still breathin'," he answered.

Two healers rolled a stretcher next to the prone fighter. With quick, efficient movements, they shifted the man onto the stretcher, raised it to waist height, and hurried away.

"Go train," Jameson said, his voice low and angry. "Don't just play the games you know. We compete in thirty minutes so make the time count."

Dalin went to his gear bag first and found one of his sealed water bottles. He checked the seal, wrapped with his special twist pattern in the adhesive, before cracking it and drinking the whole thing. His nose had stopped bleeding but it still felt swollen and clogged. The protein bars at the bottom of his bag generated interest from his stomach, especially after all the energy burned during the run. After making another blatant check for posted rules, Dalin quickly downed the protein bar and another half bottle of water. Although it still felt like someone had poured Geraldo's *salsa diablo* directly into his cranium, the pain had subsided to a low burn.

He'd punched the bully. Jin wouldn't be proud. But Jameson would approve.

Jameson was the one who taught him that self-defense meant strike to disable and end the fight. As he swished one last swallow of water around his mouth, Dalin looked at the place where the man had fallen, spots of blood still on the floor. If he believed the statistics from the flag round, he'd already killed two people. But this wasn't war, he reminded himself, this was a test.

His true test would be finding a way to win while keeping his darkness in check.

Chapter 33

Mara woke with a start, a shout ringing in her mind. Midmorning sun shone through tiny windows as Rafiq's ship made ready to land. As a smaller version of the ship they traveled on with the O Squad, the compartments could be rearranged for various purposes. Most of the medical bay had been collapsed to the rear of the craft, making room for the flight chairs.

Her pack with the rest of the currency, her book, and extra weapons had survived the fight outside Alandalus, though it was now scorched and torn. She had her sword and scabbard as well. But her main Mess uniform hadn't been salvageable and the spare was in need of repairs, so she wore a set of Rafiq's clothes, loose dark linen trousers and a linen tunic, with her boots.

"I didn't know this place existed," Halifax said from his seat. He didn't look much worse for the kidnapping, the escaping, and the fight outside Alandalus. One forearm was wrapped in a bandage to cover a long line of stitches, and he had a blue and purple bruise running down his jaw to his neck and shoulder.

"How far are we from Crown City?" Mara asked, deciding not to mention the mental shout. She'd been sleeping most of the trip, except for brief moments to eat, and her head still felt fuzzy from so many strange dreams.

Van Fuuren said, "We don't fly in and out of the main s'port in Crown City. We travel by horse because the roads are lined with sensors. This town," he pointed toward the porthole, "was created when our King began improving and extending the train system on Laska. It has many residents who are not only interested in avoiding the attention of the Commonwealth troops, but are also aligned with the ways of our late king."

"Horses?" Mara asked, hoping she'd heard wrong. As much as she'd love to ride under many other circumstances, right now they needed to hurry. Finding Dalin was imperative.

"We're about seventy-five kilometers from the capital," Van Fuuren answered. "You're still intending to reunite with Mr. de Forest?"

Mara nodded.

"And after that?" Even though the King's Man spoke, it was Halifax who raised his eyebrows and looked concerned.

Air turbulence bounced the craft as they continued the descent. Mara pressed against her seat and took a deep breath. "I'll convince him to withdraw from the tournament."

"My dear, the rules are ironclad. When your partner registered to compete, he became committed until elimination. That means losing or death."

Mara swallowed hard. They were almost on the ground. When the hatch opened, she'd be able to breathe again. "Then I'll join him in the fight."

Van Fuuren shot Halifax a look that conveyed how little he thought of that idea.

"You are free. Presumed missing or killed in the action on Iloel. All I require is that you journey with me to K—"

"No," Mara shouted. "Enough," she said with quieter force. "Our agreement was dependent on Dalin, my partner, going with us. We are here to retrieve him."

The ship landed with a series of jolting bounces. Mara closed her eyes and gripped the harness. Other people might wonder why Dalin had entered the tournament, but she knew it was because of their poorly conceived plan fueled by her guilt and distress over the war project casualties. The one they made before they knew anything about the Queen's Mess.

The stable was so near as to be visible from the small s'port, less than a kilometer away along a narrow, dirt road. Rafiq's craft was only one of three ships currently docked, with room for maybe three more ships at most.

Leaving Rafiq and Van Fuuren to confer with the s'port workers, Mara shouldered her pack, buckled her sword at her waist, and strode toward the buildings in the near distance. She took deep breaths of warm air, the sun heating the crown of her head.

"Monsoon season hit with a vengeance," Halifax said from directly behind her. "Can't believe how humid it is."

Mara paused a step, letting him catch up. "What will you do now?" she asked.

Halifax said, "I don't think I want to go back to the Mess. Eventually I need to let my family know I'm all right." He fell silent, their footfalls quiet on the soft dirt. Behind them, machines at the s'port hummed and whined. She half-expected a shout from one of their escorts as she and 'Fax kept walking.

It looked as though the landscape around the facilities and town had been cleared of trees long ago, but scrub forest closed in on two sides. It was the first significant stretch of trees she'd seen and from the window of the transport, the growth went on for tens of kilometers. These spindly trees couldn't hide the younger *gontra*, let alone a massive old Tree though. And if Laska was as under-explored as Asattha, a Tree could be on the other side of the planet and no humans would know about her.

"Our circumstances are surprising. Unexpected," Halifax said. "I'm intensely curious as to what might happen next. All great heroes need a chronicler, Mara. I want to be yours."

She whipped around to see his expression, but Halifax appeared serious.

"I'm not a great hero." She let out a sigh when she saw the two men now on the road behind them. "That King's Man thinks I'm something, someone… We'll do the tests and be done."

Halifax nodded. "Can't think of a hero who understood his or her place in human history at the moment it was happening. That's where chroniclers come in. But in the short term, might I offer my services as your bodyguard?"

Unable to help it, Mara laughed, the tightness in her chest loosening. "In your study of great heroes, did you find that most needed bodyguards?"

They were nearly at the stable now, a metal and green-painted wood structure that wasn't new, but certainly in good repair. It stood on the outskirts of a town not much larger than some of the settlements she'd visited on Asattha.

When they entered the tiny office, an elderly woman said, "How may I help you?"

"Do you work the stable alone, ma'am?" Halifax asked.

The woman curled both hands over a small metal box on the narrow counter separating them. "The boys are just in town watching that tournament on the new holoprojector. My grandson built it from parts, but it works fine."

"Our party has a reservation for some horses to ride into Crown City," Halifax began.

Mara pushed through the door and broke into a jog as soon as she cleared the corner of the stable. The town had a defined main street with a small, noisy crowd gathered at the far end.

Distance viewing of the tournament meant she might get a glimpse of Dalin.

* * *

About fifteen minutes into their remaining training time, a palace official appeared in the doorway, motioning to Jameson. While they spoke, Dalin recognized Jameson's "team player - love my government" body language and gestures that he'd used on some of their missions. Smiling, clapping the official on the shoulder, and vigorous nodding. Nothing the man would do in the course of a normal day or even month on Asattha. People didn't remember your clothes, unless they were completely wrong, like sandals in a snowstorm. But disguises only went so far. People remembered how you were, how you talked, the tone of the interaction. Despite those lessons, it was strange to see Jameson's even white teeth in a broad smile.

The minute the official was gone, Jameson whistled for the team's attention.

"Change of plans. We're straight to poison tasting. They scored enough dexterity data during your practice and need the equipment for some of the other groups. Grab your gear, we're moving out in three."

For the poison test, they were formally seated at two long tables covered in dark gold cloths set with cream-colored plates and silver tableware. Liveried palace servants brought in a soup course to start. A few grabbed spoons and started to eat. Poison tasting just before lunch was a tough draw for Team Asattha. People were hungry and not prepared to be cautious. Jameson clapped his hands and whistled.

"Exercise restraint, be suspicious, all of you. This isn't a meal. It's part of the tournament because it might be part of the champion's job. In case we have any experts among us, I've been instructed to tell you that today's possible poisons are all fast-acting. Some assassins will want a loud, agonizing, public death. That's what's on the menu for some of you lot, if you don't slow down and think."

Since the soup was served as individual portions, it was impossible to know if the whole batch was poisoned or just certain servings. Dalin lifted his bowl instead of his spoon and sniffed the steam. It looked and smelled like *mulligatawny*, with bits of chicken visible on the surface and a warm orange-yellow broth. The broth or the components of the soup could be poisoned, he reasoned.

"Do we report to you?" a candidate near Jameson asked.

"What? Oh, hold on," Jameson said just as chimes sounded from wrist units around the tables. "There you go. A scorecard was just sent to each of you. Make your notes there and submit after all of the courses have been tasted."

"Do we get real food later?" someone called.

"Not until after chess, I'm afraid," Jameson said. "But it will be a hearty meal because we've got a busy afternoon ahead of us."

Dalin took one tiny sip of broth from his spoon. It was bland. Some poisons, the better ones, were tasteless. He waited a full sixty seconds and then turned his spoon over on the saucer and pulled up the scorecard. Next to soup he marked, "no."

What followed was a traditional British-Indian meal, though the food lacked in both creativity and flavor. Only once, when he tasted the shrimp *vindaloo*, did Dalin think a poisonous agent might be present. It could have been the chili powder making his lips tingle or peppers. With a shrug, he checked "yes" next to the shrimp *vindaloo* and waited. The protein bar wasn't holding off his appetite completely, but he was really glad he'd eaten it or he'd be miserably hungry now.

Exclamations had died down after the soup and most of the candidates talked little as they tasted each dish. Jameson walked among the tables, answering what questions he could. A few muttered to themselves or each other, but quiet tension hung over the room.

When the last plates were cleared away, Jameson said, "Before we go to the chess room, raise your hand if you've never played."

About fifteen hands went up.

With a heavy sigh, Jameson said, "I was wondering about that." He tapped his wrist unit for a few moments and then chimes sounded around the tables. "This is a copy of the rules of chess. Standard tournament rules. Wipe your faces, push in your chairs, and line up in order of your experience. Most experienced closest to the front, least at the end of the line."

Once he'd started at the university, Dalin hadn't had much time for chess except the occasional game with his father. The militia station had a board, but no one played that he knew about. With an inward shrug, Dalin placed himself ten people from the front.

The heavyset man who'd struggled so much with the run stood right next to Jameson. "Chess tournament winner in my region for five years straight," he said.

"You're from Kels?" Jameson asked.

"My people come from Mullaghbrack. North and west of Tramore, closer to Mills Valley," the man said with pride.

Jameson moved along the line and with little prompting, each person gave his or her chess pedigree. Several were tournament winners, several more had been in regular chess clubs.

The person directly in front of Dalin was a petite female with large brown eyes and straight black hair held by a headband. "I play every week." She paused and let out a little breath. "I played every week with my *baba*, my grandmother."

Several people behind Dalin were regular weekly or monthly players, so he moved himself back until he reached the other occasional players like himself.

Jameson led them out with a reminder to stay in this order. They walked farther this time, from the palace to the school. Either nothing had been poisoned, or the caution to limit themselves to a taste had worked. Dalin puzzled over this until he turned the corner and saw another team approaching.

This group was in a bunch, rather than a line. They bore orange flag marks and right in the middle was Fentress. As they passed, she blew Dalin a kiss that garnered catcalls and whistles from both teams.

He shook his head and kept walking. "Isn't she the head of the Furies?" the girl who played chess with her grandmother asked.

Dalin didn't hear the response, but it triggered a few more looks his way.

"If the Queen had a selective breeding program, she'd throw both of you in it for sure," said the person directly behind him.

His startled intake of breath turned into a choking cough as he looked over his shoulder. The girl behind him, dark skin tight over the same sharp facial structure as Dr. Iskindar, narrowed her eyes. "What do I mean, 'if'? Probably got a whole slew of royally designed babies stashed around here in the interest of science."

The line stopped outside two classroom doors. Jameson said, "First two in line play against each other, and on down. Fifteen boards set up in this room. Ten boards in that room. Get your partner. Get to a board. You can't move them from their positions because of how the sensors are set to record points. Wait for the moderators' signal to begin."

As soon as he sat down across from the girl who thought he should be selectively bred, Dalin understood the purpose of the chess round. The way to win was to capture the opponent's king while protecting your own. Kook would've known that immediately. He'd have told everyone too.

Had the mental attacks impaired his acuity? Dalin half-listened to the rules and reminders while running through number progressions and the periodic table of elements in his head. Their room had two moderators walking between the pairs of players. They weren't wearing palace uniforms, so maybe they were actual chess experts?

Chess masters through the centuries had detailed and popularized many strategies for winning chess. One of Dalin's favorites, because of the challenge, was to win without sacrificing any pawns. Occasionally pawns did battle in that one, but it wasn't the traditional lose-by-layers-of-hierarchy method that most beginning players learned. He studied the board, trying to remember the moves for protecting the queen and the pawns, fighting from the middle.

The chess match was interesting but uneventful. Waiting for the next terrible thing to happen was almost worse than being in the middle of the next terrible thing. And maybe that was a different kind of test.

As pairs finished they were directed to grab lunch in the Mess Mess.

In nearly every other circumstance, Dalin would've signaled to Jameson they were leaving and probably taken charge of the group as well. Conscious that his profile was high enough already and that Jameson was supposed to be a stranger, he just stuck his hands in his pockets and followed along.

As promised, the Mess Mess had been rearranged into table groups to seat fifty. Flags in the seven tournament colors marked each team's area. To Dalin's relief, the food stations hadn't changed. The usual Mess Mess staff served from the warming pans and everyone appeared to be eating from a variety of stations.

He'd been worried that lunch would be in their room, served in individual portions. After Mara had been drugged, he didn't want to eat anything that had been out of his possession or individually prepared. Dalin really only felt safe eating at Cousins, but was willing to accept random chance in the cafeteria.

It became apparent who on Team Asattha had seen active service. The veterans filled their trays to the brim and made extra trips to fill water glasses. Then they hunched over their food and shoveled it in with complete focus. Jameson did the same thing when he arrived with the stragglers from the chess trial. But some ate sparingly, chatting with people around the table and shooting curious looks at the other teams.

Dalin didn't want to be overly full, but not knowing when they'd have another chance to eat, loaded up on complex carbohydrates and protein. He drank several glasses of water in addition to filling his water bottles and resealing them.

Rather than talk loudly over the whole group, Jameson moved from table to table saying, "Finish up and meet back in the training room in ten."

Wishing he had containers or something to wrap extra food in, Dalin cleared his tray and headed for the washroom. Geraldo probably had something he could use for perishables. It was stupid to hope that as the Queen's Champion he could keep his job as *sous* chef at an eating house in Lower Town, but with so little to hope for, Dalin clung to the idea that he'd be in that kitchen again soon.

Back in the room with Team Asattha, Jameson was directing people to have a seat with their gear. Only eight minutes had elapsed, but everyone was present.

"Right," said Jameson. "They calculated all of your scores from the four challenges this morning. Bottom ten are out. That includes the gent who had the seizure earlier."

Though a few people shifted positions, the group regarded their coach in silence.

"If I call your name, you are dismissed. No arguments. You made it this far and that's something. Everyone on this team has conducted themselves in an exemplary way. But rules are rules and we're down to forty as of now." Jameson read the names and said "thank you" after each one.

When the departing nine candidates were gone and out of earshot, Jameson said, "Not sure who's luckier, them or you. But no matter, you chose this tournament and on we go." He flicked the list in the air and chimes sounded around the room. "This is your scores, ranking you by challenge. Next step is to divide into two teams of twenty people each."

"For what purpose?" Dalin's chess opponent asked.

Jameson nodded. "That's an excellent question. Scan those scores and then we'll talk. They gave us an hour for strategy and then we suit up."

Dalin was curious about his own scores. He hadn't competed against total strangers since university. He hadn't tried to win anything in longer than that.

Across the four areas, Dalin had the second highest overall score. His run and dexterity scores were the highest, but he'd lost points during the poison test and a few more during the chess test.

The top name on the list was Ryoko Kimura. He looked around, gaze landing on the petite girl who played chess with her grandmother. Several people had scooted closer to her and were clapping her on the shoulder. Ryoko's cheeks were flushed pink and she bowed her head at each round of compliments.

"Back to this lass's question." Jameson pointed to the girl. She sat up straighter. "For what purpose will we divide into two groups?"

He had everyone's attention again. Dalin continued to be surprised at how his gruff, solitary mentor had morphed into a skilled field commander. And unlike a few of the roles he'd seen

Jameson play in undercover work, this had too many layers to be fake. Dalin would've bet a good pair of boots that Jameson had done this, been a leader of soldiers, at some point in his career.

"It's goin' to be a straight brawl. Capture the flag, but this time, only one flag. Team that wins moves on in the tournament. Losing team is eliminated, all twenty of 'em."

This produced chatter in several clusters of people. Jameson let it go for less than thirty seconds.

"So if I only wanted twenty of you to move ahead, I'd divide the teams one way. But let's say I think we have more than twenty excellent candidates ready to serve her majesty. How would we divide then?"

The mats were gone from their room, Dalin finally noticed. That's why the floor was so uncomfortable and everyone kept shifting. Conversation drifted both over and under the wall from the adjacent training space. Dalin had a good guess where Jameson was not-so-subtly leading them, but he was interested about what the rest of Team Asattha would conclude. Suppressing his natural instincts to lead had been hard at first, but now he was adjusting to hanging back.

"Ryoko and Dalin should be captains," one of the men was saying. "And then we should try to divide up the top scores in running and dexterity as evenly as possible between Team A and Team B. And, um, if you have the unofficial damage scores, you, I mean we, should factor those in as well."

"Chess skills don't matter in a brawl?" Jameson asked.

"Strategy matters in a brawl," said the heavyset man from Kels.

Jameson looked at the group, and Dalin could see what he saw, open body postures and thoughtful expressions for the most part, with a good measure of nervous movement all around.

"All right," Jameson said. "One more variable. We love our variables here, do we not?" This got a few smiles and grimaces. "Half the capture the flag rounds will take place in the stadium, rain or shine. The other half will be here, in the Box starting this afternoon."

After a pause to let that sink in, he continued, "No weapons. And you'll be wearing the advanced fight suits." An equal mix of protest and relief emerged on people's faces across Team Asattha.

Ryoko caught his eye and gave him a shy smile. "Permission to meet with my fellow captain to look at the scores?"

"Granted," Jameson said, looking up from his wrist unit. "We'll talk terrain while you do that. Now, sand versus mats?"

The scores showed Ryoko was skilled. But if Mara were his co-captain in this farce, they'd be unstoppable, Dalin couldn't help comparing the two as he and Ryoko moved to the far end of the room.

"A chess match can be won by either aggressive offense or solid defense. But you really need both," she said with a thoughtful nod. "Is this round timed?"

Dalin waved to get Jameson's attention. "Is the capture the flag round timed?"

With a frown, their coach scrolled through several pages of virtual documents. And though in many other circumstances none of those assembled would have waited silently, they sat and watched him with complete attention.

At last Jameson said, "Yeah, looks like. Fifteen minutes to get the other team's flag or both teams are eliminated."

"Aggressive offense it is then," Ryoko said.

Chapter 34

Roaring sounds, too large for the few dozen people visible, compelled Mara to keep jogging past the small and friendly looking shops. The street was made of bricks packed tight with red-brown dirt, aged and well kept, like the stable.

A circular metal dais, about three and half meters in diameter, and not quite a meter high, projected a dome-shaped image supported by metal petals at regular intervals.

"Lotus design," Halifax murmured, having followed as a bodyguard would.

This close, the noise took on the more distinct sounds of a large, excited crowd. Rows of seats were visible on the perimeter, but the center of the image was a group of fighters facing off against another group. None of them was tall enough to be Dalin, but Mara shuffled a few steps closer anyway. One of the central fighters did look familiar.

"How many is that?" Halifax asked. "Thirty?"

"Twenty against twenty," said a man to their right. "Team Dorado A versus Team Kels B."

"It's Fentress," Mara said, leaning even closer.

"What?" Halifax said. "How did she—"

The man on their right nodded. "Fentress is near the top in the wagers. She's looked really good so far."

Fentress grappled with a shorter male. They both wore the fight suits so neither could get a firm grip. Booted feet slipped on the sand. Save for a colored bit of fabric knotted around their upper arms, it was impossible to tell which team was which.

Fighters kept trying to dodge around where Fentress and the others with orange armbands fought, without success. Over their heads, a clock continued to tick down, flashing past four minutes as a person with an orange armband broke through the other side, a group distinguished by green armbands, and raced toward the far stairs. Someone tripped the runner and she bounced hard on the steps accompanied by audible dismay from the crowd. But another runner wearing an orange armband leaped over the slumped form and sprinted toward the top.

Vicious hand-to-hand continued around her, but Fentress finally dropped her opponent, first over her knee and then to the ground. She threw her head back and howled as the runner above grabbed the green flag and trumpets blared a series of high notes.

"Dorado A wins!"

"I knew it, they looked better just walking out."

"That Fentress is going all the way."

Currency changed hands as the image dimmed to nothing. For the first time Mara noticed the unusual mix of attire worn by the people around the platform. The variety of denim, tunics, leggings, sandals, and boots was more pronounced even than in Lower Town. But despite the range of clothing, one common attribute was that nothing looked new. Everything had a permanent layer of dust.

"What…which part of the tournament was that?" Halifax asked a female directly in front of him as she turned to leave.

The female ducked her chin and peered up at him through shaggy black bangs. "Did you just land?" she asked in heavily accented Origin English. "Not been watching so far?"

"Just landed," Halifax agreed. "Yes."

The female shrugged. "That was, ah, large group, mmm, capture the flag. Winners advance. Losers done. Orange armband team takes green armband team flag. Orange team win."

Mara stared at the metal dais and then checked the people standing and talking nearby. The image had hovered above it like an energy projection. But no one appeared to be manipulating or controlling the image.

"The next fight won't be on for a few hours," said the man who knew about Fentress. "You know any of the other candidates besides Fentress Elizalde?"

Keeping her hands still at her sides, Mara said, "Dalin de Forest? I think he—"

"He's going to win," said another man. "Never seen anyone fight like him."

"Someone heavier gets him to the ground, he's done," said the first man. "And," he continued, "that dumb skunk of a coach put him on Asattha B instead of Asattha A where he belongs. Everyone knows the A teams are supposed to win these capture the flag rounds."

"So de Forest's team, Asattha B, hasn't competed yet?" Mara gestured toward the empty dais.

"Yeah, they're the last fight in the stadium tonight," the other man said. "Wish I could've got some tickets."

"Thank you, we appreciate it, " Halifax said, gently tugging Mara back toward the stable.

Van Fuuren met them in the middle of the road, his face ruddy and damp. "You shouldn't be seen here," he said in the tone of an officer to a junior soldier.

But for all they were in this man's debt, they weren't under his command. "My objective is to find my partner," Mara said, matching his tone. "The woman at the stable indicated distance viewing for the tournament was taking place—"

"We could hear it," Halifax added.

"And we went to investigate," Mara finished. "We discovered that my partner competes tonight in the stadium."

Rafiq appeared at the corner of the stable. He waved them closer. "Mounts are ready. Rations from my ship are portioned out in the saddlebags. Everyone needs to top off water before we head out."

"Thank you, Mr. Malouf," Van Fuuren said. With a sharp nod he walked past Rafiq and disappeared in the stable.

"Dalin fights tonight," Mara said, keeping her voice low.

Rafiq tipped his head in Halifax's direction and raised his eyebrows.

"Oh," she said. "Rafiq Malouf, please meet Halifax—" The O Squad uniforms didn't have names on the upper chest so she didn't know his family name.

"Métis," Halifax said. "I was on the student observation squad with Ms. De La Luz and am also presumed missing in action."

When Rafiq's expression didn't change, Mara said, "Things happened on Iloel. My eyes, the drug, it changed me again and he—" She stopped trying to explain and huffed out a sigh. "You know how you like stories?" she said instead. "So does he." She nodded toward 'Fax. "Hasn't given me a reason not to trust him yet."

Unfolding his arms, Rafiq took off his headscarf and shook out the wrinkles.

"How far to Crown City?" she asked.

Rafiq squinted at the sky. "Approximately five hours. Unless it rains." He turned to the groom helping them. "How's the mud been the last week?"

"Not bad," the groom said. He cleared his throat and spit. "Been dry mostly. Only one good soaker since you left. Expectin' a big one this afternoon though."

Mara's mount was a handsome gelding, three or four years old. He stood patiently while she checked the tack, her hands and eyes following the exact order of steps dictated by Protector protocol, while her mind raced up the road.

To Dalin.

Chapter 35

Hours later, Geraldo swept Mara into a tight hug. "*Prima*, we were worried about you." He released his hold but kept her at arm's length to eye her rain-soaked clothes and hair. "What have you been eating?" His tone turned indignant. "I sent food with Rafe—"

"And it was delicious." The warmth of the eating house felt too close after the wind and the rain outside. But the familiar smells of green chile and cooking oil reminded her of comfort and safety. She swayed a little and steadied herself on the back of a chair. "It was all the days before that. Not a lot of food sources I could tr—, like yours."

Remembering herself long enough to glance around, she was surprised to see only one table occupied. "Where is everyone?"

"Getting ready to watch the last fight. Big holoprojector over in the market. Got a tarp covering most of the area so folks can still watch."

The skin on her arms pebbled with chill. Mara asked, "Dalin?"

Geraldo nodded, his expression darkening. "Rain or shine, last fight's in thirty."

Her clothes had dripped a small puddle on the floor. "Can I borrow—?"

"Go on back. Got a visitor who wants to see you anyhow. Where's *el jefe*?"

"Escorting the other passengers."

The staff door flew open and a small woman hurried out. She stopped, lips parting in a silent "oh."

As her eyes filled, Mara blinked hard. She hoped she wasn't hallucinating again.

"Mara." The woman reached a hand toward her cheek. "It's you," she breathed. "Light be praised."

"Elana?" Mara gripped the half-wall for support. "I'm not... I don't... They gave me poison and—"

With a gentle tug, her aunt pulled her into the back hallway and led her to the guest room. "I'm real. I'm here." She clasped Mara's cold hands together inside her small warm ones. "Let's get you dressed and something hot in your belly before we go out in the wet to watch your idiot partner fight."

Thoughts of Dalin dug sharp, urgent claws into Mara's consciousness. She had to get to him, tell him the mission could change. Movements stiff and uncoordinated, she stripped off her outer tunic and unwrapped her hair. But trying to hurry made things worse as her chilled fingers fumbled on buttons and clasps.

"Let me help," Elana said, and with care, unknotted Mara's boots and dropped them to the floor. Each time another piece of clothing came off and more skin was exposed to the air, cold tremors shook her frame.

The wet clothes in a heap, Mara huddled in a soft robe on the edge of the bed. Elana dug into the pocket of her trousers and withdrew a flat disk chrono like the one Jameson used.

With a gasp, Mara asked, "Is Jameson here?"

"If they're able to start on time in this weather, the fight starts in twenty minutes. I'd prefer to send you through a warm shower, but we're just going to get wet again."

Mara tilted her head to the side and squeezed a towel around her hair, not understanding what that had to do with Jameson.

"I'm in town for the tournament, same as a lot of folks. And I found work at this fine establishment. Going to help sell some handheld burritos to the good people watching the proceedings on the holoprojector in the market. Since you already work here, it's good you can come along," Elana said.

"Do I know you?" Mara asked, finally understanding the game.

"No," her aunt said. "You were away with your people for a time, and that's why they hired me on. But business is so good we can both work, at least while the tournament runs."

"Are you married?" Mara rubbed the towel over her head one last time and then ran her fingers through the worst of the tangles before starting a braid.

Elana wrapped her arms around herself, eyes sad for a moment. New lines of strain furrowed her brow. "There's a fella in the tournament. Not a fighter." She pushed her palm out in a stop motion and shook it. "No, he's a coach, I guess. There to help the process unfold as what's best for the Queen."

Mara pushed off the bed and hugged her aunt. "Jameson?" she whispered. "He's the coach?"

"On Dalin's team, or for Dalin's team, Team Asattha," Elana whispered back. "But you had to know the story." With a rueful smile, she added, "Is it too much to ask for all three of you to be safe at the same time?"

Elana and Geraldo packed an insulated rolling cart full of food while Mara dressed. Two layers of thick dry socks didn't do much inside her wet boots, but it was an improvement. At Geraldo's request, she went back for her sword and belted it around her hips.

"Expecting trouble?" she asked, ready to suggest that her aunt stay at the eating house.

"I'm carrying cash," the cook said. "That wouldn't matter most of the time, but all these people come to town for the tournament don't know what's what. Present company excluded," he said with a nod to Elana.

She smiled back and shrugged. "No offense taken."

"Watching a fight can get people charged up. And some of the ones who were eliminated been coming down here looking to make a problem."

Outside, the rain dripped down in a steady drizzle. Mara flipped up the hood of the jacket and helped her two companions arrange themselves so Geraldo could hold the umbrella over Elana and the rolling cart. She followed behind, one cold hand on the pommel of her sword.

A large crowd shifted and muttered under the patchwork of tarps. It was a marvel of Lower Town cooperation that so many individuals and businesses had contributed plastic sheets, as well as the ingenuity and work hours to string them together.

Geraldo nudged a man at the edge of the crowd. "How long until the last fight starts?"

"Any minute," the stranger said. "Looking to put some money down?" He took out a tiny glowing screen and smiled.

"No thanks," Geraldo replied. "Just here to offer warm food to the spectators. Burrito?" He gestured to the insulated rolling cart.

The man responded in the affirmative, becoming their first customer. The sale instantly attracted another three customers. It was hard to the resist the warm, delicious smells wafting through the crowd every time Elana took out a burrito.

But Mara chose to ignore her stomach and watch the people around them while keeping part of her attention on the large metal dais twelve meters away. Most everyone was wrapped in at least a coat, if not a hat or hood, and several layers of clothing. The absence of distinct garments and skin and hair changed the overall impression of Lower Town, blending shapes and genders and faces.

Weapons were visible on hips and backs, but it was better to assume every single person was armed. At the moment, the majority of the crowd was oriented toward the holoprojector, relatively motionless. The flow and churn of people moved around the last few meters of the perimeter of the market.

"Only eggs, cheese, potatoes, and vegetarian green chile. Don't want to offend anyone's gods on a night like this," Geraldo said to a potential customer. Elana looked tiny next to him, silently distributing food as the cook collected money and made change.

A shout went up from the center of the market, followed by whistles, cheers, and a significant increase in crowd noise. A hazy blue dome filled the air above the dais and the stadium appeared, looking much the same as it had earlier in the day.

The man who took wagers said, "I put some money on this one myself. Asattha A already won. That was expected. But they loaded Asattha B with some serious fighting talent, including one of my top picks."

Mara tilted her head down and realized the man was speaking to her. "Is that right?" she said, hiding her sudden interest.

"Him," the man said, pointing to the tall male figure leading a team onto the wet sand.

Leaning closer and pressing in with the crowd, Mara stared at Dalin's face. Beaded with mist, his golden hair and high cheekbones glinted in the overhead lights.

With deep breaths she took in the sight of him, suppressing a shudder of relief. He looked healthy, uninjured. He looked perfect. His eyes flashed silver as he pumped his fist in the air and yelled, "For the Queen."

"For the people," his team yelled.

The crowd in the stadium roared in approval, as did a good number of spectators in the market.

After a quick nod to Elana and Geraldo, Mara shouldered her way toward the dais. She had to get closer. She'd been away so long. Even though the image wasn't real, she needed to be close enough to touch.

Dalin stood at the point of a triangular formation, the sleek black fight suit molding the planes of his lean, sinewy body. Wearing red armbands, his team looked focused and ready for action. A crack of lightning flashed overhead. It was impossible to separate the ensuing rumble from the projector and the sound from the sky above the tarps. Fresh rain pattered down, adding to the visible puddles on the sand.

Team Asattha B was barefoot.

In her mind, Mara gave a nod of approval. Either Jameson or Dalin had made that call. In wet sand, the booties would have not only been a disadvantage, but dangerous.

The other team had entered the field. First murmurs and then cheers for Tian A burst from clusters of spectators. Not much more uniform in size and coloring than Asattha B, the Tian A team wore blue armbands. Their fight suits included booties.

The moment the leader of Tian A registered the change in her opponents' footwear, anger streaked across her face and disappeared. She turned and spoke to the two fighters directly behind her. The startling clarity of the holographic images allowed them to watch the message passing through the entire Tian A team. Audio was near useless though as only the loudest sounds made by the teams would carry over the crowd noise.

Just then the opening announcement blared over the loudspeaker and the clock lit up with fifteen minutes. The image shifted to show first the flags on either side, and then the full view of both teams advancing toward the center.

The two groups drew closer, the Tian team spreading into a wider formation as they moved. Dalin called orders and his team narrowed into a tight wedge, every individual's face intent on the other group.

When two meters separated the teams, Dalin yelled, "For Asattha," and lunged forward. With his second step, he used his momentum to punch the Tian A team leader in the face and sweep her legs, knocking her unconscious to the ground. Mara recoiled from the brutality of the hit as the crowd groaned and yelled.

From either side of the Asattha formation, a group of five split off and ran for the edges of the Tian team. Fighters in front protected the runners in the center. The Tian fighters were ready and on the one side stopped the Asattha group dead.

On the other side, a broad man from the Asattha team head-butted surprised Tian fighters. As first one and then another grabbed broken noses, he kicked out one fighter's knees and wrapped the other to drop her to the ground, an elbow to the temple. A smaller woman stayed right behind the broad man, though her intent to run for the flag was clear.

Dalin and nine others held their ground, dropping back only slightly to be clear of the downed bodies.

A group of three sprang over the Tian A leader's still form and went straight for Dalin. He kicked the center man in the chest, throwing him backward into the next line. The one on Dalin's left ducked in with a hard jab to his ribs. Dalin turned into the hit and grabbed the man's head. With a twist of his hips and one arm wrapped around Dalin's waist, the Tian fighter threw him down, water and sand splashing from the impact.

Mara clasped her hood tighter and pressed in closer. "Dalin, get up. Dalin, get up. Stand up, stand up," she chanted under her breath.

Chapter 36

Pain screamed through his shins and knees as Dalin thrashed under the combined hold of first two, and then three opponents. A gray haze filtered his vision and he yelled the first taunt he'd ever learned in Origin Chinese. "*Xiǎo yàng le ba, bèn dàn!*" Suck it, stupid egg.

Yelling keeps you breathing. A lesson Jin repeated for years.

Dalin yelled again, his favorite childhood insult, "*Jiào nǐ shēng háizi zhǎng zhì chuāng!*" May your children be born without a butthole! He laughed and choked, taking in a huge breath and then another.

The rest of the blocking team was counting on him to fight. They were under orders from Jameson to let Dalin take the double or triple attack and not interfere.

Cold water, gritty with sand, sluiced into his fight suit as he rolled and kicked one of the attackers in the head. He was far less effective as a ground fighter, all the scouting reports said so. They'd anticipated this move, but the water and the sand, not to mention the slickness of the fight suits, increased the difficulty of getting free.

"*Dalin, get up. Dalin, get up,*" a familiar voice burned with intensity in his mind.

The split second of distraction allowed the two Tian fighters pinning his arms and torso the chance to roll his face halfway into a puddle.

He resisted, took a deep breath, and rolled face down, grabbing a handful of sand with the one hand tucked under his body. He relaxed for a count of two and then used the power of the roll to kick again and throw sand in the eyes of the female holding his legs.

Freeing his other hand, he pushed to his knees and slammed the remaining two into each other. One slumped forward, the other swung for his head.

Dalin leaped to his feet, toes gripping the sand, and slammed his heel into the Tian fighter's solar plexus.

A glance at the clock showed four minutes elapsed. Precious time gone. The remaining nine fighters from Asattha B had held their formation and kept the Tian run group from advancing past their third of the stadium floor.

Relief that wasn't his own rolled through his mind. He swung in a quick circle, swiping the rain from his eyes, glad to see the Asattha B team making progress toward the flag.

A mental empathy attack? Intrusion?

"Behind you."

He whipped around and caught the blow on his shoulder, staggering as the sand moved under his feet. A quick sideways chop to the attacker's throat followed by a palm strike into the fighter's nose dropped him or her to the sand.

At least two of the rear guard for Asattha B were down.

Five of his people held their line, against only three Tian fighters still standing. They wouldn't get the Asattha flag tonight.

But if his team didn't capture the Tian flag, they would also be eliminated.

The rain prevented a clear view of the fighting on the other side of the stadium, and the wet armbands might have been the same color for all he could tell.

He lunged forward and made eye contact with a large female from his team. She grinned, showing bloody teeth, and mouthed, "Go." A fast pivot and she swung her knee into a high arc to jam it into the stomach of one of the Tian runners.

Jogging to the right, Dalin looked upfield. Clawing hands wrapped around his calf and tugged. The fighter who'd jumped on his shins wasn't completely down.

Yet.

Pulling up his knee, he aimed a kick at the fighter's face.

"Don't kill her."

Could the attack be from his conscience? Dalin flexed his toes to the side and kicked the fighter like he would a soccer ball, the blow hard enough to roll her over.

He leaped over the next two downed competitors and ran for the fight upfield.

Though his dad loved soccer, one of the few surviving sports from the Origin, Dalin hadn't played much. He grew too fast and couldn't coordinate his feet and legs with any success.

In his brief sprint, the screams of the crowd buffeting his ears, he wondered if Jin wished for a son who caused hundreds of people to cheer. And with that thought came the impulse to wave at the stands right before he jumped on the first Tian blocker, wrenching his neck around and throwing him down.

The man pulled Dalin with him and they landed in a tangle, rolling hard. Dalin's right shoulder and wrist took too much of the impact, but he thrashed to his feet and kicked water and sand into the man's face.

Deeper water flowed across the sand on this end, each step splashing wet and grit. Dalin tried to swipe at his eyes, but his right hand flopped. With a quick breath he tried to wiggle his fingers and only produced a tingling twitch.

So much for waving. With his awareness of the injury came the searing pain, as though someone had poured hot fry oil from his neck to his hand.

The two-minute trumpet sounded, launching him up the first few stairs. Wind blew the rain in clinging ropes of water, partly obscuring the desperate struggle directly in front of him. His best runner and best blocker couldn't get past the last group guarding the flag.

Dalin leaped over seats and slipped as he landed then caught himself with his left hand. He made it over five more rows before a Tian fighter caught up with him. She kicked him in the back, just under his wounded shoulder, but the kick propelled him forward. He leaped forward again, fighting for every meter.

"Thirty seconds."

He stopped and his pursuer crashed into him. But Dalin had braced for it and punched the female in the jaw, a hard hook with his left fist. His knee buckled on the follow-through and he fell on the stairs. Ten more stairs to climb.

The shouts of the crowd had changed to counting. The voice in his head counted as he limped upward, the cold syncrete slick under his bare toes.

"Five, four, three," the crowd shouted in unison.

He slapped at the wet flag dangling as limply as his useless wrist. With a scrape against already bleeding knuckles, he pulled the flag free as the final buzzer screeched.

* * *

Cheers from the holoprojector amplified the cheers and shouts in the square. Heart still pounding, Mara watched Dalin pull himself up, his face battered but serene. Proud.

But when he looked away from the crowd to count the members of his team still standing, he faltered for a split second. Only someone who knew him would notice.

The holoimage expanded the view again to show the stadium and the three people standing, arms linked, in front of the Asattha flag. They raised their arms and acknowledged the crowd.

Through the rain it was incredibly difficult to see if the crumpled figures, strewn across the stadium like broken toys, were moving, injured, or dead.

"Oh Dalin," Mara murmured.

A comforting hand slipped into hers. "It's awful," Elana said as they watched Dalin stagger down the stairs, checking every fallen contestant as he went. Healers in yellow raincoats ran out from one of the side doors and the image went dark.

The man who'd been taking bets began exchanging more currency, sometimes collecting, mostly from disgruntled Tian fans, sometimes giving out large stacks. "Told ya I picked that kid to win it all," he said to Mara. "You seemed to like what you saw. Want to put some money down on him? Little show of faith?"

Mara's throat closed, mouth tasting of blood. Sensory input from Dalin meant his shields were weak or down.

"Elana, will you and Geraldo be all right if I go back to Cousins now? I need—" She pressed her hand to her stomach, pain blooming everywhere at once. So many hits.

"Of course," Elana said. "We don't have anything left to sell. I don't have to tell you to be careful?"

Squeezing her eyes shut, Mara shook her head and heaved a sigh. "I'm sorry we left, Elana. We, I…just… We didn't know it would be like this." She swept her arm wide toward the holoprojector dais.

With a rueful smile, her aunt said, "Learning happens in a lot of ways."

Despite the early nightfall brought on by the weather, the streets of Lower Town were even more crowded than before. The noise pushed at her almost more than the people. Mara had to get to the eating house so she could concentrate on her partner. Dalin was hurrying somewhere, the pain in his wrist worse than the time he fell down some stairs as a child and broke his arm. The wrist was broken, he was sure of it, and sixteen of the team were down. Thirty-six counting the Tian team.

Mara rounded the last corner, consumed by the torrent of thoughts and impressions from her partner, and slammed into someone.

"Hey, *habibti,* looking for the back door or what?"

Rafiq. She was in the alley, not in the hallways of the stadium. Mara swallowed the panic and let some of the connection go, tamping it down with a soft thick barrier. Just to minimize the input and get herself together.

"Rafe, I, yes, I was looking for the back door. I forgot to get a key."

"Better that we go in through the front," he said, tugging on her arm, phantom pain in her wrist jangling along the nerves. "You don't look right. Need to lie down?"

Mara didn't answer until they were both inside, the smell of yesterday's *naan* calming and familiar. She went straight to the rack of mugs and poured herself some water.

The mug clattered as she tried to place it on a table, the tremors in her fingers uncontrollable.

Meanwhile Rafiq said nothing. He unwrapped his scarf and hung it over a chair and then sat to tug off wet boots.

"It's Dalin," she said. "His shield is compromised and I'm feeling everything, or almost everything he's feeling. I need to see…" *Touch, hold, heal.* "I need to see him."

* * *

Jameson met Dalin and the other three standing members of Asattha B at the mouth of the tunnel. "Report," he said.

Dalin tried to come to attention and failed when his right knee buckled. He swayed and managed to stand up reasonably straight, keeping his weight on his left leg.

The other three, who had survived guarding the flag, seemed to have similar but slightly fewer challenges. As they each reported injuries, stretchers bearing still forms hurried past, one after another. Dark stains soaked the white sheets.

When it was Dalin's turn, he said, "Broken wrist, damage to other joints, damage to internal organs, specifically kidneys, but also stomach."

Jameson nodded, the lines around his mouth tight and dark. "The healin' corps is not sufficient to accommodate this lot." He motioned toward the stretchers rolling past. "I'm bringin' in reinforcements, should be here soon. Can ya hang on?"

When Dalin pressed lightly on his abdomen, a phantom hand pressed over his own and soft healing energy flowed into him. The gray syncrete walls spun and nausea gripped him hard. "A chair?" he managed.

"Right," Jameson said. "Follow me now, quick as ya can." He turned and led the four of them out of the tunnel and into a drier, only slightly warmer hall. Dalin limped along at the back of their formation. He flinched as the same phantom hand probed the bones of his wrist, the healing light reaching into the damaged nerves and tendons.

Jameson and the others hurried, picking up speed. Dalin just needed a moment to rest his knee. He leaned on a wall, his fight suit making a wet mark on the raw plaster.

Was it possible? It had to be. *Mara.* Thank the Light, his partner was alive. Cradling his wrist, Dalin closed his eyes and reached for the connection, to the source of the energy flowing into him.

With a gasp, he opened his eyes to stare at the walls of the guest quarters behind the eating house. "*Mara?*" His body felt fine, he was just wet. Instead of the fight suit he wore a plain dark uniform.

"*Dalin? I'm here. I'm with you, your shields are compromised.*" A torrent of worry and care and giddy relief flooded his mind.

"*I need to touch you,*" he sent, unable to hold back the rush of desire, the intense need to bury his face in the wildflower and *gontra* scent of her hair.

Her response was unchecked and immediate. Her hands on his bare chest, her lips on his jaw, bodies pressed together shoulders to hips. "*I can draw from the source here. The Laskan Tree, she will help me heal you.*"

Dalin hit the ground with a thud, the sandy, gravel-strewn floor rough through the thin fight suit. Jameson and his teammates were no longer visible down the hall.

Mara.

Her presence steady in his mind.

She was near and he had to go to her.

Chapter 37

Mara couldn't get a deep breath, her blood pounding, energy burning through her system from the source, the Great Tree of Laska, wherever it was. Maybe she had the poison to thank. It didn't matter, if she could access the energy to help Dalin.

She rummaged through the spare clothes until she found a heavy coat in the back of the closet. Wadded into a tight ball, the jacket and a dry towel just fit into her pack. From the pile on the bed, she snagged an energy bar and a water bottle she'd filled from the kitchen sink and shoved those into her pockets. She adjusted her scabbard and hip belt, making sure it was buckled tight.

With a mental shout of apology to her aunt, Mara ran out the door.

The rain was just a mist now, but the streets were a mess of puddles, both shallow and deep. She sought the driest patches of street as she hurried, slowing to a jog along the more crowded stretches of road.

* * *

While Jameson moved between all the members of Team Asattha, Dalin found clothes to borrow. It was too far to his things. His feet were bare. Every step hurt and he couldn't move at more than a fast shuffle. Crowds of spectators surrounded the stadium, some trying to get in and many trying to get out. The guards couldn't be bothered with one stooped, limping man.

The road wound around the base of the stadium and turned downhill at the corner of the Mess.

Mara was running. Somehow she was sharing energy even as she ran. He accepted the flow with gratitude, letting it wrap around his knee and soothe the torn soles of his feet. Dalin stayed in the shadows, but he hurried, drawn toward her like iron to a magnet.

* * *

The crowds thinned as she turned uphill into the nicer merchant section of Palace Hill. Singing drifted from a tavern along a side street, and clusters of people chattered in what sounded like all of the Commonwealth languages at once. Lights from the permanent businesses and larger homes kept the full darkness of the cloudy night away.

Dalin was close, hobbling along, but close, his mind burning bright. She inhaled the sharp scent of mint, a thick patch nearby soaking in the day's moisture. And then she smelled it again through their connection. Around the back of the next house, a figure leaned for support against a small mahogany tree. Though his face was deep in shadow, his normally straight back hunched, it was *him*.

Mara slowed her steps. "Dalin?" she whispered.

"Here," he said and reached out a hand.

The first touch of skin to skin was like a spark to dry tinder. Heat rushed up her arms and legs, but Mara moved slowly, carefully closer. She brought his bruised knuckles to her lips and kissed them, one at a time, letting the energy flow through her and into her partner.

He was balanced against the tree, leaning hard on his mostly uninjured leg, letting the shoulder on that side take a lot of his weight as well. She moved another step closer and he wrapped a hand around her ponytail and the back of her head, pulling her in.

One eye was swollen nearly shut, but Dalin's good eye gleamed bright silver in the dim light. She leaned in and brushed her lips over the puffy lid and down along his cheekbone. With two fingers, she traced his split lip and the shadow of his jawline, more bruise than whiskers.

Mara didn't have healer training, didn't know the physiology of cellular and neural regeneration, but she could give comfort and take away a little pain. And when Dalin was ready, she could be a conduit to help him channel the healing energy where it was needed most.

"Soldier, you were out of position," she said.

A hint of a grin turned up one corner of his mouth. "I was," he said, voice rough and soft.

Closing her eyes, she inhaled until she found the *gontra* and sandalwood scent of him, under the sweat and rubber tinge of fight suit, under the slightly sweet chemical smell of Mess laundry.

"They told me," he began and stopped, swallowing audibly. "Your name was on the MIA list," he said.

The words triggered memories of his anguish, his fury, helplessness, and resignation, flowing into her mind now too. "You lost hope?"

A light tremor passed through him and he nodded. "I thought I would know if you were really gone, but...I made sure to stay on mission, just in case. And the tournament gave me a way to—" He sighed and showed her the fights at La Kill, even the worst ones. Under the words, tracking alongside the memories, were dark undercurrents and deeper feelings.

Oh, Dalin. What would she have done in his place? All she knew was him and how to fight. Without him, the fight would be all that was left. Mara kissed his forehead, salty with sweat and damp with the misting rain. "I'm here now," she whispered and kissed his temple. "You won't fight alone. We'll finish it together."

With a massive shudder, Dalin pushed her back. "No," he said. "You are free. And you should go." With the shove, he clamped down on their connection until the open flowing conduit was only a thread of energy between them.

Losing her footing on the damp ground, Mara slipped and caught a slender branch to stop herself from falling. Covering her shock, she took off her pack and unrolled the jacket and towel. She held the two items out, one in each hand.

"I'm sorry," he said. He took the jacket and slipped it over one arm. Mara moved the branches and helped him ease the injured shoulder inside. She swiped the towel inside the collar before pressing it into his hand.

"We can get a healer," she said, as though Dalin hadn't just shoved her away. She knew from experience injuries could make even a gentle horse snappish and defensive. "Will you be missed?"

Dalin shook his head and eased himself a few steps toward the street. "My mother would have many judgmental words for the way this place is run. My dad too, for that matter."

Just down the hill, rowdy singing was punctuated by unintelligible yelling.

"Most of the candidates are too injured to continue tomorrow, and they don't have enough healers so it will be at least a day, but probably three before the tournament starts up again."

Disappear with me, Mara wanted to say. Instead, she switched the scabbard to her other hip and slipped under Dalin's arm. He let her take some of the weight from his injured knee.

Clusters of people spilled into the streets, even though every tavern and eating house was open. The mood of the crowd was cheerful, but armed Commonwealth guards walked among the revelers, their dark uniforms standing out amid the color and noise.

Dalin needed a bed and a healer. Those imperatives drove Mara as she guided them both through the side streets and alleys, winding deeper into Lower Town.

He hadn't been trained as a Protector and his pride kept him from accepting help, accepting that partnership was designed for mutual support.

They were only a hundred meters from Cousins when Dalin staggered into a doorway, catching himself just before he hit his head. The overhead light gleamed on his wet hair, his breathing hard and ragged.

Mara had just handed over her water bottle when a familiar voice rang out, "Looking for some company after your victory tonight, Romeo?"

Fentress, Kailer, and a half dozen of the Furies ambled closer. "Fought like the son of Darkness, you did," she said. "Proud to know you."

Something wasn't right about the leader of the Furies. Cheeks and nose flushed bright pink, eyes reddened, she swayed and tapped to a rhythm only she could hear. Similarly, Kailer twitched her fingers and shuffled her feet, eyes darting back and forth.

"Maybe I'll even get a piece of you when the final matches roll around, if you survive—" She jerked forward, her expression lighting with exaggerated surprise. "*Madre de Dios*, it's Mara. Kailer, didn't I tell you *ese mujer* was the least likely to be killed in action in the history of killed in action?"

With unnatural strength, Fentress grabbed Mara's arm and pulled her into their circle. "The Queen herself as my witness, I said you would become a Fury the minute you returned. Isn't that right, my beauties?"

Kailer howled in response and the others threw back their heads with high-pitched howls.

Their noise would attract Commonwealth guards any moment. And Dalin could barely stand. Despite his assurances about the lack of accountability for tournament competitors, she wanted him off the street.

With a stiff bow, Mara shook loose of Fentress's hold and said, "You do me great honor. It would be my pleasure to join you at your next ceremony."

Kailer laughed as did some of the others.

"Screw ceremony, Furies are made in the moment." With a blindingly fast flash of steel, Fentress brandished a knife and drew it across her palm. "We are blood sisters, the Furies." She flipped the knife in the air, caught it by the hilt, and held it out to Mara.

With a backward glance at Dalin, and a longer look for guards, Mara asked, "What is the promise of a blood sister?"

The murmuring females drew nearer until Mara and Fentress stood within a closed circle.

"Long ago, women were not thought to be the equal of men," one began.

"Even though we fought side by side."

"Males took advantage."

"Sisters and mothers were harmed, taken, and used."

"Until the first Fury killed her attacker, strangled him with her bedsheets."

"Justice," Kailer said.

"Blood sisters answer the call of need."

"The Furies serve Justice," Fentress said. "When the law of the land does not."

"The Furies serve Justice," the assembled Furies chorused.

The energy whipped up by their words pulsed in the circle. Part of Mara wanted to break through, grab Dalin, and haul him to safety. But another part recognized the promise in serving Justice. Wasn't that what it meant to be a Protector?

She took the knife from Fentress.

"Good. I knew this was your destiny from the first time I saw you fight. Repeat after me." She waited for Mara's nod. "If I am able, I will answer the call of need."

"If I am able, I will answer the call of need," Mara said.

"For my sisters."

"For my sisters."

"Justice must be served."

"Justice must be served."

"In Darkness and in Light."

"In Darkness and in Light."

"Seal the promise with blood," Fentress said, holding out her bleeding palm.

Mara drew the sharp blade across her palm, the weight of every other promise heavy on her mind.

Fentress slapped their wounds together then kissed her on the lips.

The Furies cheered and broke the circle, clapping and hooting.

Pulling back with a teasing smile, Fentress said, "Join us to celebrate? Finish the initiation properly?"

"My partner's healing comes before celebration," Mara said, trying to hide how off-balance she felt. She now owed a promise to the Furies as well as the King's Men. And Dalin was nearly unconscious with pain. "It is my own way of serving Justice in this moment. I hope you understand."

With a wink and a tilt of her head that flashed her nose ring, Fentress said, "That Romeo *es un hombre muy afortunado*." She licked her cut. "*Hasta la lucha proxima*."

"Until the next fight," Kailer yelled.

And they were gone, without appearing to hurry, the group of females vanished up the street, leaving Dalin and Mara alone.

Chapter 38

Dalin didn't know where he was. The moment he tried to sit up, he triggered the pain in his wrist, his abdomen, and shoulder. "*Wáng bā dan*," he muttered. Son of a bitch, everything hurt, the cumulative damage from fight training and the tournament too much for short-term healing.

Air stirred and then a soft hand touched his cheek. "Sleep and heal," the voice said. The hand moved to his uninjured shoulder, easing him back to the pillow.

"Mara?" he whispered, voice hoarse with sleep and need.

A sigh came from above him. "No, she's in the next room. Our girl's not in much better shape than you. Running into the rain to find you then bringing you here, she didn't do herself any favors."

The sheets pulled tight and settled over him again. "It's Elana," she said. "Your almost big sister?"

"Elana," he repeated. "You're here with Jameson."

A soft laugh. "I'm here with you. And no action is required but sleeping. The healer worked a lot of expensive hours on you and you best make use of that skill, *Dì di*." She sighed again. "Little brother, what were you thinking?"

Dalin couldn't remember much after the Furies had pulled Mara into some kind of chanting circle. She'd been so steady with him, not a hint of injuries of her own. "I need to see her." He started to sit up again, more awake now and able to move without hurting himself.

Soft light spilled into the room as the door opened.

"He's awake?" Mara asked.

"And so are you, apparently," Elana replied. "I'm an utter failure as a healer's assistant."

As Mara hurried to the side of the bed, the long tunic she wore fluttered above her knees. The calluses of her sword hand scraped softly across his forehead and she frowned at him. "You're warm." She looked at her aunt. "Don't you think so, Elana?"

Elana laid the back of her hand against his cheek. "Maybe a little. Could just be from sleeping." She stood and opened the door a little wider. "I'll get water for both of you. Don't. Move. No fighting, running, or joining anyone's army. Are we clear?"

"Yes, ma'am," they said in unison. Mara smiled at him as she perched on the edge of the bed, sharing the tiny joke. She was here. She was alive. The tight band around his chest loosened and he took a deep breath.

"They told me you were missing, presumed dead," he said.

"I was missing, technically," she said. Reaching around, she pulled her hair to one side and combed her fingers through the ends. "But I made some stupid decisions. We didn't know." She sighed. "Our intel was terrible. Couldn't have been worse on the ground if someone had written a story instead of a report."

Dalin braced on his good shoulder and moved to one side of the bed. "I want to hear everything about your time on Iloel. And maybe you can show me too?" He folded back the sheet and patted the spot next to him.

Glancing at the empty doorway, Mara hesitated. "You might be running a fever."

"Doubtful," he said. "Just an elevated temp as a result of the healing taking place." Even to his own ears, he failed to sound confident and certain.

She reached for his hand but after a caress across his knuckles turned it over and laid two fingers over the veins in his wrist. "Same steady heartbeat," she said.

"Elana said you were injured?"

Mara shrugged. "It was an ugly fight at the end. Them with energy weapons against me and my sword." She pressed her lips together and looked like she wanted to say more. "Seems like no one knows when you need to report back for the tournament."

Grasping her hand, Dalin sat up. They needed tomorrow. They needed days and days to reconnect. He had so much to tell his partner. Holding her hand, looking at her sleep-softened face, he felt something shift inside him, settling in place like a book long borrowed and finally returned to the empty spot on the shelf.

He wasn't meant to be alone.

Elana bustled in, carrying two full mugs of water. She handed them over and then folded her arms. "Dalin, I know what you're going to say."

"Thank you for the water?"

"You want Mara in here with you. Just like when you were little."

Mara choked on her water. She coughed and then said, "I remember that. We slept at my house sometimes and at your house sometimes."

"And outside," Dalin added.

Her smile broadened and Dalin grinned back.

"*But you didn't look like that,*" she sent.

"*Neither did you,*" he replied.

"People who want to have sleepovers drink all their water and rest," Elana said. "I'll know if you don't."

They both drank quickly and handed back the mugs. "I'll be right next door," she said, pointing one of the empty mugs at Dalin.

"We're gonna sleep," Dalin said.

"Heard that before," she replied. But then her shoulders loosened and she smiled. "I need you both to stay safe and get healed. I can't tell you how relieved I feel to have you in the same place at the same time and no one's in immediate danger."

"Jameson?" Mara asked.

Elana waved a hand, batting the question away. "That's different." She blew them a kiss and left, closing the door behind her.

* * *

It took several breaths for Mara's eyes to adjust to the darkened room. "More people are against the Queen than we thought," she said.

What she wanted to do was slip under the sheet next to him and let her body and its instincts lead. But in case they didn't have tomorrow, she needed Dalin to hear what she'd discovered on Iloel. "The monarchy is going to change and likely the Commonwealth government too, with or without us."

Dalin made an mmmhmmming sound and tugged her closer.

"The Queen's Champion will be under assault as much as the Queen, maybe more." Mara resisted his pull a moment longer and then gave in. She lowered her head to the pillow and swung her legs onto the bed, tugging the sheet and light blanket over both of them.

Shifting to her side, she stroked the tips of his spiky hair and trailed her fingers over his cheekbone and jaw. Even back when they'd first traveled together, Mara had loved the angles of Dalin's face. One of the recovered memories of their childhood was her fascination with his eyes, the shape and the color of them. She leaned in and pressed a kiss to the corner of one closed eye, breathing deeply through her nose.

Gontra and sandalwood and home.

Dalin shifted closer until they were touching ankle to head. Blurred with sleep, his voice was soft in her ear. "Always want to be alone with you. Last time, so mad about the poison and the mission. Had to get money and weapons. Needed you…"

An image of the two of them wearing next to nothing and entwined on his bed appeared in her mind. But with the image came the weighted feeling of a healing compulsion to sink back into sleep.

"That's what you want?" her voice caught as she asked.

"All the time. Every night. I…never sleep. Anymore." The space between the words stretched into deep, even breathing.

The muscles in Dalin's thighs twitched and then his feet. As his big body relaxed into the healing rest, she wished for more time to *be* with him, talk with him, and more light to look at him.

* * *

Repeated knocking woke Dalin from the best sleep he'd had since arriving in Crown City. He turned his head on the pillow and in the early morning light smiled into his partner's deep blue eyes.

"It's Elana," he whispered.

"Why is she knocking?" Mara asked.

"Just in case," Dalin said, his expression turning rueful.

"Oh," Mara said. "Oh." She leapt out of the bed and shook the tunic down over her toned, muscular thighs. "Come in, Elana," she called.

Jameson pushed open the door, Elana by his side.

"Call went out for all candidates to report. You have thirty minutes until the next event," Jameson said.

Dalin's body rearranged priorities as he sat up a little too quickly, bunching the blanket on his lap. "What's the event?"

"Sounds like an etiquette quiz and then dancing."

Nothing on Jameson's face showed humor.

"What does that—?" Mara began.

"Queen's Champion is a state position, and the role has some similarities with that of an ambassador," Elana said. "But you could drop out now, Dalin. We can report your injuries—"

"I'm fine," he said. He stood and flicked the sheets back into place, his wrist and shoulder working again. Leaning slightly, he tested his ankle and got only a slight twinge. "I'm great actually."

Jameson dumped a fresh uniform on the bed, then grabbed his wife's hand and tugged her out the door. "Out front in five," he said.

"Sir," Dalin replied.

Eyes widening, Mara raised her hands in protest. "You can drop out, we don't need the plan. In fact, we need to abandon that mission completely. So many more people, more groups, whole cities and planets are working toward the same—"

As she talked, he moved toward her and she backed up until her shoulder blades touched the door, surprise choking off the flow of her words.

Dalin leaned in and kissed her the way he'd been dreaming about, at first long and lingering, relearning the shape of her lips, then deeper and possessive. He wanted her to know she belonged with him,

Way sooner than he wanted, he pulled back scant millimeters to take a breath before he said, "Would you drop out if it was you?"

"We made that plan in isolation," Mara insisted. "And we didn't know." She paused, her gaze drifting back to his mouth where it lingered. Then she raised her eyes to his and admitted, "No, I wouldn't drop out. But you should."

Dalin pulled his head back at the flash of fear he saw cross Mara's beautiful face.

"Don't you dare die."

Chapter 39

"Wish that *cabrón* could've stayed long enough to do some cooking," Geraldo said as he checked the *puercotro* stewing in a heavy iron pot. Elana looked up from chopping onions, and Mara paused with one hand in the sink.

"How did you know Dalin cooks?" Mara asked.

"Didn't you ask him to look in on us while you was gone?" the massive cook replied. "He got one taste of my paradise," Geraldo spread his arms wide and turned slightly to his left and right, "and he asked if he could audition to be my *sous* chef."

Though she was still frustrated by her partner's choice to return to the tournament, she had to smile at the vision of Dalin and Geraldo working side by side.

"He whipped up some mighty fine grub too, somethin' Chinese. Fish. Customers really liked it."

A savage yell, far too loud for the hour in Lower Town, was answered by more yelling and then punctuated by something heavy hitting the wall on the other side of the sink.

"The crowds were noisy last night," Elana said, keeping her knife as she pushed through the kitchen door. "But it's not even noon. What's got them going again?"

Mara followed close behind, emerging into the dining room as Rafiq came in through the front door, bolted it, and threw the heavy bar down into the bracket.

"The message is going to repeat unless the Crown finds a way to stop it," he said. "Our fellow citizens of Lower Town are expressing their displeasure, *cocinero*," he added as Geraldo poked his head through the swinging door.

"About what, *jefe*?"

"Come with me and you'll see." Rafiq led them down the back hall, pausing long enough to shove a knife and flat disk into his pockets. Mara belted on her sword and grabbed a large headscarf. Elana jammed a hat over her hair and hurried after them into the alley.

The morning sky was a painfully bright, clear blue, all traces of the previous evening's storm blown away by a steady breeze. The alley didn't smell fresh, but it smelled far less rank than usual. If Rafiq hadn't seemed so serious, and the angry sounds of people weren't coming from the market, Mara would have smiled at the significant improvement in her situation over the past day.

Instead, she wrapped the headscarf as she walked, draping it as a loose cowl and hood to keep her face partially obscured.

On the near corner of the open market space, a woman stood on a crate addressing several dozen people in a language Mara did not know. Her aunt slowed and tilted her head to listen.

"My Origin Arabic's not that good, but in essence she's saying that the tournament is an extravagant distraction put on by a madwoman. People who..." Elana frowned and resumed walking. "People who love their families and love the Commonwealth cannot tolerate such a monarch in the palace one moment longer."

Angry voices rose all around them as Rafiq led their group closer to the holoprojector dais. The plastic sheets from the night before were still tied in place, flapping gently, rubbing and rustling together like giant leaves.

"It's got to be a hoax," a man was saying.

"How could the Queen be murdering people and we didn't know?" said a woman.

"She murdered her grandfather. Everyone knows that," a third person added.

Trumpets blared and the light of the projected blue dome flared in the artificial shade of the sheeting covering the square.

A man in a traditional military uniform of Origin India, complete with turban and satin waist sash, stood in front of seated crowd of well-dressed people. Most likely they were the same group or some portion of the group of dignitaries in Crown City for the tournament. "Why an etiquette quiz? Why dancing, you might ask." He folded his hands and leaned on the podium.

"Her majesty has grown concerned over the changes on the planets of the Commonwealth. Her chief desire for the coming year is to travel among her people, offering a message of support and hope." The crowd in the square booed and yelled at the man, obscuring his next few words.

"…And as such, must travel with the Queen, always ready to serve. The third and final event of the day will simulate a rescue scenario and it promises to be exciting. Now, let's review the candidates who are still…with us…" He tapped his ornate wrist unit and nodded. The virtual note didn't show on the holoimage, but he began reading names.

With the sound of paper tearing, the official and the dignitaries disappeared. The word "Attention" flashed in Origin English, and then repeated six more times in each of the other main languages of the Commonwealth.

A new image of a large white room with rows and rows of occupied beds appeared. "Ever wonder why your loved ones never returned from the Queen's Military Skills and Strategy School? Your children who did not complete training and yet mysteriously chose to stay in Crown City?" A loud voice with flat intonation blared from the speakers.

While the questions repeated in Origin Spanish and Origin Chinese, Mara said to her aunt, "Is that a man talking? It doesn't sound right."

"It was altered with tech," Rafiq said. "Whoever created this fed the words into a machine and not only produced the translations but also created a false voice."

"The Mess, as it's commonly known, uses a merit system for all students, tracking them by points. Cuts are made on a regular basis to dismiss those not meeting the standards for military service. Each individual shown here was at one time enrolled in the Mess. Some have been part of this experiment pool for more than two years."

The strange, inhuman voice repeated this in Origin Arabic and Origin Hindi. Meanwhile the image traveled down the rows of beds, pausing to scan strange equipment attached to some of the people in the beds, and sometimes scanning the young, sleeping faces.

"Could they be in comas?" Elana said to Rafiq. "Is this real?"

"Where I'm from," he said, "something this rough would likely be a forgery. But here, with no precedent, and certainly the rumor base to support the content, I'm inclined to believe it."

Geraldo ambled up and tapped Rafiq on the shoulder. "Boss, this is going out across the system. Whoever sent this accessed the full tournament feed to every planet. Sent out the names of those kids in the beds, along with the date they entered the"—he gestured at the dais—"the ward, hospital, clinic, whatever that place is."

"Hold on," Rafiq said.

The holoimage flickered, making a sound like a lightning strike. In the new image, the tiny Queen with her arms and hands bare reached out to touch Emily bin Haribin.

Mara couldn't look away as the assistant information minister flinched, the woman's skin changing color as the *vishakanya* laid their bare hands on her face and neck.

Loud declarations of horror and outrage swept through the crowd. Vanora turned, the look in her black eyes cold and vicious. The Queen lunged into a crowd. Teachers from the Mess. They fell over one another, fleeing the touch of the Queen and her lethal bodyguards.

A silver flash, like a twirling staff, and Elsebet Iskindar appeared, using her fully extended flow baton as a barrier between the killers and the teachers fleeing up the stairs behind her. Just behind her, Dalin helped people stand, untangled them, urging them out of view. One of the *vishakanya* tried to reach past her and Professor Iskindar rapped the girl on the forehead.

The blow must have conveyed some kind of energy because the girl flipped up and backward onto the floor. The crowd in the square cheered as the dais went dark.

One of the merchants turned over a heavy pot and scrambled to stand on it directly in front of the dais. His gray hair and full gray beard gleamed in the soft light under the canopy, drawing attention from his plain black and brown robe. "Someone is trying to deliver truth to all of us who have been starved for it, starved by this monarchy for so many reasons."

Elana translated when he switched to Origin Hindi, appealing to the crowd to save their violence for Vanora and the evil people at the palace and elsewhere who had allowed her schemes to go forward.

* * *

Dalin grinned through the etiquette quiz. Of course he was genuinely happy so many members of Asattha A had made it to this round. And it was good to see the remaining three members of Asattha B. Good to walk with almost no limp, good to write with his dominant hand. It was time for dancing now and then the next round of names would be cut.

Inside his mental shield, he felt as bright and sparkling as Tree Square during Candle's Promise. Mara was alive and relatively unharmed. She had healed him with her warmth, her soft kisses to his face and chest; she had given him the solace to sleep the peace of a man who had his partner by his side.

And he had touched her, talked with her, kissed her. On the ride back to the Mess, he'd allowed himself to think about that kiss, about the feel of her lips on his skin. Once they'd arrived at the school, he tucked all of that in a secure vault deep in his mind.

"Dalin," his co-captain whispered, tugging him away from the wall as the music began. "You're not paying attention. Vanora will be joining us for this round."

His grin faded as he asked, "And the *vishakanya*?"

"No one said." She tapped the top button on his uniform. "Are you dosing? Is that what's going on? You seemed clean yesterday but you'll get disqualified if—"

"No," Dalin interrupted her. "I'm clean. What rules did I miss?"

Ryoko huffed out a breath. "No weapons. No fighting. Just dancing. Everyone should dance, follow the music and follow the forms. When it's your turn with her majesty, full bow. Only a few minutes and then she'll move on." She took her headband out, shook her straight black hair loose and then slid the headband back into place. "The courtiers bunched in front of the musicians are the judges."

Just as Ryoko finished her summary, Vanora, wearing a gold-embroidered pale yellow sari, gold satin gloves, and a delicate tiara, stepped onto the dance floor, escorted by the old general. Taking the cue, the music began. It was an ancient dance from Origin Europe, the waltz.

During the etiquette quiz and certainly now, Dalin felt grudging appreciation for the years of lessons his mother had forced on him.

This fork, that glass, bows of various depths, manners and titles and lines of precedence until all of it was as smooth as a parade drill and as second nature as swinging a sword.

The dance event was being held in an actual ballroom in the palace. Cold air flowed in from numerous vents and was stirred by large ceiling fans. The dark wood floor was slick with polish and the tall windows showed neither dust nor fingerprints. A few padded chairs and couches were grouped at either end of the oblong room, but no one sat.

Dalin placed his co-captain's hand on his shoulder, took her other hand, and swung them onto the floor.

Vanora stayed with the general for the full three minutes of the first song. But when it ended, she stepped away from him and waited. The next song began, incorporating more traditional Indian instruments, but also drums and a heavier beat. A candidate wearing a blue armband bowed and offered her arm. The Queen accepted and the pair joined the complicated sequence of steps.

When Vanora changed partners, the candidates changed partners also. The exchanges did not happen smoothly, triggering whispers and note-taking from the judges.

Dalin checked his mental shields as he adjusted his uniform. During the first dozen exchanges, he managed to join the forms without much trouble. Like fighting, footwork was critical for dancing. Problem was, the upper body had to be properly aligned and his height discrepancy with many in the room made physical alignment a challenge.

The musicians played traditional music from the dominant language and culture groups around the Commonwealth. For a reign with remarkably few celebrations of any kind, the dance event could've been festive. Instead the dancers performed with solemn, and in some cases fierce, concentration. As flutes and violins opened the next song, a shriek echoed across the cold room.

Dalin's dance partner, a tall awkward man less coordinated than Gunder, stopped suddenly, causing Dalin to trip on his boots.

"You killed my sister," a different voice screamed. Many of the dancers rushed toward the yelling. But uniformed palace guards shoved them aside as they sought the Queen.

Kailer had Vanora pinned to the floor, kneeling on her chest, a thin, jeweled knife at her throat. "Hands down," Kailer screamed.

Vanora's thin red mouth moved, but her words were swallowed in the chaos as the palace guards pushed through the closest circle of candidates and advanced on Kailer. The monarch kept her gloved hands on the floor.

"Release the Queen," one of the guards commanded.

"Death to Vanora, murderer of people and planets," Kailer yelled, raising the knife above her head.

Vanora spit in her face, a huge wet mass landing on Kailer's cheek. The girl jerked, blinking rapidly, and then shivered. She toppled slowly sideways, tremors running the length of her body, her hands and feet paddling the air.

Across the space created by the guards, Fentress watched, her face bone white with helpless fury. When the guards lifted her limp partner from the floor, Fentress turned away, arms folded and shoulders curling inward.

A cluster of *vishakanya* helped Vanora to her feet and hurried her out the door. The general took a mallet from a drummer and banged several times. The anxious whispers and talking stopped as everyone in the room froze to look at him. "That concludes the dance portion of the tournament. Scores and instructions for the maze rescue challenge will be sent to team coaches shortly."

Jameson raised a hand and the Asatthan team met him near a group of stiff leather chairs. No one seemed to know how to react. "Handsomely done," he said. "You comported yourselves well." Calm confidence flowed from their coach. Several candidates visibly relaxed and edged slightly closer to Jameson. "Ambassadors take their cues from the ranking official in the room," he said. "Faces calm and pleasant, everyone. That's it. See you in the training space in ten."

While Jameson patted shoulders and herded people out the far door, Dalin looked for Fentress. But she had disappeared with the Dorado team. The room was already nearly empty. Only the musicians remained, packing their instruments in the far corner of the cold, beautiful ballroom.

The much smaller Team Asattha gathered by one wall of the Box, where the dividers were back in place. Jameson was tacking a blueprint in place on the wall.

"What you're looking at," he began, "is the section of the palace where this last challenge will run. I'm going to brief all of you, but we'll get the next round of cuts before the end of the hour. If your scores on the quiz and dancing," his expression showed how little he thought of those events but his voice remained the same, "are high enough to continue, we have another hour to prepare. They want to run this before dark today and get to the individual fights starting tomorrow. Questions?"

A male from Hépíng Xīng raised his hand. "What happened to the girl?"

Jameson gave him a steady stare.

"The one who attacked…" the male trailed off.

"Her majesty has some self-defense capabilities." Jameson paused and took a deep breath.

A girl right next to Dalin said, "There was poison in her spit. The rumors say her sweat has poison too."

"A neurotoxin," said a different male. "Vanora and the *vishakanya* secrete a neurotoxin that stops the heart."

"No, it paralyzes the muscles so you can't breathe and your heart stops beating, you go into cardiac arrest," said yet another candidate.

Dalin's mind began running the little bit of information he had about the wide group of poisons, natural and otherwise, that could be classified as neurotoxins. But the thoughts scattered when Jameson slapped his palm on the blueprint to get the group's attention.

"Does it matter if the Queen of this Commonwealth is as poisonous as a rainforest tree frog? Because if it does, this is your last chance, well and truly the absolute last chance, to withdraw your name as a contestant."

Their coach wore a generic Asatthan dress uniform that was still neatly pressed. And yet every line on Jameson's face was as tight as a tent stretched by heavy storm winds. At the moment he looked sturdy, but Dalin sensed the next big blow might push him over the edge.

"This challenge is intended to simulate rescuing the Queen from a dangerous situation. The tournament organizers showed a great deal of foresight given what's happening outside the walls as we speak."

Dalin raised his hand. "I know we need to get through this briefing, but what's happening outside?"

Jameson dropped his hand from the blueprint and squared his shoulders to the group. "An additional message was inserted into the tournament information being sent to holoprojectors across the Commonwealth." He cleared his throat. "The message contained two different sets of images. The first was of what appeared to be a healing ward, rows and rows of beds with people in them. Coupled with that were the names of students thought to be dismissed from the Mess."

So the Kook had found the place, found the information stream. Dalin hid his elation that the palace torture ward had been outed.

"Is that why Kailer said the Queen killed her sister?" the girl next to Dalin whispered.

"The second inserted message was a recording of an event, a meeting of some type here at the Mess. It shows her majesty laying hands on a member of the palace staff and the woman appears to die."

Emily bin Haribin. Who had recorded that terrible moment?

"Those messages went out twice so far today. Crown City is full of visitors and by all accounts they are as upset as the folks who live here about the images they've seen. It is no secret that Queen Vanora has enemies. The necessity for a champion is real enough. But now," Jameson stared right into Dalin's eyes, "there's no telling what an angry crowd, many of whom have no ties to the city, might do."

Mara. Mara and Elana. If he withdrew his name right now, he could, at least in theory, go free. Protect them in Lower Town. And no matter what happened after that, they'd be gone from this place. He and Mara could make a different plan, resume helping Jameson, and be together.

Without consciously moving, he had somehow made it to the doorway. His room was a fast ten-minute walk from here. His gear was always packed. Behind him, the not quite two dozen remaining candidates from Team Asattha whispered and gestured to each other. They'd be fine with Jameson to guide them.

"De Forest." A heavy hand descended on his shoulder.

"I'm going to withdraw," Dalin said to his mentor.

Jameson clapped him hard on the sensitive spot right above his clavicle. A cold angry light flashed through his eyes and vanished. "About that. A Professor Iskindar sent along a reminder that since you're a staff member here at the Mess with certain obligations"—he stressed the word and his eyes went even colder as the muscles in Jameson's jaw flexed and his back molars ground together—"ya can't withdraw due to the specific parameters of your service agreement with her."

He leaned closer, the intensity in his face and the way he held his hands promising violence. "By most accounts, ye've taken at least two beatings to within an inch of your life and learned not a thing despite your alleged smarts. By all that is light and holy, boy, I'd give you another if I thought for once and all I could beat this insanity out of ya."

Dalin wanted to ask, which insanity? Instead he said, "My partner and E are in Lower Town. Their safety is more important than anything else."

Narrowing his eyes, Jameson gave his head a single shake and then swung back toward the group. "Make sure everyone has a look at those plans. Be thinking of questions," he called.

Leaning in until his face was close, he whispered, "Ya joined the bloody King's Men. Iskindar is backing you as the Champion."

Dalin never forgot anything, not the color of people's eyes or the names of their horses, addresses, due dates, the ingredients for Jin's fish sauce. Maybe the mental attacks…no. It was the unique experience of hope he'd felt this morning, the joy and Light pushing the Darkness and the memory of that idiotic pledge away.

Chest impossibly tight, Dalin could barely draw a breath. "I thought Mara was gone," he murmured. "And I wanted answers. Professor Iskindar had answers, for a price I was willing to pay at the time."

The angry gleam in Jameson's eyes dimmed. His mentor pulled him chest to chest for a rough hug. "I'm a lucky bastard. Don't think I don't know it. But despite the luck and good people in my life, I had to make decisions that brought me to this day." He released Dalin and rubbed his eyebrow. "You make choices as a man and those choices have to be about what's inside of you. That's all ye've got in the end."

Chapter 40

As the lunch crowd finally began to thin, a boy rushed in to say something to an older man and then rushed back out. The man repeated the information in Origin Hindi to his dining companions and from there it traveled to the remaining guests in the eating house.

"What—?" Mara started to ask.

"The holoprojector is warming up, auto started," Elana said. "You go and watch. I'll finish here."

Would it be the next challenge or an announcement? The link to Dalin had been quiet so far. She could sense him, but that was all. Mara untied her apron in the kitchen and buckled on her sword.

"*¿Adónde vas?*" Geraldo said, eyeing the weapon.

"*Al mercado,*" she said, unable to suppress the tiny grin of triumph, pleased that she could understand the cook's question, 'where are you going?' and respond in Origin Spanish, 'to the market.' Geraldo had started teaching her words and phrases before she left for Iloel, and it was a relief to pick up that thread of learning.

Hurrying through the back and out into the alley, Mara stopped in surprise at the noise and density of the crowd filling the road to the market.

Her mind supplied the parameters for estimating numbers of people in a given space, a type of problem they'd spent several days working in mathematics class. The students from Tian and Dorado grasped the concept far more easily than she had, and now Mara understood why. This was easily double, if not triple, the largest crowd on the busiest market day in Satri.

She began shouldering her way through the crowd, her height allowing her to see the flows of foot traffic and the hard knots of stationary groups.

The faint sound of trumpets carried over the hundreds of human voices. Mara pressed forward, but the crowd was increasingly tight the closer she got to the holoprojector.

The first images to appear were names and scores. Mara leaned forward, almost touching the people in front of her.

Dalin de Forest was at the top of the list, followed by Fentress Elizalde. Only fifty names remained from the original fifteen hundred candidates. The man who had been taking bets the other night was exchanging currency with a group of dark-haired, dark-skinned merchants. The leader gestured at the projection and clearly said, "Fentress."

It was a smart bet. If Dalin weren't in the competition, Fentress would win.

The next image to be projected was the older male official from that morning. He began by asking citizens to ignore the negative propaganda being spread by enemies of the Commonwealth. "It has come to our attention that despite the strict treaties and isolation protocols created and signed by our founding King, agents from banned systems have infiltrated our cities."

The crash of a gong reverberated through the speakers as Rafiq tapped her on the shoulder. "We miss anything?" Elana and Geraldo stood just behind him.

A bright, high-ceilinged chamber appeared. Irregularly shaped white and brown rugs were scattered across a glossy floor. A person bundled into heavy clothing scuttled into view and placed a shoe against one wall, next to another shoe, toe to heel. The view expanded to show a line of shoes stretching along the perimeter of the room, disappearing behind a blood-red velvet couch and reappearing again.

"That's crooked," shrieked a voice and then the Queen appeared in the room dressed in her black tunic, leggings, and cape. No gloves. She stretched out one hand toward the bundled figure who shrank away and adjusted the shoe, keeping his or her head low to the ground. Rapid puffs of white mist came from the servant's mouth.

Vanora turned in a slow circle, the image following her gaze and showing a colorful and varied line of shoes, toe to heel, running around the massive room. "My rooms are shrinking."

Two of the *vishakanya* entered the image and hurried to the Queen, one on each side of her. With little pats and pets they succeeded in urging Vanora to the red couch.

"The Commonwealth is shrinking," she moaned as she dropped to the cushions. "If the measurements are the same as last year I will lay hands on every member of your family, every person you speak to in the market, every person who knows your name."

Drumbeats reverberated through the square and then the dome was filled with a solid gray background and thousands of names in tiny white text. THE ROLLS OF THE DEAD AND MISSING ARE EXPANDING EVERY MINUTE. The message repeated six more times in the dominant languages of the commonwealth.

Elana stood with her hands pressed to her mouth. Geraldo was trying to read names and Rafiq faced outward, watching the people packed in around them.

"More troops," he said, his face composed. "Speaking of expanding."

Mara turned away from the list and immediately grasped his concern. Commonwealth troops, weapons out but down, ringed the market, much as the Queen's shoes had ringed her room. Additional personnel blocked the exits. Any anti-monarchy sentiment would be put down publicly and hard.

Expressions changed from dismay and confusion to anticipation as the holoimage snapped back to the live tournament feed. A few cheers rose as Fentress appeared, tall and slim, white-blonde hair gleaming in the lights. Her fingers danced over her weapons and her fight suit. She bent and checked her boots, putting her bottom directly toward the official. Straightening, she tugged the orange Dorado armband a little higher on her bicep. Her body was in constant motion, jogging in place, twitching and plucking at her suit as the official explained the rules.

Each candidate would take charge of one of the Queen's bodyguards, because they were the approximate size—height and weight—of the Queen. The candidate would proceed through the maze, fight the attackers, and get through the obstacles. The keys to winning the challenge were keeping the girl undamaged and getting to the other side as quickly as possible. Every run through the maze would be timed. Only the competitors with the top sixteen times would move on to individual fights the next day.

Fentress nodded and kept nodding at the official as he read through the remaining rules, her eyes reddened around the edges, the pupils huge and dark. A short buzzer sounded and she grabbed the little *vishakanya*, yanking her off her feet.

"Where is this?" Elana asked.

Fentress dove into the maze.

"Another part of the palace complex I've never seen," Mara said, unable to look away as the head of the Furies kicked a shrouded attacker. She shoved the girl behind her and drew her sword. The enemies were dispatched. Mara hoped it was a fake death. The ragged attackers, swathed in a jumble of clothes and fabric, reminded her of the Iloellian fighters in Samradhi.

Fentress ran on.

The first obstacle was fire in the corridor; the second was a huge hole in the floor. Fentress maneuvered herself and her charge around both. A few meters beyond the hole, the corridor veered sharply into a dark stretch the recording device and the light from above did not penetrate.

A quiet voice spoke in Origin Spanish asking Geraldo if they had burritos to sell.

And then Fentress appeared, carrying the *vishakanya* on her back. The girl's bun had come loose and dark hair fell around her head. Her bottom lip was split and bleeding.

The crowd cheered. Mara snuck a glance back at the Commonwealth troops, but they remained stationary.

Fentress's fight suit had been slashed open along one calf and across her stomach. Red-brown blood stained her hair and her hands. The buzzer sounded again and a different official called out the time, four minutes, thirty-seven seconds.

The view shifted back to the starting point with another candidate and another *vishakanya*.

They watched the next five candidates and Mara found herself curious about how the obstacles were changed each time. Side bets were going on around them about how much fire, how many attackers, and so on.

Elana tapped her shoulder and motioned for Mara to lean down. "Dalin doesn't compete until last," she said, directly into her ear. "Jameson thinks they'll take a break midway through the group. He also thinks they're planning for Dalin's run to be after the evening meal so as many people as possible can watch."

* * *

The red mark on his hand had been bothering Dalin all afternoon. It throbbed and itched and the only thing that helped was ice.

He'd visited the healers, but Sangita's room remained empty. He wondered if she was the one who supplied Kook with the hospital recording.

His fight suit had been cleaned and repaired. In its basic design elements, the fight suit was similar to the Protector uniforms. He wondered if Mara would watch him compete tonight.

"Monkey mind," he said out loud. One of the many guard/assistants took a step toward him.

"What was that?" he said.

Dalin shook his head. "Just talking to myself," he said. "Nerves."

The assistant nodded and returned to his post. "As soon as this one finishes, you'll go to the starting line."

"Four minutes?" Dalin asked.

"That's the time to beat, more or less," the assistant said. "But most of the candidates have taken five minutes or more."

Deciding to breathe and stretch, Dalin practiced the calming routine his father had taught him. He was nervous, though not for the reason the assistant might have assumed.

"Anyone die yet?" he asked. It was just the two of them in a tiny room off the main hall; the others were stationed at intervals between the ready area and the starting point.

The assistant flinched. He swallowed and touched his black wrist unit. "Yes, unfortunately. We've lost five of the *vishakanya*. They gave their lives in service to the Commonwealth."

Dalin rubbed at the red mark on his hand lodged just above the tender web between his left thumb and index finger. The tiny transmitter throbbed with his pulse, the burning radiating outward.

A beep sounded. "Time to go," the assistant said. "You're the last run of the day."

"How many candidates died today?" Dalin asked as he stood and checked the draw on his blade.

"Eight," the man said. He didn't meet Dalin's eyes.

The calm of his mind cooled and solidified into the icy steel of a space transport hull. Thirteen lives lost for a stupid game.

The soul-deep Darkness that kept him alive in the stadium fight rose eagerly to his call. He marched the last few meters, shoulders back, chin high. No false humility now. The people needed to know; they needed to see that he was their champion.

At the starting line, he executed a perfect bow for the little *vishakanya*. Unlike most of the bodyguards, this one had light eyes of the palest blue, her hair brown rather than black. As the starting buzzer sounded, he flipped her up and onto his back.

Around the first corner, a trio of raggedly dressed and hooded assailants waited, each with a short knife. Light flashed behind his eyes and his perception of Mara exploded from the one tiny point of contact he'd been maintaining all day. She showed him the maze, specifically all the obstacles she could see through the holoprojector.

Distracted, his first block went high and one of the attackers got inside his guard. But the *vishakanya* kicked the assailant squarely in the face, knocking her into one of the others. The third came in for a low strike but Dalin pivoted and slipped his sword into the attacker's ribs.

He ran on. Something whizzed overhead and then something else rolled under his feet, nearly tripping him. He caught himself on a wall, oddly warm to the touch.

"Fire. It's big. Fills the whole corridor."

"Approximate measurements?" he sent back.

"No, Dalin, don't try it," Mara said. But he also got the thought she'd tried to suppress, *two meters by three meters.*

He skidded to a halt, glad his regular boots were an option for this trial. He tugged the *vishakanya* down and asked, "If I throw you, can you land on your feet?"

As she nodded, he wiped his blade across one knee and slid it into the sheath.

Taking two steps back, he bent his knees and then sprang forward, tossing the small female up and over the fire. Without waiting, he took five steps back and then ran and arced into a long dive, like a racing dive into a swimming pool.

Heat seared his nose and stole his breath. He landed and tucked into a forward roll, his palms scorching and tearing on the smoldering boards feeding the edge of the fire.

Eyes streaming, he staggered to his feet and reached for the girl.

She said, "If we lock elbows back to back, I can kick anyone behind you."

"Next attack, let's do that." He sprinted on, the girl running behind him now, her bare feet nearly soundless.

They were attacked with rope next, then a net. Then five swordsmen in the same ragged, hooded attire attempted to trap them at a T-junction. Mara yelled, "*Left*," as he parried multiple blows from the swordsmen while the little bodyguard pressed against his back to lash out with sharp kicks.

More than two minutes had elapsed when they hit the hole. As wide as the hall and twice as long as the fire, the huge hole showed only absolute blackness below.

Dalin laughed. When would this scenario present itself in the life of the spoiled monarch?

The sound his hands had made when he'd slapped the wall... He pulled his sword free and reversed his grip, slamming the butt of the pommel through the synth wood and into the hollow core.

"Gonna make hand- and footholds to climb up and then we'll work our way along by hand. Clear?"

In the dim light, the *vishakanya*'s pale eyes almost glowed. "I'm a good climber," she said. "It's part of our training."

"After you," Dalin said, slamming the last hole into the wall.

The girl scrambled up, a tiny pink desert lizard in no way hindered by her gloves, and called down, "It's wide enough for me to walk."

She hoisted herself up, pale clothes shimmering but barely visible, high above him.

Dalin followed, hanging from the high wall, and moving hand to hand as quickly as he could. At the other side of the hole, he called, "Jump."

"*Run, Dalin*," Mara shouted. Her excitement and her view of the finish line spurred him just past the next gap. Two more attackers sprang out behind them.

With the girl tucked against his chest, Dalin leaned onto his toes and sprinted the last hundred meters. He spun his charge across the painted red line with a flourish and a grin.

"Three minutes, thirty-two seconds," the official called.

Chapter 41

With little to do but wait until the final candidate rankings were announced, Rafiq produced detailed maps and population density charts of each planet in the Commonwealth, claiming these were a smuggler's tools.

"Normally, I use these to determine which places might need certain types of goods that I might be able to provide and, of course, which places might have an abundance of a certain item that might be useful elsewhere," he said.

Elana folded her arms and raised one eyebrow.

Rafiq paused in his explanation for a slow, suggestive smile. "*Albek hullu.*"

Her aunt rolled her eyes. "My heart is beautiful? Bet that's what you say to all your burrito sellers." She jabbed her index finger toward the map of Kels. "I think I could use this information to start a revolution," she said. "Which in turn might free up access to certain goods, which might be useful across the Commonwealth."

The owner of the eating house narrowed his eyes and stroked his beard, appearing to consider Elana's bold statement as though it were a proposed menu change. "That could be good or bad for business, depending."

A tree symbol on the Asattha map caught Mara's attention. She took a pencil and sketched the same symbol next to the mark for Alandalus on the map of Iloel. "Why do we only know the location of two of the Great Trees? Asattha's Tree said she has a sister on each planet."

"The Great Tree was humanity's first alien contact. *Sentient* alien contact," Elana said. "She did not speak of sisters, that I know of, or that is included in public record, anyway." Frowning, she traced the large unpopulated landmasses of Kels and Hépíng Xīng.

"Nobody went looking, is what you're saying," Mara said. She was confident Laska had its own Great Tree; the energy she could tap was strong in Crown City.

Without glancing up from the maps, Elana said, "Again, that we know about, or is a matter of public record."

Mara and Halifax had spent too much time together on Iloel for her to miss him just yet, but he was an excellent source of information. "The student you picked up with me, Halifax, where is he now?" A pang of guilt for not inquiring about his whereabouts earlier accompanied the question.

Rafiq paused in the act of unrolling a much larger map, a star chart. "He's staying with Van Fuuren. The, um, group has a flat in the merchant section of the Palace Hill. Has remote access to some of the group's data storage."

"I was just thinking 'Fax might know something about where else to look for Trees. From what our Great Tree said, about her sisters needing clean air and water, I thought maybe some of them would be closer to cities. Maybe on these planets." Mara tapped Dorado and Tian.

"Anyone know when the individual fight schedule comes out?" Geraldo asked, emerging from the kitchen. He passed around paper-wrapped burritos.

"Jameson thinks the rounds will start after noon tomorrow. He didn't say anything about the schedule. His guess is a standard sixteen tournament progression." Elana left her burrito on the table and pushed through the kitchen door. When she returned, she had one of the tiny order pads and a pencil. "Standard sixteen tournament progression is when the top seed starts against the lowest seed. One versus sixteen, two versus fifteen, three versus fourteen, and so on."

Rafiq laughed. "Fights to the death organized like a basketball tournament." He shook his head.

"*Jefe*, when was the last time you got some sleep?" Geraldo said, shifting his bulk between the women and the owner of the eating house. "They don't know about no basketball tournament. That's a neighborhood thing in some of the densest parts of Dorado, like New Seville, *¿comprendes?*"

With a deep breath, Rafiq drew the back of his hand down one side of his beard and then the other. He said, "What I was thinking of," then paused to take a bite of his food, "was in the archaeological record of ancient cultures on the Origin. A group sometimes called the Aztec. The game now played in the *barrios* of New Seville has a few lingering similarities."

Mara studied the Dorado map as she ate. The key showed that one tiny dot on the map represented ten thousand people. Around the planetary capital, the dots were larger and incredibly thick.

"The Aztecs?" Elana said. "I don't think that group made it to the war archives."

Half-listening as she did the mental calculations, Mara estimated five million people lived in the densest area of the city called Salvación. New Seville appeared to have close to three million people.

"They held tournaments to please their gods and the losers were sacrificed. That's all I was gonna say," Rafiq said.

"Sacrificed?" Mara asked.

"Killed in a ritual ceremony," he said. "Don't think for a second these are the only dark times humanity has seen."

* * *

Everyone was up early the next morning even though the fights weren't supposed to start until afternoon. Dalin had kept their connection low, but he was planning something. Worrying had kept Mara from sound sleep, that and the perfect memory of sleeping next to her partner the night before.

Geraldo said, "Are we gonna open for any meals today?"

Mara just wanted to lose herself in the maps until she could reconnect with Dalin. The classes at the Mess hall provided tantalizing bits and pieces of information about the Commonwealth. She certainly knew more than she did when they arrived in Crown City, but it wasn't enough.

"Elana?" she started to ask her aunt about the tiny dots spread out far away from Satri.

"No," Rafiq said at the same time. He'd finished his breakfast in a few bites and was dabbing at his beard and mustache. "Took in more than we would in a normal week the past two days. Wouldn't hurt to have more of the handheld food to sell while we watch the fights, but we can keep closed for regular business until the tournament *de locos* is over."

A fist thumped against the main door. Rafiq and Geraldo exchanged a glance. Rafiq waved at the maps with a "get those out of here" gesture.

Mara laid three maps in a pile and rolled them with care. Elana did the same for her pile. Grabbing both rolls, Elana hurried into the kitchen as Geraldo slowly unlocked and opened the door.

Van Fuuren marched in with Halifax two steps behind.

"They're going to release the students from the hospital, " he announced. "One of our contacts inside the Mess sent me the information. Since we're on the outside, I volunteered to help."

He turned to Mara. "The King's Men strive to preserve life."

She looked at her aunt, whose "What is he talking about?" expression was similar to her own.

"How many people?" Mara asked.

"Between fifty and a hundred," Halifax answered. "A small crew has been adjusting the medication to bring them to consciousness. They just need us to keep the guards busy until the first people are through the main gate." He frowned and gave his head a slight shake. "First victims? Patients? Survivors? The crowd will take over from that point because the release will happen just before the first fight."

"Smart to leverage the power of an angry crowd," Rafiq agreed.

"A little market has sprung up around the lower gates," Geraldo reported. "Security doesn't like it, but no one bothered to write any regs about this, let alone post them or inform the local merchants. We can set up shop in there. Puts us in position."

A few hours later, they loaded burritos and a massive water container onto a low motorized cart parked in the alley. Rafiq and Elana climbed into the small cab. Geraldo and Van Fuuren positioned themselves in the front of the cart. Mara and Halifax took the back.

'Fax now wore two axes in his chest harness and his long knife rode on one hip. Mara had a knife in a leg sheath, one knife on each arm, and her sword at her back.

It was slow going up the hill. Low clouds trapped the heat and humidity, the crush of tournament spectators sweating as they pushed upward toward the Mess.

"I feel like I'm hearing all of the Origin languages at once," Mara said.

"Oh you are, and more than that," Halifax said. "Never been a gathering like this in the history of the Commonwealth. The coronations were exclusive affairs, so only a small delegation from each planet attended." He smiled and bounced on his toes, acting more like a tall and well-armed child than a trained soldier.

"*Mara, I need a distraction.*" Dalin's mental voice was low and urgent in her head.

"*What do you mean? You're part of this?*" She bit her lip and took a few short steps. "*Don't you have a fight in less than an hour?*"

"*Yes, that's why I'm meditating in my quarters with orders to not be disturbed.*"

It was hard to keep walking, to keep at least some visual and mental attention to the active crowd all around them. "*Why do you need a distraction?*" What was Dalin thinking taking an additional risk right now?

"*Sangita changed the medication protocols. The people in that hospital ward are awake. We need to get them out to the gates. We have to give those people a chance at surviving.*" He was nervous and cold, but the hope in his voice was tangible.

"*You're working with the King's Men? What about Jameson?*"

"*Gone,*" Dalin said. "*Not sure where. And this is happening now. I would've told you sooner, but we didn't know what the timing would be.*" He seemed relieved to be doing something besides fighting, to be working toward a solution.

"*Five minutes. We're prepped and nearly there,*" Mara said. "*Wait for my signal.*"

"*Thank you,*" Dalin whispered into her mind. And for the briefest flash of her wishful imagination, she felt his lips press to hers.

Mara banged on the roof of the cart. "Stop," she called. "I have updates."

She quickly told the group what Dalin had said.

Geraldo and Rafiq exchanged a look. "Compost piles are just this side of the Mess kitchens," the cook said.

"Back at the gates in three," Rafiq warned.

"*Oye, prima,*" Geraldo said. "*Vámanos.*"

Mara followed the cook down a side street and then up a winding alley. They popped out one tier below the palace. A staircase and a gate led to the main fence.

"Kitchen gate is always unlocked," Geraldo said. "One more thing to guard, I guess. Plus no one's ever come through here except folks deliverin' food and drink."

He waved to the two women sitting at an outside table sipping what looked like iced tea. "Is the Dragon here? It's time to place the next order. I know y'all are busy and such, but don't want no one to catch trouble for not fulfilling any palace requests for my *chile verde*."

When Geraldo ambled a little closer, he introduced Mara. "This is my *prima*, my cousin, gettin' ready to learn the trade. She's never seen a place this big."

The women greeted her but kept their attention on the cook. "About that *chile verde*," one said. "Are ya buyin' the chiles in the market or does that boss of yours have a source? I've been tryin' to make my own version and—"

The other woman heaved a sigh as she stood. "I'll see if the Dragon can spare a moment for you. When this tournament ends, the larder will be empty, so it's best to plan ahead."

"*Muchas grácias*," Geraldo said. He leaned closer to Mara and said, "You know how to start a fire?"

She nodded, heart starting to race. When was the last time she'd needed to start a fire?

The cook pressed something into her hand. "Pull the tab and drop it in the pile." Much more loudly he said, "Take a look around," he said. "This is how royalty lives."

Despite the pronouncement, where they stood looked like a large version of a side yard in the settlements. The only things missing were chicken coops and goat pens.

As promised, right around the corner were syncrete blocks containing a massive compost heap easily four meters by three meters and probably a meter and a half tall. The pungent fumes forced her to breathe through her mouth.

Turning her back on the cooks, she uncurled her fingers from the rectangular blue device with one word printed in red. *Precaución*.

She pulled the tab and lightly tossed the device onto the middle of the pile. Nothing happened.

Dalin needed a distraction. She hurried past the compost heap and on the other side found several neat stacks of boxes and crates. The crowd noise rumbled from the other side of the palace, but no immediate sounds indicated people nearby. The packed dirt and gravel under her feet scraped as she checked the wood of the nearest crate to make sure it was dry enough to burn. Satisfied, she closed her eyes and reached for the source.

Warm energy flowed through her limbs and wrapped around her body like an embrace. *"Burn,"* she whispered to the stacks. Little sparks appeared at the corners and edges.

"Fire," she commanded.

Flames scurried up the sides of the stacks, tiny red and yellow pulses gaining momentum and height.

After one last look around, she took long strides back to Geraldo. *"Me olvidó* the order tablet," she said. *"Tengo verguenza."* She looked at the ground and made a sulky pout. "Didn't mean to forget it," she muttered.

He raised his massive hand as if to strike her and yelled, "You should be ashamed forgetting an important piece of equipment. Run. Go now."

Mara sprinted through the gate, down the steps, and along the narrow alley until she met the crowd. People were packed so tightly, she had no idea how to begin wedging herself into their midst.

Strong hands grabbed her shoulders from behind. She dropped down and forward to flip her attacker, turning to discover it was Geraldo and she'd only shifted the cook up to his toes.

"Let me block," he said. "You plant the device?"

She nodded.

"Pulled the tab?"

"And threw it to the middle of the compost pile," Mara confirmed.

He looked back toward the palace. "Any second now," he said and started pushing his way into the crowd. People gave way for him. No one was bigger or more determined, though Geraldo was polite and kept up a steady stream of "excuse us," in Origin Spanish, Origin English, and Origin Hindi.

"Get ready to move," Mara sent.

A deafening wave of noise exploded behind them, heat and smoke close behind. Geraldo tugged her down as people around them screamed.

Loud horns blew in ascending and descending notes, jarring her hearing. Men and women wearing the Commonwealth uniform pounded from the direction of the main gate, the sound of their boots lost in the commotion.

A whistling noise cut through the lower tones as it grew louder and then shrieked overhead, exploding into a burst of sparkling lights. More whistles, shrieks, and lights followed until the afternoon sky resembled a sparkling garden of wildflowers.

"Did you set fireworks?" Geraldo muttered in her ear. He stood and tugged Mara to her feet.

"No." Unless the crates next to the compost hadn't been empty?

"*Perfect*," Dalin cheered in her head. "*Well done. The revived soldiers and students are on their way out to you.*"

"We have to get up there," Mara said. The gates at the top of the hill were just visible through the crowd, the yellow uniforms of healers holding open the metal bars for a thin column of people in loose white shirts and trousers shuffling forward.

The end of the line came around from behind the corner where the palace joined the Mess. More healers flanked the line, patting shoulders and bidding farewell. Mara recognized Sangita and hurried over to her, grasping the strong brown fingers through the fence.

"Who will take care of these people?" she asked the healer. "What do they need?"

"The tall one told me you were alive," Sangita said. "But I already knew from the visions written long ago. It's good to see you, Daughter." She patted one of Mara's hands and smiled. "You should rest while you can. More work will begin for you soon." The healer released her grip to turn and help a dazed-looking man navigate through the gate.

"But what about—" Mara tried again.

"Your love?" The healer interrupted. "It survives. The Daughter needs balance just as the universe does."

"The people?" Mara finished. She leaned closer and noticed how red Sangita's eyes were.

"The people, these people." The healer gave her head a sharp shake. "They need a safe place to recover."

"Are you unwell?"

Sangita wasn't making sense and Mara needed facts about the walking wounded or subjects or students, whoever they were.

The healer tugged up one sleeve to show reddened bumps running along her forearm. The bumps covered the side of her neck as well. "I've been poisoned for my treason." The older woman patted Mara's sleeve and said, "May the Light bless your journey and show your true course."

From far away, voices cheered over a low percussive pounding of feet and hands. The first fight, Dalin's first fight, was about to start.

Chapter 42

Dalin felt confident his first two fights would be straightforward.

While his opponent bounced around and stretched on the opposite side, Dalin kept still. He checked his shields and centered himself, supplanting the nervous exhilaration of releasing the subjects from the secret hospital with cold concentration.

They'd moved the walls around again to create a single fighting space, much larger than the regular fight areas used for the Friday night fights. Thin mats covered the floor with a red painted line denoting out-of-bounds.

Though the explosion and the fireworks a few minutes later had halted the proceedings for fifteen full minutes, spectators now streamed into their seats above the fight floor, the crowd noise rising and falling on currents of anticipation and excitement.

A male, in the formal attire of Vanora's court, and Shanshan, wearing a pristine gray Mandarin-style top and trousers, moved to the center of the floor. The man introduced himself as the announcer for the final round of the tournament and Shanshan as the referee. The crowd responded with polite applause.

As the announcer went over the rules, healers filed in, three on each side, pushing carts of ice, water, bandages, and other less-easy-to-identify supplies. The fights could last up to nine minutes, divided into three rounds of three minutes each with one-minute breaks in between rounds. A win would be determined by knockout, or points for legal strikes, if a knockout did not occur.

"And now, it is my pleasure to present to you your top-ranked contestant, Dalin de Forest."

Feet pounded the risers, the clapping and cheering startlingly loud. Dalin took two steps into the open and waved, suppressing a wince as females in the front row shrieked his name.

The crowd also applauded for his sixteenth-ranked opponent, though with less enthusiasm.

The male was from Tian, probably in his mid-twenties. He carried some extra muscle in his arms and chest, his movements a bit stiff.

Though his intention was to let the fight go all three rounds, Dalin knocked his opponent unconscious with a spin hook kick to the temple at the beginning of the second round. When the buzzer sounded to signal the end of the fight, Dalin waved again to the crowd then bowed to the curtained enclosure set apart for the Queen.

His next fight, a few hours later, was also against a male, the heavyset chess player from Kels. This opponent kept trying to get Dalin to the ground. Having lost two matches at La Kill to those exact techniques, Dalin escaped the holds. He struck hard and fast at vulnerable targets then jumped back. He fought to injure his opponent, but not to kill him. The chess player made it to the end of the second round before the combination of a vicious kick to one knee and a knife hand strike to the base of his neck dropped him, his body hitting the floor and rolling slightly to one side like an iron kettle.

That was it for the day.

He wasn't sure he felt particularly proud of the fights. He was glad Mara hadn't been inside to witness them.

Four candidates remained from the original fifteen hundred.

Dalin, Fentress, Ryoko, and a kid from Laska A he'd never met or seen in action.

That evening, the four of them ate at separate tables in the Mess Mess. Dalin chose a spot where he could read the stats on the holocell.

Fentress had not only killed several people during the maze rescue challenge, but she'd killed both her opponents that day, putting her in the top spot for damage points. She stalked around her table, eating in snatches between talking, howling, and reenacting her fights with the Furies standing in as opponents.

Watching Fentress, Dalin considered that being the Queen's Champion would require a lot of performing, some of the performances much like today's fights. He had chosen a private life over his mother's public life because he saw how it wore her down.

He didn't like the times when what she did and what she said didn't match, the times his mother seemed like a fake.

He'd also avoided a public life because he... He only cared about Mara. He'd failed her when she was kidnapped. He'd failed again when she'd been severely injured by a Gaishan. And then she'd been sent to another planet, landing in the midst of extreme danger; yet another failure in keeping his partner safe. The only goals he had, life, career, or otherwise centered on Mara and her living a life of peace and happiness where she was free and safe to pursue her education and her interests.

Winning the role of champion was the best way to guarantee Mara's safety. She would be free. He would tear down the Commonwealth to make sure the rest of her life was full of all the joy and all the choices she'd lost as a child.

When the matchups for the next day scrolled down the holocell, Dalin met his former co-captain's eyes. The two of them would fight first, number one versus number four.

He nodded to Ryoko. She nodded back.

He meant his nod to say, "I won't kill you."

Her nod was open to interpretation, but her kill numbers were the lowest of the four of them.

Mara had kept the connection between their minds open enough to lend some of her natural shielding and connection to the source. Ever since Mara had returned to Crown City, he'd experienced no new psychic attacks. Likely not a coincidence.

Right now she was worried about him and was also wondering where the rest of the Tree's sisters were. She was helping Elana move the people he and Kucala had rescued to the s'port. Crown City wasn't safe for them either.

Dalin didn't want Mara to catch any of his next thoughts so he closed their connection down to a single pulse.

By the end of tomorrow he would be installed as the Queen's Champion or he'd be dead.

The ancient philosopher and Chinese military general Sun Tzu had written, "The supreme art of war is to subdue the enemy without fighting." Between Dr. Iskindar and the resources of the King's Men, Kucala running the tech, and him on the inside in the most trusted position, the monarchy would fall.

Just like the Protectors never knew the true nature of their war, Vanora and her conspirators would have no idea they were engaged in battle until it was too late.

* * *

Dalin didn't want to fight his co-captain, and he certainly didn't want to kill or harm Ryoko Kimura. Not for the first time he wondered why such a capable person, with so many skills, had joined the tournament.

It bothered him that in their team sessions with Jameson, he'd never asked the group *why* they were all vying to be the next champion. Maybe the answer was supposed to be self-evident. Or maybe any other answer besides "Serve the Queen and the Commonwealth" would be considered treason.

Ryoko looked tiny standing at parade rest across the mat. Her fight suit would fit a child. She was only slightly larger than the *vishakanya* or the Queen herself.

But she'd not only survived the stadium brawl and the deadly capture the flag round, she'd earned enough points to face him today.

Why did she want this badly enough to risk death for it?

The announcer and Shanshan ran through the same explanations as the day before. Rules were posted but were subject to change based on the dispensation of the Queen. Knockout, death, points. The only change was that weapons were allowed in the third round.

Dalin glanced down and checked his blades, small knives, long knives, and sword laid in a row behind the red line, next to his staff.

Shanshan nodded at him and then winked.

"I'm here." Mara's voice in his head. *"Good fight."*

As he walked to meet Ryoko at the center of the mat to shake hands and bow, he looked for his partner. This fight wouldn't make Mara proud, but he would conduct himself with honor and do as little damage as possible. He showed Mara his regret.

"Behind you." She showed him her location. *"Nice view. Now get this done so we can go."*

Taking the ready stance, he let out a breath and gave all his focus to his opponent.

Ryoko opened with a whip-fast strike to his nose. His block caught her arm, but her hand still connected with his face. She followed up with the same hand, chopping at his neck on the back swing and simultaneously kicking at his knee. Dalin caught her arm, rotated it in the socket hard enough to bend her forward and then dropped her to the mat with an elbow against her spine.

"Why do you want to be the champion?" he asked.

Rolling toward her pinned shoulder, Ryoko got one knee under her body and kicked out with the other leg. The first kick didn't do much. Dalin could end the fight now with a variety of strikes to her skull. The darkest strand of his consciousness whispered that her neck was small and easy to break.

"Why do you want this?" he asked again and added a knuckle punch to the small of her back. She writhed in the hold, flailing out with her left hand and smacking his ear.

The crowd noise buffered anything Dalin or his opponent said. She could tell him and no one else would know.

Ryoko gave a heave, braced both legs, and launched herself out of the hold. Breathing hard, she stood. She put up her hands and motioned him forward.

Dalin smiled, deciding this would be like fighting his sister. Nuwa hated it when he let her win, so over the years he'd figured out ways to give a temporary advantage to a smaller, lighter opponent.

He faked a front kick to Ryoko's sternum, changed at the last minute to a side kick, and hit her hard enough in the shoulder to knock her backward.

Stumbling, Ryoko pinwheeled her arms then caught her balance just inside the red line. She launched herself forward, diving low and tackling his knees. He hit the mat and just managed to tuck his chin and keep his head from knocking hard. As she raised her joined fists for a hard hammer blow to his groin, Dalin kicked her in the face.

The buzzer sounded, signaling the end of the first round.

At his side of the mat, Dalin licked his lips and tasted blood. He swiped a finger under his nose and confirmed it was bleeding. Because of what had happened to Mara, he didn't bring any water with him to the fighting floor. Even his own custom-sealed bottles could be tampered with while he fought. He rolled his shoulders and swished spit around in his mouth. He could go nine minutes without a drink.

The second round went about the same as the first. For a small person with a chess background, her strategy was more like dirty brawling. And maybe that was her strategy. To keep him surprised and off-balance.

She landed a great hook punch to his jaw.

He cuffed her neck and punched her hard in the stomach.

Though it was a fun fight, he was about to end it with a knockout move when the buzzer sounded again.

The weapons round. He would never use a bladed weapon against Nuwa, so he reached for his staff. Turning, he saw Ryoko trying to pull her silky black hair back into its tight ponytail. Sweat stuck the fine strands to her forehead and blood smeared under her nose and across one cheek. She looked as young as the brand new Protectors, barely thirteen. But unlike any new Protector, she had a sword.

With regret, Dalin switched his staff for his sword and stepped back over the red line.

This time, Ryoko edged forward with caution, guard tight and high. Rather than watch her face, Dalin watched her shoulders and her hips. A slight swivel was all the warning he needed to turn and block her first swing at his midsection. He set his back foot and struck hard toward her center. Ryoko used his momentum to push his arm across his body, striking down on his elbow with her free hand.

Excellent. More freestyle fighting.

Dalin spun and jump-kicked backward, catching her on the hip. He continued the spin and pierced her fight suit just above the knee, slicing a hole with the tip of the blade.

When Ryoko came at him again, Dalin used his significantly longer reach to wrap her in a bear hug, her back pressed tight against his front, her sword trapped tight by her side.

"I have to end this," he said. "I don't fight for the Queen, I fight for the people." She struggled in his grip and didn't respond.

"Two ways to go," he said. "I can hamstring you." Which he really didn't want to do, despite the ready availability of healers nearby. "Or I can knock you out."

She got a sharp elbow into his ribs and stomped hard on his instep.

Grimacing, Dalin switched his grip on the sword and slammed his weighted fist just under her jaw. Ryoko's head bounced once on the mat and then she was still.

He forced himself to look at the fallen girl until he saw a breath move her chest.

Cheering and clapping penetrated his thoughts as he straightened and looked directly at Vanora's box. He bowed, the deep courtly bow his mother had drilled into him, and thought only of the next necessary steps to end these kinds of atrocities forever.

Chapter 43

Fentress ran out to the center of the floor amid loud screaming cheers, slapping Dalin's shoulder as she flew past. She pumped her fists and motioned for more crowd noise, her face even more pink than usual above the gray-black of the fight suit. She pointed and waved at specific females in the audience, probably other Furies. But she blew a kiss to Mara, earning Mara some whistles and looks from the audience seated nearby.

Jumping and shaking out her hands, Fentress was in perpetual motion around the floor. Meanwhile her opponent, a lanky kid from Laska with a thin mustache, laid out two swords, a dagger with what looked like gems glinting on the hilt, a staff, nunchuks, and a spear. He stretched and watched Fentress, his expression neutral.

The tall blonde finally noticed her opponent and his weapons and ran back to her bag against the wall. She produced a shining short sword and a pair of bladed sai.

"Something is really wrong with her," Mara whispered in Elana's ear.

Elana, who'd been almost holding her breath during Dalin's fight, tilted her head away from Mara. "What do you mean?"

"When I first met Fentress and when we were on Iloel, she was calm and composed. A leader. And now she's acting like this." Mara gestured toward the fight ring.

"What's changed for her?" Elana asked, smoothing her long skirt.

All around them were people talking about the fights and the fighters. According to the announcement earlier, the break between the first and second fights would only be about twenty minutes. But the final fight, in which Dalin had just earned a spot, would be that night.

Van Fuuren had acquired their tickets. Rafiq, Geraldo, Halifax, and the King's Man sat directly behind them. They were in the middle seats, four rows up from the railing. In addition to a great view of the fight ring, they also had a direct view of the Queen's curtained box and the three dozen bodyguards around it. For the first time, an additional two Commonwealth soldiers stood with each *vishakanya*.

The large clock overhead showed five minutes remaining in the break. Fentress had settled down to real stretching, and her opponent appeared to be meditating.

"Her partner died," Mara said finally. "They were more than soldier partners. Fentress loved Kailer."

Elana's expression softened to concern. "I didn't know that," she said. "How terrible. On Iloel?"

"No. Kailer was the one Vanora poisoned during the tournament," Mara said. "They didn't announce her name, but it had to be her. Kailer and Fentress were the only two Furies left."

Elana threaded her fingers together in her lap. She bowed her head for a moment. "Grief manifests in many different ways. When we lost your parents...I wasn't right, wasn't myself for a long time."

She waited for her aunt to say more, but Elana stayed quiet.

The announcer and the tall female Chinese referee walked out to the middle of the ring. They repeated the information from the first fight then motioned to the candidates to come out and bow to each other.

Fentress must have said something because the male from Laska recoiled and looked at the referee. She shrugged and motioned them back behind the red line.

At the buzzer, Fentress sprinted to her opponent. Grabbing him by the shoulders, she kneed him in the groin. As he staggered forward, she head-butted him hard enough to knock him to the ground.

The male hit the mat and pushed right back to all fours.

Fentress stomped on one of his hands and kicked him in the face with her other foot. Blood burst from his nose, running through his mustache and down his chin.

"What in the darkest hole of the universe is she doing?" Halifax said.

"This isn't a fight, it's a beating," Geraldo said.

Elana and Mara exchanged a dismayed look, both thinking that Dalin would have to fight Fentress next.

The male staggered halfway upright and Fentress jumped on his back, dropping him to the floor again. She slammed his head into the mat and then jumped up, pulling one foot high with a clear intent to stomp.

The buzzer sounded and the referee ran out. Fentress pushed her out of the way and brought her boot down hard at the base of the male's spine. He twitched and then sagged flat, either dead or unconscious.

The referee snaked a tan muscular arm around Fentress's neck, trapped the Fury's other arm, and pushed a knee into her back. As her oxygen supply dwindled, Fentress thrashed, but the referee continued speaking directly in her ear.

The announcer swung to the curtained box and nodded when a tiny gold flag waved through the opening. "Winner," he cried, pointing to Fentress.

Fentress broke free of the hold and shot the referee an angry glare. Her pink face was now nearly red, her chest heaving as she took in the much-needed air.

"Shanshan's not gonna play games with that *chica*," Geraldo said.

* * *

Mara had emptied her pack at the eating house with the intention of retrieving the few items she cared about from the locker room and her dorm. With a quick pat to her aunt's shoulder, she slipped out right at the end of Fentress's fight.

The Fury would eventually be down to the locker room, but she'd climbed into the audience and appeared to be enjoying the attention. Mara needed less than five minutes to get the wad of clothes from the back of her locker.

Thanks to a quick reset performed by Halifax, her wrist unit worked to open doors as though she'd never been gone. Alone in the near-silent room, she changed into a rumpled and less-than-clean student uniform and was in and out in less than three minutes.

The corridors between the locker room and the dorms were also quiet, even though it was the middle of the day. Dalin had reported that regular classes were suspended, so where was everyone?

Finally hearing the sounds of students, Mara took a quick detour and saw nearly a hundred Mess students in the large gym. All the mats were full of various forms of workout. For a moment, she thought she saw Annelise's blonde curls, but when the female turned, it wasn't Annelise after all.

In her little stall of the dorm room, Mara laid her pack on the narrow bed and looked around. At first she couldn't say what had changed. Then her eyes picked out the absence of the small, homey touches a few of the girls had hung on their walls or displayed on the tiny tables.

Mara slid open the drawer where she kept her clean basics like socks and underclothes to find it empty. She opened the next drawer down, empty. In quick succession she confirmed all of her things were gone, her brief presence erased.

A sharp intake of breath startled Mara. She whirled around, sword drawn.

Annelise made a warding sign. "Are you real?" she whispered.

Sheathing her sword, Mara hurried to her friend and hugged her. "Yes," she said. "Real. And not dead."

Instead of clapping and bouncing, Annelise pushed them both out of the doorway and toward the far side of the room. "Who else knows?"

"From the Mess?"

Annelise nodded, blue eyes serious.

"Only Dalin."

"Good."

"Oh, and Fentress and most of the Furies."

Annelise dropped to the end of Mara's bed, chewing her lower lip. "What a real mess," she said, looking up. "Those two in the final fight."

Mara sat next to her, her own worry amplified by Annelise's concern.

Reaching over, Annelise tapped Mara's wrist unit. "They know you're here?"

"Yes and no," Mara said. She quickly explained what Halifax had told her about tricking the wrist units.

"Gunder and I are just starting to learn how to do it," Annelise said, wrapping her hand around her own wrist unit. "But he's being shipped out." She motioned to the other beds. "Nearly half the students are being sent to other planets and satellite schools. 'S'good thing they cancelled classes because so many of us is packin' and gettin' orders…"

"You?" Mara asked, even more worried to hear Annelise's old speech pattern emerge.

"Not yet." Annelise touched the collar of her uniform. "Gunder's bein' sent to Kels. Within the next ten days. Orders say to be ready at all times."

"Do you know what happened to my clothes? To my things?"

Annelise blinked hard for a moment. "Oh, I, I packed it all and gave it to Dalin. To send home to your people. We was gonna have a service for you when the tournament was over." She leaned into Mara and wrapped her arms tight around her torso, the wiry strength in her arms another mixed gift of time at the Mess.

"I can get a ride home. For all of us," Mara whispered into her friend's mass of curls.

Annelise pulled back, expression full of dismay. "I don't want to go home," she said. Her blue gaze swept the room and she stood to lean into the corridor for a moment.

"I'm gonna stay here and learn. And when they ship me out, I'm gonna see another planet, learn more things there. Not goin' back to Asattha until I'm good and ready. And that might be never."

Mara stood, slipping the pack over her shoulders. "But you'll be safe at—"

Shaking her head, Annelise said, "Safe gets you nowhere but bored and old before your time. For most folks anyway." A tiny smile curved her lips. "But look at you. You try to be safe and trouble finds you anyway. You have big work to do, Mara. We all know it but you, seems like."

The sounds of booted feet and voices began spilling down the hallway.

"Let's go," Annelise said. "I'll walk you partway to Dalin's quarters. That'll call less attention than you walking alone."

Students hurried along as they always had, no one giving anyone else a glance. In a few short minutes they reached the junction to turn toward the Mess Mess or toward the s'port and Dalin's quarters.

358

"Can't tell you how it restores my faith in the Light that you're alive," Annelise said, giving Mara's hand a quick squeeze. "Try to stay that way."

Throat tight, Mara managed to say, "Stand strong."

"Stand tall," Annelise replied and walked away.

Moving a few paces to a corner outside of the pools of light from overhead, Mara called Dalin.

"Are you in your quarters? I need to get my things, my clothes. Annelise said she gave them to you?"

When no reply came, Mara shifted her pack, thinking through her options. She'd forgotten to ask if the gate schedule had changed. Using the fight complex gates seemed like a decent option since foot traffic would be high.

"Mara? I'm on my way to you."

She turned and began moving toward his quarters. *"Did you see Fentress fight?"*

"No, but I heard." He sounded neither concerned nor overconfident, moving quickly through the Mess. Another few steps and he was at her side. He gave her a nod and kept walking.

Mara joined his pace, skin tingling at the energy crackling around him. He wore a clean, pressed instructor uniform, his hair washed and the blood gone from his face.

Once inside his rooms, Dalin shut the door and reached for her. He pulled her close and kissed her, clever hands lifting the pack from her shoulders and dropping it to the floor. Next came their sword belts, unbuckled and dropped as well, with scarcely an interruption in the embrace.

Mara sank into the kiss, the feelings awakened the other morning shouting in approval, craving more. She touched his face, his jaw, his hair. But when he reached for the buttons on her uniform, she broke the kiss and caught his hands in hers.

"Dalin," she began.

"I know," he said and nibbled at her jawline before kissing her collarbone and unbuttoning more buttons.

"Dalin," she said again, edging away. "You have the biggest fight of your life in a few hours."

He inhaled deeply and reached for the tie that held her braid. Moving to her side, he tugged gently on the woven strands until the mass of hair was wavy and loose over her shoulders.

"I guess you could say that," he said. "The healers said to rest, but I want to see you. And you didn't get a break or a rest on Iloel, you just had to fight the next fight, ready or not."

With his fingers combing through her hair and his smoky silver gaze a caress in itself, Mara was hard-pressed to remember if she had any other reason for existing outside this moment.

Dalin changed tactics by reaching for his own buttons. "I have some new scars. Want to see?"

Mara wet her lips. She did want to see. She wanted to kiss the new scars and the old ones. Scars. Iloel. "My things?" Swallowing hard, she stared at Dalin as he slipped his shirt over his shoulders and let it fall to the floor.

"In here," he said, his grin returning as he walked into his bedroom.

No one in the history of uniforms would ever look better than Dalin did in his tank top, close-fitting pants, and boots.

"Feel the same way about you," he said as she followed him through the doorway. "May I?" Without waiting for her reply, he removed her shirt and laid it on his pillow.

A small open box sat on the floor right next to the bed. Trying to clear her head, Mara crouched down and quickly sorted through the contents of the box.

"Your worldly goods didn't encompass the difference you made in the world. You make in the world," he corrected himself.

Mara went back for the pack and began shifting everything from the box to the bag, attempting to ignore the heated flush of her skin under her tank top and her need to lose herself in Dalin's arms.

As she looked everywhere but at him, the sparse emptiness of the room reminded her of the other reason they needed to talk. "We have a ride out of here as soon as the tournament is over."

Dropping onto the bed, Dalin looked up at her. "Good. You and Elana should go as soon as possible."

"We're all leaving," Mara said, skin tingling in a different way now. "We understand that you want to finish the tournament, that you're highly visible. But afterward, you can slip away."

He captured one of her hands and brought it to his lips with reverence. "My beautiful soldier. Always planning." Dalin looked away and swallowed. He tugged her down to sit next to him on the bed. "Here's my plan. We're going to have children of our own someday."

Mara's stomach clenched and she frowned hard at him. Who was having children, exactly?

"The Commonwealth needs to be safe for our kids. They should grow up safe from cruelty and experimentation. So I'm going to bring this monarchy down from the inside. You're going to free all the Tree's sisters and bring it down from the outside. And when we're finished with those fights, we'll—"

"We need to fight together," Mara interrupted him.

"It's too dangerous for you here," Dalin countered.

"It's too dangerous for you! Did you see what Fentress did in her fight?"

He let out a breath and folded his arms. "I watched the recording."

Fingers trembling with frustration and anger, Mara reached for her pack again and fastened the straps. She felt Dalin's shields sliding into place.

"Just think about it. Please." Flush gone, her skin prickled with chill. She leaned across him to grab her shirt.

Dalin trapped her against his body and pulled an even more rumpled uniform shirt out from under his pillow. "You can have this one."

She stood to take it and slip her arms into the sleeves. "I'm sorry I interrupted your rest," she said.

"I'm not," he replied and with a flick knocked the pack to the floor. He wrapped one hand around her wrist and tossed her onto the bed, pinning her instantly.

"How do I forget how fast you are?" she murmured against his lips and then gave in to the need to kiss him again. The moment his shoulders relaxed, she flipped him over and trapped one hand over his head, dropping her full weight on his hips.

Within the memories that returned from childhood was the ongoing and painful crush she'd had on Dalin when they were little. Looking down at his beautiful face, she sighed. "Promise me you will use every advantage you have. None of this gentlemanly fighting."

He grinned at "gentlemanly fighting." "No mercy. I promise."

"All I can think is that Fentress has some of the same berserker drug in her system that I do. It's the best explanation for how she's been acting. The drug has to physically overrule me but it seems like she's riding some form of it all the time."

Twisting his hips, Dalin knocked her sideways and pulled her up next to him so they were facing each other, heads on pillows. "When I imagined you here, we weren't talking fight strategy. Or drugs."

The images he sent her next were like some of the scenes from *Dark Deception* when the two main characters got together at the end of the book. Mara flushed. "I want…" She stopped, her mouth dry, unsure what to say next.

"Me too," Dalin said.

Their faces met between the pillows for a lingering kiss that promised more.

Dalin pulled back first and pushed his forehead against hers. "Not right now. I understand."

The knock at the door startled them both.

Jumping from the bed, Dalin grabbed his shirt and buttoned it partway. He frowned and then relaxed. "It's just Kook," he said.

Mara sniffed the rumpled shirt she wore, pleased it smelled a little like Dalin. As he opened the door, she started rebraiding her hair.

A male with dark skin, head shaved bald, stood there holding a tiny tablet. "You didn't respond to my pings so I came down here to show you the blood test results—" He broke off when he noticed Mara. "Hello, Ms. De La Luz. How does it feel to be dead?"

She shrugged. "Not as bad as I thought."

The male stepped all the way in and Dalin shut and locked the door behind him. He took in their rumpled clothes and the sword belts on the floor, gaze shifting to the sleeping room doorway and back again. He coughed and cleared his throat. "I'm sorry to interrupt you but I thought you needed to see your opponent's blood work."

"Hold on," Dalin said. "Introductions. Bryant Kucala, please meet Mara De La Luz. Kucala and I went to school together a long time ago. He works here now."

She took a few steps forward and shook the male's hands. "Any friend of Dalin's is a friend of mine."

"Likewise," Kucala said. He tapped his wrist unit and opened a projection of a document for them both to see.

"Your opponent is the head of the Furies here at the Mess. She was on the student observation squad to Iloel. When she returned, she wanted a shortcut to catch up with the others who'd been training for the tournament. She put that request out there clearly and publicly and someone took her up on it. I haven't identified her source yet, but she's using a compound related to the drug they gave you, Mara."

She sagged a little and caught herself on the back of the couch. "I suspected as much when I watched her fight earlier."

"Unlike the one dose you were given—"

"A highly concentrated and dangerous dose," Dalin added.

Kucala scrolled through the document. "Agreed. The drug your opponent is taking has to be injected in incrementally more powerful doses."

"Will the berserker state become permanent for Fentress like it could for me?" Mara asked.

He shook his head. "No, the drug escalates her metabolism, which in turn causes her to burn through the drug more quickly. What they gave you took up residence in your spinal fluid."

Focusing on Dalin, as though he hadn't just delivered a double serving of terrible news, he said, "Based on the data, I think if you can tire Fentress out or better yet, choke her out, you stand a good chance of winning."

Chapter 44

Just as he had the day before, Dalin stood in the cold, empty locker room contemplating his options. He couldn't leave with Mara right now. Her safety, her opportunities to make choices, to be happy, those were all much more important than fighting together.

If only she understood that.

A tiny part of him was afraid of, was *concerned* about, the fight with Fentress. Even in the worst fights at La Kill, his death was not a possible outcome. He didn't want to die yet. He had too much to accomplish in order to create the future he wanted. His mission was to make the Commonwealth a place where people could live without fear and where he and Mara could be together. Permanently.

He checked the seams and seals on his fight suit and picked up the booties only to put them back in the locker. His life was on the line. He wasn't going to sacrifice the advantage of fighting in bare feet for science. At the bottom of his locker, under the pile of gear was a tiny square of paper written in the code he used with Jameson. He folded it and tucked the message into an inside pocket of his uniform to decode later. His mentor's sudden absence was a bit odd, but nothing he and Elana hadn't grown accustomed to over the years.

Dalin returned to the same side of the fight square. It didn't matter, really, but as the top seed, he got to choose the side. He was not allowed to place his own weapons this time, however. One of the trainers took the stack from him and laid them just behind the red line, per the newest instructions. A messenger had informed him that he was to wait out of sight until he was introduced.

The intensity of the crowd noise rose as the minutes ticked closer to the posted start time. The connection to Mara was small, just a pinprick of light, but it was enough. This was all for her. And just in case something terrible happened, he was glad she had Elana nearby.

He mentally rehearsed fight techniques and strategies to use to tire Fentress out, force her to work for every contact. But he was a killer too. It was the cold, dark void in his mind, the part of him with no conscience and no remorse that would win this fight.

Trumpets played the royal processional. The crowd clapped as, presumably, Queen Vanora entered her viewing box. It made sense that she would make her presence known for this final fight. It was the world's most deadly job interview, after all, and she was the one hiring.

The announcer and Shanshan entered through the center door. He motioned for the crowd to quiet and she folded her arms, giving the royal box, and then the crowd, a cold stare.

Once again, the announcer read through the reminders about the rules, the Queen's dispensation to change them, etc., etc. All three rounds were weapons optional, points, knockout, or death, etc.

When his name was announced, the audience clapped and yelled, rattling the entire arena. The noise doubled when Dalin stepped onto the floor and waved to all four sides of the seats. Mara was in the same place as before. He circled one more time and then bowed to Vanora, who was actually visible now, the curtain pulled back.

They called Fentress next and the audience responded nearly as loudly. Dalin stood behind the red line, close enough to reach his weapons as his opponent bounced and waved, blowing kisses and making obscene gestures.

A gong rang but Fentress continued to interact with the onlookers. Shanshan motioned her over to her spot. Fentress made a rude face, which produced some laughter, but ambled over to her place, making a noticeable effort to move slowly.

The announcer cleared his throat, stretched out his arms and lowered his hands, indicating that the crowd should quiet.

"Each candidate may begin with a single weapon. If he or she chooses, he or she may place other weapons inside the red line to be retrieved for use later in a given round. However, any weapons inside the line may be used by either fighter."

Fentress wiggled her eyebrows and mouthed what looked like, "I'll kill you with your own sword and keep mine clean."

In response, Dalin offered his most indifferent stare.

"The other option is for the candidates to leave weapons behind the red line. They may be retrieved for the same point penalty as escaping over the line during the fight." He turned to Dalin and then to Fentress. "Understood?"

Dalin gave a single, sharp nod.

Fentress bounced and gave a thumbs-up.

It was time to shake hands. Dalin approached at a measured pace, noting his opponent's reach, the muscles in her neck and shoulders, and as he got closer, the redness of her eyes that stood out against light irises and enlarged pupils.

At the announcer's request, he bowed to his opponent and then moved a small step closer to shake hands. Fentress lunged forward and kissed him hard on the lips.

For a split second, he stiffened, but then relaxed and backed toward his side of the fight square. It took everything in him not to wipe his mouth. That would let her know she'd gotten to him. He picked up his bo staff, tapped it once on the floor, and shifted to a horizontal hold and ready position.

At the buzzer, just as she had in the previous fight, Fentress hurtled across the fighting square, this time brandishing a sword. Dalin shifted just enough to avoid the charge and cracked his staff against the bones of her ankles as she went past.

He danced away from her next swing and slapped her across the face with the staff. An angry red mark and a few dots of blood showed the strength of the hit.

Howling, Fentress came in low and sliced across his knees. She cut suit and skin, but got a stab in the throat for her efforts. Dalin didn't wait for her next strike. He spun the staff in a figure eight and hit each of her ears on either side of the spin. Shifting his grip, he put his weight into a swing at her lower hamstrings, knocking her to her back.

Her head bounced on the mat and for a moment her whole body twitched. He fought the urge to close in, though he could've ended it there.

The buzzer ended the round just as Fentress rolled to her knees and staggered upright.

On the other side of the line, Dalin checked his minor leg injuries and considered his weapons. Fentress threw down her sword and snatched up her bo staff. The killer in Dalin's mind considered the slices in the fight suit, the blood dripping onto his feet, and switched staff for sword. This female was a danger to others and herself.

It was time to end this and move to the next phase of the mission.

Twirling the staff above her head, Fentress lost her balance and stumbled. She motioned him forward. Dalin obliged her by lunging forward with a high fake to her head. When she moved the staff upward to block, Dalin dropped the strike low, slicing deep into the tendons of her left ankle. She caught him hard across the base of his skull and he nearly fell, spots flaring in his vision.

Dalin sprang upward, turning to stab directly for her heart. Fentress moved, but not quickly enough to avoid a sword in the ribs.

When his weapon hit bone, Dalin yanked it out and stabbed forward again. As she fell, Fentress whipped the staff up under his chin, knocking his teeth together. Hot blood filled his mouth, the bite on his tongue deep and painful.

He took a slow breath and tightened his core. The fight was nearly over. He gripped the pommel of his sword lightly, watching his opponent attempt to stand.

She couldn't coordinate her limbs to brace herself, hold the bo staff, and stand all at once. Small and then larger tremors racked her frame, and for the first time Fentress looked at him with fear. She held out one hand, closed her eyes, and stood, with only a little sway.

Switching his sword to his left hand, Dalin approached slowly. When he was close enough, he punched Fentress in the jaw and jabbed her hard, right at the top of her nose. Eyes rolling back in her head, the Fury fell backward onto the hard mat.

As Dalin stood over her prone form, the applause penetrated the cold fog in his mind. People were clapping for this violence? This horror? He turned to acknowledge Queen Vanora, but she was looking past him back at the ring.

* * *

Bloody spit bubbles trailing from the corner of her mouth, Fentress crawled to the announcer and reached up to him. She shook her left hand and flexed the fingers, saying something, repeating something over and over. The announcer shrugged and turned to the royal box.

"Your majesty, this contestant asks that you grant her second the opportunity to finish the fight." Fentress tugged his trouser leg and reached for the amplification device. "For the honor of the Furies across the realm and more importantly for the honor of females everywhere who fight in your name," she said.

Except for a few bursts of excited whispering, the only sound was the noise of ten thousand people shifting to look at the Queen. Vanora stood and nodded to Fentress. She looked straight at Dalin and said, "I grant the request. Call your second."

Fentress pulled herself upright using the announcer as a crutch. Leaning in, she slurred, "I call Mara De La Luz as my second."

Elana gasped, face going white with anger. "You don't have to do this," she said in a fierce whisper.

But Mara had made a promise and as the thought rose to the surface, Fentress said, "Mara De La Luz is a Fury, the pledge to her sisters sealed in blood. And by the blood, I call her to finish this fight."

The amplification cut off and a pair of healers hurried to pull Fentress away. She grabbed her left arm, shook the limp hand. Panting and shivering, the Fury tried to stand on her own and fell again. Rolling to one side, she coughed up bile, body heaving with the effort.

A team of three additional healers moved in and between the five of them, carried the tall female off the floor.

"Mara De La Luz, if you are present, please report to the referee immediately."

"No. Please," her aunt said, even as Mara stood and checked her sword belt.

"Her partner's not going to kill her," Van Fuuren said.

Elana nodded at the nearest of the Commonwealth soldiers. "But what if someone else does?"

Rafiq stood, as many people were doing. "We'll spread out to the other sections and keep an eye on the guards. They shouldn't interfere. But if they're ordered to, there's ways to slow them down."

Geraldo and Van Fuuren stood as well. "See to your survival," the King's Man said. "We have a lot invested in you."

"Reset the clock," the announcer called.

The female referee was talking to Dalin while a single healer first wiped his face and dabbed at the cuts on his legs. When the healer offered him water, he shook his head no, his gaze fixed on Mara as she made her way to the stairs.

Relieved the fight with Fentress was over, Mara didn't spend a second worrying if Dalin would hurt her. In fact, she was thinking of one of their best demo fights back at Northwest Protector House. They could give the audience a good show and then offer themselves as a pair of champions for the Commonwealth.

She tried to send the images, the memory of that specific fight to him. Just behind that, she sent the idea of a pair of champions.

Dalin didn't respond. He'd blocked ninety-nine percent of their connection while he fought Fentress. Mara didn't agree with that choice, but she understood the need to focus.

At the junction where she would turn and enter the narrow hall leading to the fight ring, Lupe Bogdanovich stood. "Good job making it back from Iloel," she said. "The Furies need you now. You've got your sword. Any other weapons?"

Mara showed her the two knives in arm sheaths and the tiny belt knife from the Iloellian Tree.

Sergeant Bogdanovich nodded in approval. "That uniform will have to do." Moving closer, she smoothed Mara's shirt and brushed at the wrinkles in her trousers. She took a pin from her collar, a tiny brass representation of a woman's face on a shield, and pinned it to Mara's collar instead. "Furies fight to win," she said.

"Understood," Mara said and saluted, just in case.

A female in a royal uniform motioned Mara toward the fighting floor. "This way," she said.

From the doorway, she watched Dalin walk a few steps away from the referee and the healers to check on his weapons.

"*Dalin,*" she sent.

When he looked up, she sent, "*Remember that demo fight we did for my class at the Protector compound?*" She projected the sequence again.

He bent down to check his bo staff. "*That will get us through one round, at least. I don't want to hurt you,*" he said, finally looking straight at her across the fight ring.

From her position in the shadowed doorway, Mara smiled. "*You won't,*" she said. "*And I won't hurt you. A little friendly contact between partners makes a better show.*"

Just then, the announcer returned to the middle of the floor, the buzzer sounding in three short bursts. "An unusual situation, ladies and gentlemen," he said as the audience quieted. "One for the historians. As some of you might know, Ms. De La Luz defeated the previous champion. It is only right she be here now." The announcer bowed his head for a count of three.

The referee appeared next to Mara. "I saw your fight against the former champion. Think you can beat de Forest?" she asked.

"I'm hoping for a draw," Mara said.

"Interesting." The referee tilted her head, a tiny crease furrowing her brows. "Out you go. Let's see what the crowd thinks."

Keeping her focus on Dalin, Mara walked onto the floor. People clapped. Some of those who'd screamed for Fentress screamed for her.

"Go get it, first year," called Raymundo, who was sitting with Angelo, Fusao, and Dominique. All four waved and clapped. She smiled and waved back, enjoying a tiny moment of happiness that they were apparently safe and unharmed.

"*You can't go into the berserker state,*" Dalin sent. "*It's too dangerous.*"

"*Fighting you won't trigger it. It has to overpower my will.*"

The referee motioned them to the middle of the floor to shake hands and bow. "*Do you want me to kiss you like Fentress did?*" she asked.

Warmth zinged through her arm with Dalin's touch, and his serious expression softened for a fraction of a second. "*Definitely later.*"

Back behind the red line, Mara laid her sword on the ground and waited for the buzzer.

Just like during the Friday night fights, technique would show. They couldn't get away with faking much. Despite her intention to stay calm, battle intensity raced through Mara's frame and her muscles flexed in anticipation as she edged forward with caution. Dalin wouldn't hurt her; he would make light contact and so would she.

In response to that stray thought, Dalin threw a high kick at her head. She jumped back and then, as he closed in, parried with a spin back fist. She added a push kick toward his sternum, following quickly with a jump front kick to his throat. She snapped a jab punch at his nose and a hook to his ribs.

Dalin kicked at her ribs with his right foot and then aimed an elbow strike at her ear. Mara feinted and leaned into a jump back kick, hitting him hard in the stomach. It was the first blow to land with any power and sent Dalin staggering backward.

The Fentress faction of the audience cheered, reminding the combatants they weren't alone.

The moment she spared a glance toward the audience, Dalin closed the distance in one long stride and threw a double side kick to Mara's gut and then her face. She ducked out of the way and countered with a knee to his thigh and an uppercut under his chin.

With a flicker of a smile, he caught her fist and pushed her back. "*Faster?*" he sent.

As she opened herself to the energy of the Tree, her arms and legs tingled. She sent the energy down their connection to share with Dalin.

His blows doubled in speed and intensity, raining down from his ten-centimeter height advantage.

Mara blocked, parried, countered, and kicked. Their exchanges and combinations of moves continued, but lightning fast. The audience yelled as the partners fought across the floor. Although their intensity was high, neither landed a blow with full force. The rapport kept them in a heightened connection, each knowing the next move a millisecond before it happened.

Dalin jumped into a flying side kick. Mara dodged and dropped to one knee, sweeping his legs out from under him as he landed. Dalin fell and she pinned him, a knee on his solar plexus, one hand to his throat.

"Do you yield?" she asked, blinking sweat out of her eyes.

To her ears, it sounded like the audience groaned with one voice.

Gray eyes grim, Dalin reached back and flipped himself upward, knocking Mara to the mat.

From the ground, she kicked at his knees and groin before springing to her feet, hands up and ready.

Chapter 45

The buzzer sounded.

They both moved back behind the red line. Dalin waved the healer off. He needed to think fast.

The win had been in his hands. And that crazy female, that *fēng pòzi,* drugged out of her mind, had called Mara as her second.

Mara. His childhood crush, his responsibility, his partner, and his future, all combined in a strong, gorgeous package.

"We're going to swords," he sent. *"Can you shield?"*

She hesitated. *"Shielding is different than just allowing the energy to flow through me. I'll shield if I need to. You think you can take me?"*

Nearly a year ago, they'd fought with swords at a campsite. They'd been alone, fighting for points, with the intention to relieve stress.

As she hefted her sword and walked across the line, Dalin sent her that memory. *"You know I can take you."*

And with that, he slashed across the old scar at the top of her thigh, cutting the fabric of her trousers and drawing a line of blood.

Eyes widening just a fraction, Mara lunged forward, pushing energy down her blade. It was hard to see, just a blurring across the sharp edges, but she caught him below his guard and sliced him under the armpit.

First blood and second blood. He blocked the next strike and caught her hand, locking her close and staring at her eyes.

Still blue.

To break the contact, Mara kicked him hard in the knee, her booted foot magnifying the impact. Even as he stumbled, he switched his grip and wound up for a backhand strike at her neck.

She got her blade up in time to block and used her other hand to shoot a palm strike at his solar plexus.

Sweating now, Dalin couldn't find his calm center. The chill Darkness, home of the killer in his mind, pushed for control.

Mara faked a side strike, pulled it at the last second and lunged straight at him again. The tip of her sword caught the suit a few centimeters below his collarbone and drew blood.

His missed block dropped lower, and with the follow-through he cut a line across her belly.

His mind registered that Mara was trying to widen their connection, to communicate. She was by far the best opponent he'd fought in the tournament. And since she'd been training separately, her repertoire of techniques included surprises now.

Kicking him again, Mara jumped and switched her stance one hundred eighty degrees. She pressed the middle of her sword to his neck and leaned close. "Yield," she said, frustration filling the single word. With every heavy breath, their bodies touched on multiple points. The scents of blood and sweat filled the space around them.

Dalin's sword point pressed against her sternum. A single upward thrust would cause massive damage. "You yield," he said.

"Let's offer ourselves as a matched pair. That could be the way to fulfill the prophecy. Please."

The buzzer sounded, faint and far away. They held their standoff until Shanshan inserted her arm between them, pushing them apart.

On the other side of the line, Dalin wiped down his sword and used the same cloth to dab at his freely bleeding new cuts. Mara did the same on her side, grimacing as she tore off part of her shirt to press against the deeper slice on her leg.

He'd been provoking her, the play fight turning into a real fight. Why didn't Mara understand that she could not stay in Crown City? She refused to appreciate the sacrifice he was willing to make for her freedom.

Across the mat, she sheathed her sword and placed it on the floor. "*I want to be with you more than I want to be free.*"

A *vishakanya* sprang to the railing and balanced like a cat. Dropping, she caught the metal bar with her hands and fell to the floor, landing on her feet. Shanshan and the announcer hurried over, bending down to hear what the girl had to say, as the crowd rumbled all around them.

Shanshan glanced over at Dalin, a frown disappearing as quickly as it appeared. The announcer nodded, head bobbing, as the little bodyguard finished speaking.

He held out his hands, turning slowly until the audience quieted a fraction. "Her majesty extends praise to these fighters." Clapping, whistling, and cheering erupted from the stands. After a five-second pause, the announcer continued. "Her majesty bids the fighters to leave the swords out of the final round and requests that they be ready to improvise."

Vishakanya swarmed the railing now, dropping lightly to the floor like spiders pouring off a shaken web.

"*They're poisonous*," Dalin sent. "*Don't let them touch you.*" Even as the urgent words formed in his mind, the bodyguard directly behind Mara rolled off first one long glove and then the other.

As the buzzer sounded, he grabbed his bo staff and made it to the center of the floor in three long strides. "Behind you."

Mara hurried forward just as the *vishakanya* reached for her. She shifted out of the bodyguard's path and gripped her first throwing knife. Dalin swung at Mara's head. She ducked and stabbed him in the thigh, jabbing the thin blade in and out like a needle.

"*Shield*," Dalin demanded. "*It should protect you.*"

She trapped his next swing between her palms and pulled down on the staff with most of her weight. Shoving her to the floor, Dalin had just enough time to switch grips and slam the tip of the staff into the forehead of a *vishakanya*. He swung the staff like a cricket bat, forcing another three to back away.

He whirled at the gurgling cry behind him as another *vishakanya* crumpled, Mara's knife in her throat.

A knife jumped to her left hand as Mara stood, pressing her back to his.

"*If you stay down, they'll leave you alone*," Dalin sent, though it was more wish than truth. He slammed his elbow into her and knocked her onto her hands and knees, the knife sliding out of her grasp.

His staff kept the tiny females away as Mara grabbed the knife and got to her feet. As she faced him, the shield shimmered into place, the whites of her eyes beginning to darken.

Why wouldn't she stay down? He loosed one of his own knives, catching the nearest *vishakanya* in the face.

Mara's knife flew and sliced into the outer muscle of his shoulder. *"Why won't you fight* with *me instead of against me? We are partners."* The betrayal in her voice and the power of the throw pushed him to the edge of his control.

She held only the tiny belt knife now as two more *vishakanya* edged toward her, one close enough to test the energy of the shield.

He couldn't lose her again. The fear finally broke his control and the killer swung the bo staff with enough power to knock her to the floor.

Eyelids fluttering closed, Mara toppled to the side. The sheen of her shield dimmed. Dalin stood over her, bo staff moving in a slow circle, keeping the poisonous girls away.

The crowd rumbled and clapping broke out as Mara pushed to her knees, fingers tight around the belt knife. The cut on her stomach bled through the torn uniform shirt, the cut on her leg bleeding even more heavily. A reddish purple contusion spread along the side of her face. "Tell her majesty," she said, voice rough and strange sounding, atonal and multilayered. "Tell her we can be the first pair of champions."

Despite the injuries, Mara looked impossibly taller as she stood, posture straight and strong. Her eyes were a full, bottomless black.

He'd caused those injuries. He'd hurt Mara and broken the only vow that mattered. And yet, she wanted to continue to put herself at risk. On a fresh surge of fear and anger, Dalin sent the final blow, a combination mental strike and command. "Stay. Down."

She rocked back and then staggered forward, falling into him. Dark red blood trickled from her nose. "Dalin?" To his ears, it was the voice of the little girl he'd failed to protect.

Her muscles spasmed as she lost the strength to remain upright, sinking slowly to the floor, weight pressing against him.

"Ladies and gentleman, your champion," the announcer yelled.

Dalin stood over his fallen partner, staff out and menacing. Waves of hot and cold pulsed across his skin, each separate cut and injury beginning to throb.

The sharpest pain was in his chest, the handle of Mara's belt knife protruding a bare centimeter above his heart.

Chapter 46

Dawn painted the windows of the palace kitchen with streaks of red and orange. Dalin leaned against the heavy wooden cutting table, the surface rough and grooved from years of knife strokes. A handful of bakers were hard at work near the ovens, but that was an easy twenty meters from the prep area where he stood alone.

At this early hour, the breakfast scents were biscuits and *naan*, coffee and chai. It was possible one of the cooks was poaching eggs, and maybe a cream sauce simmered at one of the far stovetops.

Besides the few stolen hours with Mara, his happiest times on Laska had been in the kitchen at Cousins. He needed to make something, to create, and his new rank gave him free run of the palace and the Mess. Not everyone would use his newly acquired power to work in a kitchen. But this was the first morning of a new era. He intended to plan, flavor, and manipulate the structures of the Commonwealth just as he would his inaugural meal as the People's Champion.

In front of him and to the right, the heavy chrome door to the walk-in cooling unit opened. He laid his hand on the pommel of his sword, watching as a small figure emerged, wisps of chilly mist clinging to dark hair and clothes. The person stood facing the inside of the cooling unit, breathing deeply before turning to scan the kitchen.

Dalin and Vanora recognized each other in the same instant, his hands balling into fists before he bowed.

She shrugged and closed the door behind her, leaning against the metal frame with a small sigh. "You should know that we come here when the royal rooms are too warm." The red-yellow glow from the windows brought out the deep, puffy circles under her eyes and the pinched lines around her mouth. "The champion is not tasked with guarding our person, but it is best you learn our habits. As I will learn yours." On the last statement, she raised the corners of her lips in a humorless smile.

Cold air billowed around his legs, spreading a deep chill across his skin. Dalin uncurled his fingers, flattening his palms against the solid wood once more. The red mark on his hand had finally begun to fade, but seeing Vanora triggered phantom pain. With significant effort, he kept his eyes and his thoughts away from the shiny knives, sheathed tidily in a block just past his fingertips.

"As you say, your majesty," he managed to respond.

The Queen touched her thin lips with a gloved fingertip as she trilled a girlish giggle. "When we're alone, you must call us Vanora."

* * *

Head still fuzzy, Mara looked up from the rolling chair. Straps kept her torso and upper legs in place.

"You're going to be fine, sweetheart," Elana said.

"Where's Jameson?"

Slender fingers brushed hair from her face, her aunt's kind expression flickering to worry and then back again. "We don't know," she said. "He'll make contact soon."

Closing her eyes against the pain of her combined injuries and the agony of coming out of the berserker state, Mara swallowed hard. She'd been throwing up, dry heaves continuing, though her stomach was completely empty.

"Transport will be in the alley in five minutes." Rafiq's face appeared in her line of sight.

"How is it that your ship is prepped?" Van Fuuren asked.

The owner of the eating house made a "what a stupid question" expression. "My ship is always prepped. Prepare for all possible outcomes is part of the smugglers', ahem, the business owner's code."

"The rule of preparation," Mara agreed.

A frantic knocking on the door shot daggers of pain through her head. From the chair, she couldn't see the door, but she heard murmuring voices.

"Mara. Thank the Light. They took you out and then you was gone from the Mess and we, and then Dalin—"

Gunder and Annelise stood over the low chair. "You made us so worried and proud," Gunder said, tucking Annelise tight against his side. "Don't know exactly why de Forest wants a piece of that disaster, but he won it fair and square."

"He cheated, all the way around," Annelise said. "Nothing fair or square about it, especially when Vanora sent her bodyguards after you."

Wrapping her arms tightly around her chest, Mara tried not to shiver. While she remembered most of the fight, the memories of the last round were blurred and shifting. She knew the poison had taken over at the end, though no one mentioned it.

"Are you really staying here?" she asked her friends.

"I'm heading out," Gunder said. "To Kels. Last launch tonight."

"Do you know any mission parameters?"

He smiled his broad, goofy smile. "Nope. It'll be a brand-new adventure, just like when we came here."

Annelise patted his shoulder and then stretched on her toes to kiss his cheek. "I'm staying," she said. "After all that business with the secret hospital and the points, the ambassadors are demanding reforms and such like. Especially the ones from the planets with the most people. Gonna be a big fuss for a while. A lot of teachers are leaving, students too. Darkness knows I might get private classes at first, but I'm staying. Same reasons as I told you before."

"Tell her about that sergeant," Gunder said. He brushed one big palm over Annelise's curls before ambling toward the kitchen.

Cheeks darkening to bright pink, Annelise said, "Well, I was talkin', talking," she emphasized the correct pronunciation. "To Sergeant Bogdanovich after your fight. She's a Fury, used to be the head one at the Mess."

Mara nodded.

"And she says I'm good material and she needs someone like me to look after the girls for a while. Stay strong, but stay low, that sort of thing. Not a joke about my height, either. The sergeant isn't exactly tall." She cleared her throat and watched the men and Elana continue their packing and organizing. "You're leaving then?"

"Five minutes," Mara said, regret for the whole sorry almost-year they'd spent at the Queen's Military Skills and Strategy School coloring her words.

"You can't protect people that don't want your help," Annelise said. "Or don't need it, in my case. This is the best choice I ever made." She shoved her hands deep in the pockets of her crisp school uniform.

Gunder came back through the kitchen door spooning something out of a bowl into his mouth. "These are the most excellent leftovers I've had since...ever," he said. "This crew is movin' out, did you give her the—"

"Oh, oh right." Annelise reached into her pack and handed over a wrapped bundle. "This was on my bed." On the plain paper someone had printed, "Mara."

Awareness tingled through her fingers as she carefully ripped along a seam in the paper. Inside was Dalin's soft, dark brown pullover. The one he'd loaned to her on their first trip to Satri. She pressed it to her nose and inhaled, tears prickling behind her eyes, throat clogging. Something with a little weight tumbled out from the folds of the pullover. It was her belt knife with a note wrapped around the handle. The note contained only four words and bore no signature.

Until the next fight.

AUTHOR'S NOTE

The year I participated in the Denver Writing Project, one of our guest speakers was a poet named Jake York. I think I was reading *The Diamond Age* by Neil Stephenson that summer and I wanted to talk about memes. Before memes lived visually all over the Internet, Neil Stephenson, Jake York, and others explained them as repeating ideas that burrow into our collective consciousness.

The other thing I remember from Jake York's guest lecture was that knowing the beginning of a poem when you sit down to write is a gift, knowing the end of the poem (before you know the rest of it) can be a curse.

When I began writing *The People's Champion*, I knew how it had to end. And I knew the two tropes I wanted to work with: battle school and away team. To me, tropes and memes are connected concepts in the sense that when we recognize the repeating thing presented in a fresh way, we/humans get a little brain zing.

And to Mr. York's excellent point, it was a bit of a curse to know the end of the book first. You might be familiar with the young reader series *Captain Underpants*? Well, one of the things Dav Pilkey repeats throughout the books is, "Before I can tell you that story, I have to tell you this one…" And that's what it was like trying to get *The People's Champion* to the perfect ending. Before I could take the reader to that place, I had to tell this bit and set up that situation and cause this problem, etc.

Early drafts of the first book in this trilogy, *The Protector Project*, contained multiple scenes from Dalin's point of view, but for a variety of story reasons the book worked much better when kept strictly to Mara's perspective. Writing *The People's Champion* using both POVs was an exciting challenge. I felt like I knew Dalin really well and I wanted readers to know him too. He has a different frame of reference, a different vocabulary than Mara. Dalin is more intense, more angry, and self-aware enough to admit almost all of his flaws. But in a different way, he is just as vulnerable as Mara, just as in need of balance as she is. I was thinking so much of the Charles Wallace character in *A Wrinkle in Time* as I wrote for Dalin. Sometimes knowing too much can get a person in even more trouble than not knowing enough.

Every good hero/heroine needs a strong villain or the story falls apart. A monarch responsible for the widespread war experiments and the deaths of so many would have to be an extra special sort of evildoer. As luck would have it, several years ago I was attending the Rocky Mountain Fiction Writers' Conference. I found my friend Cathy in a session about poison and poisoning. It was the tail end, maybe the last fifteen minutes, and the presenter put up a slide about the *vishakanya*. The *vishakanya* are an urban legend from India about young, female assassins who were administered steady doses of poison until they became physically poisonous themselves. We all know (fictional) evil queens, but an evil queen who is poisonous? What writer's mind could let go of an idea like that?

While I was writing this book, my work office was right next to the English Language Acquisition department and all of the cultural liaisons that work there. Every day I heard snippets of at least nine world languages. That audio has become woven into my ideas about the future, specifically that what we might hear in the schools of the future will sound a lot like what we hear more of all the time in the schools of today.

A completely unscientific poll of my friends and various readers yielded a majority belief that the second book of a trilogy is the weak book. The best book is either book one or book three, according to this non-representative sample. "What about *The Empire Strikes Back*?" I would ask. And everyone would agree, yes, that was the best film of the first *Star Wars* trilogy. But it was an exception to the trilogy "rule."

The action of *The People's Champion* provides a glimpse of the larger problems facing not just one or two planets but the entire

Laskan Commonwealth. And maybe that's the trick of the second book, working through an urgent, specific, and immediate set of problems while revealing hints about the massive challenge ahead. The other trick, to my way of thinking, is to write a compelling ending that leaves us believing all is *not* lost and hoping for a great fight the next time we see our heroes.

ABOUT THE AUTHOR

Jenna Lincoln loves to read, write, and talk about reading and writing. She spent many happy years as a language arts teacher doing just those things.

After dabbling in *X-Files*, *Firefly,* and *Supernatural* fan fiction, Jenna got serious about building her own imaginary world, big enough to get lost in for a long, long time. When she comes back to reality, Jenna enjoys her home in beautiful Colorado with her husband and two daughters.

Did you enjoy this book? Drop us a line and say so! We love to hear from readers, and so do our authors. To connect, visit www.boroughspublishinggroup.com online, send comments directly to info@boroughspublishinggroup.com, or friend us on Facebook and Twitter. And be sure to check back regularly for contests and new releases in your favorite subgenres of romance!

Are you an aspiring writer? Check out www.boroughspublishinggroup.com/submit and see if we can help you make your dreams come true.

CPSIA information can be obtained
at www.ICGtesting.com
Printed in the USA
LVOW10s0109200418

574225LV00010B/295/P